I object.

Those two little words had changed everything.

Colton thought he knew everything there was to know about Sophie, but, as it turned out, she wasn't an orphan with a past that was too painful to talk about. She had family. In fact, she had a daughter.

A daughter she'd given away.

Colton knew he'd lived an even-keel sort of life. But right now his life was anything but.

He stood in front of the Valley Ridge community and announced, "I'm so sorry for the inconvenience, but the wedding's canceled. I talked to the caterer and all the food's being moved to the diner. Please feel free to stop by and help yourself. And please, those who've brought gifts, be sure to take them on your way out."

With that, he marched down the aisle and took off toward the farm. He was a simple man—too simple perhaps to know how to handle something this decidedly unsimple.

Dear Reader,

I know when you think wine, you think the shores of Lake Erie, right? Well, if you don't, then maybe you should. The hero of this book, Colton, runs a small winery and loves to extol the wonders of our grape-growing region… and he's right. And while I loved introducing Lake Erie's very real wineries in this final book of my trilogy, A Valley Ridge Wedding, this is a love story. It's a different love story.

When we left Colton and Sophie at the end of *April Showers,* their wedding had been called off because a mysterious young girl objected. Tori's trying to figure out who she is, where she came from and where she belongs. That's a journey we all take in one way or another. My particular journey echoed Tori's. I grew up not knowing part of my family—part of my history. I went looking for answers and found not only closure, but a new part of my family who I love and treasure.

My heroine, Sophie, has her past arrive at her wedding, and it ripples through her present. It threatens her relationship with Colton. But maybe with some time, some tears and some of that Valley Ridge magic, they can come out stronger because of it.

I hope you enjoy this last addition to A Valley Ridge Wedding miniseries! I've enjoyed my time in Valley Ridge so much that I'm heading back this holiday season with *A Valley Ridge Christmas*. I hope you'll come visit with me!

Happy reading!

Holly Jacobs

A Walk Down
the Aisle

HOLLY JACOBS

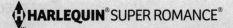

HARLEQUIN® SUPER ROMANCE®

Recycling programs
for this product may
not exist in your area.

ISBN-13: 978-0-373-71858-0

A WALK DOWN THE AISLE

Copyright © 2013 by Holly Fuhrmann

Printed in U.S.A.

www.Harlequin.com

ABOUT THE AUTHOR

In 2000, Holly Jacobs sold her first book to Harlequin Books. She's since sold more than twenty-five novels to the publisher. Her romances have won numerous awards and made the Waldenbooks bestseller list. In 2005, Holly won a prestigious Career Achievement Award from *RT Book Reviews.* In her nonwriting life, Holly is married to a police captain, and together they have four children. Visit Holly at www.hollyjacobs.com, or you can snail-mail her at P.O. Box 11102, Erie, PA 16514-1102.

Books by Holly Jacobs

HARLEQUIN SUPERROMANCE

1511—SAME TIME NEXT SUMMER
1601—UNEXPECTED GIFTS
1615—A ONE-OF-A-KIND FAMILY
1677—HOMECOMING DAY
1733—A FATHER'S NAME
1846—YOU ARE INVITED...*
1852—APRIL SHOWERS*

HARLEQUIN AMERICAN ROMANCE

1232—ONCE UPON A THANKSGIVING
1238—ONCE UPON A CHRISTMAS
1247—ONCE UPON A VALENTINE'S

HARLEQUIN EVERLASTING

THE HOUSE ON BRIAR HILL ROAD

*A Valley Ridge Wedding

Other titles by this author available in ebook format.

To George and Marilyn. I might not have found you until later in my life, but don't ever doubt that you are loved.

And to Ben, our own "Cletus." You arrived as I started writing this trilogy, and you've already enriched my life more than I ever imagined possible. Always remember, you are loved…and as far as I'm concerned, you are perfect!

A special thank-you to Julie Pfadt of the Lake Erie Wine Country and to all our local wineries. And to Jeff Ore and everyone at Penn Shore Winery for showing me the ropes…or vines, as the case may be!

PROLOGUE

VICTORIA ALLEN PARKED her father's black SUV next to the library. She purposefully backed it into the parking space so the plates weren't visible. She felt a guilty sense of dread knowing what was going to happen when her parents got hold of her, but she pushed the feeling aside. She checked the GPS on her phone and headed across the bridge and into town.

Her parents would eventually have to admit that she'd taken their car for a good reason, and it wasn't as if she didn't know how to drive. Besides, she'd followed the speed limits much better than most of the drivers on I-90.

Thinking about her parents made her feel a sense of homesickness, though she'd only been gone a couple of hours. She couldn't help but admit how much her mother would love this small town. As Tori walked down the quiet street, she thought that Valley Ridge, New York, looked like Mayberry. When Tori was younger, her mom had watched episodes of *Andy Griffith* every day at five o'clock. It struck her as ironic that her college president mother, Gloria Allen, who wore power suits and used her BlackBerry as if it was another appendage, loved such a sentimental show.

Of course, her academic, power-suited mom was a woman of unexpected contrasts. She had married Freedom Jay Allen. Though her mom called her dad

Dom, it didn't change the fact he had been born on a commune. And though he'd now joined the rest of the world, her dad was still a vegetarian, and wouldn't know a high-flying job if it bit him. He worked from home as a painter. An honest-to-goodness, brush-on-canvas artist.

When Tori was little, her mom went to work and her dad had been a househusband.

Her mother might be conventional in many ways, but she had an unconventional streak in her nonetheless.

Actually, both her parents would love this town. Now she felt even more guilty for taking their car and driving it without a license. They were going to be so pissed.

Well, her mom would be pissed, but her dad would be disappointed in her.

Disappointed was worse.

Tori glanced in a coffee-shop window and caught the reflection of a girl with blue hair. It took a split second for her to register the girl was her. Every time she noticed it, it shocked her. But she guessed that had been the point of her minirebellion. Her mother had been mad at that, too. But rather than being disappointed, her father had smiled and said, "Way to express yourself, Tori."

She wondered what her father was saying now.

They were going to be so worried once they realized she was gone.

Tori decided that maybe a coffee would calm her nerves, but the lights were off in the small shop. There was a sign on the door that read At the Wedding.

She went to the diner, which also had a Closed for Family Wedding sign on its door.

She looked up and down the street and saw that every business on it was dark.

The whole town shut down for a wedding?

It was a Saturday at the end of June. You'd think that a small town like this would get a lot of touristy people during a weekend in the summer.

Weird. Forget Mayberry. This place was *Twilight Zone*-ish. Her mom loved that show, too. And her mother liked really bad disaster films. The kind they showed on cable late at night. Her mom used the DVR for them all. Tori couldn't count how many times she'd seen the world almost hit by asteroids or the moon, or overrun by a zombie apocalypse or some killer virus. But thankfully, some B actor or actress always saved the day at the last minute.

Guilt ate at her. She knew she could head back right now and there was a chance her parents would never know what she'd done. Her mom had some all-day college thing that she'd dragged her dad to.

But Tori also knew she couldn't do that. She had to get answers. She'd tried to explain her need to her mom, but her mom hadn't understood. Tori had always gotten along with her mom and dad, even though most of her friends didn't understand it. She still loved them, but she was so freakin' angry. She couldn't seem to get a handle on her emotions. Not that it was the first time she'd felt confused. Her dad said it was normal to be moody in your teens. If that was the case, Tori couldn't wait to be in her twenties.

She checked her phone's GPS again and left the ghost town's main street, heading into a residential neighborhood. Five blocks later, she arrived in front of a house that would have made Hansel and Gretel go all gingerbread.

It was a tan one-story house. Its shutters and window boxes were bright yellow, as were the zillion flowers planted all around the tiny yard, with its picket fence and wooden arch, which had flowery vines hanging off it.

Maybe *Hansel and Gretel* was the wrong fairy tale. This was more about contrary Mary and her growing garden.

Looking at the cheery little house that seemed to scream *happy* made Tori feel pissed. Really pissed.

The anger was a deep burning in the pit of her stomach. It had been there ever since she'd seen the letter on her mother's desk. It had been addressed to Sophie Johnston in care of the New Day Adoption Agency. Her mom had been lecturing her on her blue hair, about how people's perceptions are shaped by first impressions, and what was it she hoped to say with blue hair? Tori had rolled her eyes and spotted the envelope. She'd picked it up, seen the name and then held it out to her mom, who stopped midlecture and turned pale.

That's when Tori had known the truth. Her parents weren't hers. Somewhere out there, two other people were her real mom and dad.

Fighting about hair dye had seemed like a very minor thing as she had gotten into it with her mom over the fact she'd kept such a big secret. "I planned on telling you when you were eighteen," her mom had said. Her mom had wanted her to be mature enough to handle the news.

Tori had almost doubled over from the pain of knowing that she wasn't Victoria Peace Allen, the only daughter of Gloria and Dom Allen. She wasn't sure who she was, but she needed to know.

Her mother wouldn't tell her anything. She kept say-

ing, "When you're eighteen…" As if eighteen were
some magic number. Like all of a sudden, Tori would
decide no, she didn't need to know who she was and
where she came from. Like in four years she wouldn't
wonder what kind of woman could give away her baby.

Tori opened the stupid gate of the stupid fairy-tale
house, and her anger grew. This was where her biological mother lived? In a pretty little house in a freakin'
nice little town. Not a care in the world, and certainly
no worries about some baby she gave away fourteen
years ago.

No. This woman had just handed over her child and
gone on with her life. Her very happy, gingerbread
house life.

Tori stormed up to the door and pounded on it.

When there was no answer, she pounded on the door
again, and gave it a quick kick. A black mark from her
boot marred its cheery yellowness. For some reason,
that made her feel better. Here was the tangible evidence that she existed. Something her biological mother
couldn't deny.

Tori was about to kick the door a second time when
she heard someone say, "Pardon me."

Tori turned and saw a cop car, with a young blond
guy who didn't look very coplike despite his uniform.
"Sophie's already gone to the wedding."

"Oh." Oh, so Sophie had joined the *Twilight Zone*
masses at this wedding of the century?

"Did you miss the bus to the wedding?" the cop
asked.

"Yeah," she lied. And walked over to the cop car. It
had VRPD stenciled on the doors, and a bar of lights
on the roof.

"Well, come on and get in." He leaned over and

opened the passenger door. "I'll give you a lift. I'm heading out there myself."

Tori had listened to her parents lecture her on stranger-danger since she was old enough to speak. Getting in a car with a person you didn't know was never a good idea. That's why she'd stolen her father's car. It seemed like a better idea than hitchhiking. But this was a cop. There was a box in the backseat that was wrapped in wedding paper, so his story seemed plausible. Tori opted to get in the car. A wedding would give her a perfect opportunity to observe her biological mother without being noticed.

She climbed into the passenger seat and asked, "Don't you have to protect the town from...whatever criminals do in towns like this?"

The cop didn't take offense; instead, he smiled. "I think the entire town is at the wedding. I'm predicting things will be fine if I take a wedding break." He paused, and said, "Buckle up."

Tori complied, and tried not to think about how much that sounded like her dad, and how scared her dad was going to be when he found out she was gone.

"I'm Dylan, by the way," the cop said as he pulled away from the gingerbread house.

"Tori," she said.

"Bride's side or groom's?"

"I'm here to see Sophie."

"Bride's side it is then," he said with a grin. "It's a beautiful day for her wedding, isn't it? Her and Colton..."

The cop kept on talking, but Tori wasn't really listening as she tried to digest the fact that Sophie hadn't simply gone to this wedding that shut down

Mayberry—she was the bride, the reason the entire place was closed.

Tori had just found her mother, and here she was getting married.

The anger that had burned in her belly since she'd seen that envelope blazed with new heat.

Fourteen years ago, this Sophie had handed her baby over to strangers then had carried on with her life without a second thought. She'd thrown Tori out like some unread, unwanted newspaper.

And now she was getting married to someone. Getting ready to start a new life and probably have scads of kids with him.

Kids she'd keep.

Tori didn't know what to do. She wished her mom and dad were here.

She'd found her birth mother and was going to crash her wedding.

CHAPTER ONE

Dear Baby Girl,
I know I usually write your letter on your birthday, but I wanted to share today with you. Today I marry the man of my dreams. My friends keep saying we're perfect together, and while you and I both know I'm anything but perfect, he is. And I feel as if he makes me a better person. And I'm hoping if we ever meet that's what you find…a better person.

SOPHIE JOHNSTON ROUNDED the corner of the barn, getting her first glimpse of her fiancé's surprise for her. It was a large white arbor, practically dripping with white flowers. Colton had wanted to do something special for their wedding, and she was willing to let him do whatever made him happy because there was only one thing she needed at this wedding—him.

Her two bridesmaids and best friends, Lily and Mattie, walked up the aisle, their slow step-pause gait making her crazy because, frankly, all she wanted to do was bolt down the aisle to Colton's side.

As Lily and Mattie continued their slow walk, Colton stepped into view and the sight of him in his tux took her breath away. He was not a tall man, but his five feet eight inches seemed more than ample considering she was five-two on a good-heel day. His dark hair was always cropped short, but he'd let it grow out a bit for the wedding, and had tamed it with gel or something, because it seemed to be staying in place.

As she waited for her friends to finish their laborious walk, moments with Colton flashed before her eyes.

Colton in his cowboy hat, walking by the plate-glass window at the diner. She'd been blatantly staring, and when he had turned and looked inside, their eyes had locked. He'd come in, strode over to her table and asked her out.

Colton taking her to the ridge on his farm. He'd made a picnic and they had sat in the Adirondack chairs he'd bought and placed up there for them. One blue, one yellow. They'd watched the sunset on Lake Erie. He'd told her that he loved her that night. She'd said, "Thank you."

He'd told her he loved her every day for weeks, and finally one night she'd admitted, "I love you, too." He'd said, "I know."

He'd known. He seemed to understand her in so many ways. Sometimes he understood her better than she understood herself. And there he was, waiting for her.

Mattie and Lily finally stood to the left of the altar. The guitarist nodded at Sophie, started to play the bridal march, and she finally began her own walk down the aisle.

Sophie tried to force herself to maintain the same sedate gait as her bridesmaids had, but she wasn't sure she was managing it. She was able to stop herself from running, but barely.

She was almost at Colton's side when he reached down and picked up…a cowboy hat. He slipped it on his head. A white hat.

He'd told her he wore the hat to protect himself from the sun while he was in the fields or the vineyard. She'd teased him, saying he was a closet cowboy. All heart, honor and passion for the land.

He'd told her that his greatest passion was her.

Sophie stopped her headlong race down the aisle for a moment because she was laughing so hard. Colton adjusted the obviously new hat on his head and grinned at her.

This was the man she was about to vow to spend the rest of her life with.

The perfect man for her.

He laughed with ease, but more than that, he made her laugh, as well. He accepted her as she was, and had never tried to make her be something she wasn't.

He loved her.

He wasn't a talkative man, but his every action told her he loved her.

She took the last two steps and was at his side… where she belonged.

Where she planned to spend the rest of her life.

She grasped the hand of the man she loved.

It was a perfect day. The sky was a brilliant June blue. The field next to the arbor was dotted with new green stalks that would be tasseled corn by the end of the summer. Behind her there were rows of borrowed chairs, all festooned with white ribbons and lace and occupied by most of the occupants of Valley Ridge, New York—her friends and surrogate family. The air was awash with the scent of flowers.

But none of that mattered to Sophie. It could be stormy and cold. The entire town could have ignored their invitations. The chairs could be old and ratty, and the arbor could blow down in the gale.

As long as Colton was next to her, it would still have been a perfect day.

All she needed was him.

He gave her hand a quick but solid squeeze, and Sophie knew a sense of rightness. Of wholeness.

Of love.

"Dearly beloved," the minister said as tiny wind chimes, which hung from the corner of the arbor, tinkled in the light breeze.

The minister inhaled, and Sophie could scarcely contain her joy. She wanted to scream yes right now. Yes, she'd take this man for better or worse. Yes, she'd take this man for richer or poorer. Yes, she'd take this man for the rest of her life.

Yes. Yes. Yes.

She looked at Colton and whispered "yes" to herself at the same moment that someone from behind her shouted, "I object."

Sophie turned, as did Colton. As did everyone gathered in her beribboned chairs in Colton's field. A young girl with vivid blue hair stood in the back row of the chairs. "You can't get married yet. Not when I've worked so hard to find you. No. It's not fair."

"Do you know her?" Colton whispered.

Sophie shook her head. She had no idea what to do. When she was thinking about her wedding day, she had tried to make plans for every contingency. If it rained, they'd move the ceremony into the barn, where they had held their engagement party and where their casual reception would take place.

If the minister got ill, she knew a man at one of the wineries who'd become ordained online in order to perform weddings for his winery's new reception hall. She'd call him.

If the caterer's trucks broke down, she'd call in her friends and ask them to supply a quick potluck.

If her parents showed up and caused a scene, she had Valley Ridge's local police officer as one of her guests, and he could cart them off to jail, or out of town. She knew Dylan would take them somewhere. Anywhere that wasn't here.

Yes, Sophie was sure she'd thought of everything, considered every possibility. But she hadn't ever imagined someone objecting to her marrying Colton.

He took her hand again, and together they walked down the aisle to the girl—at a pace much faster than the one she'd used walking toward Colton. Of all the catastrophes Sophie had imagined, having a blue-haired girl object to her wedding hadn't been one of them.

Colton motioned the girl away from the rows of chairs. "Who are you?"

"Tori." The name came out like a curse, filled with anger that vibrated on those two syllables. "Her daughter." She nodded at Sophie.

Daughter? Sophie started to shake. She felt as if there wasn't enough air to draw a breath. She felt lightheaded and clung to Colton's arm for support.

"That's right, *Mom*," the girl continued. "The baby you threw away has found you. Sorry to interrupt your day. Hell, sorry to interrupt your life."

Sophie studied the features of the tiny, blue-haired girl, and realized that the girl was older than she looked. Just about Sophie's five foot two inches. The girl—Tori—her features were her own. Tori's very blue eyes sparked with pent-up anger.

Then she searched her upper lip. There. The tiniest, faintest of scars. Something no one would notice unless they were looking for it. There was the scar.

Tori. Her daughter's name was Tori. The annual letters Tori's parents sent via the adoption agency never mentioned her name. They simply included a few pictures, and a page or two of their daughter's accomplishments and highlights of her year.

"Tori," Sophie whispered. It was the first time she'd ever said her daughter's name. Until now, she'd simply been *Baby Girl,* even though Sophie knew she was no longer a baby.

She gulped in air, trying to fill her lungs.

Colton said, "Sophie?" and she looked at him. She saw the moment that he realized this girl had spoken the truth. Tori was her daughter, and Sophie knew exactly three things about her. She was fourteen. She'd dyed her probably blond hair blue. And she was angry.

She was very, very angry.

"She's mine," she whispered, sure for more reasons than the girl's looks, scar or height. Something in her yearned to take this girl into her arms and hold her in a way she hadn't ever been permitted to. Something in her recognized the angry woman-child as her daughter.

"I don't know what to say," she admitted to both Colton and Tori.

Colton took charge. He led the two of them into the barn and away from the prying eyes of the wedding guests. The barn was strung with white lights, and there were makeshift tables covered in elegant white tablecloths set up with white china and linen napkins. Sophie loved the juxtaposition of the rustic setting and the formal place settings. The same contrast could be seen in the humble daisy and more formal white rose centerpieces.

The girl looked around the barn, and her anger

seemed to grow. It radiated from her every pore like some hot, red aura.

Sophie wanted to say something to comfort her, but didn't know where to begin. "Tori, I—"

The girl turned away. Sophie wasn't sure if she was crying or simply too angry to speak. But Colton obviously had a lot to say. He started with, "You had a daughter and you never thought to mention it?"

Sophie wasn't sure how to explain things to Colton or Tori. She didn't know anything about the girl's parents, but she knew that Colton's family was a loving, supportive one. They filled the first two rows of seats in the field. How could she make him understand what it had been like for her at that time?

And how could she explain to this girl why she'd given her up? What words could a mother use to make Tori understand something like that?

Sophie swallowed. "Fourteen years ago, I was little more than a child myself when I gave birth to a baby girl. I never held her, and caught only the barest glimpse of her as they whisked her away."

Tori whirled around and, rather than speaking to Sophie, she looked at Colton. "Yeah, she got rid of me. I was a burden. A mistake." She faced Sophie, and practically screamed at her, "Did you ever even meet my parents or did you just hand me over to the agency and let them pick? Did you worry that they might beat me? Maybe they'd be crazy. Maybe they would go on and have a bunch of their own biological children and remind me every day that I'm not really theirs."

Sophie knew that the girl had thrown those things out to hurt her, and even if none of them were true, Tori had succeeded. "I didn't meet your parents, but I picked them." She remembered that battle. She'd lost so many other fights then, but that had been one she'd been adamant about winning. If only the girl knew how hard Sophie had fought for at least that much—the ability to pick the couple who would raise her daughter.

"And I know that your mother had a hysterectomy, so she couldn't have had any other children. Maybe they adopted more, but they didn't have any biological kids. That's one of the reasons I chose them. I wanted to be sure you were with people who would treasure you."

Her answer didn't mollify the girl. "Yeah, well, maybe they beat me."

"Did they? Do they?" Sophie asked. She couldn't begin to count the number of times she'd had a dream like that—a nightmare. Her daughter was hungry. Her daughter was lost. Her daughter was hurt. And knowing that there was nothing she could do to help this child made it worse.

Tori was silent and finally shook her head. "No one beats me. My dad's a pacifist. He won't even kill flies."

"Oh." Sophie had so many questions. Fourteen years' worth of questions, but she sensed that the girl wasn't here to answer them. Tori wanted answers of her own.

And behind Tori, Sophie could see Colton. She could read him well enough to know that he was asking himself, if she could keep something that big from him, what else was she hiding?

She needed to explain why she hadn't told him. She hadn't lied, but she'd never told him. "Colton, I—"

"I asked you," he said softly. "I asked if you had any family. It was our second month of dating and we'd gone to my parents', and I asked if you had a family. And you said, 'not anymore.'" He paused. "It was a lie."

"Not in the way you think." She didn't know how

to make him understand. "My family is complicated. And when you asked, we'd only been dating a couple months, and I'd just met your very wonderful family. I didn't owe you answers about my less-than-wonderful one. Not then. And later…?" After that, he'd never asked again. And Sophie had been happy that she didn't have to explain.

He removed the new cowboy hat from his head and ran his fingers through his hair. She'd been right—he'd used some sort of gel in it. Sophie wasn't sure why that fact registered, but it did.

"Do you have family other than a daughter?" he barked.

"In a strictly biological way? Yes."

She waited, anxious to hear what he would say. He simply nodded. "I'm going to go talk to the caterer and we'll have them set up the meal at the diner. Then I'll tell everyone the wedding's off. You take Tori and go talk. It's obvious you two have a lot to say to each other."

He'd said the wedding was off. For today, or forever? "What about us?"

Normally she could read Colton like an open book. But now, the book had slammed shut, and all he said was, "We'll talk later. In the morning. Right now, you need to deal with Tori. I'll send everyone home. Why don't you take your…daughter, and slip out before someone corners you."

She'd hoped he'd say, *Talk to Tori, then meet me in front of the minister, we'll work it all out.* But he was calling off the wedding. They'd "talk" about it tomorrow.

Sophie had planned for any number of emergencies

with the wedding, but not this. Not a returning long-lost daughter.

And not the man who was supposed to love her leaving.

There was nothing to do but nod at Colton and watch him stride back to their guests, her heart breaking into a million little pieces. She waited, silently pleading for him to stop and come back to her, but he didn't.

"Let's go to my house where we can talk," she said to Tori. Her daughter.

COLTON LIKED TO THINK of himself as a simple man.

He knew he was a man of few words, but he tried to make the words he did utter count.

He tried to tell Sophie daily that he loved her. He tried to show her in his every action.

He tried to be there for his friends. For Finn, who'd suffered so much when he lost his sister Bridget last winter, and for Sebastian, who'd come home physically damaged and emotionally battered.

Yes, Colton had been content with his straightforward bachelor farmer's life, and then Sophie Johnston had breezed into Valley Ridge. Meeting her had changed everything. His dreams expanded to include her at his side, and raising a family here together on his grandfather's farm.

When she'd come down the aisle toward him, she'd been walking toward that simple future, as well.

I object.

Those two little words had changed everything.

He'd thought he knew everything there was to know about Sophie, but it turned out she wasn't an orphan with a past that was too painful to talk about. She had family. And she had a daughter.

A daughter she'd given away.

Colton had always lived life on an even keel. Now his life was anything but. He motioned to Sebastian. "The wedding's off. Do you mind if I have the caterers take the food to the diner? I know that means you'll have to open, but—"

His friend smacked his shoulder—a guy's form of comfort. "There's no buts. Consider it done."

"Thanks. If people ask what happened, tell them that I'll explain later. First I have to figure it out for myself."

He turned to the wedding guests. Most of them were friends he'd had since childhood. His family filled the first two rows, and he wondered how he'd explain today to them, especially when he could hardly wrap his brain around it himself.

He stood in front of what seemed like the entire community and said, "I'm so sorry for the inconvenience, but the wedding's canceled. I talked to the caterer and they're moving all the food to the diner. Please feel free to stop in and help yourself. And please, those who've brought gifts, retrieve them on your way out."

With that, he turned, strode up the aisle and raced off down the hill toward the farm. He was a simple man—too simple perhaps to know how to handle something this decidedly unsimple.

SOPHIE HAD DRIVEN to Colton's that morning. She hadn't intended on driving back to her house today. They were supposed to leave for their honeymoon tonight. No cruise or European vacation. They'd borrowed their friends' cabin in the Poconos for the week. Only the two of them in the mountain retreat. Long walks. Quiet days. A perfect way to start a life together.

And now? Sophie wanted to curl up in a ball and

cry. She wanted to find Colton and throw herself in his arms. She wanted to be back at the arbor he'd built for her, saying *I do* in front of all their friends, then walking down to the barn for their reception. She wanted to dance with Colton and cut the cake, and…

Instead, she drove the now-silent teen back to her house. "Let's go talk."

Sophie noticed the big scuff mark on her front door as they walked up the stairs but didn't comment as she let Tori inside. Sophie led her into the small but functional living room, and nodded at the red plaid couch. Tori slouched onto it and then glared as Sophie sat next to her.

"Why don't you start," she said softly. "You came to find me because…?"

"Why did I find you?" Tori's voice was quiet, but that only made it easier to hear the anger reverberating in every syllable. "Oh, I don't know. I'm going about my very normal life when I discover I'm not who I thought I was. I thought I was Gloria and Dom's daughter. I thought my mother was a college president and my dad was a stay-at-home painter. I thought my grandparents were ex-hippie farmers. Instead, I find out I'm adopted and I don't know anything about my real family. I found out that the reason I didn't inherit any of my dad's artistic genes is 'cause I don't have his genes. And I didn't get mom's academic brain 'cause I don't have her genes, either."

"So you want to know about my genes?" Sophie asked quietly. She'd dreamed of this. Meeting her daughter. But in those dreams, there had been a happy, albeit tearful, reunion.

Not being battered by wave after wave of anger.

"Hell, no," Tori barked. "I don't care about your

genes. I want to know how someone just gives their
baby away. I wanted to see you. I want a freakin' explanation. I deserve that much."

"You do deserve that much and so much more. It's a
long story," Sophie said. "I don't know where to start."

"How about with that guy you were about to marry.
I take it he's not my father?" Tori asked.

"No. Your father was my high school boyfriend. His
name was Shawn and I thought I was in love. For that
one blink of an eye, I thought Shawn and I would be
together through everything. Anything."

As she remembered those long-ago feelings, she recognized how shallow they were. She so wished Colton
had been Tori's father. He'd have stood by her. He'd
have done the right thing, no matter how hard it was.
By right thing, she didn't mean marry her. She might
have been young, but even when she was pregnant with
Tori, she'd known she never wanted anyone to feel obligated to stand by her. By right thing, she meant he'd
have stayed and helped raise the child they'd created.
Colton would have supported her against her parents,
and she had no doubt that with Colton by her side,
she'd have won.

"And the guy, this Shawn, who was my real father.
He didn't want me, either?"

She longed to say something to help Tori. To ease her
anger. But she knew what it was like to feel betrayed
by a parent, and she didn't think there were any words
that would erase that kind of pain. She'd try, though.
"Shawn. Shawn Mayburn was his full name, in case
you want it. He—we—were both kids. Not much older
than you are now. We were high school sweethearts,
making plans for our future. He'd go to college two
years before me, but that was okay, because he'd be

able to show me the ropes when I got there. We'd get our degrees, backpack through Europe and then…well, things got fuzzy then. Still, we knew we'd have a phenomenal life. We had all kinds of ideas. But we didn't plan on having a baby—at least not when we were still in our teens. Please, Tori, no matter what you think of me, you have to know you were always, always wanted. And loved."

Tori reached out and snagged a corner of the throw over the back of the couch. She rubbed a section between her forefinger and thumb, and finally asked, "So, what happened? If you wanted me and loved me, and you loved my father, how come you let me be adopted?"

"I—" This had been a whirlwind, but suddenly Sophie realized that she hadn't asked. "Where are your parents?"

"I—" This time it was Tori who hesitated.

Sophie might be brand-new at parenting, but even she could see the guilt written all over Tori's face. "Do they know you're here?"

Tori shook her head. "No."

"You ran away?"

"Not exactly." Guilt clearly replaced Tori's anger. "I ran to, not away. I ran *to* you. To find you and find some answers."

"You need to call your parents right now," Sophie said. She could only imagine how scared they must be.

"No."

"Tori, this isn't negotiable. I'll answer any questions you have as honestly as I can, but I won't tell you another thing until you call your parents and tell them where you are."

"I'm not what they want," Tori blurted out, the pain of that knowledge—right or wrong—evident in her voice. "When I found out, I realized how disappointed they must be that they adopted a clunker kid. Mom makes her living educating kids, yet has one who doesn't get straight As. I get Bs and sometimes Cs except with anything technology. Those classes I always ace, but it's not really academic, is it? I have a bizarre sense of how things work. I'll never read Proust for fun. I'm Mom's big disaster. And Dad, he'd love an artsy sort of vegan kid, and instead he has a hamburger-eating one who can paint the walls in her room, but not much else. They're both extraordinary, and I'm…I'm not. I'm an average kid."

"So you looked up your biological mom because you wanted someone to blame for your mediocrity?" Sophie asked. She realized it came out snarky, but listening to Tori, she thought that maybe her daughter needed a bit of snark if those were her biggest complaints about her parents.

Tori shrugged. "Maybe partly. Maybe I wanted to find you and find there was something special about me. And maybe I hoped that I'd find someone who understood. Maybe there was some genetic…"

Sophie filled in the blank. "A mediocrity gene?"

"It sounds stupid when you say it." She rubbed the afghan harder.

"Maybe it is. Here's how I see it. You are who you are. Part of that is the genes I gave you. Part of that comes from Shawn's genes. Part of that is the way your parents raised you. And part of that, the biggest part, is you…the essence of you. No amount of genes or environment can change that essence."

"So I'm screwed." Tori slouched even further.

Sophie might not have ever parented a child, but she'd seen Bridget, and now Mattie, holler at a kid without saying a word. She tried quirking her eyes and frowning at Tori's totally awful word choice.

It got the desired result.

Tori raked her hand through her short blue hair. "Sorry. I am sorry for everything. I didn't come here to ruin your life, too."

"You haven't ruined my life." Sophie wanted more than anything to reach out and hug this child she'd fought so hard for. This child she'd thought of every day for fourteen years. This child she loved.

But she didn't have the right.

"Maybe I didn't ruin your life, but I definitely ruined your wedding."

Sophie thought about Colton's expression when she told him that, yes, she'd had a child. The pain and the accusations there. "Colton loves me, and I love him. We'll figure it out," she said with more confidence than she felt. She needed to get back to finding out where Tori's parents were, and having her call them.

"It's just that, I got to town and everything was closed for a wedding, then I got to your house and you weren't here. This cop stopped and thought I was a guest and that I missed the bus to the wedding. *Your* wedding. I thought it was a great opportunity to see you without introducing myself, without explaining who I was. So I sat in the back, and then there you were, so beautiful and so happy as you walked down the aisle. And these ladies in front of me whispered that you were perfect, and you and Colton were perfect together. I…"

"You?" Sophie prompted.

"I was so angry. How could you be that happy when you gave me away? I was an inconvenience, and you took care of it by getting rid of it. You went on to build this perfect life…without me. I was so mad when the minister started talking and I knew that you were leaving me again. You were going on with your happy life without a thought of me. Then I was standing, objecting…"

There was so much pain. Not anger like Sophie had thought, but straight-up raw and deep pain. And Sophie knew everything Tori was feeling was her fault. She'd done this. She'd made the best—maybe the only—decision she could. She'd tried to give her daughter everything she'd never had. A nurturing, loving family. And all she'd managed to do was hurt her. "Tori, I'm so sorry—"

"No, I'm sorry." Tori had tears in her eyes. "I screwed up your life. Getting rid of me was probably the smartest thing you ever did."

"Losing you… I didn't get rid of you, I didn't throw you away. I lost you." Sophie recalled when the doctor said she'd had a baby girl, and how she shouted about wanting to hold her, but her mother had been there, shaking her head. They'd taken Sophie's baby away, and all she remembered after that was screaming until a nurse gave her a shot of something that knocked her out. Then it was the next day and her baby was gone.

She'd never held her baby. But she'd had some comfort imagining her baby's adopted mother holding her. She'd thought about how joyful her baby's parents must have been after trying for so long to have a baby.

"How did you lose me?" Tori asked.

Sophie offered a weak smile, emotions rolling and mixing together into a tsunami of feelings that she couldn't sort out. "I wanted what was best for you, and best for you wasn't being raised by a mother who didn't even have a high school diploma and who had no way of earning enough money to support you. I lost you because I loved you that much. I swear we'll talk about all of it, but not now. Right now we need to call your parents."

"Why don't you call them my adopted parents? You're my mother."

"No, I am the woman who gave birth to you when I was little more than a girl myself." That was the moment she stopped being a girl. She'd lived her entire adult life with the pain of not being able to hold her baby, or to keep her, embedded in her soul.

"*They* are your parents. They're the ones who made you feel better when you were little. They're the ones who know you best. They know your favorite color. They were there your first day of school. They came and comforted you when you had a bad dream." At least she hoped they'd done all that. Things like that were what she longed for growing up. She had wanted to give the gift of those moments to her daughter.

Quietly Sophie asked the questions she needed answers to. "Did they ever hurt you?"

"You mean like hit me or lock me in closets?" Tori shook her head. "No. They love me…or love the me they want me to be. But I'm never going to be a straight-A student. And I'm never going to be an artist or even a vegan. I can't be. They gave me everything, and I'm still a screwup."

"You're perfect," Sophie told her.

Tori snorted.

"You can't be what they envision, or even what I envision. And if no one else has ever mentioned it, let me assure you that you shouldn't try to be what any of us want. You need to be you. And you're perfect at that…at least you're perfectly equipped to do that. To be the person you're meant to be."

"So, your day job is writing lyrics for bad country songs?" Tori sniped.

"I wish someone had said those words to me when I was growing up. Even more, I wish I'd figured that all out when I was still in my teens."

Tori didn't say anything this time. Sophie pushed. "I need your parents' number."

"I won't go back."

There was a stubbornness in Tori's expression, and Sophie could hear her mother telling her, "I hate it when you look like that. Like you're almost daring me to try and get you to..."

The getting-you-to changed. Her mother had tried to *get her to* do ballet. Sophie had refused after the first few lessons. She'd hated it. If there was a rhythm gene, then she had received the antirhythm variety. There had been other attempts at getting-her-to. Piano. Drawing lessons.

Which made her think of Tori's artist father. "You need to call them."

"I came here to know you, and I'm not going back yet. I have so many questions, and if you try to get rid of me again, I'll run away and—"

"No threats," Sophie warned. "Don't say things you might feel obligated to make good on. Legally, I'm nothing to you. They're your parents, and I guarantee they're worried."

"I—"

Sophie interrupted again. "No excuses, no threats. The number. We'll call them and then we'll work something out. Even if they take you home right away, you'll go knowing that I love you. That I never gave you away. And that that was the single most painful thing that's ever happened to me. If your parents do insist that you leave now, then when you're old enough, you'll come back and we'll talk. No matter what, you'll know you're loved. Maybe you don't believe it but, Tori, of all the things you need me to tell you, that's the most important thing. You were loved. You are loved. You were wanted. You are wanted. And as far as I'm concerned, not knowing anything more about you than the fact you're tenacious, you have blue hair and you're very angry, I still know that you are absolutely perfect." And for the first time ever, Sophie leaned over and touched her daughter. She gently ran a finger over Tori's cheek, brushing against a strand of her blue hair.

It was such an easy gesture, but Sophie knew that she'd remember that one small touch for the rest of her life.

"But…" Tori started, then looked at Sophie and nodded. She rattled off a number.

Sophie dialed, and felt sick as she said, "Hello, uh, you don't know me…I'm Sophie, I gave birth to your daughter fourteen years ago. Tori's here with me now…."

CHAPTER TWO

IT TOOK A LITTLE MORE than two hours for the Allens to drive from their home outside Cleveland, Ohio, to Valley Ridge, New York. The little slip of Pennsylvania that stood between the two states didn't usually take a long time to navigate.

After she'd made the call, Sophie had slipped off her wedding dress and hung it carefully in her closet. She'd stroked the material for a minute and tried to imagine what she would be doing now at the reception. She shut the door on that fantasy. She knew that life wasn't a fantasy. She'd met Colton and, temporarily, she'd forgotten that fact.

She slipped on a pair of jeans and a blouse. She thought about taking her hair down, but there were so many bobby pins, and so much hairspray in it, she didn't think she could until she showered.

She didn't want to lose a minute of her time with Tori to showering, so she'd gone back into the living room. She'd stood in the doorway, drinking in the sight of her daughter on her couch. Anger. Pain. Blue hair. Still gripping the throw on the couch between her finger and thumb. Every inch of Tori was…perfect.

She wished she could make her daughter see that.

During those one hundred and twenty minutes they waited for Tori's parents to arrive, Tori peppered Sophie with questions ranging from her family's medical history to Sophie's educational background. She asked about Sophie's job here in Valley Ridge.

She didn't ask again why Sophie had given her up.

She didn't ask about her father.

The questions she didn't ask bothered Sophie more than the ones she did.

Tori startled when the doorbell rang. "It's them, isn't it?"

Sophie nodded. "I imagine so. Do you want to get the door, or shall I?"

"You. They're going to kill me."

Sophie got up and, before going to the door, walked by her daughter and patted her shoulder to comfort her and to allow herself one more touch. She went to the small foyer and opened the door. The woman, Tori's mother, wore a pair of black pants, low heels and a no-nonsense fitted white blouse. She was wearing a very classic set of pearls and had pearl studs in her earlobes. Her light blond hair was pulled back into a chignon.

Tori's father had on jeans with a hole in one knee, wear marks on the other and a couple of paint splotches. He wore brown loafers and a T-shirt with pictures of doors on it that read The Doors. His dark brown hair was shaggy, as if he'd forgotten to get it cut for several months.

"Sophie?" the woman asked.

Suddenly, it occurred to Sophie that she didn't know Tori's last name. She'd only mentioned her parents' first names. "Gloria and Dom?"

They both nodded.

"Thank you for calling us," Gloria said stiffly.

"Tori's in the living room." Sophie knew that Tori's parents needed to see her—to touch her, to know for themselves she was all right.

Sophie had been right. As her parents entered the room, Tori got up from the couch and was enveloped in her parents' hugs. For as completely composed and business-looking as Gloria appeared, she was unabashedly crying as she embraced her daughter. "Don't you ever do anything like that to us again."

Dom sounded heartbroken as he added, "You could have talked to us. We'd have brought you—"

Tori pulled back, the happy reunion forgotten. "No, Dad, don't say you would have supported me and brought me to meet Sophie. You didn't even tell me I was adopted. I still wouldn't know if I hadn't seen that envelope. You both lied to me my whole life."

"Victoria, it's time to go," her mother said, tears forgotten. "We'll discuss this later. Right now, you've barged in on Sophie and—"

Tori pulled back from her parents' embrace. "No, Mom. I'm not going. I got a few answers, but I need more. I need to know Sophie. If I can know her, maybe I can figure me out."

Sophie felt awkward in the midst of the volatile family confrontation. "Tori, I—"

Tori whirled on her. "Oh, I know, I'll interrupt your perfect life. I already ruined your wedding. I'm an inconvenience, but I'm not going home to Cleveland yet."

"Victoria—" her mother started, but her father interrupted.

"Tori, give us a minute."

"Where should I go? Sophie's house is small. I'll hear you wherever I am. And honestly, I think I've proved I'm an adult."

Dom had struck Sophie as a free spirit. Seeing him with Tori's mom, a decidedly unfree spirit if ever she'd met one, seemed incongruous, but in this instant, he transformed into a father—a firm but loving father who expected to be obeyed. "Tori, if anything, you've proven how immature you still are. I'm not denying that we should have told you sooner that you were adopted, but that doesn't excuse your conduct. You are fourteen, and you stole our car. Not only that, you drove it out of state."

"I read the driver's manual. I know all the rules. I think I was the only one who drove the speed limit the whole way here. And I've driven all kinds of vehicles at Nana and Papa's farm. I was confident I could manage. And I did."

"It's illegal. If you'd been stopped…if you'd hit another car…if…" All the things that could have gone wrong had obviously been playing in his mind.

"You drove here?" Sophie asked. It occurred to her that a good parent would have asked how a fourteen-year-old arrived in Valley Ridge. The town was too small for a public transportation system. That left either driving or hitchhiking.

She felt sick at the realization Tori had driven across three states. She couldn't stop the images of what could have happened. Scenes from nightly newscasts played in horrible detail, all of them with Tori as the focus.

"Go outside, Tori," her father said firmly "Find a seat on Sophie's porch and don't move from there. We'll come get you in a little bit."

"Fine." Tori whirled and headed toward the front door.

"And if you go anywhere other than that front porch, I'll track you down and I'll—"

"What? Spank me?" Tori laughed.

"I might be a pacifist, but believe me when I say, if

that's what it took to get you to understand how incredibly stupid you've been, well, I'd do it. Don't tempt me."

Tori looked taken aback by his response. She hid it by turning on her heels and slamming the door behind her for good measure.

Sophie didn't know what to do, what to say. "I'm sorry."

Dom quirked one eyebrow and Sophie thought of *Star Trek*'s Spock, which struck her as an absurd thought to have in the midst of the day's events.

"For what?" he asked.

She shrugged. "I don't know, but I can't help feeling this is all my fault, and I'm sorry."

"Let's sit down." He assumed the role of host and got them situated in the living room, he and his wife on the couch, Sophie opposite them on the chair.

"If anyone should be sorry, it's me," Gloria said. "Dom wanted me to tell Tori she was adopted from the day she arrived home, but I…" She shook her head. "I couldn't bear it. I sent you those letters every year through the adoption ageny, and part of me relished sharing her development with someone I knew cared. I was so grateful to you for choosing us. I spent days writing them. Picking out pictures. But I never told you her name or ours because I was afraid. She's mine. Every time I mailed out a letter, I'd be sick with worry that you'd realized how much you gave up and come to get her, but that didn't stop me from writing down all the details I thought you wanted to hear. I needed to prove to you that you were right to choose us. But it scared me to death."

"So that's why no names?" Sophie asked. All she'd ever known her daughter as was Baby Girl. Every year, after she read Gloria's letter, she'd write her Baby Girl a letter in response. She could have sent them to Tori through the agency, but frankly, pouring her heart out to her child didn't seem fair. At some point, she'd give her daughter the box of letters. Maybe it would help answer her questions.

"I know. Not even her first name. That was cruel." Gloria leaned into Dom with a real need to touch him evident in her expression.

"No. You were so generous sharing her moments. When I received that first letter chronicling all those milestones in her first year…" Sophie fought to hold back the tears. "For weeks, I read it every day. I can recite the letter to you word for word. But at some point, I knew I couldn't go on that like that. So, I put it away. And each year, when you sent the new letter, along with the pictures, I'd read it through, then I'd reread all the old ones. I'd write my response and put it away, as well. I gave myself one full day to appreciate them, to look at Tori and marvel at her. Then I'd put the box away and would go back to living my life. You provided that one letter to me and then went back to being her mother. I get that. You wanted to keep her safe."

"But I failed. I hurt her by not listening to Dom."

Maybe Sophie could see Gloria's guilt because it mirrored her own. She saw it and recognized that they didn't simply share a love for Tori, but also the guilt that came from wondering if they'd done the right thing.

Dom squeezed his wife tighter into the protection of his arm. "You can't know if things would have been better or worse if we'd told her. The fact is we didn't. The two of us. And now we have to deal with the repercussions. The three of us. We have to forget about blame and guilt. We need to figure out what to do for

Tori. She's in pain, and we need to decide how best to help her."

Sophie looked at these two people who'd been parents to her daughter, and a sense of peace swept through her pain and guilt. No matter what she'd done, she'd found her daughter wonderful parents. "I'll do whatever you both think is best. She's your daughter. I don't want you to think I've forgotten that."

"Thank you." Gloria studied her a moment, then repeated, "Thank you. So what do we do now?"

"No," Tori shouted from the doorway into the living room. "I've decided that I'm not going to sit outside and let the three of you decide my fate. Here's what's going to happen. I'm staying with Sophie for a while. Think of it as summer camp."

"Victoria Peace Allen—" Gloria stuttered to an abrupt halt, as if she couldn't think of what to say next.

Sophie realized that she now knew her daughter's full name. And on the heels of that thought came a single word…*Peace?*

Dom must have seen the look because he nodded and said, "Peace." He started to laugh. Gloria, then Tori, started laughing, as well.

"Dad's a hippie. A commune-living, vegan-eating hippie," Tori supplied. "So are Nana and Papa."

Dom shook his head and clarified, "My parents were the hippies. I'm merely the son of hippies." He turned to Sophie and explained, "Gloria picked Tori's first name. I got to the pick the second. My name's actually Freedom Jay Allen."

"Which is why I call him Dom," Gloria said with a sniff.

Despite everything that had happened that day, the

shock layered onto pain, layered onto utter confusion, Sophie found herself smiling.

"And you grew up in a commune?" she asked.

"Well, like any child, I lived where my parents decreed."

"Nana and Papa never decreed a thing in their whole lives." Tori turned to Sophie. "They don't live on a commune anymore. They run a CSA in Pennsylvania."

"CSA?" Sophie asked.

"Community-supported agriculture. Basically, people buy shares of their farm's crops. They're still hippies," she added in a conspiratorial whisper.

For a moment, all four of them were quiet. And slowly, the leftover smiles faded, and Tori stared at the three adults. "I get it, you know. I get what you meant, Sophie. They're my parents. They've raised me. Nana and Papa are my grandparents. They all know me. They were there when I took my first step and started school." She turned to her parents. "I get that. And I love you both. Nothing will ever change that. You are my parents. But you need to understand, I can't leave until I know…"

"Know what?" Sophie asked. "I swear, I'll tell you whatever you need to know."

"I don't know, but I need to figure it out. I need to work it out in my head. If you try to make me leave before I do, I'll run away again."

"No threats," Sophie repeated. "Remember?"

"I can't go home without knowing."

There was desperation in Tori's voice. Sophie couldn't decide if Tori was desperate for answers or desperate to be understood.

Maybe both.

She wanted to go hug her daughter. But she knew

she'd been right when she'd told Tori that Gloria and Dom were her parents. She watched them both pull Tori onto the couch between them and wrap their arms around her.

And that moment solidified the knowledge that she'd done the right thing. All those years ago, as she had read letters from people asking for a baby, she'd seen Gloria and Dom, and a feeling of rightness had settled over her. She'd known these were her daughter's parents. And they were.

"Here's what I suggest," Dom finally said. "The three of us are going to go—"

"I meant it, Dad," Tori interrupted, her anger back in place.

Dom shot her a look that shut her up and he continued, "We'll go find a hotel for the night. The three of us can discuss things, then tomorrow morning, the four of us will meet for breakfast someplace neutral and decide how we're going to handle this."

"By *this,* he means me," Tori informed Sophie.

Sophie found herself agreeing to Dom's plan with gratitude. She called JoAnn, who had two rooms available at her B and B. "It's only a few blocks away," she assured the worried-looking Tori. "And why don't we meet at the diner for breakfast? You name the time."

They agreed on ten.

As the family walked to the door, Tori turned and said, "I'm sorry about the wedding."

Remembering an old saying, Sophie told her daughter, "It will all come out in the wash."

"Wedding?" Gloria asked.

"Today was her wedding, Mom," Tori admitted, shamefaced. "I objected."

Tori's parents started talking, but Sophie interrupted. "Tori, of all the things you need to worry about right now, that's not it. If anything, you should sympathize with Colton. He didn't know about you, kind of like you didn't know about me. Sometimes people keep secrets out of malice, but sometimes, they keep them because that secret's simply too hard to talk about. Losing you…well, if I had to talk about it every day, I don't know that I'd have made it. And I'm sure your mom didn't think of you as anything but her daughter. Trying to explain there was another facet to that…" She turned to Gloria. "I get it."

"But—" Tori objected.

Sophie stopped her. "Listen, we'll meet tomorrow and try to figure out what's best for you. That's always been my number-one concern, and even though I've just met them, I know it's your parents', too. So, you three go talk tonight. I'll see you tomorrow at ten at the diner for breakfast."

Tori nodded, and Gloria wrapped her arm around her daughter's shoulders and led her toward the car.

Dom hung back for a second. "You didn't want to give her up, did you?"

"I loved her then, and now. Everything I did I did for her. I chose you and your wife because you seemed to be such a balanced couple. Your letter about longing for a child… I gave Tori the best life I could. And despite everything, I'd do it again."

He studied her, then nodded and followed his family.

The three of them were a unit. A family.

And Sophie knew that even though she'd given birth to Tori, she'd never be more than that—the woman who gave birth to her.

Tori might not realize that fact yet, but she would.

Sophie would see to it.

CHAPTER THREE

COLTON SPENT a sleepless night.

He'd picked up his phone a dozen times, ready to call Sophie. Wanting to tell her they could work it out. Needing to tell her how much he loved her.

And yet, he couldn't manage it.

Every time his phone rang, he checked the caller ID. Not one of the calls was from Sophie, but there was a distinct possibility that half of Valley Ridge had left him messages. Finn and Sebastian had tried to contact him multiple times, but he hadn't picked up. He couldn't talk to anyone until he spoke to Sophie.

And he had no idea what to say to Sophie. So he didn't call her or pick up for anyone else. Instead, he paced. He cursed. He watched the clock tick forward, and thought about what they should have been doing at each hour.

Now, we'd cut the cake.

Now, we'd have our first dance.

Now the reception would be over, and he'd bring his wife home.

Now...

None of that had happened.

At eight in the morning, he knew a phone call wouldn't work. So, he drove to Sophie's house. The house they'd planned to put on the market because she was going to move into his house after they got back from the Poconos.

As a matter of fact, *now* they should be in the car and headed to their friends' mountain retreat.

He knocked at Sophie's door. He hadn't knocked on her door for months. Not since the day she'd given him a key. As he waited for her to answer, he noticed a dark scuff mark on the door itself and wondered what had happened.

He wondered if she'd been so upset that she kicked the door when she got home, but he knew her wedding shoes couldn't have left a mark like that.

The door swung open and there she was. He drank in the sight of her. It felt as if he hadn't seen her in years rather than just hours.

"I thought you'd come," she said by way of a greeting as she opened the door and let him in.

"Kitchen?" he asked, trying not to notice the boxes that were pushed against the hall walls. She'd told him that she'd started packing her mementos and books. The only furniture she was bringing was her grandmother's writing desk and rocker. He'd told her to feel free and move in whatever she wanted. She'd hemmed and hawed about the plaid couch she loved. He'd assured her that she could redecorate the whole house if she wanted. She could buy them a pink polka-dotted couch and he'd sit on it, as long as she'd sit next to him. She'd kissed him after that declaration—only a small peck on the cheek—and told him there wasn't anything she wanted to change about the house. It was perfect.

She'd laughed then and told him that maybe, if they were lucky, in a few months, they'd change one of the guest rooms into a nursery.

The thought of Sophie pregnant with his child had thrilled him.

But that memory only served to remind him that while that child would have been his first, it wouldn't have been Sophie's first. She'd had a baby and given her away.

And she'd never told him anything about that baby.

And she'd certainly never mentioned who the baby's father was.

He felt an uncharacteristic spurt of jealousy at the thought of some unknown man with Sophie.

"The kitchen is as good a place as any," she replied, pulling him back to the present.

The last time he'd seen her, she'd been wearing her wedding dress. Her hair had been all fancy and styled. Now, she didn't have on a speck of makeup, and her hair was pulled back into a messy bun. She wore a pair of cutoff sweats and his old Gannon University T-shirt.

She looked like his Sophie again.

But he wasn't sure she was…he wasn't sure she had ever truly been the woman he'd thought she was.

She nodded at the table in the sunny breakfast nook and took a seat. He sat across from her.

Colton had planned to start slowly. To ask her to tell him what happened, but instead he found himself jumping right into the thick of it. "How could you be willing to marry me and never tell me about whatever happened in your past? You said your parents were dead."

"They were—are—dead to me. They stole the life I planned. They stole my hopes and dreams. They stole my daughter," she added softly. "I couldn't stop it. I work at forgiving them every day—not that they'd ever think to ask for my forgiveness. I work at it anyway, and most of the time I think I've succeeded in forgiving them, but I can't forget any of it. I finished school and then I left. I changed my name and I've never, never looked back."

She wasn't even really Sophie Johnston? "Who are you really?"

"Sophia Moreau-Ellis."

He tried to imagine her as Sophia Moreau-Ellis, but he couldn't. She still looked like Sophie.

His Sophie. But she wasn't his—not really. Not ever.

"And you haven't seen your parents since?" He couldn't imagine that. He was close to his family. His parents had been calling, wanting to be there for him. Normally, he'd want that, too, but this time, he simply wanted to be left alone to process what had happened.

"My parents aren't anything like yours. Image. Position. Money. Those are the things that matter. I think the fact that I'm gone is a relief to them. They can moan to their friends about how ungrateful their daughter was. But, to be honest, I can't imagine my name comes up often."

Her parents were rich. He knew that suddenly. "You have money?"

"A trust my grandmother set up."

Which explained how she could afford her house. She worked hard at her job, but since he was a member of the newly formed wine association, he knew what they paid her for her PR services. Even with the other occasional freelance jobs she did, now that he thought about it, he knew she had to have another source of income.

Sophie having a trust fund made the idea of her marrying him even more of a mystery. He'd always wondered why she'd chosen him. Sophie could have had any man in Valley Ridge.

Any man, period.

And yet, she'd picked him.

"My grandmother's father started with one small gas station. West's. It grew into a large chain in Ohio and Kentucky. The name has meaning there. That makes my mom first-generation rich. My dad's family, the Ellis family, made their money in fertilizer two generations ago. He's worked hard to get the stench of that poop off him all his life." She said the words as if by rote, as if she'd said them or thought them many times.

It all made sense now. "So, your family's rich. You're rich. A poor little rich girl? You came here and worked as a PR person. You found a simple farmer and thought, *Gee, that'll show my parents?*"

"I came here and worked at a job I'd been preparing for since birth. Public perception is everything in my family. My parents could be fighting, screaming at each other, then hold hands and be all smiles for a party. I learned how to present a public face at birth. I simply took all those tools they gave me and turned it into a job. I take the wineries and give them a public face."

For a moment, he thought she was going to cry, and that would be his undoing, but she didn't. She simply said, "And when I came here, I planned on finding a place I could build a home. I came looking for a community. I didn't plan on finding love. Frankly, I didn't plan to ever marry. Especially…"

"Especially what?" he asked. "You didn't plan on marrying, especially not a farmer? Not a man who comes home covered in dirt? A man who rhapsodizes over a new tractor, not the newest opera? A man who wears a cowboy hat and lives in a house his family has owned for generations?"

"I never planned on marrying…especially not a man as perfect as you."

SOPHIE WAITED, PREPARING herself for more of Colton's questions or accusations. "I want to tell you—" she started.

But he shook his head. "Sophie, it's obvious that you aren't the woman I thought you were. I'm not saying this to be cruel, or to hurt you. And I don't want you to think it's because you had a child. It's simply—well, not simply. Nothing about this is simple. It's that you obviously have a lot of things you didn't tell me about. Things you couldn't trust me with. I don't think I ever really knew you."

"You did," she said. She wanted him to understand. She needed him to understand. "You knew the real me. Know the real me. The *me* that my parents wouldn't recognize. The *me* I always wanted to be. That's what I found here in Valley Ridge, not only a home, but a place where I could be the real me."

When he didn't respond, she added, "That's what I found when I was with you—the real me."

For a moment, she thought she'd made him understand, but she saw in his face that he didn't. She steeled herself for him to say something hurtful, but in the end, he shook his head and stood. She followed suit and, for a moment, they stood face-to-face, not touching. Then he wrapped his arms around her. He leaned down and gently kissed her cheek.

Colton didn't say the words, but she knew that kiss was his goodbye.

"I'm sorry." He stepped back from the embrace.

Sophie realized that was it. The last time they'd ever touch. Part of her ached to step back into his arms, but the bigger part of her understood there was no going back. She took another step, putting more distance between them.

"I wish it could be different," he said, "but I can't…"

She knew what he was saying. He couldn't be with a woman he didn't trust. "I understand."

"Can we be friends?" he asked. "Not now, but eventually?"

"I'd like to say yes, but no." This was her fault, too. She'd left them nowhere to go. She should have trusted her instincts and not gotten involved with anyone. Ever. She should have learned fourteen years ago when she'd lost her daughter that there was no such thing as a happy ending.

Well, lesson learned now. What hurt the most was knowing that she'd hurt Colton in the process. She couldn't go back and undo that, but she could make a clean break of it for his sake. "No, we can't be friends. I'm sorry, Colton. We can be friendly. Given Finn and Mattie's relationship, and the fact I think there's something between Lily and Sebastian…" She paused a moment. "We'll see each other. Valley Ridge is small enough that there's no help for it. We'll be friendly. We'll smile and make small talk, but we can't be friends. Not when I know what we should be, what we could have been, if I'd been…"

She let the sentence hang, not sure how to end it. *What we could have been if I'd been honest* was her first thought, but in reality, the real end to the sentence was *what we could have been, if I'd been someone other than Sophia Moreau-Ellis.*

Colton didn't respond. He simply nodded and turned

and walked down the hall. She followed as far as the kitchen doorway. She watched as he opened the front door and walked through it. He shut it behind him softly but firmly. The sound of the door latch clicking into place wasn't loud, but to Sophie, it was defining, and something she'd remember for the rest of her life.

It would haunt her, along with the sound of her own screams as she'd begged them to allow her to at least hold her baby one time. *Please,* she'd begged over and over, crying hysterically.

She hadn't begged Colton. And she wasn't crying. She felt as if she wanted to. That maybe if she did, some of the almost unbearable pressure, which seemed to press on her from all sides, would ease. But she didn't.

Couldn't.

Colton was a simple man. An honest man. He was a man who believed in hard work, laughter and, most of all, love.

Sophie knew the truth of the situation. Colton would have accepted her past. He could have forgiven her anything…as long as she'd offered him the chance.

She'd never be able to make him understand that even now, talking about her childhood, about her pregnancy, was almost impossible.

God, she wanted to cry.

She wanted to blame her parents for ruining yet another relationship for her. She wanted to add one more black mark against them as parents.

But she knew she couldn't blame this on them.

She'd done this on her own.

She'd had the perfect man and she'd let him go.

She put her palm to her cheek, on the spot where he'd kissed her.

That was it. The last time they'd ever touch, and the

only thing that had ever come close to hurting as much as that moment they'd taken her daughter from her.

Yesterday, she'd touched her daughter for the first time ever when she'd run her finger across Tori's cheek. Today she'd touched the love of her life for the last time.

The enormity of both moments would stay with her forever.

She wanted to crawl into bed and spend the day crying about Colton, but she couldn't. She had Tori to think about.

Her baby girl.

All these years of worrying and wondering.

And Victoria Peace Allen was here in Valley Ridge.

Even though her parents would take her home this afternoon, Sophie had seen her. Touched her. She knew that Tori was loved and she'd been cared for.

Sophie knew her decision to let the Allens raise her daughter had been the right one.

In one hour she'd see Tori again.

The knowledge wasn't enough to assuage her pain at losing Colton, but for now, Sophie pushed the hurt back. Compartmentalizing was something she was an expert at. Someday she'd pull out that last scene with Colton. She'd replay it and allow herself to feel it. But not today. Today Tori had to come first.

Sophie sat at the table in the kitchen, a cup of coffee in front of her, and watched the clock.

A half hour before she was supposed to meet the Allens, she got up and walked to the diner.

The Valley Ridge Diner looked as if it came out of a scene from *Happy Days*. Vintage Formica tables, a jukebox in the corner and Hank Bennington behind the counter, a coffeepot in hand. "How are you, sweetheart?" he asked as she walked past him.

Sophie knew that he wasn't asking because of the canceled wedding. There was no sympathy or hidden question in his greeting. Hank had Alzheimer's. It was in the early stages, and some days were better than others, but she suspected he'd forgotten about the ceremony, just as he'd forgotten her name again.

"I'm fine, Hank," she said. "I'm going to take the back booth. I'm waiting for some visitors."

"You help yourself to whatever seat you want, darling. I'll bring you coffee."

The diner was virtually empty. It was too late for most of its breakfast crowd, and too early for the lunch crowd. The only other customer was Marilee from the MarVee's Quarters. It was odd to see her without her partner, Vivienne. They had a Penn & Teller sort of relationship; they were almost always together, and Marilee did most of the talking. Today she was talking to Connie Nies, who worked for Colton at the winery.

Both women looked up as she walked by. "Sophie, we're so sorry," Marilee said. "I'm not asking what happened, but if there's anything you want us to pass on, we'd be happy to."

Knowing that any news of note tended to filter through Marilee and Quarters, Sophie considered a moment, then nodded. "Two things would be helpful. You could let everyone know that Colton and I have decided to call off the wedding permanently. And you can let everyone know that it was my fault. I don't want to go into details, but Colton deserves everyone's sympathy."

Marilee patted Sophie's hand. "Sweetheart, I will definitely circulate that, but as much as I love Colton, everyone knows it takes two to make a relationship work…and two to make it fall apart."

"Maybe in most cases, but not this time. This time,

it's all on me." She turned to Connie. "You keep an eye on him when you're working, okay? He's so busy in the summer, he sometimes forgets to take care of himself." She'd planned on being the one there to see to it that he did. She'd planned on making sure he ate a balanced diet, not simply coffee and sandwiches on the go.

Her plans had popped like a bubble yesterday. "Thanks," she said, and fled to the back of the diner. She sat down at the back booth, and thought about all the things she'd planned that would never happen.

And no matter what Marilee said, she knew it was completely her fault.

Hank brought her back a cup of coffee as Gloria and Dom came in. "Let me get a couple more cups," Hank said.

"I hope you don't mind, but we asked Tori to give us a half hour before she arrived."

"I don't mind at all," Sophie said. "It will give me a chance to assure you that I will do whatever you both want. If you prefer I not communicate with Tori, I understand. I—"

Hank came back with two more coffee cups. After he poured Dom's and Gloria's, he asked, "Are you all ready to order?"

"We're waiting for one more person, Hank," Sophie said. "So, in a half hour or so, after she's arrived."

"Great. I'll check back with the coffee."

"Thank you," Gloria said to Hank, then turned to Sophie. "Tori let us know in no uncertain terms what she wants. We spent a great deal of the night discussing what to do."

"You might not have noticed, but Tori is slightly strong willed," Dom said with the right hint of sarcasm.

"That's an understatement," Gloria muttered, taking

a sip of her coffee as if to fortify herself, then jumped in. "I called the police department this morning. And spoke to some officer named Dylan?"

Sophie nodded. "Yes. He's a good guy."

"And he assured me that you're not a felon. In addition to that, he gave me a glowing report on you as a person. He swears you're one of the good ones. He talked about how you stepped in and helped when some woman named Bridget passed away this last winter?"

"Bridget was my first friend here in Valley Ridge. I met her at the grocery store. Her daughter Abbey wanted cookies, and when Bridget said no, Abbey had a bit of a toddler temper tantrum. Bridget came over and said, 'Talk to me, please? I need to ignore my daughter's outburst, and if you would make a bit of a fuss about the other two kids and how well they're behaving, she'll come around.'

"So, I knelt down and talked to Zoe and Mickey, asked them about school and praised their good grades and, eventually, Abbey came over and told me that she'd colored a cow and could she give it to me? Later that night, they all walked over to present me with my cow picture—which by the way looked like two ovals with four sticks for feet—and I went for a walk with them. After that, well, Bridget was one of my best friends in town. When she got sick, her friend Mattie came home, and Lily, who's a nurse, came to care for her, and the three of us became friends, too. It helped having someone to rely on when Bridget passed."

"I'm sorry for your loss," Dom said.

Sophie blinked back tears, knowing that if she started crying over Bridget, she'd start crying over Colton, over the fact that the life she'd planned and longed for was gone.

"Thank you," she managed.

"Dylan said the three of you practically lived at Bridget's while she was sick," Dom said.

Sophie wasn't sure if it was a question or a statement, so she simply replied, "She was my friend. And the kids needed all the support they could get."

Gloria nodded, as if that explained everything. "If you cared that much about a friend and her children, I can't imagine that you wouldn't be as careful with my—our daughter."

"*Your* daughter," Sophie corrected. "I meant what I said last night. I get that Tori is your daughter. I gave birth to her, but she's yours."

"Listen," Dom said, "my wife and daughter laugh that I'm a hippie. I tell them all the time that my parents were the hippies, and I was only a kid who went along for the ride. I grew up on a commune, and there was this woman I called Mama Rose. She ran the kitchen, and when the adults were out, she watched over all the little ones. I loved her. All the kids did. We all loved her, and I still send her a Mother's Day card every year. But that never changed the fact I loved my own mother and father. I knew who my parents were, even though I loved Mama Rose. My aunt, who is not, nor ever was, a hippie, asked my mother how she could stand that I loved Mama Rose, and my mother laughed and said, 'You can't run out of love. There's always enough to go around.'"

"I like that saying." Sophie nodded, understanding what he was saying. She repeated, "You can't run out of love."

Dom nodded. "I like it, too. I want you to understand that we're not worried Tori will forget we love her, or that she loves us."

Sophie glanced at Gloria and her expression wasn't quite as assured as Dom's, but Sophie understood that. Sophie was Tori's birth mom. She suspected having her in the picture was harder on Gloria than Dom. "I'm glad, because I might have given birth to her, but I never held her when she was sick, comforted her after a bad dream. I never hugged her after a hard day of school, or celebrated after a good one. I'd be happy to have a part in her life, but it can never be as her mom."

Something in Gloria's expression relaxed. "I'm glad you want to a part of her life because she's demanding that she be allowed to spend time with you this summer and swears if we don't, she'll run away." Gloria's voice dropped. "Tori might have a way with anything mechanical, but I will have nightmares for the rest of my life about what could have happened when she stole the car and drove here. I can't live through that again."

"So, we've decided that if you'll agree, we'll let her spend some time with you this summer." Dom reached over and took Gloria's hand.

Gloria had on a pair of dress slacks, a turquoise blouse and well-matched jewelry. She looked sleek and put together. Dom wore an old Rolling Stones T-shirt, splattered with bits of blue paint, and Sophie wasn't sure the last time a brush had touched his rumpled-looking hair. And yet, despite those differences, Gloria and Dom fit together. They were a united couple. And they were the kind of parents she wished she'd had— parents who put their children's needs first.

And though she'd always believed she'd made the right decision for her daughter, she felt reassured yet again. These two people loved Tori enough to share her because Tori wanted, or maybe needed, it. "I can take her whenever you want, for however long you want."

She felt a spurt of elation at the thought of spending time getting to know Tori. It mixed right in with her other chaotic and jumbled emotions.

"Don't you have to work?" Gloria asked.

Sophie thought of Colton's comment about her being rich, and for once her trust fund didn't seem like a thing to feel guilty about, but rather a blessing that allowed her flexibility and freedom to do whatever Tori needed. "I can work around whatever you have in mind. It's an advantage of being self-employed."

"Then, what we're proposing is we take Tori home for the week and she can pack, then we'll come back next weekend. JoAnn at the bed-and-breakfast said she'd put rooms aside for us each weekend this summer. During the week, Tori will stay with you, and we'll come down each weekend to spend time with her and get to know you better. If my daughter has her way—"

"And she always does," Dom informed Sophie.

"—we'll be seeing a lot of each other."

"You're going to let Tori stay with me?" In her wildest imagination, she'd never dreamed this particular scenario. "Really, you don't know—"

"We talked to Dylan, and you can be sure, we'll be talking to other people in town...." Gloria shook her head. "It's not ideal. I'll want Tori to call every night. But I don't know what else to do. She's very determined."

"That was an understatement," Dom agreed. "But the three of us will need to come to some agreement on a proper punishment. Stealing a car is serious. There has to be some sort of repercussion."

Listening to a man who grew up on a commune talk about repercussions sounded strange.

Dom must have sensed her thought because he

laughed. "Like I said, Mom and Dad are the hippies. I'm a father who loves his daughter enough to see to it she understands the gravity of what she's done. And I understand her enough to realize that she won't let go of the notion of getting to know you. It's not that she *wants* to know about you and spend time with you— she *needs* to. Just like she needed to see how the television worked when she was five and took it apart. She tried for a week to figure out how it worked, then—".

"She put it back together," Gloria finished, her pride evident. "She understands how things work. And not just electronics and cars, but computers. She can take them apart physically, and she can do pretty much anything with them in a programming basis. She simply gets it. And when she needs to understand things, she's like a dog with a bone. She won't let go until she does. Right now, she needs to know you, to understand you. And nothing Dom and I say will dissuade her."

"I realize having her here will disrupt your summer," Dom started.

"I would let anything and everything fall to the wayside in order to spend time with Tori," Sophie told them. She was in awe of these two people, her daughter's parents. Their putting Tori's needs first contrasted her parents' need to put image first.

"Then, we're decided," Dom said. "We'll head home today and bring her back next Friday night, and stay the weekend. Then, that Monday, she'll stay with you?"

Sophie suddenly remembered a saying about doors closing and windows opening. The sound of Colton closing that door this morning would haunt her dreams for the rest of her life, but having Tori come stay with her, getting to know the daughter she had lost—that was more than a window opening. It was as if a cyclone had blown the whole darned house to Oz. Everything was suddenly in Technicolor and anything was possible.

Sophie remembered she hadn't answered. "Yes. I swear I'll take good care of your daughter. And as for her punishment for stealing a car, I think I have an idea."

THE REST OF THE DAY was a blur. Sophie made arrangements for Tori's punishment, although in her mind, it was a wonderful way to spend a summer.

She decided that she could balance having Tori with her work. Tori would do her punishment time, but when she was off, she could come to the wineries when needed. Not that she would be needed for a few weeks. Sophie had taken two weeks off for her honeymoon, so she had unanticipated free time.

She went home and started to unpack her boxes, ignoring what she'd imagined she'd be doing with the contents when she'd packed them. She ignored the fact that she'd planned on putting her grandmother's desk in the corner of Colton's office. She ignored that she'd imagined the two of them sitting in the office in the evening, Colton working on the farm's books and herself working on winery promotions.

That future was over now.

But there was a new future. One that included her daughter.

Doors closing…windows opening.

That was her new mantra.

Getting to know Tori was her window. Tori would be here on Friday. Sophie concentrated on that fact as she studied her guest room. She wanted to do it over for Tori.

A double bed, a small dresser and nothing else. She'd removed the minutia and packed it away.

She decided she wouldn't put anything back in the guest room. She'd let Tori decorate the room. She could paint it, too, if she wanted.

Maybe blue to match her hair?

She smiled at the thought. Tori was unique. And she had parents who seemed to encourage that uniqueness.

Sophie wondered what it would have been like to have that kind of love and support.

Her doorbell rang as she started to slip into the past, wondering about what-ifs. She was thankful for the interruption, but she didn't want to answer the door. She'd stay up here until whoever was there left.

"Sophie, we know you're in there, and we're not leaving until you let us in," came Mattie Keith's voice.

Sophie didn't need to wonder who the other part of Mattie's *we* was. She went down, opened the door and found Mattie with Lily.

"Listen, I'm not really up for company…" she started, but let the sentence fade on its own because as she looked at her friends, she knew they weren't leaving until she let them in. "Fine, come on in."

"I brought some wine," Mattie said. "And Lily's got the fixings for bruschetta. That was our girls' night option. But in case we need something stronger than that, I brought…" She reached into her grocery bag and pulled out a pint of ice cream. "I bought one of every flavor they had."

"I think we might need some of both," Lily said.

Both women walked through the door without an invitation. They looked at the half-unpacked boxes. "Packing?" Mattie asked.

"Unpacking," Sophie told her. She saw understanding register in both Lily's and Mattie's expressions. "The wedding's off."

"Temporarily?" Lily asked.

"I don't think so," Sophie admitted. She'd like to think she and Colton could find a way to fix things, but she remembered his expression before he turned and walked out of her house. There was a sense of finality in it. "No, I don't think so."

"Do you want to talk about it?" Lily asked gently.

"No, of course she doesn't want to talk about it," Mattie said with an air of surety. "But she needs to talk about it, even if she doesn't know it. First some wine, then some talk. Speaking of wine, there's a chance I won't be drinking much more of the stuff. Finn and I are talking about adding to the family."

"You and Finn are that serious?" Lily asked as she put her grocery bag on Sophie's counter.

"We're talking about a quick marriage in August." Mattie glanced at Sophie. "I wasn't going to say anything, but Finn said you'd want to know. That you'd find out eventually anyway."

"Are you kidding?" *Doors and windows,* Sophie thought as she hugged her friend. "Of course I want to know. And this calls for a celebration."

She took the wine out of the bag and dug through her kitchen drawer. "I've got a bottle opener somewhere in here."

Mattie's hand covered Sophie's. "I brought one. And while I open the bottle, tell us what happened. Who was that girl?"

Sophie sat at the table and let Mattie and Lily bring over the wine and bruschetta before she answered, "My daughter."

"You have a daughter and never mentioned it?" Mattie asked, shocked.

Sophie tried to decide how to explain what it was like. How thinking about Tori, much less talking about her, hurt.

She'd known she'd have to tell her friends, but she hadn't talked to them because she didn't know what to say. Stalling, Sophie reached for a piece of the bruschetta, and as she brought it to her mouth, she caught the overwhelming scent of garlic. It wafted up her nose, and she felt a sudden wave of nausea. "Pardon me," she managed as she bolted for the bathroom.

After she was done throwing up, she sank to the floor, covered in a cold sweat.

She never threw up.

The last time she'd been sick was when she was pregnant with Tori.

"Sophie, are you okay?" Mattie called through the bathroom door.

"Fine. I'm fine," she said, thinking. Trying desperately to remember the last time she'd had a period. "I'll be out in a minute."

She sat on the tile floor and leaned against the cool tile wall. The last time she remembered having her period was when Abbey had been sick in the hospital. She'd been buying feminine products when she'd heard the news. It had been a weird period. Light. Really nothing more than splotching. She remembered thinking how odd it was, but hadn't worried since her cycles had been irregular since she'd gone off her birth control at the beginning of the year.

When had Abbey been sick?

Sophie got up and splashed some cold water on

her face, then brushed her teeth and walked out to the kitchen.

"Sophie, are you okay?" Mattie and Lily asked in unison.

She nodded. "Mattie, when was Abbey sick?"

"Why?"

"What was the date?" she repeated without answering why she wanted to know.

"April twenty-eighth. It was a Thursday and it was the scariest moment of my entire life."

Sophie watched her friends exchange worried looks as she sank into the chair. Two months. She did the math in her head, and if it was true, then sometime at the end of January, beginning of February, she'd have a baby.

She'd have a baby with a man who'd left her.

Again.

She hugged her stomach.

This time, no one, nothing, would tear the baby from her. Colton might not want to marry her, but this baby had been conceived in love. She'd stopped taking birth control pills in January because they knew they wanted a family right after the wedding, and her doctor had suggested it might take some time for her system to regulate. They'd used other precautions but, obviously, they'd failed.

Then she thought about Tori.

If it was true, if she was pregnant, what would the news do to the daughter she'd just found? Or rather the daughter who had found her? A child who already thought Sophie had simply given her away without a second thought or regret.

One week ago, Sophie had been on the cusp of marrying the man of her dreams, starting a family with him and living happily ever after.

This week, the daughter she thought she'd lost forever had stolen a car, come to Valley Ridge and objected to her wedding. Her perfect man had decided she was too much trouble to marry. And for a second time, she might be going through a pregnancy on her own.

Sophie wasn't sure if the situation was ironic, moronic or simply absurd, but a giggle escaped.

Then another.

Soon she was laughing, and tears were streaming down her face as she hugged her stomach and wondered if it was possible she was pregnant.

"Sophie, you're scaring us," Lily said. "Come on, hon. Talk to us. How is it you have a daughter, and why aren't you and Colton getting married? What's going on?"

"And, most important, what can we do to help?" Mattie said.

Sophie fought hard to get herself under control. "Do you know the saying about God closing a door, but opening a window? Let's open that ice cream and I'll tell you."

And for the first time in her life, she allowed the story to spill out. She told her friends about her parents, who cared more about image and status than her. She told how her parents had chased off her boyfriend, and their ultimatum to cut her off without a dime, leaving her no way to support her baby. She told them that she'd acquiesced to her parents' demands and gone to a home. She'd given birth in secret, like someone from a '50s movie, and how she'd fought to give the baby to people who'd love her rather than the überrich couple her parents had chosen.

And even though she told her story to her friends, she didn't tell them about her screams when the hospital staff took her baby away without allowing Sophie to see or hold her. But she saw in their faces that they knew that part.

She told about Tori finding her, about how wonderful Tori's parents were. "And she's coming to spend some time with me."

"How long?" Lily asked.

"As long as she wants, at least until school starts. Her parents will come to spend the weekends."

"And Colton?" Mattie asked.

Sophie shook her head. "I never told him about Tori. He sees that as a lie. I don't know how to make him see that it wasn't that I didn't want to tell him, or that I didn't trust him. I couldn't tell him. For fourteen years, I've allowed myself one day a year to wallow in that old pain. Tori's parents send a letter annually on her birthday through the agency. Pictures, too. That one day, I read their new letter, and I reread the old ones. I look at pictures of a daughter I never held, and I see pieces of myself in her. I write a letter to her, a letter I never send, but just add to the box. For that one day, I allow myself to mourn. If I had allowed myself any more than that, I don't think I'd have survived. And if I'd told anyone, and had to have seen the pity in their eyes daily, I would have buckled under the pain."

But suddenly that all changed. Tori was in her life again. She'd actually touched her daughter. She would get to know her.

She didn't think she could stand merely sharing the story. She wanted to shout it from the rooftops. She had a daughter, and Tori was back in her life.

Sophie's hand rested on her stomach as she laid it all

out for her friends. Well, not all. She didn't tell Mattie and Lily about her pregnancy suspicions, and they didn't ask. She had to be sure before she said anything. And then she'd have to tell Colton.

For a moment, she envisioned Colton telling her that they had to marry for the baby's sake. And part of her would long to say yes, because having Colton in her life was what she wanted. But she didn't want him that way. She didn't intend to be an obligation. He was a man who valued honor, and she didn't want to be something his honor demanded he attend to.

No, if she was pregnant, even if he offered to marry her—which she was sure he would do—she'd have to say no. She'd have to be certain he understood that she'd never keep him from his child. She was positive they could work out something amicable.

Telling him should be the hardest thing she'd have to do if she was indeed pregnant, but telling Tori, explaining it to her, would be worse. Sophie would have to find a way to tell Tori and make her understand that she'd never wanted to give up custody of Tori, that she'd done what she'd thought was best.

She'd have to be sure Tori understood that she was loved.

Then Sophie would tell her friends. These might not be the perfect circumstances, but this time, she was going to celebrate her pregnancy. Starting with telling her friends. But not tonight. Not until she was sure, and had told Colton and Tori.

"What about Colton?" Mattie asked.

For a moment, Sophie was confused, thinking that Mattie knew about her newfound suspicions, but then she backtracked on the conversation and realized she didn't. "Colton and I...we're not getting married, but we'll build a new relationship. A friendship."

That's what he'd said he wanted, and she'd said she couldn't manage anything more than friendly. Well, that was no longer an option. If she was right, being friends with Colton was a necessity.

She'd do anything for this possible unborn child, even break her own heart by pretending to be only friends with Colton when she was still so in love with him she could hardly bear the weight of it.

CHAPTER FOUR

TUESDAY AFTERNOON, Colton was on his John Deere mowing the lawn, knowing he should be in the fields but wanting to stay near the house. Yesterday, he'd worked in the barn.

He told himself that even in the summer he needed to get things done around the house. And that was true, but things getting done around the house couldn't take priority over things getting done on the farm and vineyard. He should be out today suckering the vines, or...

He spotted a car coming up the long driveway and for a moment, he thought it was Sophie. For that split second, he thought she'd come to make him listen. To convince him that he was wrong and breaking up was wrong.

It wouldn't be the first time she'd read him the riot act and made him change his mind.

For that split second, he was relieved. Sophie was going to fix things. To make him understand why she'd held so much back.

Then he saw that it was Finn's car. He could see there was someone in the passenger seat and they were sitting far too tall to be Sophie. He didn't need to be able to make out the features to know it was Sebastian.

Most days he'd welcome his two friends' company, but not today. He'd been avoiding them and dodging their calls. Hell, he'd been hiding out from everyone.

He'd realized that he had no groceries in the house because he'd planned on being on his honeymoon. Rather than shopping in Valley Ridge, he'd driven across the state line into Pennsylvania to North East to restock the kitchen.

He didn't want to see anyone.

Except for Sophie, a small part of him whispered.

But since his friends had obviously seen him on the lawn mower, he didn't have a choice. He turned off the riding mower and walked down to the house, resigned. There was no way out of their attempts to help him.

"You two couldn't take a hint?" he said by way of greeting. He removed his hat and wiped the sweat from his brow before reseating it.

"No, obviously we couldn't," Finn said.

Finn pointed to a case of beer, and Sebastian held up a bag as he said, "We brought our own refreshments, so you don't have to worry about playing host."

"As if I'd worry," Colton scoffed.

His friends headed over to the picnic table at the side of the porch.

Colton sighed, and followed them. "I'm not ready to talk about it."

Finn snorted. "Yeah, that's a huge surprise. Colton not ready to talk. I'm shocked. How 'bout you, Seb?"

"Sebastian." Their friend corrected his name automatically. "And yes, I'm shocked, too."

Colton gave in to the inevitable and sat down. "So, if you didn't come for the sordid details, why're you here?"

"We came to hang out with a friend who, though he might not be ready talk, needs us," Finn informed him. "Even if he doesn't realize he needs us."

"That's what my family says when they leave messages on my machine. They tell me that I need them. They're wrong and so are you."

"They're worried," Finn said. "We might have talked to your mom and she might have encouraged us to come out."

Sebastian looked serious as he said, "And we thought you should know that the entire town knows that blue-haired girl from the wedding is Sophie's daughter."

"How do they know?" Colton certainly hadn't said anything to anyone.

"Sophie told Lily and Mattie and asked them to spread the word. Just telling MarVee and that was taken care of."

"But why?" Sophie had never told him. She'd kept the fact that she'd had a child and given her up for adoption a secret from him, and now she wanted the entire town to know? He tried to tell himself that he felt hurt, but he knew it was a lie. He didn't feel hurt—he felt angry. He felt like a fool. How could she not tell him about such a huge event in her life? And if she hadn't told him about her daughter, what else hadn't she told him? That was the question that haunted him. What else was Sophie hiding?

Finn opened up a bottle of beer and handed it to Colton, then another and handed it to Sebastian. "Tori's coming to spend the summer with Sophie. The girl's parents are going to be here on weekends, but she'll spend the weekdays with Sophie."

Colton drew a long sip of beer when what he really wanted to do was slam it back and reach for another. Unfortunately, he wasn't a drinker, and definitely not a drink-in-anger-and-pain sort of drinker, so he sipped.

"Thanks for letting me know," he managed.

"So, are you two rescheduling the wedding?" Finn asked.

Colton took off his hat again and wiped at his brow as a means of stalling. He put his hat back on and shook his head. "No. I don't think so."

"Oh," both of his friends said in unison.

"Speaking of weddings," Sebastian said as he elbowed Finn.

Finn looked guilty and Sebastian looked awkward. Something was up. "What?" Colton pressed when they both remained silent.

"We held off saying anything because we didn't want to take the spotlight off you and Sophie, and now…" Finn's sentence died and he looked extremely uncomfortable.

"What?" Colton repeated.

While Finn took a sip of his beer, Sebastian said, "Finn's getting married in August and he feels uncomfortable telling you, given the circumstances."

Colton knew his friend needed his support, so he smacked Finn on the back and forced a smile. "Congratulations. You and Mattie? It's hard to believe you're going to marry the kid who used to make us all crazy. Do you remember that time we were sleeping over at your house, and Mattie spent the night with Bridget?"

All three men groaned in unison.

Finn shook his head. "Mattie still has the pictures she and Bridget took of us, and swears that if I ever try and leave her, she'll let them go public."

"I still don't know how the hell they got into the room and put makeup on the three of us without us waking up." Sebastian shook his head, and then glared at Finn. "There's nothing for it, you're going to have to stick with her through thick and thin, if only to save our fragile male egos."

As if realizing what he said, he turned to Colton. "Sorry."

"No, don't be." Colton looked at Finn. "I'm happy for you both, and I'm sure Sophie is, as well." He *was* happy for his friend, but he felt… Ah, hell. What he felt was a jumble of emotions. He was too simple a man to figure them out. "So, why August?"

"We want to go on a Disney World honeymoon with the kids before school starts. Frankly, I think Abbey's more excited about Disney than about the wedding," Finn told them. "You both will stand up for me? We're thinking something simple at the house…."

Colton listened as Finn laid out his plans, but his thoughts were on Sophie and her daughter. Tori. That was her name. And she was coming to Valley Ridge for the summer?

What kind of parents let their kid spend a summer with a stranger, even if that stranger did give birth to their child?

Probably the same kind of parents that let their kid dye their hair blue.

And even as he had the thought, he felt guilty. His younger sister might not have dyed her hair blue, but she had gotten her belly button pierced. His parents had a farm in Fredonia, about forty-five minutes away, and he didn't see them as much as he'd like, especially in the spring and summer. But they'd come up for a day a few weeks back. The whole family had gone down to the lake for an afternoon. Misty had on a bikini, so the piercing was right there for the world to see. He'd been shocked, and when he said something, his mom and sister both laughed. "A woman's only got a few good stomach years," his mother had said. "Your pregnancy ruined mine and any hopes I ever had of a belly button ring. I said yes, because I thought Misty should capitalize on the fact that she can still wear one."

"Plus," his little sister had said, "I didn't get a tattoo or pierce something highly visible. When I'm tired of it, I'll take it out." She'd leaned forward and kissed him. "You really are a stick-in-the-mud, you know that?"

Maybe he was a stick-in-the-mud. Maybe it was too much to ask that someone you're vowing to spend the rest of your life with tell you the truth. He knew it was impossible for anyone to know absolutely everything about someone, but seriously, how hard could it be to say, *My parents aren't dead, and oh, by the way, I had a baby I gave away?*

He forced himself to keep his mind on his friends' conversation. Thankfully they didn't expect much from him in terms of participating. That was a good thing about having a reputation as being quiet—no one expected too much conversational help from him.

As he listened, his emotions roiled about, becoming even more confused.

That was fine. He didn't need to sort them out. He was going to pick up his life where he'd left it before Sophie.

A quiet life.

A simple life.

A solitary life.

That's all he wanted.

Eventually the town would forget he'd once been engaged to Sophie Johnston, or Sophia Moreau-Ellis, or whatever other name she wanted to use.

Yes, the town would forget, and he prayed that eventually he'd forget, as well.

WHEN SOPHIE WAS PREGNANT with Tori, she'd read a book by Teresa Bloomingdale called *I Should Have Seen It Coming When the Rabbit Died.* It was a humorous account of a woman who'd had ten kids. The anecdotes and stories were supposed to invoke laughter. Knowing she'd never raise her daughter, Sophie had cried her way through the book.

But as she tried to pee into the cup the doctor's nurse had given her, she realized that the awkward experience would make a humorous vignette if she were writing a book of her own. *I Should Have Seen It Coming When the Stick Turned Pink*...or got a plus sign. Or whatever the doctor's test did. She knew it didn't involve rabbits dying, like the book's '70s title had suggested.

Dr. Neil Marshall was Valley Ridge's G.P. He birthed babies, stitched cuts and generally took care of all the community's health care needs, from immunizations to high blood pressure. He farmed out patients that needed more specialized care than he could provide, but for the most part, everyone in town saw Dr. Marshall.

Lily worked as a nurse in his office on Mondays.

And that's why Sophie was there on a Thursday.

She planned on telling Mattie and Lily about the baby, if there was a baby. But she had other people she'd have to tell first. Visiting the office on a day Lily didn't work simply made things easier.

Cup duly peed in, and exam gown flapping, she bolted across the hall into the safety of the examination room. She knew she should be hoping she wasn't pregnant. Her life was in chaos. She'd lost a fiancé in the middle of the ceremony and found a daughter. No, about the only time that could be worse for having a baby would be as a teenager.

But all she could think of was having Colton's baby. A baby she could keep. A baby she would raise and love.

She was lost in trying to decide nursery themes when Dr. Marshall walked into the room.

He didn't say anything, but nodded and watched her, as if gauging her reaction.

She burst into tears but assured him, "They're happy tears. I'm so happy…" She repeated herself until the worst of the tears subsided, then sniffled her way through his talk of ultrasounds and prenatal vitamins.

She was going to have a baby.

She was going to have Colton's baby.

And even if Colton didn't want her anymore, this baby had been conceived in love.

There was a whole host of things she would have to deal with. Coping with Tori's feelings had to be her top priority. Telling Colton a close second. Dealing with being a single mother…

But she'd figure it all out.

She was going to be a mother, and no matter what happened, she planned on enjoying every moment of this pregnancy. She felt her old familiar happiness bubble around in her chest. Normally she found joy in life. All the little things. A sunset on the peninsula, an afternoon with friends, being held in Colton's arms. But when Colton had walked away, her normal happiness had frozen. Try as she might, she couldn't find joy in anything. But it was suddenly back.

She hugged her arms around her stomach.

Around her baby.

She left the doctor's with a prescription for prenatal vitamins, an appointment in a month for another visit and an ultrasound, and a sense of apprehension. But she didn't allow herself to second-guess things. She'd talk to Tori's parents when they brought her to town this weekend and see how they wanted to handle telling Tori. But right now, she headed "north of 5" to Colton's.

She smiled as she thought of the term.

Right after she'd moved to Valley Ridge, someone had given her directions by saying "north of 5." She'd been confused, but they'd explained that it meant north of Route 5, a fairly major thoroughfare. It was the small spit of property that was sandwiched between the road and Lake Erie. The area where Colton's farm was.

She had no idea why she was thinking about directions and when she first moved to Valley Ridge. Or why thinking about something that simple made her bubble over with happiness, but it did.

Her hand slid to her stomach. It was as hard to imagine a baby growing there now as it was with Tori. She couldn't help remembering how she'd marveled as her stomach expanded, as the baby started moving. She remembered lying on her bed and watching her stomach ripple and undulate of its own accord. Always knowing that she'd be giving the baby up.

Sophie gripped her stomach fiercely with her free hand. She had her first child back in her life and she'd do whatever she could to be a part of Tori's life from here on out. She might not ever get to be Tori's mother, but she could know her and love her.

And she'd fight with everything in her to keep this child.

First step, telling Colton.

She tried to imagine his reaction. Anger? No. She couldn't imagine Colton being angry. Surprised, yes. *Shocked* was probably a better description.

And he'd try to do the honorable thing. Not that she'd agree.

When he'd kissed her goodbye and walked out the door, she'd known she'd see him. They'd interact. They'd be friendly. Not friends, but friendly.

But now, they'd be more. They'd be connected through this baby. This baby they'd created out of love.

She pulled up his long driveway. Only then did she think about the time. It was eleven-thirty in the morning. Odds were he was still out in the field somewhere, but most of the time he came into the house for lunch.

Even if he didn't come in until dinner, she'd wait. This was something that had to be done. He'd felt betrayed she hadn't told him about her daughter and had let him think her parents were dead. She wouldn't risk waiting even a day to tell him about this baby. She couldn't move forward until she'd told Colton.

Sophie parked the car by the barn. Normally, she'd have let herself into the house, but that was when she'd had a right to. She'd spent so much time here the past few months, looking at how to move her things in, how to integrate her life with Colton's.

But she no longer had that right.

She walked to the porch and sat in the rocker, which had been his grandmother's. She remembered Colton telling her about it. He'd shared all his happy memories about his childhood. Stories in the rocker, picnics at the lake, adventures with Finn and Sebastian.

She'd shared nothing of her past.

Sophie tried to rationalize that fact. She tried telling herself that Colton's sharing those happy memories was different from her sharing her own not-so-happy childhood memories, but she knew it was a cop-out.

She'd held back so many pieces of herself from Colton. She wouldn't keep this news secret.

He had to know he was going to be a father.

COLTON HAD HAD an awful day.

He spent Tuesday and Wednesday nights awake, trying not to think about Sophie and her daughter, trying not to think about lies and secrets. He had watched late-night talk shows, then late-night news, and had tried to sleep.

Both nights, he'd finally drifted off in the wee hours of the morning and had slept in later than usual.

This morning, it was ten before he started the coffee, then headed out on his tractor, only to discover he'd forgotten to fill the tank, which was why it now sat as far from his house as it possibly could.

He made a move toward the barn to get a gas can and spotted Sophie's car.

His heart gave a small jump. She was here.

His head thought, *Great. Just what he needed.*

But his heart felt something altogether different.

He spotted her sitting in the rocker, her eyes closed and her hands folded in her lap.

For a while, he stood still and simply admired her. She looked pale, not that she'd ever been overly tanned. She used to joke that her skin was almost neon, and when she wore shorts, she was a threat to drivers' safety, since the glare from her legs might blind them.

Right now, he'd planned on being with her at a quiet Pocono cabin, enjoying his first days of marriage to her.

He recalled images of their messed-up wedding, and the sinking feeling he'd had when he realized he didn't really know Sophie Johnston, or Sophia Moreau-Ellis, at all.

He stomped toward the porch, and as he stepped onto the first stair, her eyes flew open. "Colton." She smiled. He might not know much about Sophie, but he did know that smile. He couldn't count how many times she'd smiled at him like that, and how he'd treasured each and every one of those moments.

"Sophie?" Her name came out harsher than he'd intended and he watched her smile fade.

She stood, her expression now serious. "We need to talk."

He'd said everything he needed to say, so he waited to hear what had brought her out to the farm. A part of him hoped she would tell him something to make him understand why she'd hidden her past. He had never been able to find the words, but Sophie always had. He wanted her to do that now…find the words to make everything okay again.

Sophie sighed, as if his silence was somehow a great disappointment. What did she want from him? She'd certainly been silent on her past, hadn't she?

"Fine." She widened her stance and looked as if she were preparing for a battle as she inhaled a long, deep breath and blurted out, "I'm pregnant."

"What?" He'd thought she was here to try to explain why she hadn't told him about her daughter. He desperately wanted her to give him some explanation he could accept and understand. Missing her was simply too hard. He realized he wanted an excuse to take her back. But not this. "Pregnant?"

She nodded. "Pregnant. I went off my birth control after the holidays because we wanted to start a family right away, remember?"

"We used other protection," he protested.

"Yes. But obviously it didn't work."

He walked onto the porch and sat on the other rocker, and Sophie returned to his grandmother's. All that separated him from Sophie was a small table… and a million small lies.

Sophie sat patiently while he mulled over her bombshell. He wasn't sure why he hesitated, because there was only one option open to him, and even as he made the decision, he realized that he felt nothing but relief. He had his excuse to get back with her in spite of her lies. "I guess we'll marry after all."

Colton wasn't sure what reaction he expected, but it wasn't her laughing in such an un-Sophie-like way. It was laughter he didn't recognize. Cold. Hard. Cynical.

It was the opposite of everything he'd ever experienced with Sophie.

She stood again, walked off the porch, then turned around. "Thank you for the offer, Colton. But I know what a marriage without love looks like, and I'm not interested. I will keep you apprised of the baby's development, and when he or she arrives, we'll work out some sort of custody arrangement. I'd like to keep it amicable, and between the two of us, but I understand if you want to take a more formal route. If you decide on seeking legal representation, let me know. I'll give you my attorney's name."

She paused a moment and when he didn't say anything, she continued, "I'm planning on telling Lily and Mattie soon, and if you want to tell Finn and Sebastian, I understand. But if you and whoever you tell keep it quiet for a while, I'd appreciate it. I have to think about how to break this to Tori. I can't even imagine how she'll cope with the news. I gave her away. That's how she sees it. 'Threw her away' is how she put it. Not that it was like that at all. But right after she found me, she's now going to discover I'm pregnant with a baby I'll be keeping and raising. She has parents who love her, but I don't know if that, or anything I can say, will help her cope with this. So, please, give me some time to break it to her. After that, you can tell whoever you want."

He nodded.

And she spun around and left without saying anything else.

Colton sat in the rocker on the porch and watched as her car pulled down his driveway, turned and disappeared from view.

He'd thought he'd sorted everything out in his mind.

Sophie had lied to him. She'd had a relationship with someone else, borne a child and given it up for adoption. Not it. Her. Tori. Sophie had given Tori up for adoption.

And despite what she'd led him to believe, she had parents. A family.

He'd spent every minute since the wedding ceremony reviewing their relationship. Replaying and trying to analyze it in light of these new revelations.

For the life of him, he couldn't understand why she'd lied about something so simple as her real name.

He'd have accepted her, whatever she chose to call herself. He'd have tried to understand if she'd told him about her daughter. He'd have tried to support her no matter what her deal was with her parents.

She'd said she knew what a marriage without love looked like. Obviously, it didn't look good, and he was sure she was talking about her parents.

But she'd lied to him about all that, or at least omitted the information from their discussions, which was as good as a lie. He couldn't help but wonder what else she'd lied about. He couldn't know, because she still hadn't offered him a proper explanation.

Now she was here telling him she was pregnant. Yet, when he offered to do the right thing, she'd said no.

She'd acted disappointed in him, as if he was the one who'd lied.

All he'd ever done was treat her with respect, honesty and love. How on earth could she feel she was the injured party?

When he'd told her goodbye, that the wedding was off, she'd accepted the news, but then refused his offer of friendship. She'd said she'd be friendly, for their friends' sakes, but being friends was off the table.

Now she was telling him they were going to have a baby and talking about visitation and lawyers?

Colton sat in the rocker for the longest time, trying to make heads or tails of any of it.

"Colton?" Mrs. Nies said, surprising him. Connie worked at the wine shop that was on the opposite end of his property. There was a well-beaten path between the house and the shop. He'd formed a partnership with Mattie's brother Rich, so he didn't need to be on hand. Between Rich and Mrs. Nies, it was well looked after. But most days he made a habit of pitching in where he could, and he knew in the fall, during the grape harvest, he'd be around more often. He and Rich had set aside part of this year's crop to try their hand at ice wine. The winery was a never-ending source of excitement for him. But he hadn't been there since the wedding... the almost-wedding.

"Hi, Mrs. Nies," he forced himself to call out.

The woman was timeless. The kind of age that seemed set. She looked the same to him as when he was a kid. He used to joke with Sophie that Mrs. Nies was the Dorian Gray of Valley Ridge.

"I saw Sophie's car," she said. "Is everything okay? I heard that the blue-haired girl was her daughter. She had to have been little more than a girl herself when she had her. I can't imagine how hard it was deciding to give her up for adoption. In my mind, it was brave."

"Brave?" he asked. Brave to give away your own flesh and blood?

"She was young. She had to ask herself what sort of life she could give a child. What kind of parent she could be if she was little more than a child herself. She picked an option she thought was best for the girl. That's brave in my book."

"I guess," he allowed. He hadn't thought about it in those terms. Sophie, young and alone. Where was the girl's biological father? Had he stood up and offered to do the right thing, or had he left her high and dry?

"I wanted to check on you, sweetie."

Mrs. Nies was one of the very few people who could get away with calling him sweetie. Her and his mom.

"I'm fine," he said, though he wasn't sure that was true.

"Rich is worried about you. And I saw Finn and Sebastian come over the other day. I'm guessing they're worried, too."

"I'm fine," he said again, as if repeating would make it so.

"Well, you remember, whatever's going on, you have friends. You call me anytime you need something."

The older woman's offer touched him. "Thanks, Mrs. Nies."

She started back toward the shop, then turned to face him. "Rich put up another wine quote today."

His partner had installed a blackboard at the front door of the winery, and rotated out odd quotes on wine for fun. He waited, and Mrs. Nies continued, "It was by a man named Franklin P. Adams, and said something about wine, women and song being hard to control. I guess you're finding that out. We women can be hard for men to understand. Ask my husband and he'll tell you as much. But if you asked him, Mr. Nies would tell you despite the difficulties, we're worth the effort, like producing a good wine is worth it."

She only meant to help. Colton knew that. So he forced a smile and said, "Thanks, Mrs. Nies. And you go home and tell Mr. Nies that I agree…you definitely are worth any effort he made."

She laughed and headed back down the path.

And Colton went back to sitting on his porch and trying to decide what to do next.

He was going to be a father.

And Sophie wasn't going to marry him.

SOPHIE WAS SHAKING as she drove back into town.

She'd done it.

She'd told Colton the news. He couldn't accuse her of hiding the information from him, or lying.

She wasn't sure what she'd expected, but his offer of marriage like that wasn't exactly it.

Well, *offer* was a pretty generous term. *I guess we'll marry after all.*

Yeah, that was the proposal every young girl dreamed of.

She parked her car at home but couldn't face going inside the house. So she walked the few blocks to town with no real destination in mind. She simply knew she couldn't sit still alone in the house.

Valley Ridge was a blink-twice-and-you'd-miss-it sort of town. The main street, Park Street, was the business hub of the small farming community. There was MarVee's Quarters, which used to be the Five and Dime, but when Marilee and Vivienne had bought it years ago—well before Sophie had come to town— they'd renamed it Quarters because they said inflation had edged out nickels and dimes. Marilee had recently told someone in town that if they bought it today, they'd have named it MarVee's Silver Dollars. Vivienne had reportedly snorted and said no, they wouldn't have, because it would have sounded like a house of ill repute.

Vivienne's comment made the rounds through town because she tended to speak less than Colton, and that meant she was pretty quiet.

Sophie pushed away thoughts of Colton and con-centrated on taking in the sights, as if she were Tori and had never seen Valley Ridge, New York, before.

There was Mattie's coffee shop, Park Perks. Bur-nam's Pharmacy. The diner, the grocery store and Val-ley Ridge Farm and House Supplies. Annie's small antiques store, and rumor had it a new bookstore was taking over one of the vacant storefronts. One end of the four-block main street held the township offices, and at the far end of Park Street were the schools. Over the bridge that marked the end of the town proper sat the small library, which was next to Maeve Buchan-an's house.

Sophie couldn't help but remember the first time she had driven through the area. She'd felt as if she'd come home.

There were no real estate offices in Valley Ridge, but she'd stopped at the Quarters and discovered that Marilee and Vivienne knew not only everyone but everything about Valley Ridge. They'd told her about the house Sophie now owned. Well, actually Marilee predominantly told her, and Vivienne did a lot of nodding.

Sophie had bought the house, moved in, started to do some work for local wineries and eventually talked them into banding together as a collective in order to do more advertising. In addition to working for the wineries, she'd taken other freelance PR jobs. She'd never imagined that her parents' obsession with public image would lead her to a career that promoted the public image of others, but in reality, all she did was what she was trained to do from birth. She tried to shape what others would think about a particular business, product or service.

If she'd had to rely solely on her income, she would have been hurting during the tight months, but thanks to her grandmother, she would never have to worry about money.

Another fact that annoyed Colton. As if she could help the fact her family had money.

If only she could make him understand that she'd give it all away if she could have the kind of relationship he had with his family.

She sighed and found herself walking into the diner.

"Hello, beautiful," called Hank Bennington from behind the counter. "Where have you been all my life?"

"Waiting for you to find me," she responded.

Hank laughed, followed her to the booth and flipped over a cup, about to pour coffee from his ever-present pot. She put her hand over the cup, realizing her coffee days were over for a while. "Could I have ice water with lemon instead?" she asked. "It's hot out there."

"Anything for a beautiful woman," he said.

Sophie noticed Hank didn't call her by name, but

despite that, he seemed himself today. The night of their stag and drag in Buffalo, a combined bachelor/bachelorette party, Hank had gone missing and put an early end to their celebration. They'd found him at Colton's, hanging wind chimes on the arbor Colton had built her for the wedding.

Thinking of the wedding-that-wasn't was too depressing. She would celebrate, she decided.

Hank returned with her water.

"Is Lily in?" she asked.

He paused a moment, then shook his head. "I don't think so, but I can check."

She glanced at the clock. Her friend was a visiting nurse who spent her evenings helping Hank out at the diner. "No, it's probably too early."

"So what are you ordering today?" Hank asked.

Her first thought was of the baby. "A fresh greens salad, and the cottage cheese fruit cup, please."

"That won't take but a minute," he said.

Sophie realized her hand was on her stomach again. This might not be the perfect time, and it definitely wasn't the perfect situation, but she was so excited about this baby. She couldn't wait to tell Lily and Mattie now. She wanted someone to be happy for her.

She thought back to her pregnancy with Tori. Not one person besides herself had been happy about it. Well, no one but the Allens. Whenever she'd thought about her baby, she'd comforted herself by imagining how thrilled the prospective parents would be. Now that she'd met them, it was easier to picture Gloria holding Tori for the first time. In her game of make-believe, she could see Dom setting toddler Tori on a table with a paintbrush and canvas.

Her daughter had been loved. Tori had been treasured. And now Sophie had a chance to have Tori in her life.

Telling her about the new baby could be difficult—

"I went by your house." Colton stood alongside her booth and sat down opposite her. "I figured you'd be with Lily or Mattie."

"Both of them are working, so no. I'm here for lunch."

As if on cue, Hank smiled and deposited her salad and cottage cheese in front of her.

"Son, were you ordering?" he asked.

"Burger, fries and coffee, please," Colton said.

After Hank walked away, Sophie said, "I don't recall inviting you to join me."

"I don't recall waiting for an invitation." He removed his hat and set it on the seat next to him.

Once upon a time, the action would have melted her heart. She loved that Colton was the only man in the area who wore a cowboy hat. He had all kinds of excuses for wearing it. He was in the field all day, and it protected him from sunburns. A baseball cap wouldn't protect his neck. It was better-looking than an Amish wide-brimmed hat, which people in this part of the country did wear on a regular basis.

But, in reality, he simply liked the way they looked.

She tried to forget that his hat was endearing and asked, "So, what can I do for you, Colton?"

"You can't drop a bombshell like that on me and then walk away."

"Yes, I can." She was being difficult. She knew she was, but she couldn't seem to help herself.

"We need to talk about getting married," he said.

"No, we do not."

She purposefully speared a bite of salad and chewed it as he tried again. "For the baby's sake."

"I said it at your house. I've seen what a marriage based on something other than love looks like, and I can guarantee it's not good for a child. Much better to be raised by two parents who are *friendly*."

"I'm starting to hate that term," he grumbled.

"*Parents* or *friendly?*" she asked conversationally.

"Friendly."

"Sorry. Listen, I want to keep things amicable. I want to work together for this child's sake. He or she deserves to be loved by both of us. The baby deserves to have us get along. But, Colton, I need to be clear, marriage won't be in the cards."

She wanted him to leave. She'd come here to celebrate. Granted a salad and cottage cheese wasn't much of a celebration, but it was hers. She deserved a moment to revel in happiness over the baby before Colton came around offering to marry her because he had to.

Had to?

Once he'd claimed he couldn't live without her. Now he felt he had to marry her. So who was the liar?

Colton said, "You were prepared to marry me a week ago. How could you change your mind so fast?"

"I didn't change my mind," she pointed out. She'd thought that he'd be mad. That he'd come to her for an explanation, and even if he didn't understand, even if he was mad, he'd accept what she told him and love her regardless. Her parents' love had been conditional, and it turned out, so was Colton's. *Be perfect.* That was all she had had to do for her parents to love her. When she couldn't, they'd been happy to see her leave.

Turned out Colton wanted her to be perfect, too.

Well, the joke was on him. She'd never claimed to be perfect.

"I didn't change my mind," she repeated. "You changed yours."

"It's not that I changed my mind, it's that…" The sentence died off as he tried to search for an excuse.

"Colton, it's okay. I don't blame you. Really, I don't." She'd been shocked when she'd found someone to love, and had always worried that the ax would fall. So, she wasn't surprised when it did, and she wasn't really surprised that she was the one who had inadvertently set the ax in motion. "It's my fault, and I accept that. But we can't go back. So, thank you for the offer, but no, thank you."

"Sophie, I—"

She pushed away the remainder of her salad. "I'm sorry, Colton. This is my fault. All of it. I should have told you, but…" She shook her head. She could give him lengthy explanations about why it was so hard to talk about the daughter she'd been forced to give up, about her family. "Suffice to say, I didn't. I didn't tell you that I had living parents, a daughter or money in the bank. So, here we are. We're going to have to make the best of things."

"And be friendly?" he asked.

Hank came over with the burger. Colton said thank-you, watched Hank leave and waited for Sophie to answer.

"Yes," she said. "We have someone else to think about now, so being friendly is our best option."

"No, being married is our best option," he maintained. "I'll get over the things you didn't tell me."

He paused and when she didn't reply, he added, "I miss you. I want to try again."

Sophie wanted to believe him. She wanted to believe he could get over the fact she'd lied through omission. But Colton was a man with a very black-and-white view of the world. And she suspected this sudden change of heart had more to do with the baby than anything else. There were many things she was confused about at the moment, but the one thing she knew with certainty was that she wasn't willing to settle.

"Again, thank you, but no. I don't think there's any going back. I will keep you posted." She rose, pulled a twenty from her wallet and set it on the table.

Colton grabbed her wrist. "Sophie, don't go, please."

She saw the irony in the fact he'd been the one to walk away before. She'd wanted to beg him to stay and, now, he was asking her. Her answer was the same, not out of malice, but because it was her only option. For most of her life, she'd sworn she'd never marry. For a brief moment in time, she'd believed she could have the marriage and love she'd always dreamed existed, but she knew the only reason he was asking her to marry him again was because his honor demanded it. "I'm sorry, but I've got to go."

"Sophie," he said. Just her name. Part of her wanted to turn around and go back to him, but she forced herself to keep walking.

She'd fallen in love with Tori's father while she was still in high school. She had imagined them coming back to class reunions together. She had imagined their family. She knew there would be ups and downs, but she'd thought they'd weather them together.

Then he left her to carry their daughter on her own. He'd given her no choice but to acquiesce to her parents' wishes—no, their demands—that she forget about her dreams of raising their child and give the baby up for adoption. Shawn had never even contacted her afterward to see if she was okay, or to ask the gender of the baby. He'd taken off and never given her, or their daughter, a second thought.

She had sworn she was done. That she'd never trust, or rely on, a man again.

Then she'd met Colton, and slowly, he'd won her over. Again, she was sure that there was nothing, no hurdle, they couldn't overcome together. And at the first rough patch, he'd left.

There was an old saying about if you fooled a person, shame on you. But if you fooled that person again, shame on them. Well, she'd finally learned her lesson.

She wouldn't be fooled again.

She put her hand on her stomach.

She had Tori back in her life. She had friends, and soon, she'd have this new baby.

She had a full life. A blessed life.

It was more than she ever thought she'd have.

She was going to count herself lucky.

She was sure she could learn to live without Colton, just as she'd learned to live without Shawn.

She could learn again, no problem.

CHAPTER FIVE

THE NEXT DAY, Sophie was on pins and needles as she waited for the Allens to arrive.

Tori had texted and said they'd all checked into JoAnn's bed-and-breakfast and were now walking over.

Sophie's emotions changed from ecstatic to terrified to… They moved about with such speed and wild fluctuations that she was exhausted even though it was only a little past lunch. Tori would be spending the Fourth of July weekend with her parents at JoAnn's, then she'd be moving into the guest room upstairs on Monday.

Sophie had stripped it to its bare bones. She hoped that during their first week together, Tori might want to decorate it with her. She'd decided that having a project would give them something to do, some commonality to start to build a relationship over.

It had sounded like a good plan until now, but as she waited for the Allens it sounded more and more stupid.

And with the baby, she couldn't even help paint. She needed to tell Tori, but not right away. She wanted to give them some time to start to build a bond before she told her about the baby.

Sophie had bought out the baby book section at an online bookstore and paid for expedited shipping. She had the small mountain of books stashed in her closet and would keep them there until after she'd told Tori. But what she'd read so far suggested that waiting for twelve weeks to tell people made sense. Many babies were miscarried in those first three months.

The mere thought of losing this baby was almost a physical pain.

Sophie walked to the window and peered out. She paced to the living room, then back to the window.

She finally gave up and went to the porch and sat on the steps, watching for her daughter and her daughter's parents to arrive.

What an ambiguous place to be. Somewhere between mother and stranger.

Her hands rested on her stomach. She wanted this baby so much, but the thought of causing Tori one more moment of pain hurt.

Back and forth. Her emotions, her thoughts, careened back and forth.

Finally she spotted the Allens. The blue in Tori's hair had faded. Oh, it still showed, but it was as if her blond hair simply had a blue undertone.

Sophie said, "Hi," to Gloria and Dom, then turned to Tori and asked, "What happened to the hair?"

Tori grinned. "It was a temporary dye. It's meant to wash out over the course of weeks. I should be blue-free by the time school starts. I've dyed it with permanent dye before, but the time I tried out black hair convinced me that temporary was a better idea."

"What was the problem when you dyed it black?"

"I wanted to look dark and mysterious, but instead, I looked like Elvira gone to high school. It wasn't a good look."

"Sorry." Sophie had never dyed her hair. When she was Tori's age, her parents wouldn't have allowed it, and when she got older, she'd never seen the point. But she felt a jolt of admiration for the Allens, who gave Tori the freedom to experiment.

"Yeah, well, I learned my lesson." Tori fluffed her bluish-tinged blond hair. "I may dye it again." There was a challenge in the statement, as if she was daring Sophie to protest.

"Maybe I'll dye mine, as well. We could try complementary colors." Sophie smiled, hoping that Tori understood she accepted her. "You could go back to blue, and I could go with Old Glory red, and we'd fit right into this weekend's celebrations." She smiled at the Allens. "How was your drive?"

"Fine, but it took a lot longer than it should have." Gloria shot a look in Dom's direction.

He didn't seem fazed by it. "What my wife is saying is, I drove. She hates it when I drive."

"Oh? Too fast?"

"Just the opposite," Gloria said. "I think every car on I-90 passed us at some point."

"I've read reports that say gas mileage falls rapidly anytime you're driving more than fifty miles an hour. And I drove at fifty." He looked expectantly at Gloria and Tori, who said "hippie" in unison.

He simply laughed.

Sophie watched the family banter with an ease that suggested this was a normal part of their lives. Teasing each other. Laughing with each other.

Tori was the first one who seemed to remember Sophie was there, observing their interaction. She took off on another topic. "Mom and Dad said you had a job for me?"

"A volunteer job," Sophie said. "Why don't we talk about it inside?" As she ushered the family into her kitchen, she asked if anyone would like anything to drink.

"I'd love a cup of coffee," Gloria said. "If it's not too much trouble."

"Mom's an addict. Dad only drinks herbal teas. Hippie," Tori teased again.

"A child of hippies," he corrected.

Sophie had a sad selection of herbal teas. And since she'd be spending the next few months decaffeinated, she'd have to invest in a few more. But for now, she offered Dom what she had. "I have some blueberry tea, and Sleepytime."

"Blueberry," he said. "Thank you."

"Tori?"

"Juice?" she asked.

Normally, Sophie had orange juice on hand, but she'd expanded her choices. She wanted to give this baby the best nutritional start she could. "I've got orange juice or cranberry pomegranate."

"The cranberry."

Sophie bustled around, serving everyone. It gave her something to do. Almost too soon, everyone was served. She sat down with a cup of tea herself.

"So," Tori began. "Mom and Dad made me wait to get here to tell me about my punishment for stealing the car. They said you have an idea for my—"

"Probation," Gloria filled in with a smile.

"Tori, we all agree that you need some sort of consequence," Dom said. "Your mom and I understand why you stole the car. And okay, we're partially to blame. By not telling you something so important, we gave you cause to believe we couldn't be trusted to help you."

"But you didn't even try, Tori," Gloria added.

"But I—" Tori started.

"We've heard your arguments," Gloria said "Yes, you have driven vehicles at your grandparents' farm. And yes, you did read the book and obey all the traffic laws. But, Tori, you're still a fourteen—"

Tori interrupted. "Almost fifteen."

"—year-old girl, and anything could have happened. I can't tell you how many nightmares I've had thinking about all the possibilities."

"Mom's talked and talked and talked," Tori grumbled at Sophie. "Some kids get paddled or grounded— I get lectured to death. Sometimes I think getting spanked would be easier. So what torture did you think up for my probation?"

Both Gloria and Dom looked at Sophie. "It's not torture. At least I don't think it is. Valley Ridge has a small library that closed years ago. Maeve Buchanan moved in next door to it a while back and said it was almost torture to look out the window every day and see the ghost of the library she'd loved so much when she was young. So she talked to Ray, my friend, Mattie's brother, our mayor. He gave her permission to reopen it. She volunteers her time after work, so it's open most evenings. But she's wanted to open it during the day, especially during the summer when all the kids are out of school. So, I talked to your parents, and they agreed that might be a good place for you to volunteer at."

"Yeah. Don't do the crime if you can't do the time?" Tori asked. Sophie must have looked surprised, because Tori laughed. "Hippies think punishments should be useful and teach a lesson."

"Not a hippie," Dom said by rote. "My parents—"

"Were hippies," Tori finished for him. And all three Allens burst into laughter at the family debate. Sophie couldn't help but join in.

After the laughter died down, Tori asked, "So, what would I do at the library?"

"If you think you could handle it, you'd open the library a few afternoons a week. You're almost fifteen and I'd be close by if there was a problem, and there are other volunteers who will be in and out, but your parents agreed that you were old enough to handle this kind of responsibility. You'd check out books, and when things are slow, check materials back in and reshelve them."

"So my punishment is I'll be the librarian for the summer?"

"I guess that's one way of looking at it, though a real librarian does more than check books in and out."

"So, I'd be the library checker-outer?" Tori asked with a grin.

Sophie loved the entire Allen family's sense of humor. She joined in with their laughter, and realized that this was what she was going to miss about Colton's family. They laughed together like this. "Yes, you'd be the library checker-outer. Maeve thought it sounded like a brilliant idea, if you think you're up for the challenge?"

"Piece of cake," Tori said. "I like books."

"She's a voracious reader," Gloria shared.

"I was, too, when I was younger." Sophie thought of the stack of mothering books in her closet and said, "Still am, I guess. Maeve asked if you'd like to come over Monday morning and she'll show you around."

Tori shrugged and tried to look blasé, but Sophie had seen Tori's excitement at the idea. "If that's a yes, I'll let her know."

"Yes," Tori said.

"Sunday's the big Fourth of July party, so we'll have

plenty to do then, but I was trying to think of something for all of us to do today. Maybe we could drive to some of the wineries I work with. Some I don't, if you like, too. One of my friends said he'd give us a behind-the-scenes tour, if you like?" She phrased the suggestion as a question.

"That would be wonderful," Gloria said. "We have some favorite wineries in Ohio. There's a couple in Port Clinton that are amazing. The entire lakeshore region has some of the best vineyards outside France."

Sophie forced her smile to stay in place, but inwardly, it slipped a notch. She couldn't help but remember Colton rhapsodizing over his grapevines, and about how his small vineyard was on the same longitude—or was it latitude?—as some of the best French grape-growing regions. It had become a standing joke between them. He'd come home and talk about his grapes and she'd say *oui, oui* in her awful French accent. They'd laugh over it, like the Allens all did—with a sense of familiar.

"…I made her a wine rack a few years ago, after which we both decided that woodworking was not my forte," Dom was saying.

"But you should see how Dad painted it. And then he hand-painted wineglasses to go with it," Tori said. And the look she gave her father was one of utter love and pride.

"Dom doesn't like it when the wine rack has too many holes in it." Gloria's look for her husband was also love, but a different kind of love. It was one that Sophie suspected she'd once had for Colton. Her heart broke a little all over again.

"Well, I know Western New York and North East wineries. We'll have to see what you think."

"Are we going to Colton's?" Tori asked.

Sophie shook her head. She'd told him they'd be friendly. And odds were he wouldn't be there. Ray Keith would be, and/or Mrs. Nies. But seeing them would lead to questions Sophie didn't want to answer. "I don't think so. But my friend Geoff is going to give you the tour. He's been making wine for only a decade, and his enthusiasm is contagious...."

She continued to talk, ignoring Tori's expression, which lingered somewhere between disappointment and guilt.

Sophie would need to ensure that Tori didn't have any lingering feelings of remorse over the wedding, because she knew exactly where all the blame belonged.

Firmly on her own shoulders.

COLTON WALKED INTO the diner, hoping to catch up with Sebastian.

He was in luck. His friend was at the grill and caught sight of him. Colton raised an eyebrow, wordlessly asking if Sebastian had time to talk.

Sebastian held up a finger, indicating he'd slip away in a minute.

Colton walked to the most distant booth. He still hadn't decided when he should tell his friends about the baby. He wanted to be sure that Sophie had talked to Lily and Mattie first.

He wasn't sure why, but he suspected that she needed to be the one to tell her friends, and he hoped she had already told them, because she needed someone to talk to, to support her.

Once upon a time, he'd have been the one she talked to. She'd once said that one of the reasons they worked so well as a couple was that he didn't like to talk and she did. She'd laughed and said she talked enough for the both of them.

He missed her laughter. He'd dreamed about her last night. Showing him how to hold a baby. She'd laughed at his attempt. He'd woken up to the sound of her laughter. He hadn't been able to go back to sleep after that, and had gone downstairs to watch the news for a couple of hours. Her laughter had seemed so real. The touch of her hand as she handed him the baby.

On the heels of that longing came a surge of anger. For all her talk, she'd never mentioned the daughter she had given up, and the fact her parents were still alive. He understood her point that the first time he'd asked her about her family, she hadn't known him long enough or been close enough to owe him an explanation. But later, she should have clarified. She should have said something.

She should have told him.

Hank came over, coffeepot in hand. Sebastian's grandfather always had a coffeepot in hand. Even when Colton, Sebastian and Finn had popped into the diner for something when they were kids, Hank had carried around that coffeepot. He probably walked a few miles a day, circulating the diner, refilling coffee cups.

And they'd spent a lot of time in the diner growing up. Hank was always good for an after-school snack. He'd encouraged Sebastian's friends to treat the diner as home. And for Sebastian, it was probably more home than their house had been. For all intents and purposes, Hank had raised his grandson Seb here at the diner. His friend's mother had left him when he was a kid. To the best of his knowledge, Seb had never talked about her. Not to him, and probably not to Finn.

Like Sophie never talked about her parents?

"Coffee?" Hank asked.

Colton turned his coffee cup upright and nudged it toward Hank. "Perfect."

"Anything else?" Hank asked.

Colton didn't need a menu. He suspected most of Valley Ridge never even looked at one. The only thing that changed about the Valley Ridge Diner's menu was the day's special. "Ask Seb if he'll bring me out a BLT?"

"Oh, you know Seb?" Hank looked surprised.

Colton realized that Hank didn't recognize him. He remembered what Lily said and tried a gentle reminder. If it worked to bring Hank back to the present, good. If it upset Hank, stop. "Oh, Hank, after all those times you yelled at the three of us for climbing the cliffs at the lake, I can't forget Seb."

For a moment, Hank had a blank look, and then he laughed. "You three boys were almost the death of me. I know your parents and Finn's felt the same."

And he was back. Colton grinned. "You kept us in line."

"I tried to keep you in line. I didn't always succeed." He paused. "Were you ready to order?"

"A BLT?" Colton repeated.

"That's right." Hank hurried off to the counter to call back his order.

These days, someone occasionally got a meal they didn't order, but not one local would have said anything and hurt Hank's feelings. The town was aware of his dementia, and they were not only willing to eat unordered food, but the community had made it their business to keep their eyes out for Hank's roaming, especially after they lost him before the wedding.

Colton sipped his coffee and thought about Sophie

and their baby. If his child was anything like him, they were going to have their hands full.

Valley Ridge was such a wonderful place to grow up. Especially on his grandfather's farm. He'd run amok there with Sebastian and Finn.

He'd have to reconsider keeping livestock again. He'd raised a couple milk cows for his vocational-agriculture—vo ag—class, but he'd never had livestock around as an adult. He'd have to think about that. Kids loved animals. He'd want his son or daughter to grow up comfortable around them. When they were older, they could join FFA—Future Farmers of America.

If they wanted to.

He'd never force his son or daughter into a particular path or career.

His child. Sophie's child.

Sophie had talked about getting chickens. Just a couple, she'd assured him. Two hens. Hell, she'd already named their fictional hens, Thelma and Louise, and when he'd asked, assured him that he wouldn't be getting any fried chicken dinners, but if he played his cards right, he might get a quiche.

He hated quiche.

But he'd have eaten it for Sophie.

He'd have done anything for Sophie.

He'd have even married her for the baby's sake, despite whatever secrets she was keeping. But she'd said no.

How could she do that, considering she was carrying his child?

They'd planned on having a houseful of children. He'd imagined what it would be like, but never this.

He'd thought they'd go out and celebrate. Maybe to the beach. Or maybe, back in the woods behind his house. No, probably up on the ridge where Sophie could watch the sunset over Lake Erie as they ate dinner. Some women might have wanted a fancy dinner out, but Sophie would have been happier with a simple picnic.

They would have—

"BLT, anyone?" Sebastian said, putting a plate down in front of Colton. "I added the fries."

"Thanks."

Sebastian slid into the seat across from him. "So, how're you doing?"

"Fine. I wanted to ask you something."

Hank came over and poured Sebastian a cup of coffee. "Thanks, Hank." Sebastian turned to Colton when Hank walked back toward the counter. "You wanted to ask me something?"

"Has Sophie talked to Lily?" Colton popped a fry into his mouth and realized how not hungry he was.

"Recently?" Sebastian sipped his coffee.

"Yeah." If Sebastian hadn't been sitting across from him, Colton would have pushed the plate back and given up on the lunch, but instead, he took another small fry.

"I know they saw her on Sunday," Sebastian told him.

So Sophie hadn't seen her best friends yesterday. Colton couldn't imagine that she'd have told them on the phone, so odds were her friends didn't know. So, he wouldn't say anything to Sebastian.

"Maybe they should go see her," he said. Gee, Sophie not sharing important information with people she was close to? A week ago, he'd have been surprised, but not now.

"I know her daughter and the girl's parents are in

town this weekend." Sebastian lowered his voice. "The parents go home Sunday night and Tori's staying with Sophie."

Colton took a big bite of his BLT despite the fact he felt faintly nauseous, thankful he couldn't respond verbally, and he simply nodded.

Hank came over and refilled both his and Sebastian's cups. "You boys look serious."

"Seriously hungry," Colton assured him, though it was a lie.

Hank made another round through the dining room, and Sebastian reached for his cup with his left hand. He didn't hold the handle but rather wrapped his hand around the whole cup. The scars traveled from Sebastian's hand to under his sleeve.

He noticed Colton watching him. "Lily keeps insisting I need to do more with my left hand."

Sebastian had been in the Marines, but after some sort of accident, which he didn't talk about, he'd left the service. Colton knew his friend had been angry about that when he'd come home, but secretly, he was relieved that Sebastian wouldn't be going overseas again.

He thought of what Sophie had mentioned about Lily, and smiled. "Lily said, huh?"

"Yeah." That one word confirmed Sophie's suspicions.

"She's a good woman." Finn had worked with Lily at his hospital in Buffalo. He'd hired her to come to Valley Ridge and take care of Bridget when she had gotten sick. She'd done more than simply care for her as a nurse—she'd been Bridget's friend. She'd bonded with Sophie and Mattie as they all cared for Bridget.

"She is," Sebastian replied. "So, about Finn and Mattie. You and Sophie okay with it?"

Colton nodded. "I'm happy for them."

"I'd say we'd have to plan a bachelor party, or even a stag and drag like you and Soph—" He cut himself off, as if realizing he might be broaching an uncomfortable topic.

Colton ignored Sebastian's awkwardness. "Finn doesn't want one?"

"He and Mattie want the wedding to be low-key. He's planning on talking to you, but he wanted to give you some time to recuperate before he did."

How did you recuperate from a broken heart? Because as romantic as the term sounded, it was the truth. He'd thought he'd known Sophie Johnston like no one else in the world, but he'd been wrong. So wrong. "I'll call him."

"A phone call? You'll have to use words, you know."

"Smart-ass." He couldn't manage another bite of the sandwich or fries. "I don't want him to feel awkward. Sophie and I are both happy for him and Mattie." He looked at Sebastian, who was taking another sip of coffee. "And you and Lily."

"Thanks." Sebastian paused and asked, "So did you and Sophie decide to reschedule?"

"No. No, I don't think that's going to happen." Unless he could find some way to change her mind. But she had a stubborn streak, which was just one more thing he hadn't known about Sophie.

"That's too bad. You two were perfect together."

Colton shook his head. "Not as perfect as you might think."

"Is it her daughter?"

He could have accepted Sophie's daughter, but he couldn't accept the fact she'd lied to him. That she'd held so much back.

It didn't mean he didn't love her, or miss her like crazy. And it certainly didn't mean he wouldn't marry her for their baby's sake.

Even to himself, the thought sounded like a cop-out. Hell.

He grabbed his hat and stood. "I've got to go."

"Call me if you want to talk." Sebastian snorted. "Though *want* and *talk* are two words that will never go together where you're concerned. So, call me if you need to talk, or if you want someone to sit around and be quiet with you."

Colton smacked Sebastian's shoulder. "Thanks." He tossed enough money to cover his not even half-eaten meal on the table and hurried out of the diner.

How did his life get to be such a mess?

SOPHIE WAS EXHAUSTED.

She'd hovered on the edge of nauseousness all day.

And she'd been nervous, too, as she toured local wineries with the Allens. She was terrified she'd say something wrong. That she'd somehow set off Tori's anger, or annoyance....

She thought the Allens had enjoyed Geoff's tour of the winery. Geoff had taken them all out into his vineyard and had rhapsodized over his vines as if they were his children. He had talked about pulling new growth off—called suckering—which encouraged the vines to pour all the energy into the grapes.

His enthusiasm made her think of Colton.

Who was she kidding? Everything made her think of Colton.

They had walked into the winery and the smell had almost overwhelmed Sophie. She'd remembered Colton taking her for a picnic here. They'd drunk wine, shared a lunch, and she'd started to fall in love with him as he waxed enthusiastic about his plans for the farm and vineyard.

Geoff had led them inside and taken them to the rooms behind the storefront, where giant stainless steel vats filled a large room, then on to the lab, which looked as if it could have come from a movie set. It was small, but clean and functional.

When Geoff had shown them his new bottling unit, he'd practically glowed, describing how it not only bottled the wine but labeled it, as well. He had shown them how he could use either traditional corks to stop the bottles, or go with screw-on tops. Then he had given an impassioned speech about why sometimes screw-on tops were better than corks.

Sophie had half listened to him. She'd heard the cork-versus-screw-on-top discussion before. She'd watched as bottles ran through the machine. They went in empty and came out full and labeled. Colton and Rich had been talking about buying something similar. They'd come over to Geoff's and sought his opinions, and had returned home even more excited at the prospect. She'd listened to Colton talk enthusiastically about his visions for the winery. Having Rich as a partner meant he could see those dreams fulfilled sooner.

Everything in Valley Ridge reminded her of Colton.

Soon, she'd be reminded more intimately. She wondered what their baby would be passionate about. Farming? Wine? Maybe sports or…

She'd fantasize about the baby tonight. Now, she had other things to attend to. The Allens seemed to be enjoying the talk. And Geoff was in his glory, sharing his excitement with others.

Sophie had toured all the local wineries she worked

with, and it never got old. It wasn't so much the explanation of the processes, though that part was fascinating. Wine making was a perfect example of science combining with art. But that wasn't it. It was the passion that the owners and vintners used when talking about their wine.

Pride mixed in with what could only be called love.

Geoff led them back to the store and hurried to help a customer.

"I'm going to buy a couple of bottles," Sophie said to the Allens. Geoff had gone out of his way to give them the tour, and buying a few bottles was a nice way to say thank-you.

She realized that she wouldn't be able to drink the wine for months to come. Months. Her child would be in her arms in mere months.

"Us, too," Dom said.

She'd gotten lost that quickly in thoughts of the baby, and it took a minute to wind her way back into the conversation and realize what Dom was us-tooing about.

"I could help you decide what to buy if you'd change your mind about me drinking wine," Tori offered.

Her parents snorted in unison, and Tori sighed as she walked over to the bench by the door and fiddled with her phone as she waited.

Sophie picked up a bottle of Riesling and put it in her basket.

Gloria followed suit. "Sophie, we wanted to be upfront with you. You know that we've talked to that local police officer—"

"Dylan," she filled in again.

Gloria nodded. "He assured us you were okay. But I wanted to know about your family," Gloria said. "I know it sounds intrusive, but if they're going to see Tori—"

"They won't," Sophie said. There were many things she was confused about right now, but that wasn't one of them. "Maybe someday, if Tori wants, she'll look them up and meet them, but I haven't talked to them since I was eighteen. I wrote them a letter when I graduated from college, and it was sent back, marked Return to Sender. Below my return address, there was also a note that read, 'We have no daughter.' I don't want you two to think I'm unforgiving. I could forgive them forcing me to give up Tori, if they asked me to. If they felt the least bit guilty about it. Heck, if they could tell me they felt they did what they had to for my own good. But my feelings, and certainly Tori's, never mattered to them. For them, public perception was everything. And a pregnant teenage daughter would certainly have hurt their image. And I think they found it almost easier when I left."

In her mind's eye, she could almost see her parents, over cocktails, telling some new friend about their ungrateful daughter. How they had to write her off to avoid any more pain or embarrassment. And that unknown friend probably nodded and sympathized and continued to sip the cocktail.

She moved to the shelf of red wines and picked a nice table wine she'd tried before. As she put it in her basket, Gloria patted her hand. "I'm sorry."

"I can't say I'm over it, but I've adjusted my reality to the fact that my parents are what they are. I can't change them. I can't make them see that family means more than public perceptions. What matters most to me is Tori. If you tell me that you think seeing me isn't in her best interest, I'd understand and accept that."

"You might, but she wouldn't." Dom smiled. "Tori doesn't *want* to know things—she *needs* to. She needs to understand. Normally, that need to understand is mainly focused on mechanical things. I can't tell you how many electronics in the house have been taken apart."

"But she always puts them back together," Gloria assured her. "Of course, not always as quickly as she took them apart."

"The toaster," they both said in unison.

Sophie waited, hoping that they'd share the story. Hungry for whatever bits of her daughter's life they'd share.

Dom seemed to sense her need and said, "She took it apart when she was six. It wasn't functional again for weeks. Not a problem for me."

"What he's not saying is he's pretty adaptable. Me? I'm a creature of habit and my habit includes toast for breakfast." They laughed over what was an apparent favorite family story, and Sophie waited to feel jealous that she hadn't shared those moments with her daughter. There was a hint of that, but mainly there was a warm glow that she had a chance to hear the stories now and a chance to know her daughter.

They discussed Tori's job at the library and the house rules that the Allens followed, which were actually few and far between. They didn't have actual curfews but, rather, worked on a case-by-case basis. If Tori planned on being home at a certain time and couldn't make it, she needed to call. If you make a mess, you clean up the mess....

Sophie nodded, agreed and realized that those many years ago when she had looked through the prospective parents, she'd followed her heart, and her heart hadn't led her wrong.

Dom and Gloria loved Tori, and they'd raised her with love and sensible rules. They gave her freedom where they could—hence her blue-hair experiment—but they also gave her guidelines, boundaries and structure.

But mainly they gave her love.

That's all Sophie had ever wanted for her daughter.

As they left the winery, Sophie was pretty sure she'd have allies in the Allens when it came to the baby. Next week, she'd tell them she was pregnant and ask their opinion about how to handle the news with Tori. But, for this one week, she wanted to concentrate on Tori. On maybe finding a story or two of their own.

CHAPTER SIX

COLTON WALKED DOWN Park Street. This was the last place he wanted to be on Sunday afternoon, but his parents and sister, Misty, had come to Valley Ridge for the Fourth of July celebration.

"…and it looks so patriotic," Misty prattled with excitement. "Sophie and Ray did a great job." She went silent.

Colton realized no one had mentioned Sophie since his family had gotten in from Fredonia. "They did," he said, and shot his little sister a smile.

Flag buntings hung out all the shop windows, while the actual flags streamed from the streetlights. The streets were lined with cars, as people parked and headed toward the school grounds.

"So, we're going to meet the boys?" his mother asked. To her, Sebastian and Finn would always be *the boys*.

"Yes. If we can find them." He'd never seen so many people at one time on Valley Ridge's main street.

"Ray and Sophie put out a huge promotion in the region. It seems to be working." There, he'd mentioned her name. Maybe that would ease some of his family's awkwardness.

They strolled by the Quarters as Sophie and the Allens walked out.

His parents and Misty looked at him, so he forced a smile and said, "Sophie."

"Colton."

He extended his hand to Sophie's daughter's parents. "Mr. and Mrs. Allen, I'm Colton McCray."

"He's the guy Sophie was going to marry," Tori said as she glared at him.

He ignored the teen's palpable animosity and introduced his family. "My parents, Helen and Al, and this is my little sister, Misty."

"Not so little anymore. I'll be a senior next year," Misty assured him with a laugh, which probably sounded fine to everyone else present, except for him and his parents. Again, he gave his little sister points for trying.

"Are you joining us for lunch?" Mrs. Allen asked.

"No, not today," Colton said. He turned to Sophie. "How are you feeling?"

"Fine, just fine," she said, shooting him dagger looks that said, *Don't mention the baby, whatever you do.*

So she hadn't told Tori and her parents? Yeah, color him shocked at the idea that Sophie held on to secrets.

He gave the slightest tip of his head and stepped away, hoping his family would take the hint and leave.

"Everything looks wonderful, Sophie," his mom said. "Colton told us you and Ray Keith put this all together."

"I helped put together some of the promotions. Ray was the one who organized the town, and he found the money somewhere for all the buntings and flags. And wait until you see the fireworks display tonight. It rivals Buffalo's and Erie's. We…" Sophie's words tripped over themselves as she babbled along about the celebration.

That in itself was not unusual. Sophie was generally excited about…well, everything. She found happiness in the smallest things. He remembered one day as they walked down Park Street, she'd stopped at a crack in the sidewalk and pulled up a small weed. He must have shot her a questioning look. She'd laughed and told him, "It's pineapple weed." She'd squeezed the small firm yellow flower and thrust it under his nose. It had smelled like pineapple. She'd told him, "Life's like that. If you don't watch where you're going you might step on something sweet." She'd sniffed that stupid weed the rest of the way home, smiling as she did it.

That smile over the weed was much more genuine than the one she wore now.

He realized Sophie's torrential flow of words had finally ebbed. "Well, it's awesome," he said. "I'm sure we'll see you at the school."

"I'm sure you will." To anyone else listening, Sophie sounded pleased at the prospect, but Colton didn't miss the fact that she wasn't pleased at all. But she was being friendly. Oh, so freaking friendly.

His parents and Misty finally started back and Colton followed. He turned to take one more look at Sophie, who stood with her hands folded protectively over her stomach.

Over their baby.

The baby she hadn't told anyone about yet.

He sighed.

On the surface, Sophie seemed to be an open book. She wore her emotions on her sleeve. He'd never seen anyone who could cry over a diaper commercial and then roar with laughter over some dog chasing after treats, but that was Sophie.

Now for the first time he could see something more was hidden beneath her easy laughter. There was a pain there. It didn't take a rocket scientist to figure out that some of that pain had to come from her parents…the parents she allowed him to think were dead. The parents that hadn't come or, rather, hadn't been invited, to their wedding.

He'd found out that Sophie had lied to him, and thought that was that. She wasn't who she said she was.

But maybe he should have wondered why she was happy to allow him to think her parents were dead. And he definitely should have asked why she hadn't told him she had a daughter.

He'd simply been so angry. Embarrassed in front of the entire town.

He should have waited longer to go see her.

Or maybe he should have seen her sooner.

Hell, maybe he should never have let her leave without him at all. Maybe he should have gone with her and Tori to her house and found out exactly what was going on.

Things he could have done, and maybe should have done, kept occurring to him.

"Colton?" was all his mom said.

"I'm fine, Mom. Let's go check out the food booths at the school."

She nodded, and his family went back to talking about how great the town looked and how much Valley Ridge had changed since they bought the farm in Fredonia, when his father had gotten the job at the college there.

Colton glanced behind him, hoping for one more glimpse of Sophie, but she was lost in the crowd.

Should have. Could have.

Of all the things he could have, should have done,

the one that stood out the most was the fact he should have made Sophie explain.

And when she did, he definitely should have listened.

SOPHIE WATCHED COLTON'S family disappear in the crowd and realized she was practically gripping her stomach. She forced herself to stop and thrust her hands into her capris' pockets. "Shall we?" she asked.

"He's a jerk," Tori muttered.

"Pardon?" Sophie asked.

"Colton. The guy you almost married, before I objected and ruined it. He's a jerk. I mean, I know it's my fault, but if he wasn't a jerk, he wouldn't leave you just because you had a kid years ago, when you were practically a kid yourself."

Sophie shot a look at the Allens, silently asking their permission to handle this, and Gloria gave the merest nod granting it.

"Tori, please listen to me. Nothing that happened, or will happen, between Colton and me is your fault. Not at all. We had problems in our relationship, and those simply became more than the relationship could handle. It had nothing to do—has nothing to do—with you."

Tori shrugged but didn't seem convinced. "You didn't tell him about me and when he found out, he left you."

"No, I didn't tell him about you and about a lot of other things. I had my reasons, but I still hurt him."

Gloria stepped in. "It's like how my not telling you that you were adopted hurt you. When you withhold big secrets like that, the other person wonders what else you're hiding. Well, between me and you, that was it.

You were adopted and I didn't tell you because…" She took a deep breath. "Because I was afraid."

Tori didn't look convinced. "Afraid of what?"

"Afraid of losing you."

"Never," Tori whispered as she hugged her mother.

Sophie felt herself tear up as she watched them. She hoped to build a relationship with Tori, but she'd never have one like this.

She brushed away her tears. For years, she'd allowed herself to own her emotions. She cried when she was moved to tears. She laughed when things amused her. She looked for joy wherever she could find it.

But she no longer had that luxury.

Her parents had taught her the value of a social face. She hadn't worn hers in years, but it was like riding a bike. She hadn't forgotten how.

She'd faced Colton twice now, and both times she'd hidden away her heart.

"Lead on, McGuff," Dom said.

"It's *lay,* not *lead,* and Macduff, not McGuff!" Gloria corrected him with a laugh.

"Dad likes to misquote stuff all the time. It drives Mom nuts," Tori said conspiratorially.

"Oh, this lady's imagination is vapid," Dom said as they walked down the street.

"*Rapid,* not *vapid,*" Gloria groused with mock ferocity.

"Dad's bringing out the big guns when he quotes Austen's *Pride and Prejudice.*"

For the next couple of hours, Sophie and the Allens wandered through the holiday festivities. They bought kettle corn and ice cream, and prim-and-polished Gloria bought a funky set of beach glass earrings, which seemed out of character, but Tori told Sophie that Gloria had a soft spot for dangly and shiny things. They passed by Dr. Marshall, who gave Sophie a sympathetic look as he waved at them.

Dom got into a long discussion at one of the farmer's stands about organic gardening and where to buy ladybugs.

"You buy ladybugs?" Sophie whispered to Tori.

Tori nodded. "They're an organic way of controlling pests."

Mr. Tuznik, the former mayor and current crossing guard, approached their group and scooped Sophie into a hug, then whispered, "It will all work out."

She didn't need to ask what *it* was. She wanted to tell him that the distaster of a wedding was her fault. That Colton's leaving her was her fault. That everything was her fault. But she didn't say anything other than "thank you" as she patted the elderly man's back and disengaged herself from his comfort.

On his heels, Marilee and Vivienne started heading their way, so she ducked into a tent of tie-dyed T-shirts and teenage jewelry, the Allens right behind her.

When Tori bought a couple of braided bracelets, they started through the crowd again. Sophie worked hard at not making eye contact with anyone, but she couldn't miss the sympathetic looks from everyone. Between those looks and the other booths they visited, the Allens continued their banter as Sophie pointed out the sights.

She spotted Colton, along with Finn and Sebastian, over by the dunking booth. She'd known she was bound to run into them—and into Colton again. Every fiber of her being wanted to turn and walk in the other direction, or simply ignore them like she'd been ignoring everyone's sympathy, but she wasn't going to slink around

Valley Ridge, avoiding Colton and his friends. Time to practice her social face. She purposefully didn't alter her course, and smiled at the group. "Hi, guys. Finn and Sebastian, I'd like to introduce you to the Allens. Lieutenant Sebastian Bennington and Dr. Finn Wallace, this is Dom, Gloria and Tori Allen."

"Nice to meet you," Finn said, while Sebastian merely gave a brisk nod.

"We were on our way…over there," Finn said, and the two of them headed across the high school lawn at a quick pace.

Colton stared after his friends with an expression that said he had no idea what had just happened. Sophie might have clued him into the fact that his friends were snubbing her, but he'd figure it out on his own sooner or later.

"Good seeing you again. I hope you're having a good time today. Valley Ridge pulled out all the stops," he said. Making social small talk wasn't his forte, and Sophie shot him a smile of thanks, which seemed to encourage him, because he said to Tori, "I hear you're going to be helping Maeve out at the library this summer?"

Tori looked surprised.

"You're coming from Cleveland, so you might not know how small towns work, but here in Valley Ridge, news travels faster than you can tweet. Not only did I run into Maeve, but I heard it from about half a dozen other people, too."

Sophie knew that in addition to talking about Tori and her job, people were discussing her and Colton's wedding and speculating on what went wrong. She wanted to groan. She wanted to tell everyone it was all her fault. But, instead, she kept her social smile in place as Tori looked skeptical at the thought of the small-town gossip mill, and Dom said, "It was like that on the commune. If I did anything, my parents heard about it before I got home."

"I've always lived in a city, so don't look at me," Gloria told Tori with a laugh. "But I guess that there are some bonuses to that kind of grapevine. You'll hear how Tori's doing before Tori even knows how she's doing."

"You've got that right," Sophie said.

Colton cleared his throat. "I better go check on Finn and Sebastian. I'll see you at the library, Tori."

"Yeah, sure," Tori said with as much animosity as his friends had shown Sophie.

"Sorry about Colton's friends," Sophie said to the Allens. "Let me assure you, it was me, not you."

"They're rallying around their friend?" Gloria asked.

"That's not fair," Tori said. "I broke up the wedding, not you."

"You didn't break up anything," Sophie reiterated. She wouldn't allow Tori to feel guilty about that. "As for Finn and Sebastian, they're simply watching out for Colton. I like that he has friends who have his back no matter what. Everyone needs someone like that in their corner."

"But I—" Tori started.

"Not your fault. It will all work out," she said for Tori's benefit, and maybe for her own. It felt good saying the words out loud. *It will all work out.* When she'd been pregnant with Tori, her life had been as emotionally chaotic as it was now. It had been hard to believe, in the midst of it all, that things would ever be okay again.

And look at her life now. Though she'd missed Tori every day, her daughter had been raised by two wonderful people who obviously loved her. And Sophie had built for herself a life she loved.

Her hand rested on her stomach, and she reassured herself that a year from now, she'd be in a good place again. The chaos would have settled, and she'd have her daughter back in her life, and a baby to raise.

But not Colton, a small voice whispered in her head; she ignored it.

They wandered through the booths. Food. Games. Until they came to the small booth filled with paperbacks. Maeve Buchanan was working it. "Hi, Maeve," Sophie said. "Nice booth."

"The library's got so many paperbacks. We thought this was a great way to clear out some of our donations and make some money for other books we really need. Do you know we don't even have one copy of any of Shakespeare's plays?" Maeve shook her head at the thought, setting her wild red hair in motion.

She seemed to sense her hair's undulations, because she reached up and tried to smooth it into place, but it didn't help. Maeve heaved a put-upon sort of sigh and gave up, then turned to Tori. "And is this my summer volunteer?"

"It is. Maeve Buchanan, this is the Allen family, Dom, Gloria and your victim—volunteer—Tori."

Maeve grinned. "It's nice to meet you all, especially you, Tori. I can really use the help."

"Sophie said you pretty much run everything yourself and you don't even get paid?" Tori asked, as if the concept of not being paid for work was a mystery to her.

"I don't get paid in money, but I get paid," Maeve assured her. "There's something magic about suggesting a book to someone, and having them read it and get as excited as you were about it. When I was younger,

I had someone who did that for me. She'd hand me a book I wouldn't have picked up if you paid me, and because I didn't want to hurt her feelings, I'd try it and find the magic."

"Yeah, Mom made me read—"

"Suggested." Gloria humphed, which made Dom and Tori both laugh.

"Yeah, suggested in the same tone she *suggests* I clean my room, or put my dishes in the dishwasher. Anyway, I tried them because she *suggested* them, plus I knew she loved them, and I was surprised to find I love them, too. And last summer, we had Shakespeare Sundays."

"Shakespeare Sundays?" Maeve asked.

"We read the plays aloud. I hated reading them, but it was fun with Mom and Dad. Dad made the best Puck ever."

"I did," Dom said, with a modest smile.

Maeve dug through a pile of paperbacks and asked, "Have you tried this?" as she handed Tori a ratty copy of *The Hunger Games.*

"No. I saw the movie, though."

"Try the book. I love that you read Shakespeare, but you'll need some more contemporary YAs for the kids who come visit."

"YAs?" Tori asked.

"Young adults. It's a very hot genre, and I think most of the people who will be using the library in the afternoons while you're there will be kids." Maeve looked beyond their group and said, "Speaking of kids, let me introduce you to some of our more frequent visitors. Joey, come over here."

"Joe," the young boy corrected.

Maeve nodded and continued. "Joe, Allie and Mica

Williams, this is Tori Allen. She's going to be opening the library a couple of hours an afternoon for the summer."

The tiniest blonde sister, Mica, gave Tori a once-over and asked, "Do you read books to little girls?"

Tori knelt down. "I don't think I ever have, but I'd be willing to learn."

Mica considered it a moment, then nodded. "Okay. I'm Mica and I'm five. I know all about reading. My brother, Joe, he reads to me and he can do the voices. You gotta hold little kids on your lap, and you gotta do the voices. My friend Abbey and I will help you."

"I'd appreciate that," Tori said.

"We're gonna look for books at the booth. Ya got any for kids, Miss Maeve?" Mica asked.

Maeve led the girls into the booth, and Joe smiled at Tori. "Sorry. She doesn't generally accost strangers like that. She must like you."

Sophie watched as Tori blushed and answered, "No problem. I like kids for the most part."

"Me, too," Joe said. "For the most part. Do you want me to introduce you around? I hear you're going to be spending the summer here in Valley Ridge."

Tori looked back at her mom and dad for permission, and when they nodded, she said, "Sure, that would be great."

"Let's get the kids and we'll see who we can find."

Maeve sold each of the little girls a book, and the group of kids left. "See you in the morning, Miss Maeve," Tori called out.

"And that's that," Gloria said with a laugh. "Tori is a social butterfly. Before we get back next weekend, she'll know half the town."

"That's the kind of help the library could use. The

idea of having a kid there in the afternoons might make a draw," Maeve said. "I've got a bunch of people who will be helping out, too. I don't want you to think I'm simply dumping everything on Tori. But I'll be showing her the ropes tomorrow, and she'll be heading things up."

"So she won't be alone?"

"No, I've lined up some adult volunteers. Mayor Tuznik, Mrs. Dedioniso, Mrs. Esterly… We've got a bunch who will be in and out during Tori's afternoons."

"I thought your mayor was your friend Mattie's brother?" Dom asked.

"He is. Stanley Tuznik was the mayor years back. He's retired now and is the crossing guard for the school, but he still gets Mayor as an honorific," Sophie explained. "Kind of like once you're president, you're always Mr. President."

Dom laughed and nodded.

"Thanks again, Maeve," Sophie said. She walked through the crowd, waving at people and trying not to get too close to anyone who had "that look" in their eye. That's what she dubbed the look that said they wanted to hug her and assure her that everything would be all right. She wasn't sure she could take too much more of either.

So she stuck to introducing Gloria and Dom to people who didn't seem likely to swoop in for a hug. When they reached the school, they put their blanket at the corner of the football field as evening descended and it started to get dark. Sophie was alone with Tori's parents. It was the perfect time to tell them about the baby and ask their opinion. But she couldn't find the words.

Big shock there. She obviously could never find the words for the things that really mattered. "I—"

"Aunt Sophie," came a voice, interrupting her before she even started.

Abbey Langley threw herself onto Sophie's lap. "I missed you so much. So did Bear. He said come visit."

Abbey didn't wait for a response. The small redhead prattled on about what she'd done with Finn and Mattie that day. "...and popcorn. Mickey almost puked."

"TMI," eleven-year-old Zoe Langley said. "You ran too far ahead. Aunt Mattie's gonna get you."

"Uh-uh." Abbey turned to the Allens. "Aunt Mattie don't get me. She loves me."

"But I'll get you," screamed Mickey Langley, who was rewarded by an earsplitting shriek as he chased his little sister around the blanket.

"Here we are, bringers of chaos," Mattie said. "Harbingers of doom. Have you seen Finn?"

"A while back. He was with Colton and Sebastian."

"Boys," Mattie groused with a grin.

"Mattie, these are Tori's parents, Gloria and Dom Allen. They'll be in town most weekends this summer. They're staying at JoAnn's."

"My fiancé..." Mattie said, stumbling a bit over the word, as if it was still a surprise that Finn was her fiancé, "stays there. At least for a few more weeks until the wedding."

Gloria and Dom both looked at Sophie. "I'm going to stand up for Mattie." She faced her friend. "You know, we're going to have to go dress shopping."

Mattie groaned. "With Lily, the bridesmaid-zilla."

"Lily's that bad?" Gloria asked.

"Worse," Sophie and Mattie said in unison.

Mattie regaled Dom and Gloria with her disgruntled renditions of Lily's list of wedding rules.

Sophie realized that all three of them gave her concerned glances, so she forced a smile and joined in the laughter.

She noticed her hands were once again cradling her still-flat stomach. She couldn't help but notice how often she did that.

She forced her hands onto her lap. She'd tell her friends, and Gloria and Dom, about the baby next week. If these were the kind of sympathetic glances she got after a broken engagement, she'd need to gird her loins in order to deal with the looks she'd get when everyone found out about the baby.

Mattie and the kids left and returned to the blanket they were sharing with Finn, which sat next to a blanket with Sebastian, Hank and Lily, which sat next to Colton's solo blanket. Sophie couldn't help glancing their way. Part of her wished she was there with them, part of the group again.

But when Tori found them just as dusk turned to straight-up night, Sophie realized she was part of another group now. One that included her daughter, her daughter's parents and, someday soon, a new baby.

They waited for the fireworks to begin.

"Should we teach Sophie to play the ooh-aah game?" Gloria asked.

The entire family talked over one another, explaining that if you listened to the crowd when the fireworks went off, their responses seemed to alter between ooh and aah of their own accord.

When the fireworks started, they were silent a moment, and sure enough, after each burst of fireworks, the crowd oohed and aahed, which set the Allen family to laughing.

Sophie joined in their laughter, but realized that despite the fact they'd tried to include her, this was a family thing. And though she was biologically Tori's family, she wasn't really. Not in any way that mattered.

COLTON WAS SITTING slightly behind Sophie and the Allens, which gave him the perfect opportunity to watch her.

He noticed that the three Allens sat so close to one another they touched. The mom's and dad's thighs touched, and Tori held her mother's hand as they watched the fireworks together, laughing over something.

Sophie sat a bit removed. Oh, she laughed when they did, but it was apparent to anyone who really took the time to look that she was an outsider. Included, but not part of the family.

Not anymore.

That's what Sophie had said when he asked if she had a family.

Not anymore.

He'd been so angry the day Tori showed up and Sophie had admitted that she still had family, that she'd lied to him, that he hadn't asked himself what her parents must have done to make Sophie cut them out of her life.

Each time a firework lit up the sky, he could see how isolated she looked, sitting there as part yet apart. He wanted to go over and sit next to her. Wrap his arm around her and provide support.

But he'd given up the right.

And though he knew he'd been justified in calling things off, he couldn't help but wonder again what would have happened if he'd insisted that the wedding go forward, and then worked to sort things out with Sophie after.

After they were husband and wife.

After they were tied forever.

He'd have had the whole story and been next to Sophie, helping her work things out with Tori. He'd have been there when she found out about their baby.

He could almost imagine how it would have been. Something would have happened to make Sophie suspect. Maybe she'd missed a period. Maybe she felt sick in the morning. Sophie, being Sophie, she'd have shared her suspicions with him immediately. She couldn't hold on to a secret to save her life.

At that moment, his fantasy bubble burst.

Sophie obviously could hold on to a secret.

He glanced at her daughter.

Sophie had more than proved that.

How could he have married someone who couldn't tell him the truth?

How could he not marry the woman who was going to have his baby?

How could…

He forced himself to let those unanswerable questions go and watch the fireworks.

"You okay?" Sebastian asked, and Finn turned to him, waiting to hear his answer.

"Fine. I'm fine," he lied.

Maybe he could keep some secrets, too.

CHAPTER SEVEN

AT NINE ON TUESDAY, Sophie knocked softly on Tori's door. "Time to get up," she called. "You don't want to be late meeting Maeve on your first day of work, especially when she took time off from her own job to help get you settled."

Tori surprised her by opening the door, fully dressed. "I was on my way down."

"I didn't hear you get up. Of course, I had the radio on."

"Yeah, I heard."

"Oh, I'm sorry. Did it wake you up?" She should have thought that the radio might have woken Tori.

Sophie hadn't lived with anyone since she left home. Even in college, she'd paid extra for a private dorm room. Funny, when she was planning the wedding it had never occurred to her to worry that living with someone might be an adjustment.

Maybe because she had no doubts that she and Colton would mesh as well living together as they always had.

"Sophie, it's fine," Tori said. "I was teasing. And it's nice to learn you listen to regular music." She started down the stairs.

Sophie was on her heels. "Regular music?"

"Contemporary stuff, not some old guy singing

about a splinter in his shoe and in his heart because some woman done him wrong."

"I listen to country music, too. And it's not like that." Sophie listened to country music because of Colton. He didn't like *regular* music. She refused to think about him but, instead, concentrated on her daughter as they walked into the kitchen. She turned the radio down. "I'm not sure what you like for breakfast. I have granola, or we can stop at the coffee shop on the way to the library. Mattie makes the most kick-butt muffins. We can go to the diner if you want something more, or I can make eggs, or—"

"How about I grab a muffin at the coffee shop?" Tori asked. "But I'd take a cup of coffee now."

"You drink coffee at—" She was about to say *your age,* but stopped herself.

"At my age?" Tori had no problem filling in the blank. She laughed. "Mom loves the stuff, and I always had a sip of hers in the morning. I like the taste. She always limited me to that sip, saying if I started drinking it too soon, it'd stunt my growth. But then I met you and figured I'm stunted either way, and Mom agreed, so now I get one cup in the morning, as long as I promise no soft drinks in exchange."

"I like how your parents work." They listened to a rather logical argument and adjusted the rules accordingly. She had to agree with Tori's assessment… if Sophie's genetics played out, Tori was doomed to shopping in the petite section of the store for the rest of her life.

"Yeah, I guess they're better than most of my friends' parents. Mom and Dad at least listen to me. If they say no to something, but I can come up with a logical argument, or a compromise option, they'll listen. Listening isn't something most parents do too well." She paused. "Well, Mom had a hard time listening about you. But she was afraid. I hadn't thought about why she reacted so differently than she normally did to other stuff."

Tori went to the small coffee machine. The coffee pods were next to it in a basket, so she brewed her own cup of coffee, and Sophie realized it was more like half a cup of coffee, since Tori liberally added milk after the fact.

Sophie took a sip of her own decaf. She'd been trying to convince herself that it was as good as the regular, but she couldn't quite make herself believe it.

They sat at her kitchen table in the small breakfast bay of the kitchen. The silence was comfortable for a few minutes, then it started to feel more uneasy.

"So, did you want to ask any questions today?" Sophie finally asked.

"I've thought about it. About what I want to know, about…well, all of this. And I decided that I don't want you to simply regurgitate your past and my beginning to me. That's not how kids normally find out about their parents. Normally, they know that if they cry, their mom will pick them up. And then they learn that if they smile, their mom smiles back. And then…" She shrugged.

"It's not until they're older that kids even know their parents were once kids, too. I remember when Mom told me about the one day she'd skipped school. She found a dog that had been hit by a car and she carried it to the vet's, then waited for hours until it got out of surgery. That's the first time I remember realizing Mom was once a kid. The realization surprised me. The fact she saved a dog didn't."

"It doesn't surprise me, either," Sophie said. She'd just met the woman, but she knew that despite her impeccable wardrobe, Gloria would be the first one to jump out and help an injured animal.

"That's how I want to get to know you. In bits and pieces. Organically, is how my dad would put it. I don't want you to spit out the story in a rush. I want to…"

"To get to know me organically."

"Yeah."

Tori wanted to know that if she cried, Sophie would pick her up. If she smiled, Sophie would smile, too. She was amazed by this child, who she'd given birth to and who the Allens had raised so beautifully. "Then that's what we'll do. I'll try to talk about my past. It's not something I'm good at."

"Yeah, you never told Colton about me."

"No, I never did. But I don't want you to think it was because I regretted having you or was embarrassed. It hurt so much to talk about you. I've missed you every day since the moment they took you from me. I screamed out loud, begging to hold you at least once. Wanting to see you for myself. But no matter how I begged, they wouldn't listen. I don't know, maybe I figured no one would ever listen. You became something I held on to tightly, but privately. And after I left my parents for college, I didn't talk about them, either. When people asked, I'd say my parents were gone because they were. At least to me."

Tori reached out and put her hand on Sophie's. "If you forget to talk, I'll remind you when there's something I need to know. But for right now, why don't we go get those muffins? And take me to work."

Tori had gone over to Maeve's yesterday. It was nice that the Fourth was on a Monday. The town had celebrated over the weekend, and yesterday had still been a day off. Maeve had shown Tori around the library, and it was a simple system, which would hopefully make Tori's time there easy.

"Maeve said you'd only be there a few hours. When you're done, we're meeting your parents at the diner before they drive home." Gloria and Dom had thought about leaving Monday morning, but they wanted to let Tori try out a night at Sophie's while they were still in town. So they stayed the extra night. Having lunch together would give them a chance to reconnect and see that it had gone all right.

"I won't forget. And it's a short walk from the library to the diner, so I'll meet you all there when I'm done."

Sophie wanted to say no, that she'd pick Tori up, but her daughter was almost fifteen and well beyond the age of needing an escort to and from destinations. She'd driven herself from Ohio through Pennsylvania and over the border to the edge of New York—the thought still made Sophie cringe. But, given all that, she could definitely walk a few blocks solo.

Sophie forced herself not to offer to meet her and simply said, "I hope you like volunteering at the library. It's been Maeve's baby since it reopened, but she's lamented that she can only be there a few hours in the evening. With you there during the day, it will give the kids somewhere to go."

"Yeah, Maeve asked how I felt about reading books to the little kids. A story time. Mom used to take me to something like that. This lady, Miss Kitty, she was awesome. She didn't even look at the books, she knew the words and the stories. She was so excited about reading that you couldn't help but get excited, too. I don't know if I can read like her."

"I don't think the kids will care if you have to read the words."

"Yeah, that's what Maeve said. I…"

Tori talked about the library, about Maeve… She simply talked and Sophie hung on every word as they walked to Park Street. She was walking on a summer morning with her daughter.

It was a moment she'd never imagined having.

COLTON DROVE DOWN Park Street. Jerry had called Saturday to say that his special order of flagstone had come in. He'd ordered it for Sophie because, once, after a particularly wet week, she'd mentioned that they should put down some sort of stone patio. They'd had friends coming over for a picnic, and the yard had still been soup.

She'd shown him a picture in a magazine. It had been a flagstone patio. He'd thought she'd enjoy the surprise. He'd imagined placing a pink bow on the pile of stone. Sophie would have laughed, then rolled up her sleeves and helped him build the patio.

Now the flagstone was in, but he wouldn't need a pink bow.

He turned onto Park Street and spotted Sophie and Tori going into Park Perks.

Without conscious thought, he pulled into a vacant spot two doors down from the coffee shop.

He wasn't following Sophie or forcing a meeting. He simply had a sudden hankering for coffee and one of Mattie's carrot muffins.

Yep, that's all this was.

He straightened his hat and sauntered into the shop. The bell on the door jingled. Not only did Mattie look at him, but Sophie and her daughter turned toward him, as well.

Neither Sophie nor Tori said anything. It was Mattie who greeted him. "Hi, Colton."

"Mattie. Sophie and Tori." He walked up to the no-longer-blue-haired girl and saw her hair still boasted a slight blue hue.

"Sir." She eyed him distrustfully.

"Have you seen Maeve? Our librarian."

Tori's response was a silent glare, until Sophie gave her the slightest elbow. Tori sighed.

Colton ignored the exchange between Sophie and Tori, and said, "I'm sure Maeve will appreciate your help. She's wanted to expand the hours at the library for ages."

"A lot of kids need something to do during the day. A library's a good place for them to do it." She snapped her mouth shut, as if she'd realized she'd responded to him with something akin to enthusiasm.

"Speaking of the library," Sophie said in an obvious bid to rescue Tori and escape, "we'd better get you there. Maeve's got to be at work by noon. She wanted to spend the morning with you."

"Sophie, can I come over some night?" Colton blurted out. "We need to talk."

She didn't even hesitate as she answered, "No, I don't think so."

"Can you come by the farm?" he tried.

"Colton, we've said everything we needed to say. I'll text you anything that you need to know." She gave him the slightest nod of her head and he knew that anything he needed to know would center around the baby, not her. Sophie turned to her friend. "Have a good one, Mattie."

Tori shot him a parting glare as they both hurried out of the shop.

Mattie whistled a long, low sound. "Wow, you are definitely in the doghouse. That's not somewhere I ever thought you'd end up with Sophie. She adores you."

"Once upon a time, but not so much now." He'd never seen Sophie like this. She'd always been smiling. Easy going. Amenable.

"What did you do wrong?" Mattie asked.

Colton didn't answer her question and ordered a coffee, though he'd lost the taste for it.

He realized that Mattie hadn't asked the right question. The right question was, what hadn't he done wrong?

SOPHIE GOT TO THE DINER early and found Gloria and Dom already sitting at a back table. She went to join them. Hank followed her. "Coffee?"

"Ice water with lemon?" she asked.

"Sure thing, beautiful."

She sat down and studied Tori's parents. They still looked as incongruous as ever. Dom wore a T-shirt that proclaimed Paint by Numbers and had a bucolic scene half painted on it. Gloria had on a light summer sweater set and her pearls.

"So, today's the day. You'll have Tori until Friday," Gloria said by way of greeting.

Sophie nodded. "About Tori. I couldn't help but wonder if you think she's all right."

"You don't?" Gloria's expression went from friendly to concerned, and Dom's face echoed hers.

"She's too…" Sophie wasn't sure how to phrase her concern. "I almost said *nice,* but that's not it. When she showed up at my wedding and objected, she was angry. I mean, it was almost palpable. Everything about her, from her blue hair to her stance, was simply so very angry. Angry at you two, angry at me. I don't know how someone goes from that angry to not-so-much so quickly. I mean, she took the blue out of her hair, accepted the idea of this job without a complaint and has been nothing but nice to me. She told me this morning that she doesn't plan to grill me, searching for answers, but wants them to come organically." Sophie smiled at Dom as she said the word. "She wants me to talk about myself as things come up. I'm not good at that."

Sophie realized "not good" was an understatement.

She tried to figure out how to put her fears into words. "I'm afraid that I'm going to say something wrong and set her off again. I'm afraid that maybe all that anger is bubbling under the surface, and try as she might to hide it, it's going to come exploding out at some point."

Dom looked at Gloria and said, "See, I'm never wrong."

"He's insufferable, but he wasn't wrong when he said very much the same thing. Tori's a teen and even though she's talking to me again and smiling, she's still furious with me for not telling her about you."

"And I'm pretty sure she's still furious at me for giving her up."

Dom nodded. "This is the calm before the storm. We want you to know we don't expect you to deal with the fallout by yourself. We can be here in two hours, maybe three depending on the time of day."

"I'm afraid that I have news that's going to make that upcoming storm worse. I haven't told anyone but Colton, but…" Sophie might wear her emotions on her sleeve, but she didn't talk about them. She didn't share. But for her daughter's sake, she forced herself to say the words. "I'm expecting. I can't imagine how the news will affect Tori."

The Allens exchanged a look with each other and Sophie could read their concern for their daughter.

"When were you going to tell her?" Gloria asked.

"Sooner rather than later, I think." Sophie found her hands on her stomach again, of their own accord. As if by wrapping themselves around her unborn child she could protect it from the anger she feared that Tori was going to have.

"I've learned my lesson," Gloria admitted. "We all need to be as honest as possible with Tori and with each other."

Sophie nodded. "I agree. But I wanted to ask you both what you want me to do."

"Wait until we're in town before you tell her," Gloria said. "I don't know what else to offer for suggestions." She looked at Dom.

"Be honest, be loving and be prepared to deal with the outcome. We'll do whatever we can to help her through it, and to help you."

"You don't even know me." There was no hint of anything other than genuine concern in the Allens' faces.

"You're part of our family," Dom said. "Even before we met you, you were part of our family. You gave us the greatest gift anyone can give another person. How could you not be a part of us?"

Sophie started to cry. And she didn't try to stop the tears that she'd held in check since Colton had said goodbye. "I'm so happy to get a chance to know Tori, but I want you to know that I still believe I did the best thing I could by letting you adopt her. I worried so much that first year. I bought a baby book and tracked what milestones she should have reached. Milestones I couldn't witness, but you did. I worried you wouldn't realize how miraculous each was, but on her first birthday, I got your letter and it was clear that you not only recognized what a miracle she was, you treasured her. I found peace. I knew that she was loved. Not only a little, but completely. It was there in every line you shared. Thank you for that and for all the letters that followed."

Those letters that arrived like clockwork annually were a lifeline for Sophie. They kept her going.

"We marveled at every one of those milestones," Gloria said. "When I wrote the letters, I was able to share how absolutely amazing she was with someone who would understand."

"I'm so happy about this baby, but I know it couldn't have come at a worse time."

Gloria shook her head. "There's never a good time for a baby. When we got the call that you had picked us as parents for your daughter, we'd almost given up hopes of ever having a child. I'd just been given tenure at the university and Dom had been given his first solo art show. Our quiet life had exploded and we thought that things had worked out the way they were supposed to. We'd be a childless career couple. Then we got that call."

"Tori didn't sleep through the night until she was over a year old," Dom said. "That entire first year is still blurry."

"He did a painting called *Tori at Midnight*. It sold immediately." Gloria's pride was evident.

"I don't think I even remember painting it," Dom admitted. "I was that sleep deprived."

"What we're trying to say is, life happens when it

happens. You can't script it, you can't control it. Dom taught me that." Gloria reached for his hand with practiced ease. "Tell Tori, but give yourself this one week before you do. If you tell her next weekend, we'll be here for her and for you."

Sophie looked at the two of them holding hands—united. And they were going to stand by her. There had only been one other time when she thought she'd had someone standing in her corner no matter what. That was when she'd fallen in love with Colton.

She couldn't have imagined a time he wouldn't be there for her.

She'd simply never known that the first real test of that connection would lead to such an epic failure.

And now, here were two virtual strangers offering to be there for her. She choked up at the thought. "Thank you."

"Here comes the working woman," Tori called out with a grin as she approached the booth.

Sophie shot Dom and Gloria one last look of gratitude, and then turned to Tori. "So, it went well?"

Tori slid into the booth next to her, her thigh touching Sophie's.

"I've discovered I love the sound of the *ca-thunk* as the stamp hits the book." Tori mimicked the sound for emphasis. "Maeve doesn't have money for the kind of computer system that tracks books. She runs the library old-school. A card catalog, a patron catalog and a stamp. *Ca-thunk*. Maeve says even if she does have enough funding for a new computer system, she isn't sure she'd want to change 'cause she loves the sound, too. She showed me the Dewey system and..."

Tori bubbled over about the library through their lunch.

Watching Tori, listening to her—it was hard to believe that she was the same girl who had objected at the wedding.

Sophie couldn't help but wonder what would have happened if Tori hadn't said anything until after the ceremony. Would Colton have been so quick to walk away if they'd made their vows?

Sophie understood that he would be hurt, that he'd be mad, but to simply write her off?

Her parents had done that. She'd done her best to be the daughter they wanted, even though she'd chafed under their restrictions. She'd made a mistake and they'd written off all the things she'd done right. They'd written off her.

Colton, the man she'd believed would always be at her side, had ultimately done the same thing.

What was it about her that drove people away like that?

"Well, we should hit the road," Dom said to Tori. "We'll miss you, Chicken."

"Dad," Tori whined.

"Chicken?" Sophie asked.

"I liked chickens when I was little. A neighbor had a flock and I spent a whole summer telling Mom and Dad I could speak chicken."

"Ba bwak, ba bwak," Dom said.

Tori groaned while her parents laughed. Gloria was the one who grew serious first. "You call me every night. I mean it, every single night."

"I will," Tori promised.

"And you remember that even if you're staying with Sophie, our rules still apply."

Tori nodded. "I know."

Dom kissed her. "Be kind. When you have a choice, in any given situation—"

"If you have a choice, always choose kindness," Tori said, obviously repeating a quote she'd heard frequently.

"That's right, Chick."

"Thank you for allowing me...us..." Sophie was thanking them for an array of things, not only allowing her this time with Tori, but for raising her when she couldn't. "For everything."

They each kissed Tori again, then Dom started toward the door, but Gloria leaned forward and whispered, "Congratulations," in her ear.

She wasn't sure if Tori's mother was congratulating her on finding her daughter, or on the new baby, but either way, that word brought Sophie to tears and she allowed herself an impulsive move and hugged her.

Gloria seemed as surprised as she was, but she hugged Sophie back. "I'll talk to you both tonight."

Sophie and Tori watched as Dom and Gloria got in their car, parked right outside the diner, and took off down Park Street.

"Looks like it's you and me," Sophie said.

Tori nodded. "Looks like."

And suddenly, without Dom and Gloria there to serve as a buffer, Sophie felt awkward. What now?

ON THURSDAY, Colton sat in the corner of the diner, methodically eating his steak dinner. He'd spent most of his day in the field, trying not to think of Sophie as he worked. But it was hard because the arbor he'd built for her was on the far end of the field. Every time he saw it, it felt as if someone was rubbing salt into an open wound.

He'd thought about cooking something at home, but instead he'd decided to come into town and get dinner at the diner.

The fact that Thursdays were Sophie's I-don't-cook days didn't have anything to do with it. Granted, the diner might be the only dinner joint in town, but there were other towns and cities nearby, so she could have taken Tori to dinner at any of them.

But as he chewed on his steak, he caught sight of her and Tori walking into the diner. And, seeing her, something in him loosened.

He studied Sophie and couldn't decide if he was imagining it, or if she really did have a small bump where their baby was growing.

He wondered if she was having any side effects. If she was sick in the mornings, or if she had cravings.

He'd tried to figure out how far along she was, but other than knowing she'd stopped using her birth control pills after the New Year, he didn't have a clue. She couldn't be too far, could she?

He didn't think Sophie had seen him. She chose the seat that faced the window, so she still didn't know he was here, but Tori was facing him, and she definitely noticed him if the scowls she was sending in his general direction were any indication.

He tried to stare her down, but she didn't give an inch. She looked at Sophie often enough that Sophie didn't sense that anything was wrong, so Tori continued to glare.

He wondered if Sophie had told her about the baby. He was pretty sure she hadn't told Mattie and Lily yet. He wished she would because he really wanted to get his friends' opinion on what he should do now.

Tori stopped midglare and turned her attention to

Sophie, who twisted around and saw him. She got up and came over to the booth.

Colton didn't think he could see any signs of her pregnancy. "How are you?"

"Fine. Dandy. Peachy keen," she said with a sarcasm he'd never heard Sophie use before. "And how are you?"

He shrugged.

"Listen, tomorrow we have that winefest meeting. I wasn't sure if you were going, or if Rich was going?"

Colton had partnered with Mattie's brother Rich Keith in the winery so that he wouldn't have to go to things like this winefest meeting, or deal with customers at the winery. They met a few times a week to go over things, but this time of year, Colton was focused on his crops, not on the winery, so their partnership worked out perfectly.

But suddenly, he wanted to go to the winefest meeting more than anything he'd wanted to do in a while. "I'll be there. Probably Rich, too."

"I hope we can stay civil? The entire community is talking about us and I'd like to set the groundwork for a friendly relationship before our news comes out."

"Speaking about our news, have you mentioned it to anyone yet?"

"I'm going to tell Tori this weekend, and after she knows, I'll tell Lily and Mattie."

He nodded, resigned to not saying anything to Finn and Sebastian until next week then.

"I—" A look of panic swept over Sophie's face and she squeaked a polite "pardon me" and made a quick beeline for the restroom.

He was still staring after Sophie when Tori came over to the table and asked, "What did you do?"

"Huh?" he asked.

"It's my fault your wedding was ruined," Tori said. "You don't need to blame Sophie."

"I don't blame her, or you." Colton felt a sense of weariness.

"You made her cry."

"I didn't," he said. "We were talking about a meeting tomorrow night."

Tori snorted. "Sure, that was all. The fact you were ready to get married a couple weeks ago, and after I objected you called things off didn't enter the conversation."

"Not today it didn't." Their baby had, but not the wedding this time.

They seemed to be circling around and around. Weddings. Lies. Babies. Weddings. Lies. Babies... The words fell into a kind of *Wizard of Oz* lions, tigers and bears rhythm in his head.

"Yeah. Well, be nice to her," Tori instructed. "She's been sick all week and doesn't need some cowboy-wannabe making her life miserable."

"She's been sick?"

"Yeah." Some of the anger gave way to concern. "I think the stress of me and you is making her sick. She tries to play it off, but her house is small, I can hear her heaving her cookies in the bathroom."

Well, he had part of his answer. The baby was giving her morning sickness. And if her rush to the bathroom was any indication, her *morning* was in actuality all day.

He wondered if that was normal.

He wished she'd hurry up and tell people. If people knew, he could ask Finn, who was a doctor—albeit a surgeon who might not know much about babies, but Lily was a nurse and she worked with general practice patients. She'd keep an eye on Sophie and make sure she took care of herself.

Sophie came out of the bathroom and spotted Tori talking to him. He studied her as she walked across the diner, looking a bit green around the gills.

"What are you two up to?" she asked, her eyes narrowing at the two of them.

Tori answered, "We're just getting to know each other. I mean, your fiancé should know your daughter and vice versa."

"Right now, we're not labeling our relationship other than to say we're trying out being friends," Sophie corrected.

Friends? Like hell. They were about to be parents. "Not even really friends. We're trying out simply being *friendly,* right, Sophie?" The words came out of their own volition, and with more than a sense of anger. Colton saw them hit their mark.

Sophie flinched, then nodded. "Friendly. I'll see you at the meeting tomorrow night. Come on, Tori." She started back to their table, and Tori turned around to follow Sophie, somehow managing to step on his foot, which was safely under the table.

Well, obviously not too safely.

Tori whipped around and, with sarcasm dripping from every word, said, "Oh, I'm so sorry. Too bad you didn't wear cowboy boots along with your stupid hat. They might have saved your foot."

She shot him one last glare for good measure and then followed Sophie back to the table.

Colton resisted the urge to rub his foot. He wouldn't give the kid the satisfaction.

Sebastian chose that moment to come into the diner. He spotted him and hurried over. "Hey, I need to get to work soon. I told Lily I'd pay the invoices on the desk before I started my shift, but I've got a few minutes, if you have time."

Colton knew his friends were worried about him. And he'd seen how they'd given Sophie the cold shoulder at the Fourth celebrations. "I've got to run, but I have a favor to ask before I do."

"Name it," Sebastian said without waiting to hear what Colton wanted. "Anything."

"You and Finn need to stop being brusque with Sophie. She didn't do anything. The problems are on both our parts. But more than that, I wanted to suggest that as a way of showing her that you're still her friend, too, you should ask her about your campaign."

Sebastian sank into the booth across from him. "What?"

Seb—ah, hell, he was trying to remember to think about his friend as *Sebastian* since he'd declared he didn't want to use his childhood nickname anymore. *Sebastian* was running for the town council, and Colton wasn't sure why he hadn't thought of it before. If Sophie helped him, then they'd spend time together, and after Sebastian knew about the baby, his friend would tell him if he saw anything amiss in Sophie's health.

"Sophie does advertising for a living. Marketing. Look at the effort she's put in at the wineries. Even if she doesn't want to really work on your campaign, she could give you a few pointers."

"Lily was pissed at me after the Fourth, and pretty much read me not only the riot act, but called me a jerk. I am many things, but I'm not a jerk. It's simply hard not to be mad at Sophie. She never told you about her kid, and I know it hurt you that she called off the wedding."

Colton set the record straight. "*I* called off the wedding. And while I appreciate that you and Finn always have my back, I'm a big boy. I don't need you fighting my battles. And right now, Sophie and I are being *friendly,* but I'm hoping that, soon, we're more than that."

Sebastian looked surprised. "Wait. You're trying to get back together with her?"

Colton wasn't sure he could ever totally trust Sophie, but they had a baby coming, so there was only one answer he could give. "Yes. And it's not going to help my cause if my friends are being jerks."

"That puts an entirely different light on things. I've got this." He leaned across the table and smacked Colton's shoulder with his damaged hand. That was a huge change from when he'd come home and kept the hand in his pocket as much as possible.

"Thanks, Sebastian. I knew I could count on you."

"Always." He left Colton and hurried toward Sophie's table.

SOPHIE WAS A BIT THROWN when Sebastian approached her table wearing a smile. The last time she'd seen him he'd been so cold she'd pretty much had frostbite.

"Hi, Sophie," Sebastian called out, seeming genuinely happy to see her. "And, Tori, how's the library?"

"Fine," Tori said, glaring at Sebastian.

He didn't seem to notice that neither of them seemed overly pleased he'd stopped at the table.

Sebastian turned back to Sophie. "Any chance we can have a business meeting soon? I wanted to know if you could help me come up with some sort of slogan for my campaign. Frankly, I'll take any ideas at all. I need to make sure people see me as Sebastian, grown-up adult, not Seb, young hellion."

If someone had told her a blue unicorn was running down Park Street, Sophie would have been less surprised than to hear Sebastian's obvious change of heart and request. "Uh, sure. You know I'll do whatever I can to help."

He smiled again. "Great. Next week then?"

"Sure."

A sneaking suspicion occurred to her. Maybe Colton had told Sebastian, and this was his pity-the-single-mom offering.

Well, she didn't take charity from anyone. She'd cancel the meeting and tell Colton and his friends she was more than capable of handling this baby on her own, without their pity jobs.

"What was that?" Tori asked. "He was rude to you the other day at the fireworks."

She wanted to vent, to say, *Yeah, he's a total dork.* She'd handled everything that had been thrown at her up until now, but she couldn't handle anyone's sympathy. It grated.

She tried to tamp down her anger and smiled at Tori. "Sebastian's Colton's friend. I hurt Colton, so he was mad at me. I can't blame him."

"I can," Tori muttered. And there, under the surface, Sophie could sense the anger she'd seen that first day at her wedding. It still seeped from her. Tori had simply been working to hide it, but Sebastian gave her a target to aim some of it at. "You didn't do anything," Tori said. "I did. I showed up and broke up your wedding."

Sophie reached across the table and placed her hand on Tori's. What she wanted to do was hug her. She wanted to hold her, but she didn't have the right. "I keep telling you—and will keep on telling you until you believe me—you didn't break up my wedding. I did. I didn't tell Colton about a lot of things. I don't think I ever really stopped to think about how much I didn't share with him. And I certainly never asked myself why I didn't tell him things."

"You said it—you don't like to talk about your past."

"I've been mulling over why," Sophie told her daughter. "Let me start by asking you, why do you think your mom and dad didn't tell you that you were adopted sooner?"

"Dad wanted to, but Mom didn't until I was old enough." More of that anger, laced with frustration, trickled into that sentence. "But I was old enough a long time ago."

"So why didn't she tell you?" Sophie pressed.

Tori thought about it a moment. "She was afraid of losing me. Or maybe she was afraid I'd see her as someone who wasn't my real mother."

"But she is your real mother," Sophie assured her.

Tori nodded and a light flush of blue was obvious as her hair ruffled. "Yeah. She is my real mom." She looked nervous, as if saying that would hurt Sophie.

Sophie offered Tori a comforting smile. "So your mom didn't tell you, because she wanted to keep thinking of herself as your real mom and, more important, because she wanted you to think of her as your real mom. How you thought about her mattered a lot to her."

"Yeah," Sophie agreed.

"I think the reason I didn't tell Colton about a lot of the stuff in my past was because I wanted him to keep seeing me as Sophie, the woman he fell in love with. The woman I worked so hard to become. I didn't want him to pity me. I didn't want him to feel bad that he has an awesome family, and I didn't—don't. I didn't want…" She shrugged. "I held on to you—you were mine. I didn't tell anyone, not because I was embarrassed or anything like that and…" She felt the tears gather in her eyes. "And I kept you in my thoughts and my heart every day. You were mine. It seemed almost blasphemous to share that."

"You wanted to hold me," Tori stated, but it sounded as if she needed reassurance.

Sophie, who'd never really talked about her pregnancy or delivery, knew she had to now. She'd sworn to herself she'd be honest in all her answers to her daughter. "I so wanted to hold you at least once. To have that memory of you. But they took you while I was still on the delivery table. The very first time I touched you was when we were at my house talking after the wedding. I touched my finger to your cheek right before I called your parents. It was a small gesture. Something most people wouldn't think twice about, but I swear to you, I will remember that moment, that one touch, with clarity for the rest of my life."

"What happened after they took me?" Tori asked.

"Someone gave me a shot of something. Some drug that knocked me out. When I woke up, I was in a regular hospital room, and my parents tried to pretend I'd never been pregnant. They wanted me to carry on with the life they had planned for me and to forget you."

"But you didn't."

"I couldn't go back. Having you changed me. I wanted to keep you so much, but I let you go because I wanted the best life possible for you, and I knew I couldn't give that to you. Not then. I was too young. I'm glad your parents waited and didn't tell you about me because that's what I wanted for you. A normal life. I wanted you to be loved. And you had that?"

Tori nodded.

Sophie smiled. "Then when I talk to your mom tonight, I'm going to thank her. I know it hurt you to find out like that, but your mom and dad gave you exactly the life I wanted for you—the life I couldn't give you."

"The life you never had?" Tori guessed.

"The life I always dreamed about," Sophie agreed. Parents who loved her more than they loved themselves—more than they loved their public image. Parents who would put her needs first.

That's what she'd always wanted and, though she'd never had it, she'd given that to her daughter.

"I always wanted to be loved unconditionally, but that's not how my parents' love worked. I didn't care about giving you rich parents, or perfect parents. I wanted to give you to people who would give you unconditional love. And from what I've seen, I did that."

She'd given her daughter something she'd never had. Unconditional love.

She realized how desperately she'd wanted that for herself, as well.

She'd thought she'd found it with Colton, but she'd been wrong.

CHAPTER EIGHT

LILY AND SEBASTIAN came over on Friday. Helping out a friend was definitely a better idea than sitting and angsting about the fact it was Friday and Sophie had decided to tell Tori about the baby when she returned from the library. She was so afraid of losing the daughter she'd just found.

Of course, she didn't have a clue what help she could be to Sebastian's campaign. She'd found that sometimes concentrating on anything but a problem helped spark her creative juices, so she had pulled out her winefest folder.

She had a long to-do list for the fall winefest and had crossed off only the most urgent, which included calling the printers and setting up an appointment with them to go over some of the advertisements. It was almost mid-July, and though a few months sounded like ample time, it was nothing when planning an event this big. North East did an annual winefest, and she didn't want to step on their toes, so they'd planned theirs around North East's date, exchanging coupons and information.

Cooperation Not Competition was her catchphrase as she worked with neighboring community's wineries.

A catchphrase.

She didn't know diddly about politics, but she knew

that she wanted something short and pithy to identify Sebastian as a candidate.

Sophie spent the rest of her morning surfing the internet and looking for ideas.

Granted, this wasn't a presidential campaign, but the more she thought about it, the more she wondered if maybe a local politician wasn't more important to a town. She thought of Ray Keith, Mattie's brother and the mayor of Valley Ridge. He'd helped the community ride out the recession with the help of the town council—the very council Sebastian was running for.

She dialed Sebastian's number and, when he picked up, she said, "Don't think. I need you to answer this question as concisely as you can. Why are you running for town council?"

There was a short pause and he said, "I guess to serve my community."

"Great. See you in a bit." She hung up.

To serve.

And in a flash, she realized that Sebastian had spent his adult life doing that. Actually, according to Colton, Sebastian had grown up serving customers at the diner. He'd gone into the military and served his country.

And now he wanted to serve his community on town council.

It was an honest, simple and concise message.

He wanted to help his neighbors. He wanted to make the community a better place.

All of that could come under the heading of serving.

He wanted to serve his community on town council because that's what he'd done his entire life. Serve.

Sophie was practically bubbling over with excitement.

She hadn't felt this happy since…since the morning of her almost-wedding.

To serve.

Sebastian could weave that message through any ads, throughout any speeches or debates. What was his goal? To serve.

By the time Lily and Sebastian arrived at her house, Sophie could hardly contain herself. Lily hugged her and Sebastian came in behind her and nodded at Sophie.

She waved them both into her tiny home office.

"I'll confess, I've helped a few local businesses out, and I'm about killing myself planning the Valley Ridge Winefest, but I've never done anything political, so I wasn't sure exactly what to do for you, or how to help you. I went online and did some surfing and discovered that many campaigns have a central theme. A lot of times, it's *the other party is wrong,* or *the other candidate is wrong, vote for me.* I don't like that kind of campaign and couldn't imagine you would, either, Sebastian."

"No, that's not what I want." He sounded a bit put out.

She couldn't blame him for taking Colton's side and being mad at her.

She was mad at herself.

So she ignored his ramrod-stiff back and his less-than-cordial demeanor, and smiled. "I didn't think that kind of campaign would suit you. Which is why I called you, and your answer was perfect. That's the theme of your campaign…*to serve.* It's what you've done your entire life—at the diner, in the military and now on town council. You've built your life around service."

"It sounds better the way you say it than simply saying I waited tables and joined the Marines."

"Any campaign, political or otherwise, is as much about how you say something as what you say. You need content, but you also need to know how to present it."

"To serve..." He mulled. Then nodded. "I like it."

Sophie spent the next half hour talking about simple, inexpensive ideas on getting his message out. She advised that he weave the two words into any public speeches, and added, "But I think the most effective way is to talk to people, one-on-one, or in casual, informal settings."

Sebastian thanked her and seemed decidedly less frosty.

"So, how are you?" Lily asked. "I mean, really, how are you?"

Thinking about the Allens coming to town today, and knowing she needed to tell Tori about the baby, Sophie wasn't sure how she really was. She went with a safe answer and said, "Okay. As okay as I can be. And right now, how I am is on my way out the door. I have a quick meeting for the winefest, and I want to be sure I'm home when Tori gets here."

Lily frowned. "You're avoiding me."

She was, but only because she wanted to tell Lily about the baby, but felt she needed to tell Tori next.

"I'll tell you what, Tori's parents are in for the weekend. Maybe we can convince Finn to keep the kids and give Mattie a night off and we can have a girls' night out?"

"Perfect. And thanks so much for helping out Sebastian."

"My pleasure. I've never done anything like that, but I think it's a solid idea."

COLTON HADN'T PLANNED on coming to the winefest meeting. Meetings were one of the biggest reasons he'd taken on a partner in the winery. Meetings were definitely Rich Keith's bailiwick.

Using the word made him think of his father. His father was known for his odd phrases and terms. He'd dropped in the other day because he was in the neighborhood. Considering that his parents owned a farm forty-five minutes away and rarely came back to Valley Ridge except to visit him, it was a bit suspect.

And then his dad had told him women are like roses. They look pretty, they smell good, but sometimes they have hidden thorns.

He'd tried to explain that Sophie didn't have any thorns. She had secrets. And he'd felt betrayed by that.

He'd thought he knew her inside and out, but he hadn't.

His father's retort had been, *Guess you need to ask yourself why she had such a hard time telling you, or anyone, about her family and daughter.* Why hadn't she told him?

"Hi, everyone," Sophie said as she hurried into the meeting room at the township building. "I appreciate you all coming out." She looked around the room, including everyone in her greeting…everyone but him. She'd done her best to make him invisible.

"This is going to be a quick meeting. I'll catch you up on where I am and what we need to do from here. For those who missed our last discussion, we can't use the school fields for our tents. No alcohol for whatever reason on school property. And that makes sense. So, I discussed with Mayor Ray and we talked to Maeve, and they both don't see any problems with our using the library parking lot. Maeve's thinking she'll put out some sort of donation kettle. Plus all our main street shops are getting involved, and we can have nonalcoholic vendors on the school's property. Now, I wanted to talk to you all about taking part of our ticket price and donating…"

She continued talking about printing and promotion.

Colton didn't make much of an effort to keep up. He was far too busy studying her. She looked tired. He wondered how she was sleeping—*if* she was sleeping.

He wondered if she was still having problems with morning sickness.

He wondered how things were going with Tori, and had she told her daughter about the baby yet? If she had, what had been Tori's reaction? And if she hadn't, when was she going to tell her?

When was her next doctor's visit?

Round and round. He asked himself questions he wasn't comfortable asking Sophie.

He didn't feel he had the right.

And yet, he was also convinced he had every right.

Damn, this was a convoluted mess. He needed to talk to Finn and Sebastian, but wouldn't until he knew that Sophie had told Mattie and Lily.

He realized the meeting was over and everyone was clearing out.

He strode to the front of the room and stood directly in front of Sophie, leaving her no choice but to acknowledge him.

"Yes?" she asked, staring through him.

He wanted to make her see him. He wanted her to look at him the way she used to. But he didn't know how to accomplish that. "Have you told the girl, or your friends?"

"The girl has a name. It's Tori. And I'm telling Tori today, Mattie and Lily after that."

He nodded. "Fine."

"I'll be seeing you." She turned away from him and began gathering up her things.

"When's your next doctor's appointment?" he asked.

"Why?" she countered without turning back around.

"I'd like to come with you, if you'll let me."

"I'll text you the day and time. But I do have to go now."

"You can't avoid me forever."

She didn't respond, but hurried out of the meeting room.

Well, she'd said he could go to the doctor's with her. That was something. Maybe the doctor would ask some of the questions Colton wanted answers to.

SOPHIE GOT HOME moments before Tori walked in.

"How was your day?" Sophie asked.

As usual, Tori bubbled over about her work at the library. "Joe Williams came in with his little sisters again. Mica and Allie asked me to read them a book. They said I tell stories much better than Joe does."

From her expression, Tori considered that a huge compliment. "So, we found an old book, *The Wild Baby Book,* and I thought Mica was gonna pee her pants laughing when the baby in the book fell into the toilet.

"I told Joe he was lucky to have his sisters, but he snorted and said I could take them home with me. I told him I was tempted."

This was the perfect opening. Talking about sisters, and taking them home. But before Sophie could get the words out, Tori continued, "Then Maeve got in and said she got two calls about me. People told her that I was doing a good job. And Mrs. Esterly came in to help for a while today and said I was a natural storyteller."

Sophie said the words she'd always wished her parents would have said. "I'm proud of you. I never doubted that you could handle this job."

Tori blushed. "I wasn't sure, but now I feel pretty good about it."

Sophie loved this past week. Tori had been so excited about work and so accepting of her. There'd been no angry outburst, no recriminations. She'd like to hold on to the secret of her pregnancy a little longer, but she knew now that secrets always came out. Even if you kept them for the best of reasons, they surfaced, and they hurt people. The last thing she ever wanted to do was hurt her daughter again.

"Listen, Tori, your mom and dad are coming soon."

"Yeah, I miss them, but I liked staying with you."

It was almost as if Tori knew exactly what to say to keep Sophie from telling her the news. "I love having you here, too. And I want you to know that you'll always have a place in my home. Your mom and dad are your parents, but I love you."

"I've been thinking about it," Tori said. "You're more like a sister. A big sister to me. I had a friend at home whose big sister is almost twenty years older than her. You're not that much older than me."

"No, I'm not. And I want you to know, I love you. I loved you from the moment I found out about you, but now that I'm getting to know you, I love you differently. I love you for you, if that makes sense."

Tori didn't look as if she were sure if it made sense or not, but she nodded.

"You were so mad when you got here." Sophie did not want that anger to come back, but feared it would.

And she couldn't blame Tori. Nothing about this situation was easy.

"I'm still mad," Tori admitted, "but I'm trying not to be. I like you. I wasn't sure I would. I thought maybe I'd hate you for throwing me away—"

Before Sophie could object again to that phrase, Tori held up her hand and said, "I know now that it wasn't like that. But still, I'm mad, but I'm happy, too. And I love my job here and I like staying with you and getting to know you, but I miss Mom and Dad. I miss my friends, too, but I'm making new friends." She shrugged. "I'm a mess."

"You're perfect." Sophie knew she was as messed up as Tori—as confused about everything.

"You keep saying that, but I know I'm not."

"You're perfect to me." This time, Tori didn't argue. Sophie wanted to leave the conversation there, but she knew she couldn't. She forced herself to continue. "I need to tell you something. You and I have both learned that hiding things and avoiding talking about difficult things doesn't work."

Tori shook her head. "No, it doesn't."

"So I'm telling you before I even tell my friends. I've only told Colton, and your mom and dad. I told them first because I wanted to ask their opinion on how to tell you."

Tori looked nervous and started thumbing the edge of the throw on the couch. "What?"

"I'm pregnant."

For a moment, Tori didn't say anything. She didn't look up or meet Sophie's eyes.

Sophie braced herself for the upcoming storm and added, "I can't think of a worse time. I've played out all the things you might feel and I understand and accept that whatever you feel—if you're mad at me, if you're mad at the baby—that's okay. It's understandable. No matter how mad you get, I still love you."

"You're keeping this one, right?" Tori asked, still without glancing up.

That question cut at Sophie. It was all she could do not to look down and see if there was some gaping hole in the vicinity of her heart.

Tori finally looked up, and Sophie forced herself to meet Tori's eyes as she nodded. "Yes." Then she added, "I would have kept you if I could have. I waited until today, knowing your parents were on their way and you'd have some time away from me to decide what you want to do."

There was no burst of anger. No swearing or re-criminations. Tori simply asked, "What do you mean?"

"Well, I thought if you were angry enough, you might not want to see me for a while. And I'll hate it, but I'll understand. I want you to know I meant what I said. I love you. I always loved you. Whatever happens from here on out can't change that fact."

"So are you and Colton getting married right away?" Tori asked.

Sophie shook her head. "No."

"Not right away, or not ever?"

"I don't think we're getting married ever." It broke her heart to say those words, but they were true.

"What a jerk." Finally, Tori showed some anger, but it was directed at Colton, not Sophie.

Sophie stared her down over her choice of words.

"Yeah, sorry. But, man, you've got the worst luck with guys, don't you? My dad left, now Colton's leaving."

Having Colton compared to Tori's father, Shawn,

was unfair. "Your father was young, and my parents had a lot of power and a lot of money to throw around. But Colton asked me to marry him, and I said no."

"Why? You love him and he loves you."

Sophie's earlier thoughts on unconditional love played again in her head. "Maybe. But the only reason he asked me was because of the baby. I deserve more than that. I deserve more than being someone's obligation."

Tori dropped the blanket's edge back onto the plaid couch and stood. "I've got to think about this."

Sophie nodded. "I know. But one more thing."

"Yeah?"

"I've given this a lot of thought. I would have given anything to keep you and raise you, but if I'd done that, you wouldn't have your mom and dad, and you wouldn't be the amazing young woman you are right now. I'm sure you'd still be amazing, but you'd be different. And since I happen to not only like your parents and love the girl they raised…" She tried to find the words. "I love who you are. You're a girl who doesn't hold back. You see something and you go for it. You find something you like and you give it your all. You're amazing and I love you."

Tori stared at her a moment, a blank expression on her face, then simply said, "I'm going to text Mom and Dad and meet them at JoAnn's, if that's okay."

"Sure." As Tori walked toward the door, Sophie couldn't help but wonder if that was it. If her daughter was walking out of her life. "No matter what you decide to do next, I'll respect it. Just remember, I love you. Nothing can ever change that."

Tori didn't say anything. She nodded and shut the door behind her.

Sophie watched her go, and wondered if that was the last she'd see of her daughter.

"YOU'RE SURE?" Finn asked Colton on Saturday.

"I'm sure I'm fine with it, but if you'll feel better, I'll talk to Sophie and make sure she's okay with it."

"Thanks." Finn hung up without saying anything else.

Colton was relieved to hear a dial tone. Finn had wanted to know if Colton and Sophie would mind being paired together in the wedding party, since Lily and Sebastian were an item. And more than being fine at being matched with Sophie, Colton was also very fine with an excuse to see her, even though he'd just seen her at the meeting.

She was planning to tell Tori about the baby, and he wanted to know how that had gone. Rather than call and allow Sophie to send him straight to voice mail, he drove to her house.

Sophie opened the door looking disheveled. Normally he forgot how tiny she was. He always told her that it was easy to overlook her lack in stature because she made up for it with her oversize spirit. She'd laughed and told him he was biased.

She wasn't laughing now. She scowled at him, but it did little to disguise the fact she'd been crying.

"Are you okay?" he asked.

"I saw you at the meeting. I was fine then, and I'm fine now."

"Liar," he said. "Are you going to invite me in?"

She paused, and for a moment he thought she'd throw open the door and let him in. Instead, she positioned her foot behind the door, as if she was worried he'd push his way through, and said, "No."

Colton sighed. "We need to talk."

"No. Everything that needed to be said has been said." She turned her head slightly, probably to disguise the fact she was wiping at her eyes, but he saw it. "We've said it all, Colton."

She was wrong, of course. There was so much more he should have said at the wedding, and even after. There were questions he should have asked.

But he didn't say or ask any of those things now. He was pretty sure she wasn't ready to answer. "It's about Mattie and Finn's wedding."

"That's all you want?" Her suspicion was apparent in her eyes.

"That's all." He crossed his heart and held up two fingers with one hand, and crossed his fingers on the other. He wanted so much more than that.

"Fine," she said grudgingly. "Come in. But the first time you deviate from the topic of Finn and Mattie, you're out of here."

He followed her into her kitchen. There were certain things about Sophie's house that said *home* to him. The fairy-tale look of it from the outside. The bold plaid couch in the living room that she liked to curl up on, under her clashing plaid quilt. And this kitchen. It wasn't so much the look of it, but the smell of it. Cookies, bread, coffee…it smelled of comfort. Those scents always made him think of Sophie.

She pulled out a chair at the table and nodded her head to indicate he should take the one on the far side, as far from her as she could put him. "Shoot," she said.

As he took the seat she'd indicated, the fact she'd been crying was even more apparent here in the window's light. He wanted to ask what was wrong. He wanted to ask about Tori, about how things were going between the two of them. He wanted to say so many things, but he was a man of few words, which normally didn't bother him, but now, when there was so much he wanted to say and didn't know how to, it did.

He settled for saying, "Finn's worried that I'd feel awkward being paired with you in their wedding party. But they'd really like to put Sebastian and Lily together since they're together and so that leaves you and me."

"That's fine." Sophie wasn't being quite as monosyllabic as she used to accuse him of being, but she was coming close.

"That's what I told Finn, but I'm not sure he was buying it."

"I'll make sure Mattie understands," she assured him.

He nodded but didn't say anything more.

"So is that it?" she prompted.

"How are you really? I saw Tori leaving when I pulled up." He didn't want to know; he needed to. He missed so many things about Sophie. He missed her smiles, her laughter. He missed her sharing bits of her day and asking him about his. Oh, he was never overly effusive, but she didn't seem to mind. She accepted statements like *I planted the corn. Got in a load of manure.* It didn't matter what he said, she accepted it, and seemed to be pleased she was sharing his day.

She stood. "Okay, that's it. You're out of here. You got your answer to your question—one that could just as easily have been texted to me, or I could have answered while you stood on the porch. So, go."

"Not to point out the obvious, but you're carrying my baby." He was getting tired of this. She was acting as if she were the injured party. As if he'd lied to her. Well, he'd always told her the truth. She'd met his family and friends. She'd seen his mother's collection of his embarrassing baby pictures and heard about all his childhood missteps.

And she'd shared none of her own past with him. Not that she had living parents. Not that she'd given birth to, then given up, a daughter.

She was not the injured party and, yet, as she stared at him, taking a deep breath as if trying to calm herself, she had the look of someone who'd been hurt. Someone who'd been hurt badly.

Once they'd talked about everything and anything. Okay, obviously not everything. But what they had discussed they'd done so with ease. Nothing about Sophie was easy anymore.

She spoke quietly but firmly. "And if you'd asked about the baby—who's fine, not that you did ask—I'd have answered, but you didn't. And I warned you to stick to the Finn and Mattie topic. You didn't listen. So go."

He stood and looked down at her. "When did you get so stubborn?"

She wasn't the least bit cowed. She took a step toward him, and said, "There's a good chance I was always this stubborn, but I simply hid it away."

"Well, I think the two of us should hope that stubbornness is not a genetically inherited trait."

"Yeah, well, I guess we should also hope that loyalty—or lack thereof—isn't genetic, either." With that parting barb she simply walked out of the room. He heard her stomping up the stairs.

Evidently, that hadn't gone well.

And what was her crack about loyalty?

He'd never been anything but loyal, and truthful, too, he might add.

But somehow she felt he'd been less than that.

CHAPTER NINE

SUNDAY MORNING, Sophie waited nervously for Tori and her parents.

She'd spent the past day replaying her last argument with Colton. She'd accused him of not being loyal, and that couldn't be further from the truth. He hadn't shown her a lack of loyalty, but rather... She groped for the right word.

She wanted him to give her a chance to explain about not telling him about Tori and her parents. She wanted him to understand how much thinking about her childhood had hurt—still hurt.

She wanted him...

She wanted him to love her. Maybe be angry. Maybe be disappointed, but to simply love her, regardless.

Her parents' love had always been conditional. *We love you if... If you're the best. If you get straight As. If you are polite. If you don't make waves.*

She got up and looked out the window, watching for the Allens' car.

Well, she wasn't going to do that to Tori, or to the baby. Her hand rested on her stomach, as if she could protect her child.

No matter what Tori decided to do today—stay the week at Sophie's or return home—Sophie would accept her decision and be supportive.

She watched as the Allens pulled into the driveway and Tori got out, backpack in hand.

Sophie let out her breath. That was a good sign. A good indication that Tori was staying.

She opened the front door before the family even walked up the stairs. "Good morning," she said.

Tori didn't respond, but walked past Sophie as if she were invisible and then straight up the stairs.

Gloria and Dom came in, and Gloria patted Sophie's shoulder as she walked into the house. "She's angry."

"I don't blame her," Sophie admitted, and led the couple into the living room. Gloria and Dom sat on the couch, and Sophie took the chair. Watching them sitting close enough to touch, despite the fact they had the whole couch, made her feel alone and isolated in the chair.

"I wasn't sure she was coming back," she admitted.

"She claims she had to come back because she has an obligation to the library," Dom said. "And while that's part of it, I don't think she's ready to leave, even if she's angry."

"I offered to spend the week at JoAnn's, if Tori wanted, and she said no," Gloria added.

Sophie wasn't sure what precisely that meant, but she took it for a good sign. "I understand that she's mad at me. I've disappointed her again."

"It will all work out," Dom promised.

Gloria reached over and took his hand. "That's my husband, the quintessential optimist. It's one of the reasons I married him."

"That and my manly good looks."

Gloria snorted.

They were trying to hide their worries in order to calm her own. She gave them a small smile.

"There, that's better," Dom said. "Just remember that Tori, despite her maturity and intelligence, is still only a teen. That, in and of itself, is more angst than anyone should have to deal with. This entire situation is confusing. She worries that if she likes you too much, or loves you, she'll somehow diminish what she feels for us."

"We've tried reassuring her that we're not threatened. Well, at least Dom's not threatened, and I'm not threatened most of the time. I worry that she's still mad I didn't tell her, and that she's going to discover that she likes you more and wishes you'd raised her."

Sophie started to protest.

Gloria held up her hand. "Those moments are few and far between. Dom's right—she can't have too many people loving her. And she's decided to stay with you, which is a good sign. It doesn't mean she won't make your life a living hell this week, but remember, you can call us anytime. And if it gets too bad, I'm only two hours away. Less if Dom's not in the car making me obey the speed limit."

"I'll call," Sophie promised, and she chatted with Tori's parents a few more minutes, then walked them to the door. "Tori, your parents are leaving."

Tori stomped down the stairs, kissed her parents goodbye and, after they'd pulled out of the driveway, said, "I'm going to go over to Joe and his little sisters' house."

It wasn't exactly asking for permission, but at least Tori had spoken to her. Sophie liked Joe and his sisters. They were regulars at the library, and she knew that Sebastian was particularly close to the family. "Okay. If you go anywhere other than their house, please text me."

"I'm staying there for dinner," Tori added.

There went any hopes of talking to Tori at dinner.

"Okay. Remember, home by eight."

"This isn't my home," Tori threw back as she walked out of the house, slamming the door behind her.

This was going to be a very long week.

SOPHIE MADE IT THROUGH the silent treatment Sunday night when Tori arrived home at precisely eight and stomped up to her bedroom.

She didn't hold out much hope of Tori's silent treatment lessening the next morning…and she wasn't disappointed.

Before Tori walked out the door, Sophie said, "I'll be out tonight. I didn't think you'd mind. I'll leave your dinner in the fridge."

"I don't need you to cook for me," Tori responded.

"Fine. But there's money in the jug on the counter if you want to buy something to eat. I'm going to the diner to meet Mattie and Lily. I want to tell them about the baby."

This gave Tori pause. "You really haven't told them yet?"

"Really. I told Colton, since he deserved to know. And I told your parents because I worried the news would be hard on you and wanted them to be ready to help you."

"But Mattie and Lily are your best friends."

"Yes. But I needed to tell my family first. Now that you all know, I'll tell them. I didn't think you'd mind having the house to yourself. But like I said, if you want dinner you can come join me and Mattie and Lily, or you can take money out of the jug and sit somewhere else there. Whatever you want."

"Sophie, I…"

Sophie didn't respond. She simply waited.

"I'm pissed, and I know it's not fair to you or the baby, but still it's there. I thought I was done being mad at you. You've been nothing but nice to me. But when you told me, all that anger I had earlier bubbled back. I want to scream, Why keep that baby and not me?"

"Tori, I—"

"Yeah, I know. You didn't want to give me up. I had a nightmare about you crying to hold me, only I wasn't a baby, I was me, and…" She shook her head. "I'm not really mad at you. I'm just mad. Dad says I've gotta own my feelings, so I'm owning it, and trying to work it out. But it's not really you."

"Well, maybe it's partly me," Sophie teased, and was rewarded by the smallest smile. "You take whatever time you need. You can be as mad at me as you need to be. You can even be mad at the baby."

"It's not the baby's fault," Tori protested.

"No, it's not."

"And I know it's not really yours, either." Tori sighed as if it would be easier to be mad at Sophie if it were indeed her fault.

So Sophie offered, "Would it help if I did something totally wrong and unfair you could be mad about? I mean, I could make you go change your outfit, but I like it and it's tasteful, so that won't work." Tori had on a cute pair of pink jeans, an orange tank top and a pale yellow cardigan. The colors sounded as if they'd clash, but they all blended perfectly. "Or I could…" Sophie let the sentence fade as she mulled over another unfair act.

"Yeah, you're truly the big evil if the best you can come up is threatening to make me change my clothes." Tori laughed. It was a bit stilted, but it was something.

"That was always my parents' concern. How I

looked. Mom made me change my outfit more than once." Sometimes her mom didn't insist that she change; she'd simply say, *You're going out looking like that?* And Sophie had known that "like that" meant her outfit didn't stand up to the Moreau-Ellis standards.

Tori looked sympathetic. "Sorry."

"I didn't say it as a sympathy ploy," Sophie said.

"I know. But still, I'm sorry. You go see Mattie and Lily. What time are you meeting them?"

"At five," Sophie said.

"Well, maybe I'll come over around five-thirty, after you've told them, and grab my dinner with you." Tori was looking at some indistinct spot on the floor.

"I'd like that."

She glanced up and said, "I'm still pissed."

"That's okay."

Tori sighed. "You know, it would be easier to be pissed if you didn't seem to accept my anger as your due."

"But it is my due. I abandoned you and now I'm having a baby that I'm keeping. I accept your anger because I understand where it's coming from."

"You did what was best for me, and you gave me to Mom and Dad. I wouldn't be the me I am now if you hadn't. And you like this me." Tori echoed Sophie's own words back to her.

"I do."

"Yeah, sometimes I do, too." Tori opened the door. "I'm going to be late if I don't leave, but even if I'm still pissed, I'm not pissed at the baby. It's my little brother or sister. Last night, I watched Joe with Allie and Mica. They adore him. They make him crazy, but he adores them, too. I couldn't help but think, I'd have a sister or brother like that. I'm pissed, but it's not a bad thing."

Sophie started to cry. "Sorry. I spent years allowing myself to own my emotions, but even if I hadn't, these pregnancy hormones would have made holding them in impossible."

Tori hugged her and said, "I gotta go," then left.

Sophie watched her daughter flee down the block toward the library.

She glanced at her watch and hurried off to her meeting with Rich Keith. She'd arranged to meet him offsite, not wanting to run into Colton.

Right now, it was all she could do to handle Tori.

COLTON PARKED ACROSS from the township building, because as far as he could tell, half of Valley Ridge was on Park Street today. The main street of town was generally busy, but this was ridiculous. He admitted that a city person would scoff at the idea of this being busy, but he didn't live in a city for a reason.

He didn't wonder if it was always this busy and he'd never noticed because he rarely came into town during the summer. He was too busy at the farm. Which was where he should be now.

He looked straight ahead as he marched past buildings and a few people. He wasn't in the mood for small talk. He wasn't in the mood for doing much of anything but sitting home and brooding, and that wasn't an option.

Especially not after Mrs. Nies let it slip that Rich and Sophie had a meeting this morning at the coffeehouse. Neither were there when he arrived, but Mattie let it slip that Sophie was going over to the diner.

He walked into the diner and wished he could silence the stupid merry bell that rang as the door opened. He scanned the crowded dining room and spotted Sophie at a back booth. He marched through the tables filled with friends and neighbors, and stopped in front of Sophie's booth. "You're here."

"Thank you, Captain Obvious." She looked apologetic as she said, "Sorry, that wasn't necessary. Yes, I'm here."

If she felt bad for being snarky, maybe she'd be easier going. "May I sit down?" He shot her what he hoped was an endearing smile.

She scowled. "No."

Obviously, feeling bad about snapping at him hadn't softened her attitude. Colton sat anyway. "You met with Rich at the coffee shop."

"The coffee shop is still part his, and it's Mattie's. I needed to see her about tonight, so it worked out well. I came here to wait for Lily and do some paperwork." She nodded at the files on the seat next to her. "Not that I owe you an explanation."

"You were talking to him about the winefest."

She nodded. "Yes."

"Well, the winery is mine. I still own controlling shares. If you want to talk about it, talk to me," he said calmly. "You're avoiding me."

"No, I'm not," she denied. "I'm not seeking you out, but not avoiding you."

They had to stop going round and round in circles, rehashing the same things. Colton switched topics. "Have you told Mattie and Lily?"

"That's what tonight's get-together's about. Thank you for waiting. You have every right to tell Sebastian and Finn."

Well, she seemed to have softened her attitude, so he tried, "About that next doctor's appointment?" When she didn't answer immediately, he lowered his voice and stage-whispered, "It's my baby, too. And I plan on being involved."

"My appointment's on Friday." She pulled a card from her pocket. "I'll meet you there."

He took the card and realized that if she'd had it in her pocket, she'd obviously been planning to give it to him. So, why make him work so hard for it? "You're acting as if you're the injured party. As if you're mad at me."

"Oh, no. I'm sure you are the injured party. Poor Colton. I mean, I suffered painful experiences, things I couldn't talk about with anyone. And I tried…you'll never know how hard I tried to tell you, but how do you explain to a man who has a wonderful family and such great memories of his childhood what it's like to not have any of that? Plus, I didn't want your pity."

"I don't pity you. I feel bad that you didn't trust me enough to share—"

"No," she said, her voice escalating with what he thought was frustration. "It wasn't that I didn't trust you enough to share, it was that I trusted you enough *not* to share. I trusted that you'd have my back no matter what. That you'd take my side no matter what. And that was obviously not the case."

He was about to protest when Tori appeared at the side of the table. "What are you doing here?"

It didn't take a genius to know she was talking to him. "Having a discussion with my fiancée."

"Ex-fiancée," Sophie corrected.

"Well, I'm hanging out with Sophie until her friends come, so you can go."

He was being dismissed by a fourteen-year-old? "Sophie and I—"

"Are done." She leaned down and whispered, "It's

not good for my sibling to have some doofus upsetting Sophie."

Not knowing what else to do, since Sophie seemed okay with letting a teen kick him out, he stood. "I will be at that appointment on Friday."

"Fine," she spit out.

"And we will talk about the rest of this again."

"No, we won't. Baby. Mattie and Finn's wedding. Even the winery. Those are all valid topics, but nothing more."

He strode out of the diner. And headed back toward his truck.

He played Sophie's words again in his head. She'd trusted him enough *not* to tell him.

"Hey," Tori said, obviously having followed him.

He turned to the tiny spitfire. She still had light blue undertones in her Sophie-colored blond hair. She stood, hands on hips, ready to take on the world. "What?" he asked.

"Leave her be. You've already made her cry enough. She doesn't need any more."

Tori, too? "She didn't tell me anything. I'm the injured party."

"Yeah? What about her? If Sophie didn't talk about her past, it must have been something awful. Something that hurt her so much she couldn't. Did you know she wanted to hold me when I was born, but her creepy parents wouldn't let her? They took me out of the room and Sophie screamed so hard the doctors gave her some shot that knocked her out and when she woke up I was gone. The first time she ever touched me was the day I came here. I was pissed at her this weekend, but that doesn't mean I left. It doesn't mean I kicked her out of my life. It meant I was pissed. I'm a kid and I can figure out that being mad doesn't mean walking away. Being hurt doesn't mean leaving. I came here before Sophie met with her friends so I could tell her I'm still angry, but we'll work it through. That's what family does... they work things out. That's what my dad says. Families, they get pissed, they get over it. You walked away."

"But..." He wanted to pull out his righteous indignation like some suit of armor, but it failed him. He needed to think. He needed to talk to his friends.

He needed to find a way back to Sophie. "I screwed up."

"Ya think?"

He had turned to leave when Tori said, "You know what my hippie dad says about mistakes?"

Colton stopped and faced the girl. He realized he wanted to know what Tori's dad said. He wanted advice on what to do. "What does he say?"

"Well, his favorite quote is from Jim Morrison, who supposedly said the worst mistakes in his life had been haircuts, but my dad normally only pulls that one out when mom tells him he's looking shaggy. When I make a mistake, he likes to quote some old English guy, James Froude. Something about experience teaching slowly and at the cost of mistakes. Basically, you screwed up, learn from it and fix it."

Tori wasn't telling him something he didn't know. He'd messed up royally and now he had to fix it. "Hey, Confucius, thanks."

"Don't think it means I like you. I don't get to quote my dad quoting Morrison every day." Tori walked back into the diner. Colton watched through the plate-glass window as she went back to Sophie's booth.

Trust.

That's what it all came down to. He thought that Sophie hadn't trusted him enough to share her past, but maybe he hadn't trusted her enough.

He should have trusted that she hadn't told him about the baby she'd lost in an effort to hide it but rather because it simply hurt too much to talk about it.

He saw Sophie laugh at something Tori said.

He wasn't part of it.

And he had no one to blame but himself.

SOPHIE WATCHED COLTON LEAVE. He stood at the plate-glass window, looking in. As if he wanted to come back and say something more.

Tori returned to the booth and sat down in the seat Colton had vacated.

"What did you say to him?" she asked.

"Well, he's still a dork, but maybe not as bad as I thought," Tori answered without really answering. "Just like when I had the chicken pox. There were only a few spots on my stomach, so they weren't as bad as they could have been, but they still itched."

Sophie laughed. "So he's still a dork, only he's not as big a dork as you thought?"

"Exactly." She glanced at the door. "Here come your friends. I'll let you tell them your news. I wanted to stop in and say I'm going to be cranky for a few more days, but I wanted you to know I'm glad I'm going to have a little brother or sister."

Hearing Tori refer to the baby as a sibling made tears well up in Sophie's eyes. She tried to hold them back, but there were too many of them. They streamed down her cheeks and her nose started to run.

"Sophie, what's wrong?" Lily asked, shooting a look at Tori that said she blamed the girl.

Lily being fierce was a sight to see. She was normally the more easygoing of Sophie's two friends, except when it came to planning the wedding. Mattie had called her a bridesmaid-zilla then.

Thinking of the wedding-that-wasn't only made her tearier. "It wasn't her," Sophie managed, trying to save Tori from more of Lily's glares.

Tori got up and said, "I'll let Sophie tell you." She walked over and gave Sophie an awkward hug. "I'm really glad."

Lily and Mattie slipped into the bench across from Sophie.

"Now tell us what's wrong," Mattie demanded. She had a look about her that said whoever had upset Sophie was going to get it.

Sophie had thought she'd lead up to her announcement with care, and sort of ease her way into it, but she found herself blurting out, "I'm pregnant."

After that, her tears were joined by Lily's, and Mattie, who wasn't a teary sort, grinned so hard it made Sophie laugh.

"So, you and Colton…" Mattie started, then stopped short as Sophie shook her head.

"Oh, it is Colton's baby, but we won't be getting back together because of it." Mattie started looking as upset as Tori had, so Sophie added, "And that's my choice. He asked me to marry him."

"Too little, too late?" Mattie half asked, half growled.

From Mattie's expression, Sophie was glad that Colton had left, or else Mattie would have torn into him. "Just be happy for me? After what happened with Tori, I want a pregnancy that's celebrated and a baby I keep…."

That's all it took. Both Lily and Mattie smiled and

congratulated her. Both volunteered to be her birthing coach, though Mattie appeared decidedly green at the thought and finally mentioned that since Lily was a nurse, maybe she should do it. Mattie would make sure that Sophie's freezer was well stocked with healthy food for after the baby was born.

As they discussed the baby, then Mattie's wedding, Sophie realized this was the first time she'd ever shared the news of a baby and had it greeted with excitement.

She listened to Lily talk about dragging Mattie out to look for a wedding dress, and Mattie grouse about Lily being a bridesmaid-zilla, and Sophie started laughing. She laughed until she was crying again.

Lily and Mattie were more than friends. They were family. Here was what she'd always wanted. A family. A real, accepting, unconditional-love sort of family.

They accepted her, and so did Tori, who was still upset but had taken the time to let her know that she'd eventually get over it.

Her life was pretty perfect.

A picture of Colton, smiling at her as she walked down the aisle, flashed through her mind, but she blotted it out. She'd learned early on that things were what they were. She'd always wanted a family like Colton's, or Mattie's, but that wasn't what she'd gotten. Her parents could never be that, and nothing would change that. She'd wanted to keep Tori, but instead, she'd given her daughter the best family she could find. And nothing could change that.

She'd thought that Colton was perfect. Turned out, he wasn't. But neither was she. They weren't destined for some happily-ever-after perfect life. But that was okay. Her hands rested on her stomach. Her life was pretty perfect.

Pretty perfect was good enough for her.

CHAPTER TEN

ON THURSDAY, Colton was supposed to be on his way to a meeting in Ripley with Rich, but at the last minute, the other winery owner canceled. That was fine with Colton. There was always some job on the farm that needed his attention. This year there were more jobs than normal because he'd lost so much time with the wedding, and now with the aftereffects.

His to-do list was a mile long.

But rather than crossing something off it, he found himself walking through his grapevines. Row after row of grapes. He could name them all. He had Concord and Niagara grapes, which the region was known for, but he also had Cabernet Sauvignon and Chambourcin. He stopped at one of the Cab vines and pulled a sucker from the base of the vine.

He'd talked to his pal Geoff about a new vine he'd put in. He was excited about—

All thoughts of grapes and new vines vanished as he caught sight of something at the top of the hill.

He'd put Adirondack chairs up there because Sophie so loved watching the sunset over the lake from the ridge. She told him she'd watched sunsets from many spots on Lake Erie, but the most perfect spot to see it was from his ridge.

He'd bought the chairs as a surprise. If he'd bought them for himself, he'd have simply put some stain on them to protect them from the elements. But they'd been a gift for Sophie, so he'd painted them. One a bright yellow, because the color had reminded him of his fiancée, and the other a more manly blue for himself. She'd of course proclaimed the colors sunshine-yellow and baby blue, which didn't sound all that manly. But because it seemed to delight her, he let the description stick without complaint.

He stood now, hidden by the vines, and watched.

Sure enough, someone was sitting in one of the chairs. In Sophie's yellow chair.

There was something in the way she sat that made him sure, even from this distance, it was Sophie. He knew that she wouldn't want to see him. Every time they saw each other lately, they fought.

But Tori's words haunted him.

He's messed up. And it wasn't a bad haircut decision. It was not trusting Sophie. It was not giving her a chance to explain.

It was up to him to fix things.

He started up the hill. The crest was a narrow band of somewhat level ground. The path that led to it wound along the edges of his vineyard.

As he grew closer, he realized she was crying.

Sophie had always worn her emotions close at hand, whether she was laughing, smiling or crying. But these weren't tears of joy. These were gut-wrenching sobs.

He quickened his pace. "Sophie?"

She turned and wiped at her eyes. He didn't have the heart to tell her that no amount of wiping could disguise the fact she'd been crying as if her heart was breaking. She clutched a piece of paper in one hand, and the other rested on an antique-looking wooden box.

"I thought you were going out with Rich?" Her question was punctuated by a small hiccup.

Well, that explained why she was here. Not to see him, but to visit one of her favorite spots in his absence.

"The meeting was called off," he said.

"Oh." She glanced over her shoulder, as if looking for an escape route. "I should go then."

"Sit," he said, and took the seat next to her. "What's wrong? Is it the baby?"

"The baby's fine. The appointment's tomorrow. I gave you the time." He nodded and she continued, "And other than feeling some weird fluttery sensations, everything's fine."

"Then what?" he asked, and steeled himself for her to tell him to bug off or mind his own business. He held his breath, hoping she'd forget she no longer owed him an explanation.

"It's Tori's birthday," she admitted, her voice little more than a whisper. "Her parents came to get her this morning. They're going to Niagara Falls for the weekend to celebrate. They invited me, but I said no. They've been so generous, sharing her with me. I'd have been a fourth wheel."

"The letter?" he asked, nodding at the paper in her hand.

"Every year, on Tori's birthday, Gloria wrote me a letter care of the adoption agency." She hiccuped again. "She never signed her name, or mentioned Tori's. She always referred to her as 'your baby girl.' When they came to pick Tori up today, Gloria handed me this. She said, 'There's no reason to break tradition.'"

"So you came here to read it?"

"I didn't think you'd be home," she said, as if that explained everything.

He didn't say anything, and when the silence started to feel uncomfortable, Sophie continued, "Gloria's letter normally got to me a day or two early, but I'd save it until it was Tori's actual birthday. That's been my personal celebration for the last fourteen years. On that one day, I'd revel in the fact I had a daughter. I'd read through all the other letters, then read through the newest one. I was so hungry for news. Gloria always sent a few pictures, too."

"Can I see?"

She hesitated. For a moment, he wasn't sure she was going to share, but finally she nodded and passed him a small stack of photographs.

The first was the pudgiest baby he'd ever seen. "Wow, she was…healthy."

Sophie laughed. "Gloria said that Tori was the hungriest baby she'd ever seen. She never slept a night through until she was more than a year old. But Gloria said she didn't mind. She wrote about those late-night feedings. How the only light was from the streetlight outside Tori's window, or sometimes a full moon. But she didn't need the light to know every curve of Tori's face. She wrote about the songs she sang. Lullabies her mother sang to her. Songs she thought might never be passed down because she couldn't have children. She closed out that first letter by thanking me for giving her someone to share her lullabies and late nights with."

The next photo showed a much thinner toddler, walking around with her hands in the air and slightly extended. "That, Gloria said, was Tori's Frankenstein walk. She always kept her hands in the air like that when she learned to walk. Most babies cruise around furniture using it for support. Not Tori. She figured out how to walk and didn't want any help, not even from a coffee table.

"I knew all these snippets about her. Facts. I knew that her first tooth wasn't a front tooth, like most babies. It was her canine, and Dom called her Snaggletooth and would growl when he saw it. Gloria said that Tori laughed every time he growled, and that she didn't have a particular first word, like most babies. She had a first growl."

She sobbed a bit and said, "I thought that's all I'd ever have. Only these tiny pieces of my daughter's life. Glimpses. The letters got a little longer every year. Gloria said she spent the whole year writing them. Adding things as they occurred. And the pictures grew more endearing. Every year on her birthday, I'd open my grandmother's memory box, where I had stored them all, and I'd reread each one. I'd look at each picture and try to memorize her. When I ran into children her age, I studied them and tried to imagine they were her.

"I never thought I'd have more than this—" she waved at the box "—but now, she's here. She's spending her summer with me, and I've discovered that all these years, all these stories and facts, couldn't paint the whole picture. They couldn't really show me what a wonderful, amazing girl she was."

She paused and added, "And now she's part of my life. Even when the summer's over, she'll be a part of it. You can't imagine how amazing that is."

"She's an amazing girl. Fierce," he added.

Sophie shot him a questioning look, and he continued, "The other day at the diner, Tori told me that you'd told her about the baby. She said I'd made you cry, and then told me how badly I'd messed things up. I wish I could undo my reaction. I wish—"

"My grandmother used to say that if wishes were horses, beggars would ride. For the last fourteen years, I've wished I could have kept Tori. From the letters, I knew she was in a good home, but still, I wished. But not anymore."

"What changed?"

"I met her. I met Gloria and Dom. I realized she wouldn't be who she was without them. And Gloria wouldn't have had anyone to share her lullabies with. How could I wish things were different?" She pointed to the box. "Read them yourself."

SOPHIE CRIED WITHOUT making a sound as Colton read through the letters. She gazed out at Lake Erie and occasionally raised her hand to brush away a tear.

Colton read snippets of the letters aloud.

"'…she doesn't like the word *no*. I thought about it and realized, neither do I. Her not liking being told no is normal.

"'…she rode her bike into a parked car last month. She bit through her lip. The E.R. doc wanted to simply butterfly it, but I insisted on a plastic surgeon. I didn't want to leave a scar on her face.'"

Sophie glanced over and saw the letter he was reading. "That scar was how I knew Tori was my daughter. In the next year's letter, Gloria said, 'The plastic surgeon did a wonderful job. The scar is already so faint that hardly anyone notices it. The doctor said someday it will be so faint, you'll only see it if you know where to look. Just to the right of the center of her lip.' When Tori showed up, I noticed the blue hair, her tiny stature and then looked for that scar. It's there, but so faint you probably never noticed."

Colton's first thought was he hadn't ever noticed Tori

had a scar, but of course, she was generally scowling at him, so that would have distracted him from noticing anything.

But his second thought was that Sophie had memorized each of the letters. He took the next one in the pile. And, sure enough, Sophie quoted it accurately.

He continued reading through each year's letter and looking at the pictures. Sophie commented on them occasionally.

"She won the school's spelling bee. She beat all those upperclassmen that were years older than her."

Sophie could tell which letter was which, even from a distance—she'd read them so many times. "Yellow. Gloria said everything Tori bought that year was yellow. Dom called her Big Bird, and rather than minding, Tori learned to imitate him. I've meant to ask her to do her Big Bird voice for me."

When he finished the letters, he put them back in the box and gently closed it.

He fingered a pile of sealed letters, wrapped in a yellow ribbon.

"Those are my letters to her. I wasn't sure I'd ever meet her, but I wanted to tell her so many things."

"Every year?" he asked.

"Every year," she confirmed. "Since I moved to Valley Ridge, this spot has become my place. All those happy memories we built here. All the picnics and sunsets. They made it easier to read through the letters. I could imagine you here with me as I read them."

"I'd have been here in person if you'd have let me. If you had told me." He didn't mean for his anger to creep into his voice as he said the words, but it obviously had, because Sophie's expression flashed from sad to angry instantly.

"We've had this discussion, and I'm done with it."

"So, you can unilaterally decree what we're allowed to talk about?"

She sighed. "Not today, Colton. We've gone round and round about who did what, who disappointed who. I kept secrets. If you want to have a fight about that fact yet again, could we have it tomorrow? I'll pencil you in. Today... I can't shoulder anything more today."

There was such weariness in her voice his anger vanished.

"If I ask, would you let me hold you? Just for a minute?" He wanted to hold her for all the years she had read those letters alone, memorizing each one. Only seeing her daughter in photographs. Only knowing her through someone else's descriptions.

"No, I don't think that would be wise. This probably wasn't, either, to be honest." She leaned over and snatched the box away from him.

"I'm really sorry," he said.

"I know. Me, too."

"Can we try again?" He wanted her to say yes. *Yes, Colton, let's put this all behind us and pick up where we left off.* But he knew her answer before she said a word. He knew what it would be because he realized there was no going backward.

"No. I could never know that you wanted me for me—warts and all. I don't think you'll ever know, either. You're a man who believes in things like honor and honesty. And that's all well and good. But I put more stock in love and acceptance. And in forgiveness. I don't think we can bridge what happened so we have to find a new relationship."

Colton realized she wasn't talking about him bridging the past and forgiving her—it was her being able to let go of the past and forgive him. She was saying that she wasn't sure she could ever see him as anything other than the man who had let her down…just like everyone else in her life had.

Well, this time, he wasn't going to let her down. He wasn't going to leave her alone to suffer through remembering how much she'd lost and all the pain she'd gone through. "Fine. I won't hold you, but I am going to sit here with you for a while."

She looked as if she were going to protest, but then thought better of it and nodded.

She sat stone-faced, in a very un-Sophie-like way as she stared resolutely at the lake.

She could have been a statue for all the emotion she was showing.

"Soph, you can cry if you want," he offered. "Your shoulder's still here." He patted his shoulder, hoping she'd remember.

"It's not my shoulder anymore," she whispered. "It's yours. Your shoulder, and nothing of yours is mine."

"My baby is yours," he pointed out.

"It's my baby. You're…the sperm donor."

He felt her barb hit its target. "Listen, you can call me any number of names and I wouldn't take offense, but not that. Not ever again. We made this baby out of love. It's a miracle. Our miracle."

She shrugged and went back to staring at the lake, as if she'd find comfort or answers there. And all Colton could do was sit next to her, trying to wrap her in his support even if she wouldn't let him wrap her in his arms.

He'd truly made a mess of things.

And frankly, he didn't know how he was ever going to straighten them out.

He watched her, holding her box of memories and struggling not to cry.

He'd done the one thing he'd sworn he'd never do. He'd hurt her.

"I won't give up on us." He wasn't sure who he was promising…Sophie or himself.

Maybe both.

SOPHIE SLEPT LATE the next day. It was almost nine when she finally woke up. Much later than normal. Truth was, she'd had a hard time falling asleep last night. Thoughts of Colton kept plaguing her.

Him offering his shoulder. Him whispering he wasn't going to give up on them.

The offers felt hollow. He was trying to be honorable and marry her because of the baby. Well, she was worth more than that.

Thankfully, she had that doctor's appointment at ten and Tori was still with her parents, so she had the morning to herself. When the alarm had gone off at seven, she had taken great delight in whacking it, then rolling over and going back to sleep.

Now she crawled out of bed and actually headed toward the coffeemaker before she remembered she couldn't have coffee. Oh, she could make decaf if she wanted, but really, if she couldn't get the caffeine, why bother? Instead, she poured herself a glass of juice and took a sip when she realized she wasn't the least big nauseous. She patted her stomach and said, "Good baby," then felt foolish talking to her stomach.

She took her juice and went to the front porch, where the paper waited for her.

That was a good thing about sleeping a bit later… the paper was always waiting. If she got up at her normal time, it was hit-or-miss whether the paper would be there.

She turned to go back inside when she heard, "Sophie, wait up."

She didn't need to look back to see who it was. "Colton, what are you doing here?"

She heard his feet thud up the steps. "I came to go to that doctor's appointment with you."

"That's not for more than an hour and it's a five-minute drive if there's traffic." The doctor's office was on Route 5, outside town.

"Yeah, I'm early." He held a brown bag aloft. "Mattie made these for you. They're called Baby Bump Specials."

Sophie groaned. "She didn't."

"She did. But don't worry. She didn't get more specific than that. They're on her special board, along with a caveat—*they're not just for pregnant moms.* Rumor has it that Hank thought they were quite the thing and ordered a couple dozen for the diner, too."

She thought about turning around and leaving him and his bag on her porch. But she couldn't quite force herself to manage it, so she took the bag. "Thanks. I'll see you at the doctor's office." She turned to go back inside, not feeling overly hopeful that her plan would work but trying anyway.

"Really?" His tone was incredulous. "You're going to kick me out onto the streets to wander around aimlessly until the appointment? It doesn't make sense to drive back out to the farm, and then back into town again." He heaved a put-upon sigh. "I guess I'll sit here on your porch then. Out in the July heat."

"My porch has got to be cooler than riding around in your field," she said, trying not to give in.

"Maybe, but the kitchen would be cooler yet."

She sighed. "Come on in then."

"Thanks. Don't mind if I do."

He followed her back to the kitchen. She could hear the muffin bag make a crinkly noise right behind her.

"I'm going to eat my muffins, read my paper in peace and quiet, then shower."

"Care for company?" He wiggled his eyebrows in a suggestive way. Once upon a time she'd have laughed at that expression, but those days were over.

She shot him a look that made him laugh. He clarified, "For the paper, not the shower, though I'm open—"

"What are you up to, Colton?" Yes, he was definitely up to something. His offer to hold her yesterday. His more suggestive offer to shower with her now.

"I don't know what you mean." Innocence practically dripped from his every pore.

"Mr. Come-Shower-With-Me, muffin-bringer, here's-my-shoulder guy. What's your game? You don't need to butter me up to see the baby or come to a doctor's appointment."

"You said yesterday we could talk," he said.

Sophie shook her head. "I changed my mind."

"But—"

"Listen, I'm pregnant and hormonal. I changed my mind. I don't want to talk about us. I don't want to talk about our past and I really don't want to talk about my past. To be honest, I don't want to talk to you at all, but if we have to talk, our topics of conversation are the baby…and the baby. You can read the paper with me if you want. You can make yourself some coffee even. I'm stuck with juice until February or so."

"Do you have a due date?"

"That's what I'll get today. They can measure the baby when they do the ultrasound and get a fair idea. But given my cycles, I think February."

He nodded, made his own coffee and settled into the paper with her.

Sophie had a déjà vu feeling. It wasn't that long ago that they'd started a lot of days in companionable silence reading the paper, either here at her house or out at his farm. The quiet turning of pages was only interrupted by an occasional comment on an article.

Today there were no comments, and the silence was anything but companionable. It was thick with things unsaid.

Sophie ate the muffins, but only because Mattie made them. Not because Colton had brought them. She drank her juice. And she occasionally flipped the newspaper page, even though she hadn't really read a word.

"I'll be down soon," she said as she went upstairs to shower and get ready for the appointment.

"I'll drive," Colton said as they got ready to leave.

She nodded silently.

The drive took minutes...minutes that felt like hours as she sat on the truck's bench seat and found herself thankful for the armrest that separated them.

They sat wordlessly in the waiting room, and when her name was called she said, "I'll have them call you back for the ultrasound." She waited for him to argue and tell her he wanted to be at the entire appointment. But he didn't. He simply nodded and took a seat in the waiting room.

Sophie felt relieved to have a few minutes to herself, even if she spent those minutes peeing in a cup, then wearing a paper gown.

"Hi, Sophie," Dr. Marshall said. "How's everything?"

"Fine. I'm a little more tired than normal, but I didn't have any morning sickness today, and that was nice."

He nodded and made small talk as he did the exam, then pulled over the ultrasound machine.

"Wait," she said. "I promised to call Colton in for this part."

"In the waiting room?" the doctor asked, but didn't wait for an answer. Flat on her back on the table, with a sheet covering her lower bits, and the paper gown covering her upper ones, Sophie felt exposed.

Then Dr. Marshall came back with Colton in tow. He had his hat in hand and looked out of place as he took the chair next to the exam table. He reached for her hand as if it were a natural gesture, but she pulled it away.

The doctor took a bottle of goo out of a holder. "A warmer," he informed them both as he squirted the goo on her stomach.

He rubbed the wand around her belly, firmly but not uncomfortably. He was quiet as he studied the screen. "When did you say your last period was?"

"I remember having one when Abbey was sick. That was the end of April. It was a very light period. Hardly worth noticing."

"I suspect it wasn't a period at all. Some women have minor spotting the first few weeks. Some throughout their entire pregnancy."

It took Sophie a moment to realize what he was saying. "So, I was pregnant in April?"

The doctor studied the screen, occasionally moving the wand or pressing a button. "If my calculations are right, yes. You would have been six weeks pregnant already."

Sophie tried to do the math but couldn't quite manage it. "Wait a minute, then when am I due?"

"Mid-December."

"A Christmas baby." Colton grinned. "That's a wonderful time of the year for a miracle."

Sophie knew he'd thrown that term out to remind her of their conversation yesterday. To remind her he wasn't only a sperm donor.

She'd known even as she'd called him a sperm donor that the words were unfair, but she wouldn't take them back then or now.

"Do you want to know the baby's sex?"

The doctor's question startled her. "Wait, you can tell already?"

"Yes." They hadn't talked about finding out the sex or not. Hell, they hadn't talked about anything.

Colton sat next to her, not saying anything with words, but she could read him as easily now as she could a few weeks ago when they were in love. When they were promising to spend the rest of their lives together.

"Yes?" she asked, just to clarify.

He nodded.

She looked at Dr. Marshall and he grinned. "It's a boy."

A boy.

She was going to have a son.

Colton squeezed her hand, and she realized that she must have unconsciously taken his. She glanced at him and knew that he didn't care about the gender, but knowing the baby was a boy made the baby—made him—seem more real. And he would be here sooner.

A son in December. Not February.

The doctor slapped Colton's back and congratulated him as they left the room. Sophie changed back into her clothes. She knew her stomach protruded a little more than it had in the past, but eighteen weeks pregnant? It didn't seem possible.

It didn't seem possible that in December she'd have a son.

She set up her next appointment with Dr. Marshall and found Colton standing by the office exit.

"So, are we going to talk now?" he asked. "December's not that far away."

"December or February, it doesn't change anything between us."

"Sophie, this baby changes everything."

She couldn't argue with that. "I guess in a way it does—he does. We'll never have the clean break I anticipated. I thought we'd get to a point where we'd smile and nod at one another, but the baby means we'll have to talk. Talk about discipline and schools. Talk about schedules and… So, we'll talk about the baby, but otherwise, nothing's changed."

Colton waited until they were in the car, then he blurted out. "What about the baby's last name?"

"What about it?" she asked.

"I want it to be McCray. I understand if you don't want my last name, but I think a son should have his father's last name. And since you won't marry me…" He let the sentence fade right there.

Sophie was thankful he stopped. She was too overwhelmed by the thoughts that the baby—her son—would arrive in December to pick up that same argument again.

And frankly, she hadn't thought that far ahead to

consider what the baby's last name should be since she wasn't married to Colton.

Colton kept asking for things she couldn't or wouldn't give him. This one request was easy to acquiesce to. "I've never been particularly proud of my real last name. The Moreau-Ellis names never brought me anything but pain. And Johnston was simply a name I made up, so that's fine."

There. That was almost civilized. If they could stick to this kind of conversation about the baby, they'd do okay.

"I want your last name to be McCray, too," Colton insisted.

Of course, Colton couldn't leave things at settling the baby's last name. She shook her head and sighed. "That's not going to happen."

"Why?" he said. "You loved me a few weeks ago. You were ready to say *I do* and tie your life to mine. I'd say we have more at stake now than we had a few weeks ago."

"Twenty days ago," she said without thinking. Tomorrow they should have been married for three weeks.

"I know you. You don't fall in and out of love. You loved me then and you haven't stopped loving me twenty days later because I made a mistake."

"No, I didn't stop loving you. A part of me will always love you, and now we'll be tied together because of the love of our son." Despite the argument, she reveled in saying those words. Our son. My son.

"So, marry me," he said.

"No." She knew what she wanted, and Colton couldn't give it to her. It had taken her a while to put a name to it, but now that she had, she wouldn't settle for less than complete, unconditional love.

"I hurt you, and I'm sorry. I was so mad that you'd lied to me. You let me think your parents were dead. You lied about your last name, and you never told me about Tori. I was so angry. I never stopped to ask myself why you lied. I walked away from you when you needed me most. I can't apologize enough for that. But I'm here now. I'm not going anywhere."

"I wouldn't expect you to. This would be easier if one of us had done something big and unforgivable. But for us, it comes down to trust. I can't trust you to be there for me if I mess up again. And you can't trust me because I lied. All that being said, I know that you'll be here for the baby. I know that." And she did. Colton would give their son the unconditional love she'd always craved. She might not have done a lot right, and she might not be destined for that fairy-tale love sort of ending she'd always longed for, but she'd done that much. She'd given her son a father who would walk through fire for him.

"I want to be here for you, too."

She wished she could simply say yes. *Yes, Colton, I'll marry you even if I know you don't love me the way I want to be loved.* But she didn't have it in her.

She got out of the truck and walked around to the driver's side. Colton's window was down, so she was glad to have the door between them as she said, "I thought I could change. For so many years I kept myself separate. I didn't want to trust anyone because so many people I'd believed in had let me down. No, not just let me down, they hurt me in a way I can never describe. When I needed them, they walked away. I never thought you'd do that, but you did. I needed you to stand by me and love me even when I didn't deserve it. But you didn't. You walked away. Well, you can't keep walking because of the baby, but I've learned my lesson."

"I won't give up on us," he said, repeating his words from yesterday.

"Then I'm sorry."

She looked at the man sitting in his truck, wearing his heart on his sleeve and his cowboy hat on his head. Once it would have been enough. But she wanted more than Colton's heart on his sleeve. She wanted him to give his heart to her fully and completely, and he couldn't.

"I've got to—" She was going to say *go in,* but at that moment, the Allens pulled into the driveway, effectively blocking Colton in her long, narrow driveway.

"Sophie, guess what?" Tori called as she bolted from the backseat of the car. "I got something for the peanut." She pulled out a cotton T-shirt and held it out. It read My Big Sister Went to Niagara Falls and All I Got Was This Dumb T-Shirt. "Look how small the lettering is. I got a nine-months because Mom said I grew out of my newborn and three-to-six-month stuff real quick. I figure my brother or sister will, too."

"Brother," Sophie said. "Colton and I came from the doctor and it's a brother."

"Really?" She turned to Gloria and Dom, who hadn't bolted and were well behind her. "It's a boy."

"Colton and I went to the doctor's," she explained to Dom and Gloria.

Tori moved between Sophie and Colton, who was still in his truck, her back to him, as if protecting Sophie from him. "Did the doctor say anything else?"

"Only that my calculations were wrong. He'll be here in December, not the beginning of February."

Colton got out of the truck and neatly stepped around Tori.

"Congratulations," Dom said.

Colton acknowledged the group and said hello to everyone.

"Jerk," Tori muttered.

Sophie didn't think her parents heard her, as she wasn't facing them, but Sophie shot her a look. Tori simply looked back with defiance in her eyes.

"Why don't we all go inside? Colton, maybe Dom will move the car and let you out?" Sophie tried.

"Oh, that's fine. I have time to stay," Colton said. "I'd like to get to know Tori's parents."

Tori did a most fantastic eye roll and walked into the house. Dom and Gloria didn't seem aware of it, and Sophie didn't rat her out.

Sophie had shut the screen door when she heard, "Hey, Sophie."

Mattie and Lily walked onto the porch. "What are you two doing here?" She realized that didn't sound very welcoming, and she smiled and added, "It's always good to see you."

"I've got an hour before my next house call," Lily said.

"Mom's watching the shop for an hour and Finn's got the kids, so we brought snacks." Mattie held out a giant box.

"We wanted to hear how the doctor's went," said Lily. "I thought about trying to find someone to call in sick so I could fill in at the office today and be there when you came in."

It looked as if the Allens were going to meet everyone today. "Come on in. The Allens and Tori got back."

"And is that Colton's truck?" Mattie asked.

"Yes," Sophie sighed. "I can't seem to get rid of him."

Her friends ignored the last part and grinned. She could almost see little hearts floating out of romantic Lily's head, like some kind of comic-book bubble.

"He's here because of the baby," she assured them in a whisper.

"This is almost a party," said Lily.

"Almost? Let's get Finn and Sebastian over, and we'll be all the way there," Mattie said.

"Lily, don't you have a house call?" Sophie tried.

"It's Mrs. Rogers. It was only a well-check. I'll see if I can stop over there tomorrow instead."

"But before she makes the call, how was the appointment?" Mattie asked.

Looking at her friends, who were obviously thrilled and excited about the baby, reminded Sophie of how lucky she was. How lucky this baby was. Her hands shifted to her stomach. "Everything's fine. As a matter of fact, the baby will be here sooner than we thought."

"Was it far enough for Neil to tell the gender?" Lily asked.

Sophie nodded. But before she could tell her friends, Tori bellowed from inside the house, "It's a boy."

She found herself enveloped in her friends' arms as they laughed, cried and congratulated her.

"Oh, you're going to have your hands full if Mickey is any indication of how boys act," Mattie told her. "Remind me to tell you what he did yesterday. But, first, let me call Finn."

Sophie watched as Lily and Mattie whipped out their cell phones and started making calls. Mattie's mom was going to close the shop for her, and Finn was bringing over the kids. Lily had called Mrs. Rogers and bumped her appointment to the morning.

They all went into the house and Sophie immediately looked for Colton. She told herself that she simply wanted to be sure he wasn't in the midst of another spat with Tori, but when she saw him talking to the Allens, she didn't immediately look away because she was satisfied all was well. Her gaze lingered on him.

He appeared a little haggard, as if he wasn't getting enough sleep or enough to eat. She remembered what it was like before she'd come along and she knew that when Colton got busy on the farm in the summer, he frequently forgot to take care of himself. Sleep and food fell to the wayside when he was busy…and summer on a farm was always busy.

"So, are you telling people?" Mattie asked.

"I don't know how much longer I could keep it a secret." December. Sophie hadn't had half a chance to really digest what that meant.

She'd have a baby in her house by Christmas.

"Probably not much," Mattie teased.

Sophie's house was too small for parties. She couldn't help but think that if things had gone as she'd planned, she'd be at the farm right now. And the farm was certainly big enough to handle any size party.

She started to pull the lawn chairs from the garage, but she got caught, and everyone told her no more lifting.

"They're only chairs," she protested, not that anyone was listening. Mattie and Lily took charge. Chairs were scattered on her back patio. Everyone, including herself, had a drink in hand. Finn arrived with the kids, and Sebastian showed up moments later.

"Sophie's going to have a baby," Tori, aka the town

crier, announced. The Langley kids went crazy. Abbey proclaimed that she was going to be the baby's babysitter and best friend. Mickey overflowed with happiness at the thought of not being the only boy in the group. And Zoe pulled Tori aside. Sophie could only imagine the big-sister horror stories she was sharing.

"Soph?" Colton had come up behind her while she was busy watching everyone else.

"Yes?"

"I know you didn't plan this free-for-all, but since our friends all know, I'd like to call my folks?" Colton half asked and half said.

"They're welcome to come join the party," she offered. Colton's parents lived a bit less than an hour away, and she hoped they'd decline because in all honesty, the last thing Sophie wanted was to see Colton's family. She'd always envied his close relationship with them. Even though they lived outside Valley Ridge now, they still saw each other frequently, and she knew they always had Colton's back.

Which meant they weren't overly fond of her right now. They'd broken up. There was no reason she should have to deal with them.

But when Colton called them and told her they were on the way, Sophie forced a smile. Her parents' game face was really getting a workout since her wedding-that-wasn't.

Let the party begin.

CHAPTER ELEVEN

As the impromptu party progressed, Colton kept his eyes on Sophie. She was playing hostess as everyone spilled from her small house onto her tidy lawn and mingled.

His sister seemed to get along well with Tori. Misty had taken the slightly younger girl under her wing and they were both entertaining the younger kids. Finn and Mattie had their bunch there, and Sebastian had brought over the Williams kids. Their father was one of Lily's patients. Joe was about Tori's age and frequently helped with his younger sister, and Sebastian and Lily seemed to have taken on all three of them. Joe Williams seemed like a nice enough kid, but Colton found himself keeping an eye on the boy. He seemed inordinately interested in Tori, and he caught her casting sideways glances at him.

"You, too?" came a voice.

He turned and saw Tori's father. Her mother was as prim and proper a woman as Colton had ever met, but Dom Allen…wasn't. He had on holey jeans that were so aged they were almost white. The only real color to them was the small paint splotches here and there. He wore a T-shirt that proclaimed Home Grown, Best Grown: Join a CSA.

"Me, too, what?" Colton asked.

"I couldn't help noticing you glaring at Joe. That

boy keeps eyeballing Tori, and she's definitely looking at him, too, though she's more circumspect. I'm trying to remember that I'm the cool parent. Gloria is the toe-the-line, rules-are-rules parent. But no matter how hard I try, I'm finding it hard to be cool when I think about Tori with boys. Even nice ones."

Colton felt as if he'd crossed some boundary he shouldn't have. "I don't want you to think I'm overstepping. I thought I'd keep an eye out."

Dom waved his hand as if brushing aside the notion. "No, it's cool. I don't think there can be too many people watching out for Tori. I grew up with parents who lived their lives by the motto It Takes a Village to Raise a Child."

"Your daughter doesn't like me much," Colton admitted.

"Tori blames herself for your wedding blowing up and Sophie being hurt by it. But she's a teen and doesn't want to own the guilt, so she's pinned it all on you. That's how kids are. She'll get over it eventually."

"She *accidentally* stepped on my foot earlier." Okay, so when had he reverted to grade-school tattling?

"Want me to say something to her?" Dom asked with a grin.

"No, we'll work it out eventually," he assured Tori's dad. "I know she'll be visiting Valley Ridge and Sophie, so she'll have to get used to me being around."

"Around the baby, or around Sophie?" Dom asked. "See, other people can overstep, as well."

Colton found himself genuinely liking Dom Allen. "Both."

Dom nodded his head. "Yeah, that's what I thought. Does Sophie know you're still interested? I mean, she told us the two of you were over."

Colton shook his head. "She's mistaken. I hurt her. I thought I was the injured party, but I can see now that she was, too. I was so mad to discover she'd kept secrets. Not things like she was young and once shop-lifted a tube of lip gloss, or got busted for underage drinking. This was big, life-altering stuff, and she kept it from me. That's all I could think about…me. I was hurt and angry. But the more I've learned, the more I know what she needed from me wasn't anger but ac-ceptance, and maybe even forgiveness. She needed me to love her. She thinks I want her back because of the baby, but it's more than that. Nothing's felt right with-out her."

"Did you tell her all that?" Dom asked.

"Some," Colton admitted. "But I'm not sure she's ready to listen." Actually he was sure she wasn't read-ing or willing to listen. "But I plan on trying to win over both your daughter and Sophie. It's going to take some work."

At that moment, his dad came over to join them. "Al McCray," he said, thrusting his hand out.

Dom shook it. "Dom Allen."

"I heard you talking about Sophie? So when are you going to marry the girl, Colton?" His dad gave him the same look he'd used when Colton was eight and had snitched a pack of gum from the store. It was a look that said, *You know better, now fix it.*

"As soon as I can convince her." If asked a few weeks back, he'd have said Sophie was the most easy-going person he'd ever met. He'd have thought she'd forgive him anything in short order.

The fact that she hadn't told him how much she'd been hurt.

His father nodded his approval. "Your mother and

I didn't ask for details about what happened because we thought that you two had plenty of time to work it out. You don't have nearly as much time now. A baby. In December. It's already mid-July."

"I know." Christmas. They'd have a baby at Christmas. And he knew that he wanted Sophie and that baby coming home to the farm with him. He wanted his son to grow up in the house that so many McCrays had called home. He wanted his son to run the backwoods like he'd done with Finn and Sebastian.

He wanted his son to grow up there.

But this was more than that. He knew that the farm would never feel like home again without Sophie in it.

His life wouldn't ever feel complete unless she was back in it.

"So, win her back," his father said.

"I'm going to try, Dad," he promised. "I've been trying."

"What are you all talking about?" Misty asked as she approached the group with Tori and Joe at her side.

"Talking about how Colton's going to win Sophie back," his dad said.

"Your brother hurt Sophie really bad," Tori said to Misty. "He's going to have to think of something really big to make her forget."

That's all his romance-reading younger sister needed. She started throwing out ideas for winning Sophie back and everyone else joined in. They went on talking as if he wasn't there.

As Colton listened, he realized that despite the fact they had the best of intentions, they were wrong. Sophie wouldn't be swayed by flowers or chocolates any more than she'd be influenced by romantic dinners or even dinner cruises.

He'd won her over the first time around with small gestures. Picnics. Building her an arbor. Reading a book she casually mentioned in order to be able to talk to her about it.

Listening to her.

Being there.

He thought he'd done a good job at the listening and being-there part, but obviously he'd only listened to what she'd said and completely ignored what she hadn't.

Even when he'd thought her family was dead, she hadn't ever shared any warm childhood memories in the way he had.

He should have paid more attention.

He could talk about books she'd read or her projects at work.

He knew she loved the color yellow, and that while she loved people, she needed moments of solitude.

She'd once said she never wanted to fall in love and marry. He'd thought she was joking and had laughed, but now he knew it had to do with her parents.

He'd thought he was a great listener, that he knew everything about her. But knowing her favorite color and that her favorite season was autumn didn't amount to anything real. That was surface stuff.

What he should have been asking about was what went on under the surface.

Evening came, and still their friends, Tori's family and his family stayed. Fireflies started blinking in the yard. The older kids helped the younger ones catch a jarful.

Misty, Tori, Joe and Zoe shrieked along with the younger set as they watched the jar of fireflies blink merrily while the adults watched the kids from the porch.

Sophie stood a bit apart from the crowd, at the edge of the yard. Colton made his way over to her. "Someday this will be Cletus."

"Cletus?" she asked.

"Cletus." He thought he remembered Sophie saying that all she'd ever been able to call Tori was Baby Girl. He wanted something more than that for her with this baby.

His impromptu baby nickname did its job. Sophie started to laugh. "When did you come up with that?"

"Just now. We'll have to talk about real names, but when we do, I thought we might want to keep our ideas to ourselves." This would be something the two of them could share, but it was more than that. "I know that when Bridget had her kids, she wouldn't tell anyone their names until they were born, not even her brother. She said she didn't want to give Finn too much time to mangle them."

"Mangle them?" Sophie asked, leaning toward him. She was standing so close now. Not touching him, but more at ease with him than she'd been since the wedding.

"Bridget made the mistake of telling Finn that she wanted to name Zoe 'Allison Jane.' He spent weeks calling her and leaving her new little ditties on her voice mail. Allison Jane, she's such a pain. Allison Jane, she's—"

Sophie laughed. "I can see why she went with Zoe."

"Harder to rhyme," Colton assured her.

She continued to watch the kids as they ran around her yard. "You're right. And I think keeping a name to ourselves is a good idea."

He liked the idea of having something that was only theirs.

After a half hour, Joe's father, Ron, came by to pick up the kids. They asked if he'd like to stay and have some now-cold pizza, but he declined.

The departure of the Williams kids seemed to be a signal. After they left, everyone else started picking up their things and saying goodbye.

Sophie was hugged by one and all.

Tori was heading over to JoAnn's B and B with her parents. "But I'll be back tomorrow night," she said.

"I'm glad," Sophie told her. "I was afraid you wouldn't."

"I told Maeve I'd help for the summer, so I'm sticking." Her parents started toward the street, but Tori came back to Colton. "You don't deserve her."

"I know."

Tori nodded, apparently satisfied with his answer, then followed her parents.

His mom, dad and Misty were the last ones. "I want to say," his father said without preamble, "that whatever happened between the two of you doesn't matter. I have a grandson on his way, and he deserves to have two parents who are married and raising him together. So, whatever happened, fix it."

Sophie made a subtle move and put herself slightly between him and his father. "There's no fixing it, Mr. McCray. But I want you all to know, Cletus will need you, like he'll need his father. I'd never do anything to keep any of you from him. He doesn't need a marriage certificate for me and Colton—he needs us both to love him and put his best interests first. And that's what we're planning."

His dad shook his head. "You're wrong. The two of you are wrong about so many things."

His mom touched his father's arm, and that was enough to silence him.

"Whatever happened or happens, you're part of our family, Sophie," she said. "We love your daughter and her parents, and we're going to try and be the best grandparents any baby's ever had."

"Ma'am, that was already a given," Sophie said.

His parents left, his dad shooting him one more fix-it look.

"Dad's not going to let go," Colton told her.

Sophie stood straight, as if standing at her maximum height would add authority to her pronouncement. "And I'm not going to change my mind, so I'm afraid your dad's banging his head against the proverbial wall." She paused a minute then said, "Well, good night."

"I thought I'd help clean up." He didn't want to leave.

"There's not much to do," Sophie said. "Everyone already put their cans and bottles in the recycling bag, so there's only a few pizza boxes to toss out."

Colton couldn't bear the thought of going to the farmhouse, because she wouldn't be there. "Then sit with me?" he asked.

"What do you want from me?"

"Sit with me for a minute. We'll watch the fireflies and talk about the baby. About names, about hopes and dreams. For just a few minutes, let's forget everything else, and simply revel in the fact we saw our baby boy. They said he looks strong and healthy. And he'll be here in December."

SOPHIE WANTED TO SAY NO. She wanted Colton to go home. She wanted to be alone with her thoughts. With her dreams for this baby.

She wanted to readjust her timetable and get used to the idea of having the baby for Christmas.

Once, she'd imagined what it would be like to be pregnant with Colton's baby. She'd imagined the joy and utter glee she'd feel as she announced her news, as they told their friends and family. Maybe they'd have done a party like the one they'd had tonight.

But there wouldn't have been a strained wall between her and Colton. They'd have held hands and exchanged looks. They'd both have been bursting with the news and with their plans and hopes for their unborn son.

Cletus. That one unexpected decree had caught her by surprise. For one moment, she'd forgotten the walls between them and had simply laughed as they talked about baby names.

But that moment was fleeting. She knew that sitting on the porch with him wouldn't be what she'd imagined it would be. But maybe she could indulge herself a little and sit with him, pretending it was.

"Fine. But only for a few minutes," she allowed.

They sat on her front porch. Her backyard was private and dark enough for fireflies and intimate talk. She definitely didn't want that kind of intimacy with Colton.

Out here on the front porch it was safer. There were streetlights and lights from neighbors' homes. The occasional car drove by. She felt as if they had chaperones.

"How did Tori take the news?" he asked.

"She's so hard to read. One moment, she's angry at the entire world, the next she's offering her parents up as the baby's surrogate grandparents."

"Did you tell your own parents?" His question was cautious, as if he wasn't sure how she'd react.

"Not yet, and it won't be in person. I haven't talked to them since I left for college. I do get the obligatory holiday cards, and every year they send me a birthday card. They sign it Samuel and Marsha Moreau-Ellis." She laughed as if it didn't bother her, but she could see Colton's expression well enough in the streetlight to know he wasn't buying it. "I will send them a very polite note informing them that I'm once again pregnant and unmarried. I'm sure they'll be as thrilled as they were the first time round."

"About that—" he started.

"No, don't start," she said. She had to be very clear about this. "We can talk about the baby, but nothing more about my parents or us."

He was silent a moment. She thought he might argue, but finally he nodded. "Fine. Have you thought about names? I mean, I love Cletus, but we're going to have to come up with something better than that."

She could see he was trying, and she appreciated it. "I love names that carry a child's history with them. Named after someone or something."

"Did you have someone's in mind?" he asked.

"My grandmother was the only family that ever felt like family. Her maiden name was Sturgis. Her family homesteaded in Pennsylvania in Crawford County. There's still a road named after them. I thought it would be a great middle name."

"And a first name?" he asked.

"I thought we could name him after your grandfather." She felt guilty, realizing she knew so much about Colton's family—even the name of his grandfather. He was right; she hadn't been fair not telling him anything about her family.

"Benjamin Sturgis?" he murmured.

"Benjamin Sturgis McCray." He looked surprised that she used his last name, and she repeated his words. "A boy should have his father's name."

She might not have Colton's last name, but she wouldn't deny her son his legacy.

"I like it," Colton said, nodding.

"I'm glad. But you have a say, as well. If you had something else in mind—"

He cut her off. "No. I couldn't have come up with anything more perfect."

"Well, that was easy to settle," she said. That's how it had always been between them. Easy. When they'd talked about where to live after the wedding, they'd both known she'd move to the farm. They had planned their entire wedding in an evening. Small, intimate, on the farm, where Colton's parents and grandparents had married.

Colton nodded. "Too bad the rest of what's between us couldn't be settled so easily."

No, she wasn't going to do this. She wasn't going to talk about them, about what happened, so she turned the conversation. "So what were you and Dom so intently talking about?"

"Well, both of us plan to keep an eye on Tori and that Joe Williams. I mean, Sebastian says he's a nice enough kid, and since Joe's mom left, he's been helping his dad with his younger sisters, but Tori's still young."

"Really, you're keeping an eye on Joe?" she asked, surprised to hear how protective Colton sounded. Tori didn't like him, and she hadn't thought he cared a bit about Tori.

"Well, Dom's back in Cleveland all week. I'll be around, so I volunteered. Plus, I have Sebastian to help me. He's taken Joe under his wing."

Sophie couldn't help but imagine Tori's reaction to her father and Colton keeping an eye on her and Joe. "Oh, yeah, Tori's going to love that."

"I'm not dumb enough to tell her." He snorted. "After that, it was all about farming. Dom's parents own a CSA in Port Clinton, Ohio. I've thought about doing something along those lines, but I've never followed through. He said he was sure we could get a tour anytime."

She heard him slip and say *we*. As if she'd be involved somehow. She thought about correcting him, but he was so excited that she kept silent and listened as he went on to describe what he and Rich were planning to do at the winery. They were importing some older grape varieties and starting a new vineyard on his back three acres.

Colton was a man of few words. Monosyllabic responses were his specialty. And if he couldn't hone a response down to one syllable, he tried for as few as possible.

But his conversation with Dom had obviously inspired him. The last time she'd heard him this excited he'd been talking about bringing Rich Keith in as a partner at the winery. He'd still have some control, but he'd leave the day-to-day work to Rich while he concentrated on the farm.

She looked at the man she had almost married. A man she'd once thought was perfect. It was sad to learn he wasn't. That he was, after all, simply a man.

He wound down and said, "Sorry, I monopolized the conversation."

"Not so much a conversation as a soliloquy." The excitement drained from his face, and she realized they were no longer in a place where they could tease each other. She hurriedly added, "No, really I loved hearing you so excited about something. And I love the idea of a CSA. I'd join."

"I was hoping that you'd research this with me, and come on board to advise me how to advertise it if I did it." There was something in his tone that said he expected her to say no.

Sophie knew she should say no. Friendly. Not friends. Not lovers. Not husband and wife.

They needed firm boundaries in place before the baby came.

But sitting here next to him, listening to him worry about Tori and then wax on about a new venture, she wanted nothing more than to reach out and take his hand and share his excitement. Before she did, she stood. "I need to get inside. And you need to head home."

"About the CSA?" he asked as he stood.

Sophie knew she should say no, but she found herself saying, "I'll give you whatever advice I can."

"If I set a visit up to Dom's parents' farm, would you come? Maybe next weekend?"

"You can take time off from the farm to drive to Port Clinton?" Colton rarely took time off for anything in the summer.

He nodded, though. "I can if you can."

A line in the sand. Just one firmly placed, friendly line. That's all she needed. But she couldn't make this new idea that had so captivated Colton that line. She nodded. "Fine."

"Do you think Tori will come with us?" he asked. "I don't think spending a day in the car with me will be high on her list of things to do."

"But she's talked about how much she loves her grandparents, so I think that might win her over."

"Let me talk to Dom and get back to you." He stood there, looking awkward. Once, he'd have swept her into his arms and hugged her good-night.

Once he wouldn't have gone home, or if he had, he'd have taken her with him.

Now, neither of them were exactly sure how to act. "Okay, you talk to Dom and get back to me."

"Call if you need anything," he said, not moving toward the stairs.

"I won't." She took a step toward the front door.

He said, "Call if Cletus needs anything."

She chuckled again. "Cletus." The name was going to stick. But before she could get too delighted and forget that line she was supposed to be implementing, she shook her head. "Cletus is fine. We're both fine. We don't need you."

Colton looked hurt by her pronouncement, but Sophie didn't take it back or apologize. She didn't need anyone.

She'd forgotten that for a while, but she remembered now and she wouldn't forget again.

NEWS TRAVELED through Valley Ridge faster than…

Sophie had tried to think of the perfect analogy, but she had never been able to. She settled on simply acknowledging news traveled fast. It felt as if Valley Ridge, New York, had utilized a Twitter feed long before that social networking tool was invented.

By the week after Sophie's impromptu party, everyone seemingly knew about the baby. She'd spent those seven days receiving congratulations from friends and merely acquaintances. Most left it at that. Some, however, nosed around for updates on her plans with Colton.

She kept saying they were both thrilled and tried to leave it at that, but for some people there was no leaving it. They kept pushing and prodding, as if her private life was somehow their business. She'd dug through her childhood training and simply asked, "Why would you need to know that?" in response to any question she found intrusive.

Usually, the nosey person let it go.

But she found more and more excuses to stay home.

She used Tori as an excuse, and that was a big part of it. Every moment she could spend with her daughter was precious and she didn't want to waste one. But a huge side benefit to her evenings at home with Tori was escaping the town gossips.

Which might be why the idea of leaving town for a day struck her as a good thing. It had nothing to do with the man in the driver's seat, she assured herself as they sped west over I-90 toward Heritage Bay, Ohio, a small town on the outskirts of Port Clinton. She'd never heard of either place, but she'd heard of Put-in-Bay, so she had a vague idea where they were headed.

Though they might be separate states, the Lake Erie regions of New York, Pennsylvania and Ohio weren't very far apart. It took a little over three hours to go from Valley Ridge to Heritage Bay.

Sophie had always loved driving this tree-lined section of the interstate. Every now and then, Lake Erie's wide expanses came into sight.

But if she'd been driving only with Colton, it would have been a long and tension-filled trip. Thank goodness for Tori, who had put aside all teenage moodiness today and simply bubbled over with excitement.

"Papa can't wait to talk to you, Colton," Tori said. "He's thought about putting in grapevines since he's so close to the lake. It's supposed to be good for the grapes?"

"Our region is one of the best in the world for grapes...." Colton jumped on his bandwagon about how the Lake Erie wine region was on par with some of France's most respected vineyards. "The market is growing so fast."

Tori chuckled. "Yeah, Papa's going to love talking to you. And Nana will want to feed you. That's what she does. Feeds people. Dad said the only thing that kept him from weighing as much as an elephant was that Papa made him work off all the food Nana fed him."

"I'm looking forward to meeting them, too. Your grandfather can pick my brain about growing grapes, and I'll pick his about setting up a CSA."

As if she'd suddenly remembered she was talking to the enemy, Tori added an ominous, "Yeah, *they'll* probably like you."

Sophie could hear the implication that *they* didn't include Tori.

Colton couldn't have missed the point, but he ignored it, and said, "Of course they will like me. They won't be able to help themselves. I'm a very likable guy."

Tori snorted. "Yeah, I—" she started.

Sophie cut her off. "Now, both of you, no fighting. It's not good for the baby."

"You're going to pull that out a lot, aren't you?" Tori asked on a sigh.

"Yep."

THE REST OF THE CAR RIDE went smoother than Colton expected. Tori shared stories of her visits to her grandparents' farm growing up. He realized they had a lot in common. He'd loved going to his grandparents' farm when he was a kid. Every child should have a grandparent's unquestioning love and the freedom a farm provided. The baby would definitely get both from his parents.

"…and Nana said the moment she saw that screened-in back porch, she knew she was home. Now, Papa, he says you couldn't prove it by him. Nana gave him her list of projects. He swears he worked decades getting the house fixed up, but Nana says it was only a year. They're funny. They fight and argue, but they never mean it. Mom calls it squabbling. Mom and Dad do it, too. They're only teasing. When I was five…"

Colton kept glancing at Sophie. She was staring out the window, taking in every word that Tori uttered. He could imagine she was storing the words and memories away like those photos and letters she allowed herself to pull out once a year.

When Tori returned home in the fall, he could picture Sophie taking out those stories of Tori's, the memories they built this summer, and going through them one by one.

The thought of her crying over those memories like she'd cried over those letters on Tori's birthday tore at him.

Everything in him wanted to be there to comfort her if she did cry. He wanted nothing more than to hold her when the memories hurt.

"I love driving on I-90," Sophie said. "There are so many trees, and if you keep an eye to the north, you get glimpses of Lake Erie. I can't imagine living somewhere without the water."

"Me, too," Tori said. "After I found you, I realized

we might have lived with Pennsylvania in between our states, but we both lived by Lake Erie. My whole life, you were there, on the lake, missing me, and I didn't even know you existed. I'm still mad at Mom about that. Sometimes I'm so mad about...everything. And other times I'm happy that Mom and Dad are my parents and I get to know you. I'm a mess."

Colton glanced over at Sophie, who had tears in her eyes, so he said to Tori, "I get that. I think all kids are a bit of a mess. I spent my teen years wanting to be nothing like my dad. He had cows. Not a ton, but a small herd of milk cows, and every morning my chore was milking with him before I went to school. The farm was what our world revolved around. I couldn't stay up late because I was up so early milking. We couldn't go on vacations like normal people, because summer was so busy on the farm and during the rest of the year there was school.

"I swore I was going to go to college, get a degree and have a job that didn't start at four-thirty every morning. I was leaving the farm and never going back." Colton remembered those feelings. He'd wanted to break away. To become his own man.

"What happened?" Tori asked.

"I went to college a business major, and ended up with a minor in business and a major in agricultural science. My mom and dad owned their farm in Fredonia, so when Grandpa was ready to retire, I bought his place." He felt rather proud that he'd steered the conversation into an area that seemed to be less fraught with teen angst.

An hour later, they were driving through vacation homes on the lake and down a long hill to a sprawling farm.

He spotted Dom and Gloria's car as they pulled down the long driveway. They came out onto the front porch with another, older couple.

"Nana, Papa," Tori called as she sprinted from the car the moment he had it in Park.

She was still hugging everyone when he got to the porch with Sophie.

"Colton and Sophie, these are my parents, Marv and Sunny Allen. Mom, Dad, this is Colton McCray, our farming friend I was telling you about, and this is our Sophie," Dom introduced.

Colton glanced at Sophie as Dom introduced her as *our Sophie,* and she was glowing at the designation. The whole Allen family had taken possession of her. He wondered if she even realized how completely she'd been adopted.

Colton had warned himself to give Sophie her space. He was spending a day with her, and he didn't want to spook her. So, he turned his attention to Dom's parents. Marv Allen didn't look like a man who'd once lived on a commune. He wore a well-worn pair of overalls and a tan work shirt. His hair was steel-gray and as short as Colton's own hair. His wife, Sunny, on the other hand, looked as if she'd never really left the commune. She wore a long, rainbow-colored skirt with a blousy top and a lot of beads. Her snow-white hair was in a thick braid down her back.

"Come in," she said. "Come inside. I'll give you a quick tour and you can have some refreshments before Marv drags you out to the fields."

"The only dragging there will be will come from Colton if we take too long inside," Sophie said with laughter. For a moment, it felt as if the problems they were having didn't exist. She teased him as she'd always teased him.

They went inside to the spartan yet homey house. The main decorative features were paintings. A huge painting of the farmhouse hung over the old fireplace. "That's Freedom's work."

Dom sighed and his mother corrected herself. "Dom."

A smaller picture hung next to the fireplace. The painting seemed out of place. It was abstract at best. "And that's our Tori's. She was only five years old when she did this portrait of me and Marv."

After some experimenting, Colton discovered that if he squinted and turned his head to the right, he could almost make out that the painting was supposed to be people.

"That's our Tori, a chip off her father's block," Marv said, hugging the girl to him. And then as if he realized what he'd said, he turned to Sophie. "I'm so sorry. I didn't mean—"

"That's all right, Marv," Sophie assured him. "I knew what you meant. And I also know how lucky Tori is."

They had fresh cinnamon rolls and coffee, then Colton headed out to the field with Marv and Dom. He listened as Marv talked about how he'd come to start his CSA. He'd had a more traditional farm at first, then Sunny had opened up a small roadside stand one fall. It was on the honor system. She put out fresh produce in the morning, and a list of prices, then people took what they wanted and left the money. "There was always a bit more there than there should have been. If people didn't have the exact change, they rounded up. I found I made good money there. Then I went to a conference and talked to a farmer who'd started a thirty-member CSA. Community-supported agriculture was the wave of the future, he assured us as he raved about it. I talked to Sunny, and that first year we had ten members. Now, we have fifty. In the summer, I give internships to kids majoring in agricultural fields, and I guest lecture on the subject across the country...."

Walking the diverse fields and listening to Marv wax poetic about community-supported agriculture, Colton felt as if he had a private class on running a CSA. Marv's enthusiasm was contagious, and Colton couldn't help but wonder how viable a venture like that would be in Valley Ridge. He knew there were a couple CSAs in Ripley. Probably more in the region. He'd never really researched doing something like that. But if he diversified his crops, and added in some of each year's wine...

He couldn't wait to talk to Sophie about it on the way home.

And he lost the thread of Marv's conversation for a moment as he realized that, as always, his first thought was to share something with Sophie. And it wasn't only that she was a great sounding board or generally had good advice—it's that he wanted to share everything with her.

That's what had hurt the most: she hadn't felt the same.

He forced himself back into the present as Marv led them through a small plot of eggplant. "The trick is getting enough of a particular crop in to satisfy your members, and not so much that you overwhelm them. I have a number of members who buy full shares, and one who buys double shares and preserves the bulk of what I send over. Most of my members buy half shares. That's enough to keep them stocked in fresh produce throughout the growing season. Sunny started sending along recipes for some of our not-so-common vegetables. We're having a bumper crop of rutabaga this year, but that's not something most people eat anymore, so she's got a bunch of recipes lined up for when they start going in the baskets...."

They got back to the farmhouse in time for lunch.

Sunny had a huge tomato salad and a grilled eggplant salad, along with egg-salad sandwiches. "Nana has chickens, Colton. Have you seen them?" Tori asked around a mouthful of sandwich.

He glanced at Sophie. He remembered all her comments about her two future hens, Thelma and Louise. She'd even found a portable chicken coop she wanted. He told her it was a farm; the chickens didn't need be cooped all day. She'd looked horrified, and said she wasn't afraid of Thelma and Louise escaping as much as them getting hit by a car, or injured by a dog or some of the more-and-more-plentiful foxes in the region.

He'd ordered the chicken coop that day from Jerry at the Farm and House Supplies. It was being made by an Amish craftsman in Crawford County and was supposed to be in by August. Because it was a special order, he hadn't been able to cancel it after the wedding, and now he didn't want to cancel it. He wanted Sophie to move to the farm and have her chickens and her flagstone patio.

He wanted to see their child grow up there.

He could almost imagine her and a toddler, spreading feed for the chickens, collecting eggs together.

"What?" she whispered, as if she could read his mind.

It wouldn't have surprised him if she could. Sophie

had always known what he meant without his having to explain. Why couldn't she see what he felt now?

"What?" she asked again.

He shrugged, not sure how to make her understand how much he missed her. How sorry he was. How much he loved her.

After lunch, Sunny and Gloria shooed them all outside while they cleaned up the dishes.

Marv and Dom wouldn't be shooed and stayed behind to help.

Tori had disappeared and left Colton and Sophie alone on the porch. She sat in one of the weathered rockers, staring out at the yard.

"A penny for your thoughts," he said as he sat next to her.

Sophie burst into tears.

"Hey, hey, what's wrong?"

"No, they're not sad tears. They're happy tears. Sunny said I was a guest and wouldn't let me help, so I sat on a stool and chatted with her, Gloria and Tori as they made lunch. I got to really watch the three of them in action, and it hit me. I did exactly what I wanted to do. I've screwed up so much, but I managed to do this one thing perfect."

"What's that?" he asked.

Sophie sniffed. "I gave my daughter the family I always wanted. Not just parents, but a family. They were talking about an annual fall family picnic here on the farm. Everyone tries to come in on the weekend before Labor Day. They invited us."

She sniffled again. "Like we were members of the family. And Tori told Sunny about the baby and said she was giving us Dom and Gloria as the baby's grandparents, and then asked Sunny if she'd like to be a great-grandmother. Sunny started talking about making Cletus some baby blankets, and then asked if I'd thought about spit clothes. I don't know if I've ever even known I should think about spit clothes, then she told me she makes them out of cotton flannel and not to worry—she'll see I have a supply."

Sophie started to cry again in earnest. Colton reached for her by instinct, and she pulled away. "You can't know. Your mom, the other day, she said she made you this plaid corduroy bear that you loved when you were little. She's making one for Cletus that's like it. She didn't scold me or treat me any differently than she always had."

"Why would she?" he asked.

"Because you did," Sophie said, tears streaming down her cheeks. "After you found out about Tori."

Before he could protest, that he'd been angry but had long since gotten over it, she said, "You grew up with a mother who made you plaid bears." She paused a moment and said, "I sent my parents that card about Cletus. I got a note back. All it said was, 'Another baby out of wedlock? Nothing's changed. Don't contact us again.'"

"I'm so sorry."

"That's not why I told you," Sophie said. "I sat in the kitchen and watched Tori with her mother and grandmother and realized I gave my daughter the family I never had. A family where someone makes spit clothes and hangs up a child's artwork with all the reverence they'd use for a Picasso. I gave her that. And we'll give Cletus that. Maybe not a conventional family, but he'll be surrounded by people who love him. You, me, our friends, your family, Tori, her family. This baby will have so much love and support."

"You never had that." He'd known that, but he wasn't sure he'd really understood how lonely that would have been until now.

"My grandmother loved me. If she'd been alive, she would have been disappointed I got pregnant in my teens, but I think she would have helped me. That's something. It's enough."

It wasn't enough, though.

Sophie deserved the kind of family Tori had. One that thought she hung the moon. One that loved her no matter what.

He'd give her that.

If she'd let him.

CHAPTER TWELVE

ON MONDAY MORNING, Sophie, Mattie and Lily pulled into Harper Akina's Wedding or Knots bridal salon before lunch. It wasn't a long drive, just a bit over an hour. And though she talked and laughed with her friends, Sophie couldn't help reflecting about how much had changed since their springtime visit to the same shop.

That time, they'd come to pick up the dresses for her wedding. It seemed like a lifetime ago rather than mere months. Sophie remembered how she'd felt as she looked at her reflection in the mirror. She'd felt so beautiful in her wedding dress. She'd stared at herself for a long while, imagining the perfect life she'd have with Colton.

Perfect? Her life definitely wasn't that. But despite the upheavals, the pain, she was…happy.

She caressed her rapidly expanding stomach. Come Christmas, she'd have her son. He'd be too young to remember his first Christmas, but she'd store away memories for both of them.

"Are you okay?" Lily asked as they climbed out of the car.

"You don't have to come in and—" Mattie started.

Sophie interrupted her. "Of course I'm coming in. Harper said she'd found the perfect dresses for us."

Mattie still looked unsure. Sophie reached out and took her friend's hand. "Listen, I love you and I am so thrilled to be standing beside you when you marry Finn. And as long as I'm telling you how happy I am, I'm going to add, I'm extremely pleased you're getting married sooner rather than later. Otherwise, we wouldn't be shopping for a dress for me, we'd be shopping for a tent."

"You look lovely," Lily said staunchly.

"Oh, come on. You're the bridesmaid-zilla. You know you're feeling relieved I'm not waddling up the aisle."

Lily shook her head and offered up her standard response. "I'm not that bad."

Sophie and Mattie chimed in unison, "Yes, you are."

As they walked into the shop, Mattie joined Sophie in laughing and assuring Lily she was, but they loved her anyway. The door hadn't even swung shut before Harper Akina was standing next to them. "I've been waiting for the three of you. Wait until you see."

Harper was one of the few people that Sophie knew who made her feel tall. Even with her mile-high heels, Harper was a tiny woman. Her sleek black hair fell down to the middle of her back, and it was easy to believe if she let it grow any longer, it might outweigh her and topple her over.

"I had everyone's size from—" She clapped a hand over her mouth, as if realizing she'd been about to mention Sophie's interrupted wedding.

"It's okay, Harper," Sophie said. "Things probably worked out for the best."

Her two friends and Harper looked at her as if they didn't believe a word of it. Well, that was fine, because Sophie wasn't sure she believed a word she'd said, either.

She loved Colton, and maybe that would be enough.

He had asked her to marry him for the baby's sake. He must still love her at least a little.

She'd given up so much in order to see that Tori got the kind of life, the kind of family, she deserved. Could she do less for this baby?

All the pain she'd gone through for Tori had worked. Watching Tori interact with her family at the farm had assured Sophie how well it *had* worked.

Maybe she should settle and marry Colton for Cletus's sake. She smiled as she thought of the name. She knew how much Colton loved this baby already. Maybe that would be enough. Maybe she could give up her dreams of marrying someone who loved her for herself. Loved her no matter what.

Maybe giving up that dream would be worth it in the end.

"...and I saw these and knew," Harper said as she led them into the back.

Three garment bags hung on hooks, and she opened two at once. "Mattie, I know you said that you and your Finn were having a quiet ceremony in your backyard. You told me it was going to be even less of a to-do than Sophie's."

Harper looked horrified. "I'm sorry, Sophie. So very sorry."

Sophie wasn't sure if Harper was apologizing for mentioning the wedding again, or for the fact there had been no wedding. "It's okay, Harper. Really. I don't know how we could be here and not mention my almost-wedding."

Harper nodded but still looked upset as she removed two pale yellow sundresses from their garment bags. Sophie knew that a lot of brides assured their bridesmaids that they could wear their dresses again, but this time it would be true. They were simple yellow-and-tan-striped cotton knee-length sundresses.

"Oh, they're perfect," Mattie said.

Harper grinned and opened the third garment bag. It was a white sundress, with slightly thicker straps over the shoulder, and a couple of small fabric flowers in the same material on the right shoulder. It was simple and feminine without being too froufrou, an utter no-no in Mattie's book, Sophie knew.

Mattie sighed and smiled. "That's perfect."

"Well, I have a confession. I didn't find them through any of my suppliers. I got them at a department store. I was shopping for myself and saw them and knew they would suit your, uh…"

"Rather relaxed style," Lily supplied.

Harper shot Lily a look of gratitude. "Yes, your relaxed style."

"And yet they're weddingish enough to suit… What's my nickname again?" Lily asked, though she knew perfectly well.

"Bridesmaid-zilla," Mattie supplied.

Lily nodded. "Yeah, that's it," she said as if it were the first time she'd heard the term. "Well, they look enough like a wedding to suit me, too."

"So tell me about your other plans while you try them on," Harper said.

"It's going to be simple. A potluck in the backyard," Mattie said from inside one of the dressing rooms.

Sophie knew that Mattie's house's backyard was actually considered big for a house in town, but she also knew how many people would want to come to Mattie and Finn's wedding. The entire community had grieved when Finn's sister had died, and had tried to support Mattie as she came home to care for the kids.

And the entire community had cheered as Finn and Mattie had fallen in love. No one was going to want to miss their wedding. Mattie's dreams of a small potluck were pipe dreams at best.

Lily's bridesmaid-zilla's expression had fallen at the word *simple*.

Sophie had the beginning of an idea. She was pretty sure Colton would agree, but she could no longer speak for him, so she pulled out her cell phone and texted him as Mattie continued telling Harper about her plans.

"...then Finn and I are packing up the kids and heading to Disney World for a honeymoon."

Sophie climbed out of her clothes and slipped on the sundress. Thankfully, the waistband rode high and rested just under her ever-growing bustline. The fabric was pleated under it and fell gracefully over her stomach.

"You're honeymooning with three kids?" Harper asked, laughing.

"Hey, but we're not taking the dog," Mattie said. "So, that's something."

"You're hopeless," Lily called out from her dressing room. "And by the way, I ordered a cake."

"I was going to buy some cupcakes at the grocery store."

Sophie listened as Lily made a strangling sound from her room. "That's what I was afraid of and that's why I ordered a cake. A real wedding cake. I even had them put a bride and groom wedding topper on it."

"Bridesmaid-zilla," Mattie called out.

Sophie was the first one to step out and look at herself in the huge mirror. Even if her stomach continued to expand at an alarming rate, she should fit into the dress.

Harper eyed her up and down. "How far?" she whispered.

"You don't have to whisper. They know. And almost five months."

"Wow, that's much further along than I thought. You're carrying well. Congratulations?" A question more than a statement.

Sophie smiled. "Thank you. I'm so excited."

Her phone pinged and she hurried back into the dressing room to read Colton's text.

Harper was admiring Mattie's and Lily's dresses. "If I do say so myself, you all look beautiful."

"Thanks to you, Harper. You truly have a magic touch."

"I love what I do. My grandmother was a matchmaker. I mean, an honest-to-goodness, people-paid-her-to-find-them-someone-to-love matchmaker back in the days before online dating. She helped countless people find their true loves. She told me once that she'd get a feeling about two people. She'd realize they were a good match, even if they didn't appear to be compatible on paper. I get that same feeling about people and their dresses. Some brides come in here with an idea in their head, and sometimes they're right on target about what they want, about what sort of dress will flatter them. But sometimes, I know what dress they belong in. I saw these and knew they were meant for the three of you."

Lily looked starry-eyed as she said, "That's a gift, Harper."

Mattie rolled her eyes and asked Harper, "You'll be at the wedding?"

"Definitely. To be honest, I loved Valley Ridge…uh,

the last time I visited. I'm happy to have an excuse to come back for a day."

"You don't need an excuse. You're always welcome," Lily assured her.

Dresses hanging in their garment bags, the three friends headed back to Valley Ridge.

Sophie sat in the backseat of the car, texting Colton and listening as Lily peppered Mattie with questions about the wedding and offered suggestions, while Mattie snorted and assured her it was all under control.

He'd said yes. Not that she was surprised. Colton was a man with a generous heart.

She stopped Lily midsentence. "I'd like to throw out an idea. An offer, really."

"See, even Sophie thinks your backyard wedding needs some help. Tell her, Soph," Lily said.

"I think your backyard wedding sounds perfectly wonderful. I have only one small concern," Sophie said.

Mattie glanced in her rearview mirror. "What's that?"

"I don't think you can fit everyone who wants to be there in your backyard. *Everyone* will want to be there. Tori has made more than one comment about how most of the town shut down for my...uh, wedding." She hardly hesitated over the word *wedding.* That was progress. "You know that many or more will want to be at yours and Finn's."

"I know. We're going to keep tight hold of the guest list. Finn keeps adding people to the list. He even wanted to invite our lawyers." She snorted. "I mean, mine was nice enough, but I didn't find it too hard to cut him off the list."

Finn and Mattie had been at odds over custody of Bridget's children, and now they were getting married. The thought lifted Sophie's spirits. Surely, if the two of them could not only work things out but fall in love, she could find some sort of amicable relationship with Colton.

"Your lawyer was the one who suggested you try to work it out with Finn," Lily said. "He should get an invite because, in a way, you could look at him as a matchmaker."

Mattie glanced at Lily and shook her head. "If anyone gets that designation it's Sophie and Colton." She looked in the rearview mirror again. "Being paired in your wedding helped bring us together. We'll cut the attorneys and Finn can simply keep his guest list down."

"Or…" Sophie drew out the word, then added, "I texted Colton to double-check before I suggested that you and Finn get married at his farm."

"Sophie, that's where you were going to be married." Lily sounded aghast, as if the idea of anyone else marrying there offended her.

"I know. We decided to get married there not only because the farm's been in Colton's family for generations, but because it's big enough to accommodate anyone who wants to attend. And we don't have to worry about food for extra people, since it's potluck and…"

"I couldn't do that to you, Soph," Mattie said.

"I would love it if you would. So would Colton. Seeing you and Finn get married…well, it's something absolutely wonderful. Please?"

"I'll have to ask Finn," Mattie said.

That's all it took for Lily to kick into high gear. "Oh, he'll say yes. So, now we have a big enough venue. What about decorations?"

"Got those totally under control," Mattie said.

Lily's expression said she wasn't quite sure she could rely on Mattie's plan. "What do you have in mind?"

"Abbey's enlisted Joe's sisters, Mica and Allie, and they're drawing wedding pictures. So far the Cinderella glass carriage is my favorite."

"Do you wish you had a horse-drawn carriage?" Lily's question was laced with even more excitement, as if she'd relish finding a horse-drawn carriage for Mattie.

"I wish this whole thing was over," Mattie said. "I wish I was at Disney with the kids and Finn. I thought about suggesting we get married there, but I figured you might have an issue."

"Not me. Half the town would be in revolt and packing to head down with you all." Lily laughed. "And finding enough matching T-shirts for a family T-shirt day would be tough if you had to find them for half the town."

"Family T-shirt day?"

"Don't you worry. I have you and Finn and the kids covered. I figured you didn't know about it any more than you know about shower stuff, or wedding stuff, so I ordered you all T-shirts that read Wallace-Langley Family Vacation. And underneath in small italics it says *and honeymoon.*"

Sophie couldn't help it; she started to cry.

"Soph?" Lily asked. Mattie pulled the car over to the side of the road and turned to look at her.

"See, it's bothering you about us getting married at the farm. The backyard will do just fine."

"No. That's not it." Sophie tried to get herself under control, but knew she wasn't doing a great job of it, as her friends patted her shoulders and looked concerned.

"Don't mind me. I can't control tears. That's so

sweet, Lily. You might be a bridesmaid-zilla, but you are simply one of the sweetest women I've ever met. The way you stepped in and helped Hank, as well as all the people in the community. Well, you're sweet. I know that's redundant, but I think the baby has eaten away at my internal thesaurus. You, too, Mattie. You might not have Lily's Miss Manners–worthy knowledge of what does and doesn't work for a wedding, but the fact you don't care about the wedding as much as the family it will create…well, you're sweet, too."

Mattie blustered a moment and finally managed, "I'm not sweet, either. I'm tough. I'm feisty. I'm adventurous. Sweet? I grew up with brothers. I'm not sweet. Lily's sweet. Hell, you're sweet."

"And so are you. You put your life on hold to come take care of Bridget, and then stayed for the kids. I hope you and Finn are happy together. I wish…"

She couldn't seem to stem the tears as she realized that what she wished for Mattie and Finn was all the things she'd thought she'd have with Colton. Love. The perfect marriage. A family.

Both her friends looked so concerned about her mini-meltdown that she sniffled back the tears. "Really, I'm fine, you guys. The baby is messing with my hormones."

"Don't blame the baby," Mattie teased. "Last I knew, you wore your emotions on your sleeve."

Lily's and Mattie's teasing eased up and then they starting planning Mattie's hurried wedding in earnest. The scenery flew by as they planned. Well, mainly Lily planned and Mattie argued. Neither needed much input from Sophie, which was just as well because she couldn't help but think about the baby. Her thoughts kept circling back to Mattie's attorney. So far everything had been amicable with Colton, but what if things changed? What if he found another woman and she objected to a casual custody arrangement? What if he decided he wanted Cletus to live with him on the farm?

The thoughts of Colton taking their baby from her created a spurt of panic. She didn't think Colton would ever do anything like that, but what if he did?

Maybe she should go talk to Mattie's attorney and see what she should do to safeguard her rights. To nail down a custody arrangement on paper.

By the time Mattie pulled the car up to Sophie's house, Lily and Mattie had come to an understanding on the wedding, and Sophie was halfway to a full-blown panic attack. She was thankful that she'd been in the backseat. It made it harder for her friends to see that she was upset. She tried to school her expression as she got out of the car. "That was fun."

"Are you sure about Colton's?"

"I'm sure. Colton's sure. Talk to Finn and let us know, but truly, Mattie, I'd love to see you married there."

Mattie didn't look completely convinced, but she nodded.

Sophie waved as her friends pulled away, then she went inside, garment bag in hand, and found Tori waiting in the living room. One look at her expression was enough to let Sophie know something was wrong.

She hung the garment bag on the door's frame and sat down on the couch next to Tori. "What's the matter?"

Tori didn't say anything but seemed to vibrate with pent-up anger.

"I thought you were hanging out with Joe today?" Sophie prompted.

Tori's anger-laced words tumbled out, one after another. "Joe's mom showed up in town after she walked out on him and his sisters. His dad says he's gotta see her and spend time with her, but he doesn't want to, and I don't blame him. I don't think it's fair. Grown-ups are always trying to tell us what to do. Like when I found out about you, and Mom said I had to wait until I was eighteen to find you."

"Come here." Sophie patted the cushion next to her and Tori scootched over to it.

"I get it," Sophie said. "More than you'll ever know, I get it. I wasn't allowed to make any decisions, or do anything I wanted when I was growing up. Everything I did reflected on the family, so my parents made everything I did a family discussion. No, not discussion, because that would mean I got a say. They ultimately made all the decisions. And they weren't based on what was best for me, but what was best for them—for their image. They made me give you up because an unmarried, pregnant daughter would have been an embarrassment. And I resented them for making that decision. I still maintain that the reasons behind their decision were wrong, and how they handled it was bad, but I realize that you were meant to be your mom and dad's daughter. You three are a family. And your grandparents."

"Yeah, but that's not what I'm talking about. Joe's mom left him. No one forced her. And he shouldn't have to see her if he doesn't want to."

Sophie searched for an answer that might help the situation make sense. The best she could come up with was "Maybe there are things between his mom and dad he doesn't know."

"Then they should tell him."

"Honey, maybe they should. Or maybe it's something they need to keep to themselves because it would hurt him more to know than not to know." Sophie reached out and brushed her daughter's cheek with her fingertips. "Parents are flawed. They screw up. But just because someone messes up doesn't mean you get to write them off. Joe's mad at his mom. Maybe seeing her won't change how he feels about her leaving, but maybe someday down the road, something will have come from this meeting that made a difference in his life."

"You're trying to make me not mad at my parents for trying to keep me away from you, for lying to me."

Sophie was going to ask, *You're still mad?* but realized that the question wasn't necessary. The anger that Sophie had seen the first day she'd met her daughter was back and burning just as bright. She wanted to reach out and hug Tori. She wanted to make everything all right for her daughter, but she realized she couldn't do that.

"No, I'm not trying to make you not mad. I'm simply sharing what I realized, and then I'll point out that your parents love you. Nothing they did was ever malicious. Everything they did was what they thought was best for you. Maybe it wasn't, but that was their goal. I wish my parents had asked themselves even once what was best for me. That was never their driving concern. They worried about what was best for them."

"I think I'm over being mad at them, or even you, but then it comes back again." Tori raked a hand through her hair.

"There are moments, like when I watched you at the farm, that I tell myself I need to get over being mad at my parents for forcing me to give you up. Everything turned out like it should have. But then…" She shrugged. "We can't help how we feel, but we don't have to act on it. We don't have to be ruled by it."

For a moment, Tori tried to maintain her angry expression, then gave up and burst into teenage giggles. "Really, honest and truly, do you ever get truly pissed off? You're always so nice."

"Is that an insult or a compliment?" Sophie asked. "Sometimes it's hard to tell with you."

"Both." Tori tried to sound grumpy but didn't quite pull it off.

Sophie laughed as well as she watched the anger ebb in her daughter. And she reached out and hugged her. For a moment, Tori sat unmoving, but then she hugged Sophie back.

Sophie tried to memorize every little detail of her daughter. Her blond hair that had lost all trace of the blue dye except from the very ends. The feel of her daughter's body pressed against hers, their arms wrapped around each other.

"I love you," she whispered.

"I love you, too," Tori admitted.

They sat back and Sophie asked, "Feel better?"

"Yeah. But I'm still worried about Joe."

"He seems like a great kid. Sebastian and Lily adore him and the girls. Sebastian told me he took odd jobs in order to send his sisters to camp?"

"Yeah. That's where they are now, and he says he's glad because he doesn't want his mom messing with their heads. Allie cried for weeks after their mom left. Joe said both girls had nightmares. He got up with them a lot when his dad was so sick."

"He really sounds like an amazing kid. I can tell you that when you're going through something difficult, having friends around can make all the difference in the world. I was out with Lily and Mattie today, and I realized that fact all over again. We talked about the wedding. Mattie kept trying to keep it simple and Lily kept insisting that there are certain wedding traditions that cannot be ignored."

She thought about Mattie walking toward Finn, who'd be waiting under the arbor, and she felt a pang of…not really jealousy but a wistfulness. She wished things had worked out with Colton. She glanced at her daughter and couldn't regret that Tori had shown up that day, even if it meant her marriage plans had fallen apart.

"You said Lily was like that at your shower and wedding?" Tori said. "Sorry. I didn't mean—"

"No, it's fine. And Mattie called Lily a bridesmaid-zilla. She had all kinds of rules. Like, did you know that shower decorations need to be pastel?" Sophie laughed at that memory.

Tori giggled. "Really?"

"In bridesmaid-zilla Lily's world they do. You should have heard her and Mattie go around and around about how things were done. Mattie would get married in jeans if she thought she could, but both Lily and little Abbey would be aghast. She compromised on a pretty sundress."

"Do you think Lily is going to want to throw you a baby shower?"

It hadn't occurred to Sophie, but as Tori said the words, Sophie knew that Lily probably would. "It's highly likely. The only reason Mattie's not getting a wedding shower is she refused. She says she and Finn have a toaster that works and plenty of dishes, so if Lily threw a shower, she wouldn't go. Lily sighed over that for weeks. I don't know if I can come up with some excuse to get out of a shower for Cletus."

"And if you did, you'd probably break poor Lily's heart," Tori pointed out.

"Probably."

"If I asked, do you think Mattie and Lily would let me help? I mean, I know I'll only be this baby's half sister."

From angry back to sweet. Sophie put her hand over her stomach and wondered if teenage boys had such mercurial temperaments. "There's no half about you, Victoria Peace Allen. You are Cletus's sister. And I know Mattie and Lily would love the help."

"Okay," Tori said. "I'll ask them. And since I'm now free tonight, do we have any plans?"

"Let's go over to the diner for dinner. Rumor has it Sebastian has a new frittata that's to die for."

"A frittata at a diner?" Tori did not seem positive that was a good thing.

"Only in Valley Ridge. Afterward, let's stop at the Quarters and see what movies Marilee and Viv have on the shelves. I'm thinking this might be a perfect chick-flick night."

"And popcorn. Not the bag stuff, but the stuff you make." Tori had developed a taste for stove-popped popcorn.

"Definitely," Sophie agreed.

Later that night, Sophie sat thigh to thigh with Tori on the couch, popcorn between them, watching *The Big Year*. It wasn't quite the movie she'd thought it would be, but she was absolutely in love with the quiet film about birding. Tori wanted to put up some bird feeders and started making plans.

"We could start a notebook and log the birds that visit, like in the movie," she said.

Sophie agreed and promised to take her to the Farm and House Supplies store and buy feeders and bird feed.

Sophie reflected that she'd thought this would be a big year for her because she was marrying the perfect man. It didn't turn out that way, but it was still a big year. She'd found a daughter and was going to have a son. She had friends, and she had a community that had become a big extended family.

It was all pretty big.

COLTON WASN'T SURE why he was on Sophie's porch at nine o'clock at night, but he was sure that if he didn't see Sophie, he'd be spending another sleepless night.

Traditionally farmers were early-to-bed, early-to-rise sorts.

That's what he'd been until the end of June.

He loved getting up at the crack of dawn. There was something about walking through his fields or his growing, expanding vineyards as the sun peeked up over the horizon, all pink and orange.

He remembered the first time Sophie had spent the night. He'd gotten up before dawn and there had been enough moonlight filtering through his window for him to watch her sleep. Her eyes had been darting back and forth under their lids, and the faintest smile had played on her lips. He'd wondered what she was dreaming. He'd wondered if there was any way she was as happy as he was.

When she'd woken up and smiled at him, he'd known she was happy, too.

They'd walked his vineyard that morning. He could have talked about his visions for growing the winery or about the farm. She could have talked about her expanding PR business or any number of other things.

But that first morning, they'd walked through the vineyard in silence. They'd climbed up to the top of the ridge, where they'd sat next to each other and watched the sun turn his vineyard and fields flame-colored.

And at some point he'd realized they were holding hands. He hadn't even noticed it until that moment because it had felt as if her hand had always been there in his.

As if it belonged in his.

And then he'd realized that everything about Sophie felt as if she was part of him. A part of him he'd never realized he was missing until he'd met her. Oh, it sounded lame to even think it, but now that she'd left him, he realized with even more clarity that she was part of him. Without her he didn't feel whole. Yeah, it might sound lame, but it was the truth. He'd read articles about amputees having phantom pains and feelings in their missing limbs.

That's what it felt like to him. As if some vital part of him had gone. He could still feel her. When he crawled into his bed at night, he swore he could smell her perfume.

He'd doze off and reach for her…and touch nothing but a pillow.

After that, he'd be awake.

Everything came back to Sophie.

Which was why he was here.

He thought that maybe, if he could see her right before bed, he might be able to sleep for more than an hour.

He knocked.

She opened the door wearing her beat-up Mercy-hurst sweats and a tank top. Typical Sophie sleepwear.

"Colton?" she asked fuzzily. She'd been dozing, probably. She had that soft sort of look he recognized.

"Mom sent these over for Cletus and I thought I'd drop them off." He handed her the bag.

She took it and still looked puzzled. "Isn't this about your bedtime? Past it, actually. Generally by now you'd be on your way up to bed saying, 'Early to bed, early to rise, Sophie.'"

"Things change," he muttered. He felt foolish. He shouldn't have come. "I should go. You're ready for bed."

"I finished a movie with Tori. She's on the phone to Sebastian's Joe now." She opened the door wider. "As long as you're here, come on in."

He didn't need to be invited twice. He followed Sophie into the living room, and as he sat on her couch, a wave of exhaustion swept over him.

"So, why haven't you been sleeping?" she asked.

He shrugged. He wanted to tell her he missed her next to him. He wanted to explain that she was his phantom limb, that he could feel her and smell her, and every time he woke up, the realization she wasn't actually there hurt so much.

"Let me get you something my grandmother always made me if I was at her house and had a nightmare." She stood and started toward the kitchen.

"You liked her?" he asked, stopping her in her tracks. "Your grandmother?"

"She loved me no matter what. So, yes. I liked her. I loved her. They put her in a home, you know. She'd gotten frail and fallen. We had this huge house with six bedrooms. My parents could have brought her home.

They could have afforded nursing help. My grand-mother could have afforded that herself. But my parents felt it would be too much of a bother. So, they put her in a home and then forgot about her. I visited almost every day. They didn't visit once the last year she was alive. The last few weeks, she didn't talk anymore. She mainly slept. And one night, she simply didn't wake up. When we went to the funeral, my parents, they cried such crocodile tears, telling all their friends how much they'd miss her. It made me sick. Literally."

She fled the room as she finished the sentence.

Colton realized that was the most intimate look at her childhood she'd ever given him.

Maybe she did trust him after all. It wasn't much, but he could build on that.

He leaned his head back and the couch smelled like Sophie's house. There was a hint of floral, and there was a spicy scent—cinnamon, maybe. As if she'd just made cookies.

He leaned farther back and realized exactly what the couch smelled like.

Home.

SOPHIE RETURNED WITH a cup of warm cinnamon milk and saw that Colton had passed out on her couch.

Tori came up behind her. "What's he doing here?"

"He brought me some books his mom sent over for the baby."

"Are you going to wake him and kick him out?" Anger was once again festering in Tori's words.

"He's exhausted. This is more than his normal summertime's-too-busy-for-sleep sort of exhaustion. I could pack for a week's vacation in the bags under his eyes so, no, I don't think I will wake him. He knows his way out if he wakes up."

She'd thought she'd talk to him about custody, about having something official on paper, but that conversation would have to wait. She gazed at him and almost ached with how exhausted he looked.

"You still love him," Tori stated. Not accused.

Sophie wasn't sure how to explain her mixed-up feelings to Tori when she barely understood them herself. "I do still love him. I don't know how someone turns off that kind of love."

Obviously that wasn't enough of an answer, because Tori asked, "He asked you to marry him again, so why not say yes if you love him?"

"Because…" Sophie couldn't think of anything else to add. Because he was simply another person she'd thought would love her without reservation and who didn't. It sounded stupid. It sounded childish. But there it was. Despite everything, all the promises she'd made herself after Tori's father left her, she'd opened herself up and trusted him.

And once again, she'd been let down.

"Loving someone doesn't always mean you can be with them."

"That's dumb." When Sophie didn't respond, Tori sighed. "Adults are complicated."

"You can say that again," Sophie agreed. "Come on, let's go to bed and let Colton get some sleep. Go on up and I'll check that everything's locked tight down here."

Tori went up the stairs and Sophie checked the doors were locked, then got the throw off her rocker and spread it over Colton. She watched him for long minutes. He had darkly smudged bags under his eyes. There were lines on his forehead she didn't recall seeing before. She wanted to reach out and smooth them, but she didn't.

Heck, she longed to get onto the couch next to him. She knew from experience that he'd reach for her. He'd draw her into his arms and tuck her up under his chin. So many nights they'd slept like that, her wrapped in Colton. She'd thought she'd spend the rest of her life sleeping like that.

She pulled herself away from that fantasy and continued studying him. His hair was longer than it generally was in the summer, as if even the act of taking a razor to it was too much for him.

She was right when she'd told Tori she still loved him. She did. But she didn't trust him to stand by her no matter what. She realized she couldn't trust that he'd be fair about the baby, either. She thought he would. She hoped he would. She wanted to believe that they could keep things friendly and share. But she was going to have to get something in writing. She didn't need financial support, but she did want to spell out visitation. She needed to have some paper in hand that guaranteed he couldn't come take this baby from her.

Sophie didn't think she'd survive having another child ripped away from her.

She wished he'd loved her enough to stand by her, even though she knew she'd been at fault. After her parents, she'd sworn she'd rather go through life alone than to feel as if she had to be perfect in order to gain someone's love. "I can't be perfect. I only wanted you to love me warts and all."

She turned off the light and headed upstairs. Tori's door was open so she popped her head in. Tori had taken her permission to make the room her own to heart. She had put up on the wall a couple of posters of bands Sophie didn't recognize. She had placed books on the shelf and the nightstand, and there was a pile next to her bed. Sophie had told Tori she could decorate the room however she wanted, and other than the posters, Tori's biggest decorating feature seemed to be books. She smiled at her daughter. "I wanted to say good-night."

She started to shut the door, but Tori said, "Sophie?"

She turned around. "Yes?"

"You were talking about me. Loving someone, but not being able to be with them. Right?"

"Yes, in part."

"I get why you let Mom and Dad adopt me. But I don't get why you can't be with Colton."

"I'm not what he really wants. He wanted who he thought I was. For a long time, I pretended my past away. I thought if I didn't talk about my parents, about how much they hurt me, and if I didn't talk about you and how much I missed you, that I could somehow pretend to be who he wanted me to be. To be honest, I liked seeing myself through Colton's eyes. He saw someone who was better than I could ever be. But he was wrong. I'm flawed. Damaged maybe. I can't go back to pretending, and that pretender is who Colton fell in love with. The woman who tried to be perfect. Well, I'm not perfect. And I won't go back to trying, or pretending to be."

Tori wrapped her legs around her arms. "I guess I get that. I'm not perfect, either. Overall, I'm a mediocre student."

"Yeah, well, I can't balance my checkbook, even though I took accounting basics in school," Sophie confessed. "I mean, never. I've never once balanced the thing to the penny. I always show too much or too little and I simply use whatever amount I come up with and trust that I'm close enough."

Tori offered, "I hate gym class. I couldn't hit a softball to save my life. My jock friend Laurel was team captain once, and she still picked me last. I didn't blame her because I'd have picked me last, too."

Sophie realized that, in her whole life, she'd never told someone she loved about her flaws. She offered up another. "I painted the whole house, but I'm a horrible edger. Look at the ceilings sometime—they're practically waves."

"I can't cook," Tori said. "Not like my grandmother. She'd tried to teach me, but I'm a mess."

"I can't shave my legs without missing a section. And I don't notice the section until I'm somewhere in public," Sophie said.

Tori laughed. "I bite my fingernails."

"I hate pedicures. Really, I don't like touching my own feet. Why would I pay someone else to do it?" Sophie slept in socks in order to avoid her feet touching anything. Colton had bought her a box of wild socks last year for Christmas. He'd collected them all year. There were chick socks for Easter, pumpkin socks, striped socks...."

They both burst into laughter. "We're hopeless," Tori said.

Sophie sat next to her daughter. "We're perfectly imperfect. I wouldn't change one thing about you."

"Nothing?" Tori asked, as if she didn't quite believe that.

"Not one single blue hair...or whatever color you dye it. You are everything I ever hoped you'd be. I'm so lucky to have you back in my life." She threw her arms around her daughter and hugged her. She held on, holding Tori and crying. "Fabulously, perfectly imperfect."

Tori hugged her back. "I love you. Sometimes I'm still so mad, but even when I am, I love you. Mom and Dad know it, and don't mind. Mom said she loves you, too."

"Sometimes I'm so mad, too, and ditto. I love your parents." She reluctantly let go. "Now, you have to be at the library in the morning, so we'd both better get some sleep."

"Did I tell you that I started a donation jar at work?"

The comment seemed to come from left field, but Sophie went along with it. "No, you didn't."

"I put it out on the counter, and wrote a little card that said, 'Your change could change someone's life... help us buy a book.'"

"That's a lovely idea."

"Yeah, but sometimes, maybe we need to change our own life. Maybe you need to figure out what you want and go after it."

Sophie knew that Tori was talking about Colton, and she did want something from him, but not what Tori thought.

"Thanks. That's good advice."

She left her daughter's room determined to see to it no one ever took Cletus from her. Not even Colton.

CHAPTER THIRTEEN

COLTON WOKE UP with a start. He drew in a deep breath. Rather than the fresh farm air, he smelled…cinnamon.

Sophie.

He'd spent the night at Sophie's. On her couch.

He realized that she'd covered him with an afghan. He pulled it up and sniffed. Home. Sophie.

He felt more refreshed than he'd felt since their almost-wedding.

He sat up and glanced at the clock on her shelf.

A quarter after nine?

That couldn't be right.

He got up and headed into the kitchen. Tori was at the counter. She spotted him and scowled. "I've got to get to get to the library early, Soph." She turned and went out the back door without saying a word to him.

Sophie had her back to him so he cleared his throat.

She whirled around and said, "Good morning. I trust you slept well."

"Yeah. I'm sorry about that. I didn't mean to come and crash on your couch."

"No problem." She nodded at a chair, and he sat down. She brought him a coffee and sat next to him. "I wanted to talk to you about something."

"That sounds ominous."

She looked nervous. She fumbled with her cup, twirling it around and around as she said, "Well, first, let's start with me saying thank-you for saying yes to Mattie and Finn getting married at the farm."

"I should have thought of it myself." Sophie didn't say anything else so he prompted, "And?"

"Listen, I said I wanted things with us to be friendly and I do. But yesterday, when Mattie was talking about keeping the guest list down because their yard was so small and I thought of the farm, well, she also mentioned that Finn had wanted to invite their attorneys from when he'd planned to sue her for custody, and it got me to thinking about the issue of custody and visitation. The more I thought about it, the more I realized that it all should be put down in writing."

Sophie studied him a moment, then hurried on. "So I thought I'd go see Mattie's attorney about drawing up documents for us. Or we could go." Her words came out in a breathless rush.

Colton let his coffee mug thump onto the table and weighed his words. He could tell she was nervous about her proposal. He thought about Tori, who'd stormed out of the room. He thought about what she had said that day about Sophie screaming for a chance to at least hold her baby.

"You need to respond with real words. Preferably English ones," Sophie prompted. "I know you're probably mad. And you're going to say I should trust you. But I can't afford to do that. I would never keep you from the baby, but I need to know that you won't ever try to take him from me."

Need. He was pretty sure that was the accurate word. Not want. *Need.* And he could understand that need. He could understand her needing to be sure the baby would never be taken from her.

"I don't want any child support. We've already covered that I've got plenty of money. But I'm not saying that to make you feel insulted," she quickly added. "I am worried about the custody arrangements, not so much the money. I… I'm making a muck of this, aren't I?"

He reached over and put his hand on hers. "Sophie, it's okay. I get it."

"You do?" she asked. She sounded surprised.

He nodded. "You go ahead and make the appointment. See what Mattie's lawyer says. I'll sign anything that's reasonable."

"You're not mad? You haven't said much of anything, though that's not unusual."

"One of the beautiful things about our relationship is you find the words for me when I can't find them on my own. You laid it all out and I understand. Just make the appointment." He rose. "Thanks for letting me crash last night."

"Are you sure you're all right?"

He didn't answer that one, not because he couldn't find the words, but because he didn't want her to feel guilty when he said no. *Hell, no.* He wasn't all right. He was going to sign over custody of the baby. He wasn't marrying Sophie. And last night was the first night he'd slept through in weeks.

But mainly he wasn't all right because he realized he'd let down the woman he loved more than life itself. When she'd needed him most, he'd walked away.

No, he wasn't all right by any stretch of the imagination.

"Have the lawyer put down whatever you need to feel comfortable and I'll sign it."

"But you'll have some things you want."

"There's a lot I want, Sophie. But none of it is going

to come from a paper that a lawyer draws up." He turned and headed back to the farm.

Once he'd have called it home, but he realized that the farm wasn't his home anymore. Home was wherever Sophie and their baby were.

SOPHIE PONDERED Colton's quiet acquiescence over the next week as she was thrown into a whirlwind of wedding preparations. She worked at juggling that with her winefest duties and spending time with Tori.

She'd dug out a folder containing some of her old school stuff. They'd spent an evening roaring at her yearbooks, and looking at her childhood artwork. She'd pulled out her report cards and pointed to her less-than-straight-A grades. "Look at that—D in gym."

"How did you get a D?" Tori had asked.

"I absolutely refused to climb the rope in gym class and the teacher failed me that day."

"You refused?"

"I got my first period that day, and wasn't confident that nothing would show."

They bonded over periods, grades and embarrassing school moments.

The one thing Sophie did not do that week was call Colton. She did text him about her appointment with the attorney on Friday, but he'd simply texted back, Do whatever you need to do.

Which was why on Wednesday she walked into the Ripley office of Mattie's attorney, H. T. Aston. Mattie had said his first words to her were *Call me Tim,* which must be his standard greeting because it was the one he used with her. She told him what she needed. A custody agreement saying that the baby would live with her and when he or she was old enough, the child would spend weekends and whatever other days they agreed on at the farm, as well as every other holiday.

"I want to be fair, but I also want to protect my rights."

He had papers drawn up that morning. She'd stopped at his office at lunch. Ripley was another small town like Valley Ridge, North East and a dozen others in the region. Fairview, Girard, Greene Township, Harborcreek…

None of them felt like home the way Valley Ridge did.

As she walked to Mattie's house with Tori, the custody agreement tucked into her purse, Sophie wondered what made Valley Ridge so special. Tori talked about her day. She'd just finished reading Tolkien's *Lord of the Rings* for the first time. "…and once I got past the way he wrote it, I loved it." She spotted JoAnn on the porch at the bed-and-breakfast. "Hi, JoAnn." She ran to the porch and talked earnestly to the older woman for a moment.

Sophie watched as JoAnn laughed, and Tori ran back.

"I told her that the book she wanted is at the library."

"What book?"

"Another Jan Karon book. I told her that I think she's got a crush on the hero, Father Tim. Anyway, I'm going to check it out for her tomorrow and drop it off after work. She's got a whole family checking in. I'd have brought it with me today if I'd known."

Tori went back to chatting merrily, and Sophie knew that her daughter had fallen for Valley Ridge, too. It had become her second home, and the people had become her second family.

Sophie thought about her own almost-wedding. The

night before the big day they'd had a stag and drag, a local variation of a bachelor/bachelorette party. Hank had gotten lost and—

"Sophie, you're awfully quiet." Tori wore a worried expression.

"Sorry. Just lost in thought." She pointed to an old stone house. "You know, when I moved here, I walked the streets—"

"Oh, you walked the streets?" Tori's tone said she was teasing.

"Not like that," Sophie said with a laugh. "But I walked all the streets. I fell in love with my house, but the rest of them are so picturesque. I thought mine looked like—"

"A gingerbread house. At least that's what I thought that first day. Then I changed my mind and decided it looked more like Mary, Mary, Quite Contrary's house. It made me mad that you lived some fairy-tale life despite giving me away. That's why I kicked the door," she admitted apologetically.

"No, you, angry?" Sophie teased, and then marveled that she had a relationship with Tori that allowed her to tease her like that and be met with a grin. "And the smudge cleaned right off, and those are good enough descriptions for my house. How about JoAnn's house?"

Tori considered it a moment and said, "The Snow Queen would live in that one."

They played pick a fairy tale or nursery rhyme for the houses on the rest of the walk to Mattie's. When they got to her friend's, they saw Mickey and Abbey tearing across the front lawn, chasing after the huge dog. Sophie and Tori looked at each other and said, simultaneously, "An old woman who lived in a shoe?" Which made them both laugh.

Mattie came to the front door and spotted the kids. "You two stop tormenting Bear." Then she turned to Sophie and Tori. "What are you two laughing at?"

"Don't tell her we called her an old woman," Sophie whispered.

Tori nodded and ignored Mattie's question. Instead she asked, "Want me to go save the dog and snag the kids?"

Mattie nodded a little too enthusiastically. "Thanks, Tori. I can't tell you how much we appreciate your helping out tonight." She shook her head. "I told Finn we should leave the Disney World honeymoon a surprise. They've been in Mickey Mouse overdrive all week."

"I'll help with them at the wedding, too. We'll consider it my wedding gift."

"That may be one of our best ones." Mattie glanced at the side yard, where the dog started barking maniacally.

"I'm on it," Tori said, and sprinted around the corner.

"She's a great kid," Mattie said.

Sophie looked toward the corner, then back at Mattie. "She is. Her parents get all the credit."

"Nature. Nurture. I think nurture matters, but genes play a role, too, and she got a good batch of those. So come in the back and save me, would you?"

"What's up?" They heard a great deal of noise, then a little girl's shriek from outside.

Mattie noticed her looking and assured her, "It was a happy shriek. They're probably still chasing the dog. It's been like that for days. It's not only the kids excited about Disney next week, it's Lily. I think she's about to burst with her pre-wedding excitement."

Sophie noticed that Mattie looked a tad green. "Are you okay?"

"I feel a bit…" Mattie paused, obviously hunting for the word. "Claustrophobic, if that makes sense. For so many years, I was out on my own. Then I came home to help Bridget, and my life keeps on changing. I mean, I liked changing locations, but huge life upheavals make me…"

"Claustrophobic?" Sophie filled in.

Mattie sighed. "Yes."

"I know that change can be overwhelming," she said, "but these are good changes. You and Finn belong together. Despite your rough start, you're a perfect fit."

As she said the word *perfect,* she couldn't help but think of all the times people had told her that she and Colton were perfect together.

Her purse felt heavier, probably because of the custody agreement she hoped Colton would sign, and her conscience felt guilty because she knew that people's perception of them being a perfect couple had been based on faulty information.

The backyard was crowded with the wedding party and Mattie's family.

Sophie did her best to run interference between the very excited Lily and the grumbling Mattie, as well as help with the two younger kids, who continued to race around the yard, followed by their dog, or following their dog—with Zoe and Tori on their heels. She passed out drinks and made the rounds, visiting with everyone.

She told herself that she was being a good friend and helping out.

But she knew she was actually avoiding Colton.

He obviously knew it as well because he kept shooting her questioning looks.

When it was Abbey's and Mickey's bedtime, she volunteered to put the youngest two Langley children to bed. The party was winding down, and she hadn't seen Colton to give him the papers. She assured herself that it was all right. She had months to give him the papers and work out the custody.

Odds were, despite what he said, he'd want to add or subtract things from the agreement as it was written.

She got the kids showered and left Mickey reading a book in his room as she took Abbey to her room and read her a story. When she finished and closed the book, she happened to glance up and see Colton at the door.

"Aunt Mattie gets a new name tomorrow 'cause she's marrying Uncle Finn," Abbey said, then yawned and snuggled down into her pillow.

Sophie pulled up the covers. "Yes, she does."

She smoothed Abbey's hair. She'd done this many times when Bridget had been sick, but not recently. She missed bedtime routines.

She kissed Abbey's forehead.

"And then we're gonna go to Disney World on our honeymoon. Maybe you and the new baby can come? Tori, too. We like her."

"Well, the new baby won't be here until Christmas, so maybe we'll wait until after that to go."

"Tori, too?" Abbey asked.

"Yes. Tori, too, if she wants."

"Oh, she'll want to. Everyone wants to go to Disney. But it's good to wait for the baby, 'cause when it's in your belly it can't see much."

"No, he can't. But he's lucky. You'll be able to tell him all about Disney after you've gone."

"Hey, yeah, I can." Abbey popped back up like a jack-in-the-box. "Maybe I'll bring him a present."

Sophie tucked her back in. "I'm sure he'd like whatever you brought him, but I'm also sure he'll like you telling him about the trip the most."

"Okay. Night."

She kissed the little girl's forehead again. "Good night, sweetie." And knowing there was nothing more to do, she went into the hallway, shut the door behind her and faced Colton.

"I got your message saying you wanted to talk, then you spent the evening avoiding me."

"I didn't." She stopped because her denial was a lie and Colton deserved better than that. "Okay, I did avoid you all night. I... This can wait."

"What can wait?" he pressed.

"I went to the attorney's and he drew up some custody papers saying I have primary custody, at least until the baby is weaned and can spend nights with you, but otherwise, we share all parenting decisions. Co-parenting. I'll be the custodial parent. He said that doesn't mean you don't get a say, and if you don't like the way it's written up, we can change it—"

He interrupted. "Breathe. It's okay." He studied her a few long seconds, then added, "You really need that put in writing?"

"Colton, I do." She wasn't sure how to explain. "I trust you. I know you think this means I don't, but I do. It's just that I need it guaranteed. I don't think I'd survive losing another child. I—"

"Sophie, it's okay. I get it. Give me the papers and I'll return them tomorrow."

"I don't need them that fast. I simply thought it made sense to take care of it before the baby came."

He looked at her and she nodded. They went back downstairs and she grabbed her purse from the floor near the table. She opened it and pulled out the envelope. "If there's anything you feel is unfair or want changed…"

"The changes I want aren't something a document can give me." He leaned down and kissed her. His lips pressed to hers with a hunger, an urgent need that begged her to respond.

And she did. For a moment, Sophie simply opened herself up and kissed him back. Kissing Colton felt natural. It felt right.

It felt like coming home.

She felt as if something important had been missing and she'd rediscovered it.

But she knew they couldn't go backward. So she slowly disengaged herself and said, "Thank you."

COLTON WASN'T SURE if she was thanking him for taking her damn papers or for the kiss.

He'd like to think it was the kiss, but as he opened the papers and skimmed the legalese, he suspected it was his willingness to look at the papers.

This was what she wanted? Everything neatly spelled out. He'd have access to the baby at will, though he had to call first.

When the baby had weaned and was able, he could have overnights.

And…

Pages of rules and contingency plans.

Neither of them could move away without the other's approval.

Major decisions would be made jointly, unless… A list of possible exceptions were listed.

This was what Sophie needed to feel safe. To relax and not worry that someone was going to take the baby from her.

He continued reading through the papers. Finally, he made up his mind about something he hadn't even known he was considering.

He picked up a pen and ran a line through all the pages of lawyerly gobbledygook and on the last page, he simply wrote, "I give complete and absolute custody of this child to Sophie Johnston. The only thing I want more than being an integral part of this child's life is to be a part of Sophie's life. For better, for worse. For richer, for poorer. For the rest of my life. But I'm willing to walk away from both of them, from my very heart, if that's what Sophie needs."

He signed the papers and went to bed.

He might not be able to take back the pain she'd endured years ago, and he certainly couldn't undo the way he'd acted when he'd found out about Tori and about Sophie's parents, but he could do this.

He couldn't even give her his love in a way she'd believe in.

But he could give her peace of mind.

Sophie needed to be sure no one would ever take their child from her.

And he loved her enough to see to it that's what she got.

He'd give her the papers at the wedding and he'd hope that someday she could forgive him for letting her down.

CHAPTER FOURTEEN

COLTON AWOKE the next morning refreshed. He'd slept well, mainly because he was at peace with his decision.

He made his coffee and stepped out onto the porch. He wondered if Sophie would ever stand here again in the morning.

Just a few short months ago, he'd known if she woke up before him, he would find her here. She loved curling up in a chair or simply sitting on the porch steps *watching the farm wake up.* That's how she'd put it. It was as if the farm was alive in her mind.

They'd sat on the porch steps a few mornings before the day they almost got married and she'd pointed to a spot between the house and barn. She'd told him it would be the perfect place for her chickens. She'd be able to see them first thing in the morning. She'd told him if he played his cards right, he'd get fresh eggs for breakfast.

He stood by himself on the porch remembering, heavy with the knowledge that he hadn't played his cards right.

Until now.

All he could do was trust Sophie to realize it. He had to trust that she'd eventually forgive him for letting her down like everyone else in her life had. He'd done all he could.

He got ready for the day—Finn and Mattie's big day.

He greeted people as they arrived. He didn't need to point anyone to the field behind the barn. They'd all been there in June and knew the way.

And though he'd known she'd be there, he felt a surge of relief when Sophie finally arrived. He watched as she parked then walked up the gravel driveway, teetering a bit on her high heels whenever she hit stones or depressions. He wanted to go help her but knew that wouldn't be welcome, so he simply waited as she made the walk in her sunny yellow dress.

"Good morning," she said formally as she approached.

"Where's Tori?"

"She's coming with her parents."

He nodded and tried not to stare at her stomach. The dress sort of draped over it, but as the slight breeze wafted the material, he thought he could see the outline of her stomach, and he was pretty sure there was a definite baby bump.

He wanted nothing more than to put his hand on the place their child rested, but he knew Sophie wouldn't welcome the intrusion.

And really he wanted so much more. And because he wasn't sure he could simply stop at that, he resisted the urge.

He had to trust her. She'd figure out that even though he'd made a mistake, he loved her.

And the first step to her realization was in his pocket. He took out the envelope and handed it to her. "Here."

She stared at the envelope a moment, then back at him.

"You can go over them later," he said. "I think you'll

find everything's in order and your mind should be at ease."

"Thank you for being so nice about this."

"I get why you need to know you'll never lose this baby. And even if you don't trust me anymore, I need you to know that I'd never do anything to take this baby from you. I'll do everything in my power to see to it you never worry about that." He leaned down and kissed her. Not like last night—not with all the pent-up desire and longing he held. But a simple, chaste kiss that he hoped she realized was full of his love.

"I'm here, Sophie. I'll do whatever you want. Whatever you need. Even if that means walking away." Walking away from the thing he wanted the most. "Mattie's upstairs," he told her.

She didn't say anything as she entered into the house.

Now that he'd given her the envelope, he went down toward the barn where Finn and Sebastian waited.

"So, are we ready for a wedding?" he asked as he went into his barn, which once again was decorated for a party.

They'd set up a ministage for the band, and long tables lined a wall where the potluck reception food would go. Tiny white lights were strung on every available beam.

His friends sat at one of the tables.

"What was up with you and Sophie?" Finn asked.

He'd told them he'd be by as soon as he'd seen her. "I needed to give her some legal papers."

"What kind of papers?"

He shrugged. "Just some papers that spelled out custody and responsibilities for the baby."

Finn frowned. "Mattie said Sophie wants primary custody."

"Finn, today is your wedding. Worry about that. You and Mattie had your own custody issues and look how well that turned out. So, trust that Sophie and I will work it out as successfully. Worry about your wedding, not about how I screwed up my relationship with Sophie."

Sebastian looked angry. "I've always liked Sophie. I mean, not liking her would be like not liking a kitten or a rainbow. And I know she helped out my campaign. I mean, her slogan seems to be taking off. And I owe her for that, but damn, Colton, she still pisses me off so much. She's hurt you. She lied to you. And I know you asked her to marry you again, but she said no. It's almost as if she thinks she was the injured party. And now she needed you to put a custody agreement in writing? As if she couldn't trust your word?"

"She has every reason not to trust me. When she needed my love, support and acceptance the most, I walked away. She is the injured party," Colton said with utter surety. "She's always been the injured party. Sebastian, you, more than anyone, should get that. Your parents walked away and left you with Hank. They simply left. Hers never left, but they were never there for her. When she needed their love and support, they thought of themselves." Just like he'd done. He'd thought of his embarrassment at the wedding, not about Sophie's pain.

"They took Tori away from her. They never even let her hold her daughter."

He wasn't sure he truly understood the depths of that pain until now—until he was about to become a parent himself. Just the thought of someone taking the baby from him made him ache. If he closed his eyes, he could see her tears, hear her calling out. "What kind of parent could do that to their child? What the hell kind of love is that? And Tori's father? I don't know the whole story. I don't know if Sophie's parents bought him off or threatened him, but despite his promises, he deserted her, too. You had Hank. You always knew you had Hank in your corner. And you had me and Finn. Sophie was only a kid and she had no one."

Colton wanted to go find Sophie now. He wanted to wrap his arms around her and tell her he'd never leave her or the baby. But that wasn't what Sophie wanted. It wasn't what she needed.

"After all that, you blame her for not talking about her past? Really? The fact that she found so much to be happy about, that she found the ability to love after all of that only shows what an amazing woman she is. She might not have told me about all her wounds, but she put her trust in me. She counted on me to love her no matter what. To stand by her no matter what came our way. And what did I do? I betrayed that love and faith she put in me as certainly as her parents ever did. As surely as Tori's father did. I walked away from her when she needed me the most."

There was nothing he could ever do to make up for that. It was the ultimate betrayal. "Those custody papers I signed? They give her sole custody. Complete control. She needs to know in no uncertain terms that this baby can never be taken from her. Not even by me."

Colton added, "If she asks me to sign over my farm, the winery, the whole damn thing, I'll do it," Colton assured his friends. "If she needs me to walk away and leave her, I'll be tearing out my own heart, but I'd do it."

Finn nodded, finally understanding, but it was clear

that Sebastian didn't. "But you're the injured party," he maintained in that stubborn Sebastian way. His friend had changed in so many ways since they were kids, but in his blind devotions to his friends, he was exactly the same.

"You're wrong, Sebastian. You're as wrong as you can be. And I'm telling you, I signed away my parental rights and hope Sophie lets me be a part of my son's life. But if she does ask me to walk away, then I need you and Finn to be there for her and the baby. You'll both have an in because of Mattie and Lily, and I'll need you to take it. I'll need you to be what she won't let me be…someone she can rely on. And I'm not asking. I'm telling. We've been friends too many years for you not to do this for me. She loves Mattie and Lily. She won't turn you away because of them. You'll be there if I can't."

Sebastian still looked as if he wanted to fight someone, but even if he didn't understand, he nodded. Finn nodded, as well. His friends would be there for Sophie and the baby if he couldn't, just as Colton knew they would. And something inside him eased knowing that his child would be loved and looked after. "I love her enough to do, and be, whatever she wants and needs no matter what it does to me." He turned to Finn. "You give me hope. You sued Mattie, and yet she's marrying you today. And Sebastian, you came home with the biggest chip on your shoulder and, still, you and Lily—"

"We aren't announcing it until after Finn and Mattie's wedding is over, but we're getting married around the holidays," Sebastian admitted.

"Like hell you're not announcing it," Finn finally said. "You're going to give me a wonderful toast and then I'm going to toast your upcoming wedding. I'm assuming you're going to ask me and Colton to be your groomsmen."

Sebastian shrugged, but his huge grin marred the nonchalant gesture. "I guess I'm stuck. I don't seem to have any other best friends in town."

They talked about Sebastian's wedding, and Colton was able to laugh and smile along with his friends because he knew they'd keep their promises to look after Sophie and the baby. And he'd keep his. He'd be whatever Sophie needed, sign whatever she wanted to feel safe. He loved her. He'd never stop. He'd never quit trying to regain her trust and earn her forgiveness.

He loved her completely and unconditionally.

Somehow she'd realize that eventually. And he'd be here waiting when she did.

"REALLY, MATTIE, you can't wear flip-flops," Lily said as Sophie walked into the bedroom.

"Sophie, save me. Tell bridesmaid-zilla there that these aren't flip-flops, they are most definitely sandals. Very weddingish sandals, as a matter of fact."

Lily held the white shoes in question in her fingertips, as if she might be contaminated by their unweddinglike nature. "Do they make a noise like this—" she made a clicky sort of sound "—when you walk?"

Mattie ignored Lily's question and turned to Sophie, her eyes pleading for help. "Sophie?"

"I think they're beautiful and sensible. Unlike these." She held her foot aloft showing her high heels. "I love that Mattie knows who she is and what she wants. I'd wear something that comfortable if I wasn't afraid of wandering into the midst of a corn field and not being able to find my way out."

"You're not that short." Lily sighed and handed over what she considered questionable footwear.

"In high school, our lockers were two parts. Two thin, side-by-side long lockers for coats on the bottom, then two stacked areas for books over top of those. Every year, they assigned me a top locker. I could barely reach it, and couldn't see inside to save my life. The first two years, I had to get the person next to me to switch lockers."

"And after that?" Mattie asked, slipping the sandals onto her feet.

"I discovered that tiny women should learn how to walk in heels. Big heels."

Mattie looked lovely in the white sundress. Lily had tried to convince her to get her hair styled for the day, but Mattie had put her hair in a simple bun and done her own makeup, as well. "If I get too dolled up, Finn won't recognize me," she said. "You wait until it's your turn, Lily. You'll realize that all the external stuff doesn't mean a thing. It's that guy waiting for you at the end of the aisle that matters."

For once, bridesmaid-zilla Lily didn't say a thing. She got a misty, faraway look, and Sophie knew with utter certainty that Lily wasn't going to be waiting very long for her own trip down the aisle. "Lily?"

"What?" Mattie asked, realizing she was missing something. "What's going on?"

"Lily and Sebastian are talking about getting married?" Sophie half asked.

"Lily?" Mattie asked again, obviously looking for confirmation.

"We're not saying anything until after your wedding. We don't want to steal your thunder."

"Since when is sharing good news stealing anything,

you dork? Oh, man, I can't wait to see your wedding. You're going to be a basket case with all your rules about how things should be done. But you'll see. As long as Sebastian shows up, it will all be fine."

"Aunt Mattie," Abbey hollered from the doorway. "You gotta come. Me and Zoe are all ready and want to go."

"I'd better see to them," Mattie said.

"And Mickey says he's going to climb the tree and watch you and Uncle Finn from up high," she added.

Mattie sprinted for the door. Lily was hot on her heels calling, "I'll help."

Sophie wanted to go with them, but first she wanted to check that Colton had indeed signed the papers.

It wasn't that she didn't trust him, but she needed to see it in print.

"I'll be with you in a second," she called after Lily, who waved and sprinted down the hall.

Sophie held the envelope for a moment. Then slowly opened the flap.

There were her very official-looking custody papers, and all those very legal words were crossed out.

She flipped through the pages. They were all crossed out.

She was thinking that she was going to kill Colton McCray as she flipped to the final page.

"I give complete and absolute custody of this child to Sophie Johnston. The only thing I want more than being an integral part of this child's life is to be a part of Sophie's life. For better, for worse. For richer, for poorer. For the rest of my life. But I'm willing to walk away from both of them, from my very heart, if that's what Sophie needs."

He'd signed it.

Absolute custody.

No one would ever be able to take this baby from her.

Colton would walk away from her and the baby if that's what she needed.

Of course he would.

Sophie sat at the window of the room she'd thought would be hers by now and cried.

How could she be so stupid? Colton loved her.

Not just any kind of love. Complete and unconditional love.

She was the one who couldn't give him that kind of unconditional love back. She couldn't trust him.

He'd been hurt and angry, but it didn't take him long to get over that and come back to her. He'd asked her to marry him again not because of the baby, but because he loved her. She reread his handwritten note and traced her finger along the curve of his signature. She cried even harder. Of course he loved her.

He'd been surprised and needed a moment to adjust, but that moment had passed soon enough and he'd wanted to make things right. He wanted things to go back to what they had been. She'd known they couldn't go back, but it wasn't until this instant that she realized they could go forward not separately but together.

Tori stood in the open doorway. "Sophie, is everything okay?"

"Come here a minute." She wrapped her daughter in her arms. "I need you to know with absolute and utter certainty that I love you. That I'm proud of you. I don't care if you're a straight-A student. I don't care if you take apart my toaster and never get it back together. I don't care if you dye your hair blue, orange or rainbow colors. I don't care if you become rich and

famous or live a quiet ordinary life. All I want for you
is a life filled with happiness. I know that your mom
and dad are your parents and that they love you. Unconditionally. You've had a great life, and I have found
peace because I know that. I've also found such joy this
summer, having you in my life. But I need you to know
that no matter where you go or what you do, I love you.
I loved you from the moment I found out about you.
And all the years without you? I loved you then, too. I
simply love you."

"I love you, too." Tori hugged her long and tight,
then pulled back and asked, "So why are you sitting
here crying?"

"I'm crying because…" She sighed. "It's what I do.
For a while, I thought I could hide my emotions away,
but they're here and there's no hiding them. I was crying because I'm so happy for Mattie, Finn and the kids.
They're a family. And I'm crying for Sebastian and Lily
because they're going to have a wonderful life together,
too. A life built on love. I cry at weddings and engage-
ments and all of that. But mostly, I'm crying because
I realize you were right a while ago when you told me
Colton loved me. He does. Completely. Absolutely."

"Duh." Tori grinned. "Took you long enough to figure it out."

"I was too afraid to admit it." Sophie had tried to
ignore the deep-seated fear that somehow she wasn't
deserving of happiness. It seemed that particular bit of
baggage had always been with her. She could ignore it.
She could work around it and find some semblance of
happiness in spite of it, but it was always there.

Until this very moment.

She did deserve to be happy. She did deserve to be
loved.

And she was both.

"But you're not afraid anymore?" Tori asked.

"I have this very brave daughter who came to find me, not knowing what she'd find. How can I be afraid of telling Colton that I love him when I know exactly what I'll find?"

"What's that?" Tori asked.

"His open arms. His love."

"So, why are you sitting here talking to me?" She gave Sophie a little nudge.

"That is a very good question." She got up, leaned down and kissed Tori's cheek. "I'm absolutely in love with the woman you're becoming."

Tori snorted. "You're biased."

"True, but it doesn't mean you're not amazing and perfect. I need you to remember that. Now, pardon me, I've got a wedding to attend, and then I have to ask a certain man if he'll marry me."

She walked out of the house and stood on the porch a moment, taking in the farm. Colton's farm. His home and someday soon, if things went the way she thought they would, her home. Their child's home.

Sophie tried to force herself to be tuned in to Mattie's wedding. But she couldn't help thinking, *Colton loves me and I love him,* in between the bouquets and the walk to the field. She proceeded up the aisle and saw him, and knew he was still waiting for her as much as he had been waiting on their wedding day. It had just taken her longer than she thought it would to get there.

She listened as the minister said the words to Finn and Mattie, and in her heart she was echoing them for Colton. She did promise to love him, to stick by him…

She looked at Mattie, so very much in love with Finn, and Lily just as in love with Sebastian.

She wished she had a mirror because she knew that she had that same besotted expression on her face.

She thought her heart would burst with happiness as she started down the aisle.

The only thing that would make this day better was if their friend Bridget were here. She thought of Bridget. Her friend had been the bravest woman she'd ever met. She'd faced her death not with fear but with love. With planning for her family. And she'd given her children a new, complete family.

Sophie looked at Bridget's children, waiting near the arbor with Finn, Sebastian and Colton. Zoe, on the verge of womanhood. Mickey, still a rascal. And Abbey…wearing her princess crown. And she knew that Bridget was very much present here today.

She shot Colton a smile and hoped he could read her thoughts in her expression.

She loved him. And after the wedding—after she celebrated her friends' marriage—she'd tell him so.

SOPHIE SCANNED the reception. Sebastian had his arm around Lily, firmly anchoring her to him. She reveled in the fact they'd be announcing their wedding soon. Sebastian had come home…damaged. It wasn't the physical scars, but some deep emotional ones. She didn't know the whole of it, but she knew he'd felt guilty about not being with his friends. Somehow Lily had helped him truly heal. And together with Hank, they were a family.

She looked at Tori, who was talking excitedly to her parents. Sophie refused to worry about semantics. Tori was her daughter, but she was Gloria and Dom's daughter, too. And she knew she was loved. Dom and Gloria caught her eye and grinned. Dom gave her a little thumbs-up sign. She knew that Tori had told them, and she had their approval. She also knew that when Tori found her, she'd not only been reunited with her daughter, she'd gained a family. She waved back.

Yes, she had a family. Colton, the baby, Tori, her parents, their friends…

Valley Ridge as a whole was her family.

Maeve Buchanan, who'd been so good with Tori, was her family.

Mattie's brother Rich, who was Colton's partner in the winery, was her family.

Dylan Long, Valley Ridge's police officer, Stanley Tuznik, the former mayor and current crossing guard. Vivienne and Marilee of MarVee's Quarters were family.

Mrs. Nies, JoAnn from the B and B…

Colton's yard was full of her family.

For years she'd felt like an orphan, but she hadn't found a home when she'd moved to Valley Ridge, she'd found her family.

She'd worked hard over the years to face life with a sense of optimism and a smile. She tried to find the glee in…well, everything. Sometimes she could hardly contain it. And at this particular moment, she didn't even try. She was so immensely happy she could hardly stand it. She knew with absolute and utter certainty that Colton McCray loved her.

As she gazed at him, his cowboy hat and wedding clothes in place, she didn't have a fear in the world. She was so in love there simply wasn't any room left for fear or doubt.

She walked up to him and smiled.

He looked at her and smiled back. "What happened to you?"

"Dance with me."

"They turned the iPod off. I think they're going to cut the cake or something," he said.

She didn't need music to dance with the man she loved. "Well, until they do, music or no music, dance with me."

Colton didn't argue, didn't fight, he simply swept her into his arms and turned a slow circle on the lawn. "I was going to tell you that—"

Sophie put a finger over his lips. She didn't need him to tell her anything. She already knew. "Shh."

He peered down at her. "Something's changed."

"Nothing's changed," she said as they turned lazy circles. "I simply figured a few things out." She tightened her hold on him and she knew she'd never let go again.

"Like what?"

"You love me," she said with utter certainty. She looked up into his eyes and repeated, "You love me unconditionally and absolutely."

He nodded. "Yes. That's not a change."

"And you love the baby that same way, already," she continued. "You'd do anything—and I mean absolutely anything for him."

He nodded again. "I would."

She had to step on tiptoe to reach the brim of his hat, but she gave it a small tug. "You are a cowboy in the truest sense of the word. Not because of the hat, but because you're kind and honest, and faithful—"

He snorted, interrupting her list of his finer qualities. "You make me sound like a dog."

Sebastian stepped up onto Colton's makeshift stage. "Hi, everyone. For those who might not know, I'm Sebastian Bennington."

"I serve," someone in the crowd yelled.

Sebastian laughed.

"I'm about to ask you something, but I already know the answer," Sophie whispered.

Sebastian continued, "I wanted to say a few words about Finn and Mattie because I'm pretty sure my few words will be longer than any speech Colton would give."

Everyone laughed and turned to Colton, who waved, then he whispered to Sophie, "What question?"

"Colton McCray, will you marry me?" She said the words with utter certainty both of his answer and of the fact that he loved her.

"…and that first day of school, Finn's sister…"

"What?" he asked.

"Marry me. Make an honest woman of me. Let me move here to the farm with you. I know I kept secrets from you, but you love me despite that. You trust me." She thought about the papers and about his words to his friends. "You'd do anything for me, even if it hurt you."

"…the first time he saw Mattie she was wearing a diaper…"

"I would," he said. "I'd walk away if you needed me to, but I'd never stop fighting to make you see I love you."

She nodded. "And that's why you don't have to fight. I see it. More than that, I feel it. Marry me."

"You name the time, place," he said. "Tell me when and where and I'll be there."

"…then he really saw what we'd all seen, he loved her…."

"Here," she said, feeling more certain about this than she'd ever felt about anything. "Marry me now. The minister's still here. We still have a valid license.

There's an arbor up in the field that you built for me. Marry me. Mattie won't care that we're using their date. Finn won't care." She knew that, too. Mattie and Finn were their family. They'd share a wedding date with perfect happiness.

Colton didn't need to be asked again. He grabbed her hand and practically dragged her over to the porch, where the newly married couple listened as Sebastian wound down with, "So, congratulations Finn and Mattie. I hope your life brings you nothing but joy."

Sebastian spotted him. "You had something to say?" he asked Colton loudly, then added, "Don't worry, folks, this won't take long."

Colton nodded and jumped onto the porch next to him, pulling Sophie up, as well. As if he were afraid to let her go.

"Finn and Mattie," he said, "I feel as if Sophie and I get some of the credit for you two falling in love. I mean, you witnessed what true and everlasting love looks like when you saw us together. And we kept putting you two together, despite your difficulties, for our wedding. So, I'm going to ask you a big favor."

"Anything," Finn promised.

"Let us share an anniversary with the two of you. Sophie said she'd marry me and I'd like to seal the deal before she changes her mind."

"I'm not changing it," she assured him. "I'm not changing it ever."

Colton reached into his pocket and pulled out her engagement ring. "I don't have our wedding rings, but I've been carrying this with me since you took it off." He held out the ruby ring. "I'd like it to stand in for our wedding rings, if that works for you."

"Ring, gum-machine plastic or no ring, I'm marrying you."

FIFTEEN MINUTES LATER, Sophie was walking down the field toward the arbor that Colton had built. Her friends and the Valley Ridge community stood crowded on either side. It was reminiscent of their almost-wedding. Lily and Mattie stood to the left of the arbor, Finn and Sebastian stood to the right, next to Colton, who was watching every step she took down the aisle.

Sophie walked toward the man she loved. She was aware that she was surrounded by friends, but her eyes were only on him.

He might not be perfect, but he was perfect for her. And he'd seen all her imperfections and loved her anyway.

Sophie normally thought of herself as a happy person, but at the moment, she was so much more than happy. The only word she could think of that even came close was *gleeful,* and even that was not enough.

Colton had his hands behind his back, and he pulled out his hat.

Her cowboy.

In a community of farmers, vintners, business people, he was her cowboy.

She reached his side.

"Dearly beloved," the minister started. "Here we are again. Not only for a second wedding today, but for a second time with Colton and Sophie. And just to settle everyone's nerves, let me ask, before we start, if anyone has any objections to their marrying."

Everyone turned toward Tori, who laughed and called out, "The only objection I have is you're taking too long."

"There you have it then. Dearly beloved, we are gathered here…"

Sophie lost herself in the words. In the feel of

Colton's hand in hers. In the waves of love that seemed to beat against her like waves on the sand.

She looked at the man next to her. He was her happily ever after.

No, this wasn't the end of their story. It was only the beginning.

EPILOGUE

TORI FELT A SENSE of being home as the winefest wound down and she walked along Valley Ridge's main street, Park Street, with Joe at her side. His little sisters ran up ahead of them. "I'll miss you," he said. "It seems like you just got here."

She felt a little shiver at the words. She wanted to tell him that she would miss him, too. That she hated leaving Valley Ridge, and him. But she didn't want to go too fast. She was a kid and so was he. They lived in two different cities, and though they texted a lot and used Skype, too, it wasn't the same as living in the same town.

Plus, there were her birth parents to think about. They'd been young when they'd fallen in love. They'd thought they had the future planned, but then Sophie had gotten pregnant and...

No, she wasn't in a hurry, so she slugged Joe lightly on the arm and said, "I've been here since Friday. That's the whole weekend. Plus, you talk to me every day."

"Texting isn't seeing you." He paused, then asked, "Are you going to come spend all of winter break with Sophie?"

"Well, she's out at the farm now, and we don't drive—"

"You do," he teased.

"Well, I know how, but I've learned my lesson and I'll be waiting for a learner's permit like everyone else. So, even if I'm here the whole break, you still won't see much of me." He looked disappointed and Tori felt sort of flattered that he wanted to see her that much. "But I'm sure Sophie and Colton will let you come out and spend time at the farm. Sophie got her chickens and she's trying to talk Colton into a horse."

Joe laughed. "He'll do it. He'd do anything for her."

She spotted her mom and dad standing in front of a vacant store next to Hank's diner. "Hi, what are you guys doing staring into that mess?"

"I wouldn't say it was a mess," her dad said. "Just imagine it painted and cleaned up."

Her mom sighed. "Your dad's a dreamer."

"That's why you love me." He leaned down and kissed her mom's cheek, right there on the main street of Valley Ridge where anyone could see them. Where she and Joe had to witness it.

"Gross," Tori said with emphasis.

Joe laughed. His two little sisters had reached the corner and turned around to come back to them.

"This is where the ghosts live," Mica said in a small, serious voice.

"Joe said if we're bad, he's gonna make us come sleep over with the ghosts. I had a bunch of bad dreams, and Daddy yelled at Joe and he said there's no ghosts, but…" Allie let the sentence trail off.

"Joe," Tori said, "that's horrible." She knelt down and looked at his little sisters. "There are no ghosts."

"Yeah, that's what Daddy said," Allie said, though neither girl looked convinced.

Still shaking her head, Tori stood and asked her parents, "So what were you looking at?"

"I was saying that this would be the perfect storefront for an art studio. I was talking to Mattie's brother Ray, the one that's the mayor, and he said the town has a growing tourist business. A small art gallery, maybe with some specialty books on the area and…"

"Wait, are you thinking about buying it?"

"No, not really. Your mom works in Cleveland and I…" He shook his head. "No, I'm only dreaming out loud."

But there was something about the look her mom and dad shot each other that had Tori wondering.

"You better go find Sophie and say goodbye. We need to hit the road soon. Tomorrow's a school day." Her mom threw in the school-day part as if it was something to be excited about, but Tori wasn't excited. She would never be as excited about school as her college president mother.

"I'll go find everyone and say goodbye, then meet you at the car."

"Sophie was at the diner," her dad said.

"I should probably get these guys home," Joe said. "They've got school tomorrow, too."

"We're girls, not guys," Mica said, all proper and prim.

"Well, girls, I'll see you next time I'm home." Tori turned to Joe. "I'll talk to you."

"Text me on the ride home?" he asked.

"Yeah."

He nodded, took his sisters' hands and started back down the block.

The crowds were thinning out. It had been crazy

busy in town this weekend because of winefest. Sophie had been so happy.

Tori walked into the diner, and saw Sophie, Colton and their friends at a back table. But there were a lot of people to get past before she reached them. She started to make her way through the crowd, and though hugging wasn't something she did any more often than crying, she found herself being hugged by everyone. Marilee and Vivienne, Mrs. Nies and JoAnn.

She'd made it through the bulk of the crowd when Sebastian's grandfather, Mr. Hank, came over. "Leanne, what did you do to your hair?"

Tori, like everyone else in town, knew that on occasion Mr. Hank's memory wasn't very good. She didn't know who Leanne was, but she didn't care. She simply played along. "Do you like it?"

"It has a blue stripe in it. You look…cute, though."

This time she didn't wait for someone to hug her, she reached out and hugged the older man, hoping he thought she was this Leanne. "I'll see you soon."

"Don't be gone too long. I miss you when you're not here. I love you."

She stood on tiptoe and kissed the older man's cheeks. "I love you, too."

Sophie was surrounded by her friends. Mattie and Finn, with their kids yammering at least a dozen times over the course of the weekend about their *honeymoon* at Disney.

Tori didn't even need to guess what Lily was talking about as she approached. "And I'm getting in a truckload of poinsettias for the church…."

Tori stood behind Lily, listening as she described her wedding again. It was going to be just after Thanksgiving, but before Christmas, and Lily was as excited as a kid with presents under a tree over it.

Tori looked at the three couples. Colton and Sophie, who was now so pregnant that Tori wasn't sure she'd be able to walk if the baby got any bigger. Mattie and Finn. They weren't much for mushy displays, but he had his arm over Mattie's chair, and they sat close together as they both listened to Lily. And Sebastian. He was looking at Lily, nodding as he used his scarred hand to raise a glass to his lips.

Sebastian caught her staring at his arm. "Frankenstein, huh?"

"No, it gives you an air of danger," she teased.

Sebastian started to laugh, and Lily leaned into him and took his mangled hand in hers.

It was kind of gross to see grown-ups so totally in love, and kind of nice, too. That's how she tended to feel about her mom and dad.

Lily took a breath and Sophie said, "Sit down, Tori."

"I can't. I wanted to say goodbye to everyone."

"We'll see you at the wedding, right?" Lily asked.

"I wouldn't miss it."

Sophie got out of her chair with a great deal of difficulty and waddled over to Tori. "I'm going to hug you now, but Cletus is kicking up a storm, so you'll probably get kicked when I do."

And, so saying, she pulled Tori into an awkward-because-of-her-size hug.

"Were you this big with me?" Tori asked.

"Yes. It seems when you're just a bit over five feet, there's really nowhere for the baby to go but straight out."

"I'll call," Tori promised. "And we'll be back for the

wedding and the holidays. Mom and Dad said they're really going to try to get me here for when the baby comes."

"Your brother can't wait to meet you."

"Yeah, my brother." It still felt weird to think of having a sibling. Weird, but nice. "So, I'll see you."

Sophie leaned close and whispered in her ear the word *perfect.* It had become her standard goodbye. And even though she knew she wasn't perfect, Tori felt sort of warm all over knowing that Sophie and her parents thought she was.

"Bye." She hurried out before she got all teary like Sophie always did. Then she ran back and whispered in Sophie's ear, "I love you."

She dashed out before Sophie could cry, and she practically ran over Maeve outside the diner.

Maeve smiled when she saw her and ran a hand through her very wild red hair.

"Why are you out here?" Tori asked.

"I needed a breather," Maeve said. "I think everyone in town is celebrating the winefest's success at Hank's tonight."

Tori realized that Maeve always seemed a bit removed from the rest of the town. She came to the parties and the like, but she never appeared to be totally a part of them. It was as if she was always sitting on the front porch while the rest of the town was in the backyard.

She seemed…lonely.

Tori felt kind of sorry for her. "Well, if this were the *Wizard of Oz,* I'd be Dorothy climbing into my balloon and telling you goodbye."

"And I'd be?" Maeve asked with a smile.

"Scarecrow. You taught me so much, Maeve. I know Mom, Dad and Sophie thought spending my summer working for free at a library would be a punishment for stealing the car—"

"Yeah, don't ever do that again," Maeve said.

"I won't. But working with you wasn't a punishment. I know what I'm going to go to college for."

"Oh?" A piece of Maeve's hair blew across her face, though there didn't seem to be a breeze. Maeve shoved at it, trying to push it back with the rest of her curls, but it didn't want to go. It crept to the edge of her hairline.

Tori loved her boss's crazy hair, though Maeve muttered about it all the time. "I'm going into library sciences. I want to be a children's librarian. I want to do story times, and help kids find books. Thanks for that."

"Well, thank you for all the work this summer. And for helping out this weekend at the book fair tent."

Maeve had put many of the donated books she couldn't use up for sale at the winefest.

Tori had just hugged half of Valley Ridge, but she realized that Maeve didn't feel like someone who was used to hugging. So she moved in slow and hugged her boss. "See you in a few weeks."

Man, Sophie was rubbing off on her. She'd turned into a sappy, teary-eyed mess.

Tori hurried down the street toward her parents and looked back over her shoulder at Maeve. She was beautiful and had singlehandedly reopened the library. All summer she'd passed Tori books, and always helped anyone who needed it at the library.

But standing there by herself, she seemed like the loneliest person Tori had ever met.

As her family got into their black SUV and started

driving out of town, Tori began making a list of eligible bachelors in Valley Ridge. Someone she could fix Maeve up with. There was that cop, Dylan. And Mattie's brothers Rich and Ray were both single....

A text message from Joe interrupted her musings— Come back to Valley Ridge soon.

Oh, she would. She'd be coming back soon and often.

* * * * *

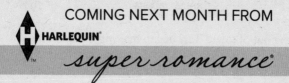
#1860 BETTING ON THE COWBOY
The Sisters of Bell River Ranch • by Kathleen O'Brien

Brianna Wright has ventured to the Bell River Ranch to make peace with her sister. She's *not* here to be romanced by Grayson Harper—no matter how good-looking he is. But working together on the ranch proves he's more determined than she guessed, and he just might win...her!

#1861 A TEXAS HERO • *Willow Creek, Texas*
by Linda Warren

Abby Bauman has found her ultimate hero. Detective Ethan James brought her through a terrifying kidnapping, but will he be there for her in the days that follow—when she needs him most?

#1862 ONE-NIGHT ALIBI • *Project Justice*
by Kara Lennox

A disgraced cop. An heiress. A night of passion and a murder. Now top suspects Hudson Vale and Elizabeth Downey must fight their attraction *and* work together to prove their innocence by finding the real killer.

#1863 OUT OF HIS LEAGUE
by Cathryn Parry

Professional athlete Jon Farell is the nurturing type, and there's no one he'd rather have lean on him than Dr. Elizabeth LaValley. Though she seems to enjoy their kisses, she wants her well-ordered life back. Well, Jon will just have to show her how much fun a little chaos can be!

#1864 THE RANCH SOLUTION
by Julianna Morris

Mariah Weston keeps her distance from the city dwellers who visit her working ranch. Then she meets single dad Jacob O'Donnell and his troubled teenage daughter. Try as she might, Mariah can't get Jacob out of her thoughts, no matter how wrong for her he might be....

#1865 NAVY ORDERS • *Whidbey Island*
by Geri Krotow

Chief warrant officer Miles Mikowski fell for lieutenant commander Roanna Brandywine the first time he met her—but she's repeatedly turned him down. Now a sailor's unexplained death draws them both into an undercover investigation. And that means working together. *Closely* together...

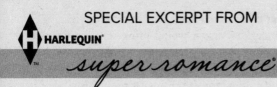

Navy Orders

By **Geri Krotow**

On sale July 2013

Chief Warrant Officer Miles Mikowski fell for Lieutenant Commander Roanna Brandywine the day he rescued her mother's cat. Too bad she's always turned him down. But now they're working together investigating a sailor's death and the attraction is growing. Then, one night to avoid detection, Miles kisses Ro...
Read on for an exciting sneak preview!

"That was a surprise." Ro's voice was soft but Miles heard steel in its tone.

He traced her cheek with his fingers. "I'm not sorry I had to kiss you."

"You did it to keep the wing staff from seeing us, didn't you?"

"Yes."

"Is this how you usually run an explosive ordinance op, Warrant?"

"Out in the field, the guys and I don't do much kissing." He saw her lips twitch but no way in hell would she let him see her grin. Ro was so damned strong. He knew it killed her to let go of her professional demeanor, even in civvies.

"No wonder, because it would prove way too distracting. I hope you don't plan a repeat maneuver like that, Warrant."

"I do whatever duty calls for, ma'am."

She glared at him. She didn't usually show this kind of heat, and it took all his control not to haul her onto the bike and take off for his place.

"What we're doing will not call for that kind of tactic again, get it?"

"Got it," he replied. She'd enjoyed it as much as he had, he was sure of it. But this discussion was for another occasion, if at all. "It's time to get to work, Commander."

**Will this _really_ be the last time for that
kind of tactic? Or will circumstances keep
pulling Miles and Ro together?
Find out in NAVY ORDERS
by Geri Krotow, available July 2013
from Harlequin® Superromance®.
And be sure to look for other books in
Geri's WHIDBEY ISLAND series.**

HSREXP0613

REQUEST YOUR FREE BOOKS!
2 FREE NOVELS PLUS 2 FREE GIFTS!

HARLEQUIN®
super romance®

More Story...More Romance

HSR13R

Love Western?

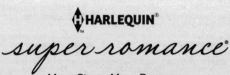

Willow Creek, Texas

Enjoy a new trilogy from
Linda Warren!

July—A Texas Hero

October—A Texas Family

December—A Texas Child

A disgraced cop...

An heiress. A night of passion. A murder.
Now top suspects Hudson Vale and
Elizabeth Downey must fight their attraction
and work together to prove their innocence
by finding the real killer.

One Night Alibi
by **Kara Lennox**

AVAILABLE IN JULY

W9-APC-032

ON THE EDGE

James Barry

Sharon Siamon

Glen Huser

Published in 1994 simultaneously by:

Nelson Canada,   *and*   The Wright Group
A Division of Thomson   19201 – 120th Avenue NE
    Canada Limited   Bothell, Washington
1120 Birchmount Road   98011-9512
Scarborough, Ontario   U.S.A.
M1K 5G4
Canada

ISBN 0-17-603953-8   ISBN 0-17-604362-4

2 3 4 5 /WC/ 97   1 2 3 4 5 /WC/ 97 96 95 94 93

I(T)P ™
International Thomson Publishing
The trademark ITP is used under license

Project Manager: Lana Kong
Assistant Editor: Carolyn Madonia
Senior Production Editor: Deborah Lonergan
Art Direction: Bruce Bond
Cover Design: Stuart Knox
Cover Illustration: Richard Parisi
Series Design: Janet Riopelle

Printed and bound in Canada

Canadian Cataloguing in Publication Data

Main entry under title:
On the edge

(Nelson mini-anthologies)
ISBN 0-17-603953-8

1. Readers (Elementary). 2. Readers (Secondary).
I. Barry, James, 1939– . II. Siamon, Sharon.
III. Huser, Glen, 1943– . IV. Series.

PE1121.05 1993   428.6   C93-094686-3

Series Review Panel

Table of Contents

1
ON THE BRINK OF DANGER

Flames on the Water . . . . NON-FICTION 8
John Melady

The Case of the
Unused Seat Belt . . . . PUZZLE 20
Donald J. Sobol

Madeleine . . . . NON-FICTION 22
Arthur Prager and Emily Prager

Ordeal in the Arctic . . . . NON-FICTION 30
Robert Mason Lee

2
ASTONISH ME

The Wish . . . . STORY 40
Roald Dahl

Lot 87 . . . . STORY 46
Joy Burnett

Encounters of the Old Kind . . . . . . STORY 53
Reid Van Melle

A Hell of a Story . . . . STORY 58
H. R. F. Keating

3

IN THE LINE OF FIRE

Hijacked! . . . . NON-FICTION 66
John Melady

The Shooting of
Dan McGrew . . . . NARRATIVE POEM 82
Robert Service

Just Lather, That's All . . . . STORY 87
Hernando Téllez

4

WATCH YOUR BACK!

Dialogue Behind a Curtain . . . . . . STORY 96
Victor Canning

If Cornered, Scream . . . . STORY . . . 106
Patricia J. Thurmond

The Most Dangerous Game . . . . . STORY . . . 110
Richard Connell

On the Brink of Danger

▲ ▼ ▼ ▲ ▼ ▼ ▲ ▼ ▼ ▲ ▼ ▼ ▲ ▼ ▼ ▲ ▶ ▶

Courage is the price that life exacts for
   granting peace.
The soul that knows it not, knows no
   release
From little things;
Knows not the livid loneliness of fear,
Nor mountain heights where bitter joy can
   hear
The sound of wings.

Amelia Earhart

▲ ▼ ▼ ▲ ▼ ▼ ▲ ▼ ▼ ▲ ▼ ▼ ▲ ▼ ▼ ▲ ▶ ▶

▲▼▶▼▶▲▼▶▼◀▲▼▶▼▶▲▼▶▼▶▶

FLAMES ON THE WATER

by John Melady

Anna Lang survived a terrible car crash—but,
more than that, she rescued her friend and
her friend's young son. For that, Anna
received the Cross of Valour.

Anna Lang of Nauwigewauk, New Brunswick,
looks back at the events that led up to her winning
of the Cross of Valour as if they were all part of a
terrible dream, a nightmare that somehow came
true, a hell so horrible she is amazed she escaped it.

At noon on Tuesday, September 9, 1980, 42-
year-old Lang and her friend, 31-year-old Lana
Walsh, were returning from Saint John where they
had been working out in a city gymnasium. With
them, in the rear seat of Anna's new red two-door
Buick, was Walsh's four-year-old son Jaye. Anna
was driving.

Because the day was warm, Lana had opened
the window on her side of the car. The radio was
on, but neither woman paid much attention to it.
They were too busy chatting, discussing the events

of the morning and the dangerous situation they knew existed at the Hammond River bridge, some ten kilometres ahead.

The highway approaches to the bridge are hazardous at the best of times because drivers coming from either direction must first negotiate a series of sweeping downhill curves immediately before reaching it. On this day however, the major hazard at the Hammond River involved the bridge itself. For over a week the south lane had been closed.

"They were replacing the right guardrail of the thing," recalls Anna Lang today. "I had driven over it several times when it was under construction, but it always scared me. Because one lane was closed, they had traffic lights set up at each end. The only trouble was, you could be halfway across and the lights would change and cars would start coming towards you. That happened to me one night, and I had to crowd into the construction area to let them pass. That was why I hated the bridge, and why Lana and I were talking about it as we went along. Both of us said we knew somebody would be hurt there before long. It was just too dangerous."

As the two women continued their journey, neither knew that a large gasoline truck was behind them. Although it was still out of sight, it was rapidly drawing closer. The huge 22-wheel, 50-t Brunswick Petroleum transport was driven by 34-year-old Charles Steeves, a trucker with 14 years of accident-free experience behind him. The tanker carried 45 000 L of gasoline.

In the meantime, on the bridge ahead, most of the guardrail rebuilding was halted while the construction crew ate lunch. Several men had gone to their cars for sandwiches, or to the nearby Mandarin House restaurant for a hot meal. Because of the hour, only a handful of workers remained on the job. The time was 12:35 p.m.

As Anna eased her car around the long curve that leads down onto the western end of the bridge, she noticed that the temporary traffic light facing her was green. She saw no vehicles coming towards her, nor did she realize that Charles Steeves's gasoline tanker was less than 20 m behind.

"He's Not Going to Stop!"

Just then, the light turned red.

"When the red came on, I automatically stopped the car," explains Lang with a shudder. "Then I looked in the rearview mirror. All I could see were two headlights and a grille. Perhaps I saw the body of the truck but I can't remember it. The grille seemed to fill my whole back window and his horn was blaring and I was screaming: 'Oh God, Lana, he's not going to stop. He's not going to stop.'"

Up in the cab of his truck, Charles Steeves was terrified. He jammed on his brakes and sounded his horn. Yet he knew he could never stop in time. "My God," he thought to himself, "I'm going to kill them all."

The careering tanker then smashed into the back of the Lang auto, demolishing the entire rear end and ramming the trunk against the front seat. In the same instant, the back window exploded inwards and hundreds of jagged glass particles were driven into the interior of the car. Little Jaye Walsh was knocked flying into the front seat.

"When the back window popped, the glass made the inside of the car look like a cave with ice crystals hanging down," Lang recalls. "The ice kept coming until it covered the roof, the sides, and even the dash. I remember being pushed forward and then crawling back to the seat again. My head hit the steering wheel and my glasses were thrown off. The whole thing seemed to be in slow motion. Everything was so slow that it's still imprinted on my mind. It was as if you were watching a movie and all these things were happening at once—but they were barely moving. Lana was thrown around as much as I was."

Walsh was tossed screaming against the windshield, shattering it. At the same time, with a mother's instinct, she grabbed Jaye and held him to her. The possibility that he would be harmed bothered her far more than the thought of injury to herself. She also knew that her husband would be devastated if anything happened to the boy.

The few remaining construction workers on

the bridge were momentarily transfixed by the loud crash and its suddenness. Near them, however, a young man named Steve Hickey, who along with his three-year-old nephew Kevin had been walking to the other side, did not even pause to see what was happening. Hickey scooped Kevin off his feet and raced with the child across the bridge and out of danger. As he did so, the onrushing car and truck, now locked together in a fatal embrace, hurtled forward in a wild cacophony of terror.

In a desperate last-second attempt to avoid hitting the car in front of him, Charles Steeves had tried to swing the behemoth he piloted to the left, into the narrow space between the Lang auto and the side of the bridge. He had failed. As his truck telescoped the car, the two vehicles ploughed through black and yellow traffic barriers and construction equipment, and finally rammed the cement forms and steel reinforcing rods with which the new guardrails would be built.

"The impact of the crash tore the tires from my car," explains Lang. "Then there was a loud, grating, grinding sound, like a teacher scratching her nails across a blackboard—only a hundred times as loud. Sparks were flying and everyone was screaming and by this time the truck had jackknifed and we were still moving forward."

Two seconds later, both vehicles veered to the right and plunged into space.

"I tried my best to keep my truck on the bridge," Steeves said later. "I never dreamed we would both end up in the river. There was no guardrail, and when I saw that my truck was headed for the edge, I thought 'I have to get out, she's going to blow.' I jumped at the last minute, and I could feel her starting to go when I jumped. I don't remember hitting the ground. I jumped up and hollered at the men working there to run and get off the bridge."

Jumping from his moving truck, Steeves fell headlong into a series of steel reinforcing bars that were imbedded upright in cement. Despite the fact that his side was badly lacerated and one of the rods was driven into his leg, he got to his feet and scrambled to safety, blood spurting from his leg as he did so.

The Wild Inferno

Then the first explosion came.

Bystanders watched in utter horror as the flying sparks set off by the collision ignited the gasoline that gushed from the ruptured tanker. The fuel seemed to burn evenly for a fraction of a second, then shredded the steel of the truck like the burst of a bomb. A waterfall of fire poured from the bridge as the compartmentalized fuel bays were torn open, one after the other. As each exploded, the sound ricocheted along the river, shook buildings a kilometre away, and sent a tower of flame higher than the trees. This was followed by a pall of smoke seen in Saint John.

Anna Lang's battered Buick hit the water, right side up.

"When we were being pushed along the bridge, there was so much racket," says Lang, "but when we went over the side my car seemed to spin around and I could see the [Mandarin House] restaurant. I knew it should have been behind me, though, and for a minute I had no idea where I was. I suppose the car was in the air at the time. Then I guess we went into the water. For a minute everything was silent and I can recall thinking, 'Oh God, it's all over.' Suddenly, there was water in the car."

A moment later the transport tractor fell into the river on its roof, a metre away. Then the shattered tanker landed on its side, disgorging burning gasoline into the water in shimmering, scorching, deadly waves. Further explosions came, each adding more fuel to the wild inferno. The leaping, crackling, roaring flames obliterated all signs of life.

But there was life.

"My car sank right away," explains Lang, "and water started pouring in. I kept holding my breath until I thought my lungs would burst. The next thing I knew, Lana was holding Jaye and I was floating over them, out the right window. I remember hitting the surface and gasping for air, but the whole river was burning and I could still hardly breath. It was so *hot*.

"Because we had been to exercise class, both

Lana and I had a lot more clothing on than we normally would have. I was wearing jeans and a couple of heavy sweaters over my tights and leotards. As soon as the jeans and sweaters got wet, they weighed a tonne so I knew I had to get rid of them if I was going to be any help to Lana and Jaye. By this time they had got to the surface, so I started swimming for shore.

"As I was swimming I was saying, 'Lana, I'll be back, I'll be back.' She never heard me say that and I never heard her say, 'Anna, please come back for me.' I guess we both thought these things but we never mouthed the words."

Now the fire was spreading farther and farther over the river. Rings of flame alternated with patches of clear water as Anna fought her way through the inferno towards shore, 40 m away. "I tried to duck under each ring and then get my breath in the clear spaces," she says, "but that was not always possible. It was so hot on top, I felt better if I stayed under. Then I remember getting to shore and trying very hard to quickly take my outer clothes off. When I finally got rid of them, I went back in."

The Rescue

While Anna was struggling with her wet clothes, Lana Walsh and Jaye were having difficulties in the water.

"I was trying to hold Jaye up," she said later.

"We had gone down several times and I was getting tired. So tired. And the heat was unbearable. Everything was burning. My big sweater was pulling me down and I was getting so tired that I was starting to give up. I wanted to save Jaye, but the heat was so bad. Everything was burning and I had to keep pushing his head under the water. Then I looked and he wasn't moving, and I thought he was dead. But then his eyelids moved. The water was burning and Jaye's hair was on fire. Then I saw Anna on the shore, but she seemed so far away.

"I saw blood pouring down her face. She was taking off her jeans and sneakers, and I can see her now splashing into the water. She came back for us. The water was burning but she really came back for us."

"As soon as I couldn't feel the bottom anymore, I started swimming," recalls Lang. "I decided to grab Jaye instead of his mother because I was afraid she might panic and drown us all. I knew if I got Jaye, she would hold on. That's what happened. He had taken swimming lessons the winter before and I think that's what saved him."

The young boy floated on his back and his mother held onto him with her left hand, keeping herself afloat with her right. When his hair began to burn, she pushed him under to put the flames out. "I finally got to them and grabbed Jaye by the shoulder and started pulling both of them after me. Every so often my hair would go on fire and I had to keep ducking to put it out. I believe Lana was in too much shock to do that.

"As we got closer to the shore, everything seemed to be so quiet. Jaye was very quiet and so was Lana. I guess there were people up on the bridge watching, although I was not aware of it. I was just too busy."

But not everyone was on the bridge watching.

Two local youths, Eric Sparks and Jack Chaisson, both 18, had been in a car behind the gasoline tanker. They had witnessed the accident, but had been able to stop before becoming involved in it.

When they saw the vehicles plunge off the bridge, they left their car and made their way down the south embankment to the edge of the river. Almost without thinking, Sparks took off his pants and waded into the water to help with the rescue. By this time Anna was approaching the shore with Jaye and Lana in tow.

"There was still a lot of burning gas around us, but I could see those guys ahead of me," recalls Anna. "They were standing on the bank and one had no pants on. I remember thinking, 'Why is he in his underwear?'" Then I saw him coming into the water. I kept saying, 'Please help me God. I'm not going to make it.'

"Eric got to me just as my feet touched the bottom again. He grabbed Jaye and handed him to Jack and then he got Lana. They had to carry them because Lana wasn't able to walk. At this point, I didn't want to look at her, or at Jaye. I didn't know what they looked like, if they were cut, had broken arms or anything. I didn't know what I had done to them."

Finally Anna managed to pull herself up onto the rocky shore, her head, face, and neck now severely burned, her face bloody, and what was left of her clothes in tatters. She would not know until later that she had two cracked vertebrae in her back.

Even though they were now on shore, they were far from safe. Across the water the crackling flames engulfed more and more of the tanker, but still the flow of gasoline had not abated.

"We've got to get out of here right away," Jack said. "That thing is going to blow again."

He had no sooner said the words than the last of several explosions boomed across the water, spewing a geyser of steam, mud, flaming gasoline, and hunks of shattered steel into the air. The earth shook and little Jaye clasped Jack Chaisson in a terrified but silent bear-hug. Eric knelt on the ground beside Lana, placed his arms under her back and legs, and hoisted her into his arms. Anna, by now so exhausted she felt she would drop, wobbled unsteadily for a moment, then straggled along after the others, away from the flames. Steadily, painfully, doggedly, the group made its way along the rocky shore, crossed under the bridge and then, helped by several others including trucker Charles Steeves, managed to reach the top of the bank and safety.

The first ambulance arrived four minutes later.

Anna, Lana, and Jaye were all hospitalized as a result of their ordeal. Anna's injuries were the most serious and she was incapacitated for the longest time. Her back healed on its own, but the third-degree burns to her face and head required skin grafting, plastic surgery, and hair transplants. She was well enough, however, to fly to Ottawa two years later to receive her Cross of Valour—although she still claims she did not deserve it. She and Lana Walsh are still friends.

To this day neither feels safe crossing the Hammond River bridge.

▲ ▼ ► ▼ ▲ ▼ ► ▼ ▲ ▼ ► ▼ ▲ ▼ ► ▼ ▲ ►

THE CASE OF THE UNUSED
SEAT BELT

by Donald J. Sobol

Just another fatal car accident? See if you can
solve this mini-mystery as quickly as ace
inspector Dr. Haledjian does.

When Inspector Winters slammed on the
brakes, Dr. Haledjian would have been pitched
through the windshield but for his seat belt.

The reason for the inspector's sudden stop
was horribly evident.

A red sports car had come racing around the
hairpin turn on the mountain road ahead. Out of
control, the car had crashed through the guard rail.

The impact didn't stop the car, but it flung the
driver straight up. He seemed to hang in the air a
moment before plunging out of sight.

Haledjian and the inspector scrambled down
the 60-m precipice.

The driver's body was a shattered mass of
broken bones and blood. About 30 m beyond, the
sports car lay on its side, a total wreck.

"Strange," muttered the inspector, pointing to the seat belt, obviously unused, which lay in the fresh blood that covered the driver's bucket seat.

"I doubt that even a seat belt could have saved his life," said Haledjian.

"I better telephone the state police," said the inspector. "It looks like one more traffic fatality for the year. Do you think he fell asleep at the wheel?"

"No," said Haledjian. "He was murdered."

Why murder?

Solution

The fact that blood soaked the driver's seat though he had been cast free of the car when it hit the rail indicated he had bled before the accident: i.e., he had been killed and placed in the car, which had then been sent down the mountain road.

MADELEINE

by Arthur Prager and Emily Prager

During World War II, many brave people fought behind enemy lines. At any moment, they could be seized, then tortured or executed. This is the true story of one daring spy, a young woman whose code name was Madeleine.

It was the summer of 1943 in occupied[1] Paris. A pretty young woman hid behind some leafy plants in the greenhouse of the Pasteur Institute. She had shoulder-length dark hair, olive skin, and large brown eyes.

A portable radio transmitter sat on the stone floor in front of her. She tapped urgently at the telegraph key, sending a coded message across the English Channel. A secret listener somewhere north of London would receive it. She was a British agent—a spy.

From time to time she looked anxiously toward the door. The Gestapo[2] were searching for her. Their trucks were moving back and forth through the streets with their radio direction-finding antennas straining to pick up her signals and follow them to her hiding place. Quickly, she finished her message and signed off with her code name, MADELEINE. Then she took her transmitter apart and folded it into its carrying case.

MADELEINE was not her real name. She was Noor Inayat Khan, and she was half Indian. In her own language this meant "Light of Womanhood." Her family had sent her to school in Paris. She made many friends there. Later she wrote children's books. French children loved her books so much that she was asked to read her stories aloud on the radio. But then the war came, and the Nazis invaded France. India was part of the British Empire, and that made Noor an enemy to the Germans. She escaped to England just before the first German troops arrived in Paris.

Safe in England, she could have resumed her career as a writer. But the country was at war. The Germans were her enemies too. She joined the Royal Air Force and was sent to radio school. Because she knew several languages, she was asked to volunteer for duty in British Intelligence. It was dangerous work, but Noor knew that she was needed. She knew she would make a better spy than most English girls. She could hide in Paris because she had many old school friends there.

After two months of training, she was dropped behind the German lines in occupied France, to join the PROSPER network, which helped the French resistance[3] to hold up the advance of the German armies. PROSPER blew up bridges and rail tracks, and sent important news about military movements to the British War Office.

Noor's message from the Pasteur Institute reported terrible news. Most of the agents of the PROSPER network and many of their French friends had been arrested by the Nazis.

A telephone on the wall of the greenhouse buzzed sharply. Noor put the receiver to her ear without speaking. It was her lookout, calling from an upstairs room in the Institute building, where he was watching the street below.

"Hurry! Get out! They've just turned the corner."

An ominous gray command car painted with the black swastikas of the German Army had entered the street. It crawled slowly toward the Institute. On its metal roof an antenna rotated slowly, round and round, tracking and searching.

Noor snapped the locks on the suitcase, which held her transmitter. It looked like a small overnight bag. She slipped out of the greenhouse and across a grassy lawn, through a gap in a hedge into the next street. There she mingled with the afternoon crowds. No one would have suspected that she was a spy.

Noor ducked into an alley, past rows of rubbish bins, and into the back door of a small, red brick house. She ran up the stairs to an attic room. There a short, stocky, bearded man dressed in the blue smock of a French worker was waiting for her. He was her control, and his code name was SERGE. No one knew what his real name was.

"It was too close this time, MADELEINE," he said. "A few more minutes and you would have been in a Gestapo interrogation unit. The other PROSPER agents have all been arrested. Now the Nazis can use all of their tracking equipment to locate your transmissions. It is only a matter of days before they succeed in trapping you. You must leave. We can smuggle you to the coast of Normandy, and back to England."

England meant safety. A place where Noor would be able to sleep at night without the constant fear that the Gestapo would break down her door and drag her away to prison and torture. It was tempting. It was also impossible.

"I am the only trained radio operator left," she told the bearded man. "Somebody has to report to England. Without my transmitter, the Paris resistance would be cut off from English supplies."

"It could mean your life, and the lives of your friends."

"We are at war. There are thousands of soldiers whose lives are in danger. They can't ask to be sent home from the battle front just because they might get hurt."

SERGE looked at her sadly. "As you wish," he said.

He read the copy of the last message she had sent to England. Then he touched a match to it and watched it burn to ashes. Noor slipped out of the house and back into the crowded street.

In a country house somewhere north of London, another woman in uniform of the First Aid Nursing Yeomanry, handed a folded yellow paper to her commanding officer.

"Latest message from MADELEINE, sir," she said, standing at attention.

"Are you sure she sent it? It could be the Germans sending us false information."

"I'm sure, sir. I was at radio school with her. I know her 'fist'—her touch on the telegraph key. That's why I was chosen to be her 'godmother' on this end, to receive her messages from France."

After dismissing the young woman, the colonel locked the door. Then he decoded and read MADELEINE's message. Opening a safe behind his desk, he drew out a green folder stamped MOST SECRET. A typewritten label on its cover said simply, MADELEINE. It gave Noor's history, her record in radio school, and how she had impressed the officer who approved her for intelligence duties with her courage and her quick mind. She had given up the chance for an officer's commission in the Royal Air Force when she chose to be a radio operator behind the German lines. The PROSPER network was her first assignment.

The colonel closed the folder and stared out of the window at the ancient elm trees in the garden. He thought of Noor. He remembered how she had been shunned at first by the other girls at the radio school. She was strange to them, a dark-skinned foreigner. Later, when they got to know her, they all loved her. Then he thought of the information he had received only that morning. The arrests of the other PROSPER agents were not just the result of good German police work. There was a traitor among them. They had been betrayed to the Gestapo!

MADELEINE was still free because she was a recent arrival in Paris. The traitor had given away the agents' names before she had come. But the Germans would find out about her soon. Perhaps they already had. There might still be time to bring her back to England and save her life.

But what about her messages? Could British Intelligence and the French resistance forces spare her before a new network could be set up? Even a week or a few days would be precious. Was her life important compared with the thousands of lives that might be saved by the information about German troop movements she might send from Paris?

The colonel shook his head and put Noor's folder back in the safe. Noor would stay in Paris.

Noor moved around Paris, from hiding place to hiding place, helped by old school friends who knew they were risking their own lives by sheltering her. But she could not move fast enough. One afternoon, as she sat transmitting a coded message to England from a house in the Paris suburb of Clichy, the door of her room crashed open. She found herself face to face with a detachment of German soldiers. Behind them were two Gestapo agents in long, black leather coats. One of them pointed a Luger pistol at her. It was useless to resist. She was handcuffed and brought to Gestapo headquarters.

The Nazis questioned her about her work and about the people who had helped her. She refused to tell them anything. They beat her, but she still refused to talk. While she was being moved from the interrogation room to her cell, she broke away from her captors and tried to escape. She was recaptured and cruelly beaten again. Nothing the Nazis could do could force a single word from her.

One night Noor and two other British prisoners managed to climb out of a window to the roof of the building. They crawled to the edge of the roof. Then they jumped to the building next door. But the street below was full of German soldiers. They were captured. Once again Noor was severely punished.

The Gestapo commandant realized at last that she would never talk. He stamped her records PARTICULARLY DANGEROUS, and ordered her sent to a prison in the Black Forest region of Germany. There she was chained like an animal in a cell so tiny that she could neither stand up nor lie down. She had to stay in a crouching position. They kept her that way, half-starved, for ten months. Still she refused to talk.

At last the Germans lost patience with her. It

was clear that they would not get any information out of her. They sent her to the death camp at Dachau, where she was executed by a firing squad.

When news of her death arrived in England, King George VI held a special ceremony at Buckingham Palace. He read the story of her courage aloud, and then, even though she was no longer alive, he awarded her a medal, the George Cross, which is given only "for the most conspicuous courage in circumstances of extreme danger."

1. **occupied**: under the control of ("occupied" by) enemies, in this case Nazis
2. **Gestapo**: the secret state police of the Nazis
3. **resistance**: a secret organization of people working to fight against ("resist") the enemy

ORDEAL IN THE ARCTIC

by Robert Mason Lee

When a Canadian Forces Hercules aircraft crashed near the North Pole in October, 1991, the story made headlines around the world. One of the passengers was Sue Hillier. The other survivors knew Sue and fellow passenger Bob Thomson were too badly hurt to move. They left them outside, covered with a tarpaulin, while they took refuge in the tail section of the wrecked plane. More than a day later, help had not arrived, and hope was running out.

Sue had heard someone through the wind, had seen the beam of light.

"Guys ogay?"

He sounded so cold; his voice was shaking, his words half formed.

"Okay."

"Godda go."

She was alone again. Bob no longer talked to her. He said he was tired. She imagined he had gone to sleep.

She was on her back, and the snow came in from the sides of her shelter. It drifted over her face. She waited until it was several centimetres thick before brushing it away. She didn't have the strength. She let it pile up until she could no longer breathe. Then she found the strength and brushed it, as high as she could, to either side. Snow drifted back down the sides and covered her face again. She didn't have the strength.

She decided to get up. She brushed the snow away, removed the diesel-soaked rag over her face. She worked her elbows up her side, and actually levered herself into a semi-upright position. This was achieved at great expense in pain. She fought the nausea and the fainting. She believed her neck to be broken; it was too painful to support her head. She leaned on one elbow, grabbed her collar with the free hand, trying to support the neck. She heaved on the collar and managed to poke her head above the shelter.

Blackness. The wind blasted her face, and ice spicules pricked her skin. It hurt, and then her face was numb.

She sank back down. She couldn't move for quite a while. She thought about her pain for a long time. It felt as if someone had cut off her head with a guillotine.

She worked the rag back over her face. The smell made her feel sick. She wondered if she could still make her legs move. She reached down and tugged at one leg, trying to make it respond. She felt the flesh tearing, her hand being soaked in new blood. Then she lay still.

She had, until now, made a routine of raising her back off the ice, to save her kidneys and vital organs. She did this by arching her hips and raising herself on the points of her shoulder blades. But her shoulders had frozen and been rubbed raw against the ice. She had felt the frostbite enter them, felt the flesh being rubbed off the bones. She no longer arched her back.

The snow drifted over her mask, piling several centimetres high. She let it.

She imagined her future, saw herself frozen in her ice coffin until spring, when the thaw would reveal her body. Perhaps the animals would get to her body first; in any case, she would not be returned to her parents until spring. She thought of the grief this would cause them, felt their grief, and she cried, and heard the baying of wolves.

I'm not going out a nut case. I'm going to be calm.

Sue prepared her list, including everyone who was important to her. She was a gregarious woman, and the list was long. Her primary relationships were at the top of the list. She spent a long time talking with her mother, and let her go. Then she dealt with Adrian, her boyfriend. She had many things to say to them, private things.

She went to her father, and her sisters, visited with them. Then her relatives and her friends, her clients, everyone she was leaving behind. She did not mind so much the going, but she wanted more than anything to go on peaceful terms. She made her peace, and she heard the snuffling of an animal by her ear.

A polar bear?

It padded around the outline of her body. She felt the weight of it on the packed snow. It walked the length of her, rounded her feet, and came up the other side.

Maybe it will go away.

It stopped at her hips. It began to dig. She felt it digging towards her hips and thighs, where the flesh was laid open to the bone.

It's the blood. It's the same leg I was digging at. It smells fresh blood. It would start there; it would start by gnawing at her hip bone.

Its snout entered the cavity it had dug, and snuffled for the blood. She felt its breath on her skin.

It withdrew.

Nothing happened for a while. Then it crept up her belly and chest. She felt its paws. It stopped, with its weight on her chest. She heard it panting.

Not without seeing my face.

She summoned the last of her will. This was not courage but a type of stubbornness. She moved her hands, pulled the rag from her face. Snow fell into her eyes and mouth. She lunged almost upright, ignoring the stabbing protest from her neck. Snow fell from her face. She let out a scream.

She opened her eyes, looked directly into his. He blinked, once, and pulled his head back; then he moved his nose towards her face. Sue pulled her head back in astonishment. They considered each other.

A white arctic wolf, the most beautiful animal she had ever seen. His face was radiant, seeming to glow in the darkness. His fur was long and spiky, and there was soft white down underneath. There was a black flash running from his forehead down his nose. His tongue was pink, and white vapours marked his panting.

His eyes were striking—as striking as Sue's own. A pale, iridescent blue. They shone. They stared into Sue's eyes, neither malicious nor curious. They simply regarded her.

Sue screamed again.

The wolf cocked his head. He turned, not hurriedly, and stepped off her chest. He padded away, stopping once for a final look back. Then he disappeared into the darkness.

Sue sank back.

I'm not dying here. And I'm not getting eaten by some wolf. I'm not freezing to death. If I have to, I'll crawl to Alert.

Sue went back to the people on her list, starting from the top. She told them she'd be coming home.

The Canadian search-and-rescue technicians—SARtechs for short—parachuted into the crash site during a howling blizzard. They broke all the rules for paratroops: they could not see because of the darkness and blowing snow, they jumped far too close to the ground, and in a fierce crosswind. The SARtechs risked their lives, even though they were not sure anyone from the Hercules crash was left alive.

"Black," said one of the SARtechs. Code for dead.

"Another one. Another black."

The tail, Arnie thought. The others must have gone inside the tail and died there. He made for the tail section, hunched against the storm, calling: "Hello? Hello?"

The wind was in his face; there were no voices on the wind. He reached the entrance of the tail and shouted: "Anybody in there?"

Aw, damn. After all this.

"Hey! Anybody hear me?"

"Ahhss."

Was that a noise? It sounded like something between a hiss and a moan.

"Anybody here?"

The voice, struggling with the word "Yes," would have alarmed a less composed man. It was an old voice, thickened almost beyond recognition by pain and cold.

"How many? How many are you?"

"Leven."

Eleven. That's what he'd said. Hot dog! Arnie felt something marvellous. He tried to focus on the feeling, pin it down. It was joy.

"In here, boys! Let's go!"

Arnie told his men to rig chutes over the opening. He stepped inside. He stepped on someone, who moaned in agony. He cast the beam from his headlamp around the tail, lighting walls thick with ice and a huddled mass of humanity, filthy and black. They looked like rats in a stinking hold. The tail smelled of burnt things, fuel, and urine. It smelled like a crash site. It smelled wonderful.

One of Arnie's SARtechs stepped in beside him.

"Careful," Arnie said. "The floor's alive."

There was a shuffling movement. Someone said something.

"Who's that?"

One of the figures lifted its head. Arnie shone his light. The man's face was streaked and grimy, the skin beneath the smudges white as snow. The lips were grey, or blue. The man looked like the risen dead.

"Smee."

"Jesus. I know you."

Sgt. Paul West's ghastly face blinked in the beam of light. "Whos air?"

"I'm Arnie Macauley. I'm the SARtech leader from Greenwood. And these are my boys."

Other survivors were beginning to come around; cutting the wind from the tail was already having an effect. So was the human presence. The SARtechs heard curious, nonsensical mumbles.

They moved carefully about the tail and went gently to work. They spoke to the survivors and listened to them babble on, in voices thick and slow.

One of the SARtechs pulled a pair of mittens over the hands of a survivor. "It would be a privilege for me to give you these," he said, with odd formality. "My mother made them for me."

Many of the survivors, returning to themselves, began to cry uncontrollably. Many of the SARtechs, without ceasing to work, cried with them, wrapping them in parachutes. Every survivor was in the severe, final stage of hypothermia, perched on the thin ledge between stupor and death. Methodically, expertly, the SARtechs went about the delicate task of helping them off that ledge.

Bob and Sue were shouting in their tombs. Both had heard strange voices and started to call out at once. Each was surprised to realize that the other was alive.

"Here!" they called. "We're aliiii!"

One of the search party thought he heard something. He walked downwind.

"Where are you?" he hollered into the wind.

"Here! We're here!"

The SARtech walked about in the storm, seeing nothing but crusted snow and rock. He passed within a metre of them more than once.

"I can't see you! Where are you?"

Bob still had his one good hand. He closed it around his little metal spar. He still had one good hand and a metal spar. He tried to poke at the tarpaulin.

The SARtech thought he saw something move under the snow.

Sue and Bob survived, as did 11 others from the plane. (Five people died, including the plane's pilot.) By the time the SARtechs reached them, the survivors had spent 34 hours in the midst of a howling blizzard, during which temperatures dipped to −60°C. It was amazing that anyone survived at all.

Astonish Me

▲▼▶▼▶▲▼▶▼▶▲▼▶▼▶▲▼▶▼▶

It was a dark and stormy night.
Suddenly a scream pierced the air ...

Charles M. Schulz, Peanuts *cartoon (1988)*
with a nod to Edward Bulwer-Lytton (1840)

▲▼▶▼▶▲▼▶▼▶▲▼▶▼▶▲▼▶▼▶

▲ ▼ ▶ ▼ ▶ ▲ ▼ ▶ ▼ ▶ ▲ ▼ ▶ ▼ ▶ ▲ ▼ ▶ ▼ ▶

THE WISH

by Roald Dahl

"Step on a crack—break your mother's back!"
Remember avoiding cracks in the sidewalk, or
jumping over the last step in a staircase, in
case something bad happened? Roald Dahl
takes this childhood obsession a terrifying
step further.

Under the palm of one hand the child became
aware of the scab of an old cut on his knee-cap. He
bent forward to examine it closely. A scab was
always a fascinating thing; it presented a special
challenge he was never able to resist.

Yes, he thought, I will pick it off, even if it
isn't ready, even if the middle of it sticks, even if it
hurts like anything.

With a fingernail he began to explore cautiously around the edges of the scab. He got the
nail underneath it, and when he raised it, but ever
so slightly, it suddenly came off, the whole hard
brown scab came off beautifully, leaving an interesting little circle of smooth red skin.

Nice. Very nice indeed. He rubbed the circle and it didn't hurt. He picked up the scab, put it on his thigh and flipped it with a finger so that it flew away and landed on the edge of the carpet, the enormous red and black and yellow carpet that stretched the whole length of the hall from the stairs on which he sat to the front door in the distance. A tremendous carpet. Bigger than the tennis lawn. Much bigger than that. He regarded it gravely, settling his eyes upon it with mild pleasure. He had never really noticed it before, but now, all of a sudden, the colours seemed to brighten mysteriously and spring out at him in a most dazzling way.

You see, he told himself, I know how it is. The red parts of the carpet are red-hot lumps of coal. What I must do is this: I must walk all the way along it to the front door without touching them. If I touch the red I will be burnt. As a matter of fact, I will be burnt up completely. And the black parts of the carpet … yes, the black parts are snakes, poisonous snakes, adders mostly, and cobras, thick like tree-trunks round the middle, and if I touch one of *them*, I'll be bitten and I'll die before tea time. And if I get across safely, without being burnt and without being bitten, I will be given a puppy for my birthday tomorrow.

He got to his feet and climbed higher up the stairs to obtain a better view of this vast tapestry of colour and death. Was it possible? Was there enough yellow? Yellow was the only colour he was allowed to walk on. Could it be done? This was not a journey to be undertaken lightly; the risks were too great for that. The child's face—a fringe of white-gold hair, two large blue eyes, a small pointed chin—peered down anxiously over the banisters. The yellow was a bit thin in places and there were one or two widish gaps, but it did seem to go all the way along to the other end. For someone who had only yesterday triumphantly travelled the whole length of the brick path from the stables to the summer-house without touching the cracks, this carpet thing should not be too difficult. Except for the snakes. The mere thought of snakes sent a fine electricity of fear running like pins down the backs of his legs and under the soles of his feet.

He came slowly down the stairs and advanced to the edge of the carpet. He extended one small sandaled foot and placed it cautiously upon a patch of yellow. Then he brought the other foot up, and there was just enough room for him to stand with the two feet together. There! He had started! His bright oval face was curiously intent, a shade whiter perhaps than before, and he was holding his arms out sideways to assist his balance. He took another step, lifting his foot high over a patch of black, aiming carefully with his toe for a narrow channel of yellow on the other side. When he had completed the second step he paused to rest, standing very stiff and still. The narrow channel of yellow ran forward unbroken for at least five yards and he advanced gingerly along it, bit by bit, as though walking a tight-rope. Where it finally curled off sideways, he had to take another long stride, this time over a vicious looking mixture of black and red. Halfway across he began to wobble. He waved his arms around wildly, windmill fashion, to keep his balance, and he got across safely and rested again on the other side. He was quite breathless now, and so tense he stood high on his toes all the time, arms out sideways, fists clenched. He was on a big safe island of yellow. There was lots of room on it, he couldn't possibly fall off, and he stood there resting, hesitating, waiting, wishing he could stay for ever on this big safe yellow island. But the fear of not getting the puppy compelled him to go on.

Step by step, he edged further ahead, and between each one he paused to decide exactly where next he should put his foot. Once, he had a choice of ways, either to left or right, and he chose the left because although it seemed the more difficult, there was not so much black in that direction. The black was what made him nervous. He glanced quickly over his shoulder to see how far he had come. Nearly halfway. There could be no turning back now. He was in the middle and he couldn't turn back and he couldn't jump off sideways either because it was too far, and when he looked at all the red and all the black that lay ahead of him, he felt that old sudden sickening surge of panic in his chest—like last Easter time, that afternoon when he got lost all alone in the darkest part of Piper's Wood.

He took another step, placing his foot care-fully upon the only little piece of yellow within reach, and this time the point of the foot came with-in a centimetre of some black. It wasn't touching the black, he could see it wasn't touching, he could see the small line of yellow separating the toe of his sandal from the black; but the snake stirred as though sensing the nearness, and raised its head and gazed at the foot with bright beady eyes, watching to see if it was going to touch.

"I'm not touching you! You mustn't bite me! You know I'm not touching you!"

Another snake slid up noiselessly beside the first, raised its head, two heads now, two pairs of eyes staring at the foot, gazing at a little naked place just below the sandal strap where the skin showed through. The child went high up on his toes and stayed there, frozen stiff with terror. It was minutes before he dared to move again.

The next step would have to be a really long one. There was this deep curling river of black that ran clear across the width of the carpet, and he was forced by his position to cross it at its widest part. He thought first of trying to jump it, but decided he couldn't be sure of landing accurately on the nar-row band of yellow the other side. He took a deep breath, lifted one foot, and inch by inch he pushed it out in front of him, far far out, then down and down until at last the tip of his sandal was across and resting safely on the edge of the yellow. He leaned forward, transferring his weight to this front foot. Then he tried to bring the back foot up as well. He strained and pulled and jerked his body, but the legs were too wide apart and he couldn't make it. He tried to get back again. He couldn't do that either. He was doing the splits and he was properly stuck. He glanced down and saw this deep curling river of black underneath him. Parts of it were stirring now, and uncoiling and sliding and beginning to shine with a dreadful oily glister[1]. He wobbled, waved his arms frantically to keep his balance, but that seemed to make it worse. He was starting to go over. He was going over to the right, quite slowly he was going over, then faster and faster, and at the last moment, instinctively he put out a hand to break the fall and the next thing he saw was this bare hand of his going right into the middle of a great glistening mass of black and he gave one piercing cry of terror as it touched.

Outside in the sunshine, far away behind the house, the mother was looking for her son.

1. **glister:** sparkle, glitter

▲ ▼ ▶ ▼ ▶ ▲ ▼ ▶ ▼ ▶ ▲ ▼ ▶ ▼ ▶ ▲ ▼ ▶ ▼ ▶ ▶

LOT 87

by Joy Burnett

Poor old Fosdick! He certainly didn't know what he was getting into when he bought that beautiful painting of a flower at an auction.

The heat was stifling in the back room of the country hotel, where the auction was being held. The attendance was sparse, and even those present appeared indifferent to the various lots offered for sale if the prices being paid was any indication. The Auctioneer's voice droned on,

"Lot 87—a floral painting by an unknown artist. Probably of Oriental origin."

It was a fairly small canvas, but completely dominated by a splash of royal purple—one flower of seemingly gigantic proportions. On one of its lower petals was a small black spider. The whole effect was garish—vulgar perhaps would have been a better description. Before the Auctioneer could start the bidding, a man in the front row called out

"£30[1]." For a moment a silence hung over the room, and then, as if unable to believe that such a price was offered for a mediocre work, the Auctioneer asked "£30?" The man who had bid nodded. "Thank you, thank you very much, Sir," was the reply. Then recovering his composure the Auctioneer asked, "Any advance on £30?"

Silence. Three times his hammer knocked.

"Sold to the gentleman for £30."

Eagerly the buyer put down his money, and hardly waiting for the painting to be wrapped, left the building clutching his new possession.

This strangely eager buyer was called Fosdick. He was an employee of a local insurance firm, and though holding a fairly responsible position, his whole life was centred on the past. The past when he was in the Army—Major Fosdick he was known as in those days. It was a glory Charles Fosdick could not forget, and he clung to it, still having his letters addressed to the rank he was no longer officially entitled to. Locally he was known as a bore—old Fosdick with his everlasting tales of battles long past, hot moonlight nights, gin slings, and incidents at the Club. To hear him talk, one would think he was the only one to have been east of Suez, was the general comment.

Now having reached home he unpacked the picture. Its cost momentarily pricked his conscience—£30, nearly half of what he had saved for a long-wanted holiday but quickly he dismissed this thought. What were two miserable weeks in some seaside hotel compared to this—a reminder of the past, and one which would long outlive any fortnight. How well the sight of that garish, purple bloom brought back thoughts of hot tropical nights, dances, and receptions at the Club, when people were pleased to make the acquaintance of Major Charles Fosdick.

After careful consideration, he decided the best place to hang the painting was on the wall over the fireplace. There it could be seen from any position in the room; it would be the first thing he saw when waking in the morning, and the last thing at night before switching off the bedside lamp.

He was still standing in the middle of the room admiring his handiwork when there came a knock at the door. It was Ogden, who had the apartment across the hall. He was a man who had lived for many years in the East, the one thing he had in common with Fosdick, whom he considered to be something of a fool. Now, Fosdick beamed at him, and pointing to the painting asked, "What about that, real beauty, eh?" Ogden looked from the picture to the man, then back to the picture. Was the old fool serious? Surely he recognized what it was—that common weed, prevalent in swamps, which gave off a stench to be avoided by all humans, but which attracted every insect, spider, or bat. He stepped forward to see what was on one of its lower petals. No doubt about it, the painter knew his subject, for he had included a spider. Looking at Fosdick, he found the man's enthusiasm for his new possession almost pathetic. Fortunately it was unnecessary to pass an opinion as Fosdick rattled on about jungle flowers and tropical beauty, so with a few nods of assent, he went, glad to escape the tirade, and forgetting what he had originally come for.

It became a routine for Fosdick to look at the picture when he first opened his eyes in the morning; and when he opened the door on returning from work, his head would swing round to look at the wall over the mantelpiece. And in the course of the evening while sitting in front of the fire reading his paper, his eyes would lift at intervals to the picture.

It was while thus sitting one evening, about a week after its arrival, that Fosdick's attention lingered on the painting. It was impossible, and yet, he could swear the spider had grown. He went to various parts of the room and viewed it from different angles. No doubt about it; whereas before it could only be seen as a small black spot from a distance, its shape and characteristics could now clearly be distinguished across the room. Several times that night when he was in bed, Fosdick switched on the lamp to view the painting, and it was many hours before he slept.

During the next day Fosdick was preoccupied, and the puzzled staff at the office commented among themselves. That night, he rushed home, eager to open the door and eager to find it had all been an illusion, and the painting normal once again. But it was not to be. With horror, he saw that the spider had grown even bigger. For some moments he felt panic, followed by suspicion, then anger. Was someone playing a practical joke on him? He took the painting down. A meticulous search failed to reveal any defect in the back of the canvas—it was the same as when he had first hung it. Before re-hanging it Fosdick stood for a considerable time staring at the picture, as if willing the spider to return to its normal size.

The next morning, haggard from a sleepless night, Fosdick was glad to leave the room and get to work. He found he was dreading entering the room that night, something completely different from his usual eager anticipation.

He opened the door and stood with his back to the painting. Perhaps if I don't watch it will diminish, he thought, but the compulsion became too strong and he looked. Good God? the thing was bigger than ever!

That night Fosdick spent sitting in his chair—watching and thinking. What would the ultimate outcome be? How big would it grow, and what would happen? In the early morning, starting awake from an exhausted doze, he forced his burning, aching eyes to once again concentrate on the monster, for monster it now was. And then as he stared, it happened—the spider moved, twitching as if awakening from a long slumber. With a howl of anguish Fosdick fled the house.

Work was impossible. He telephoned and gave the excuse of illness, and spent the day, walking, thinking, and slumbering on park benches. Towards nightfall it started to rain which forced his steps homeward. With sodden clothes, dishevelled, and near complete exhaustion, Fosdick stumbled along, while his tired brain went round in circles. I mustn't look. Every time I do it grows larger. Don't look! Don't look! Destroy it! That's it—destroy it! Burn it!

On entering his room he fell exhausted into his chair, his face turned away from the fireplace, and his eyes tightly shut. For some moments he sat thus, then gradually the compulsion overcame him—just a quick glance to make sure no further horror had occurred. He opened his eyes, and pure horror froze him. The thing was bigger than ever, and twitching as he had seen it do in the morning. But now, as he stared, it made a dash to the edge of the frame. Fosdick felt his hair rise up—*the spider was coming out!* In a second it was on the mantelshelf where it ran to the corner and paused, as if debating the best way to reach the floor. With a yell of terror, Fosdick ran from the room, down the stairs, out of the house, running anywhere to escape from the nightmare.

Hearing the noise in his room opposite, Ogden clicked his tongue in disapproval. The old fool must be ill, he thought, certainly his manner the last few days had been most odd. He went out into the hall, but there was nothing to see. He looked at Fosdick's half-open door, and then his eye was attracted downwards. Scuttling out of the room came a monster spider. Ogden stared at it with stupefaction—never in all his travels had he seen the like. A huge black, furry body with two bulbous, malicious eyes, the whole surrounded by a splay of wiry legs that looked almost muscular in their black, hairy strength. It made a lightning dart towards his leg. With equal speed Ogden brought his foot down upon it, crushing it beneath his heel. As in a dream, he saw it crumble into powder and from it arose a stench which made him gag.

At the same moment there came a resounding crash from Fosdick's room. Ogden flung the door open. The empty room with its overturned chair and spilt ashtray bore signs of the hasty departure of its late occupant. It was the painting which had fallen and in doing so had brought down several ornaments from the mantelpiece. It now lay face downwards among the debris in the fireplace, impaled on the steel spike at the top of the hearth stand which held brush, shovel, and tongs. There was a large, jagged hole in the canvas, with a split extending from edge to edge. Removing it from the spike, Ogden turned it over to assess the damage.

There was no longer any bloom of garish purple. All that remained was a dead, brown withered flower.

1. approximately $60 Cdn.

▲▼▶▼▲▼▶▼▲▼▶▼▲▼▶▼▲▼▶▼▲▶

ENCOUNTERS OF THE OLD KIND

by Reid Van Melle

Reid Van Melle was a grade nine student in
Saskatchewan when he wrote this story.
Perhaps it was inspired by a train journey to
visit relatives. On trains, time often seems to
stand still—or even go backwards.

Get off the train, go to Terminal 3, and
Grandma will meet you there." The plans ran
through my head. They finally decided I was big
enough to go on my own and it was about time.
Ever since I was five, I've been going on the train
twice a year to visit Grandma, but always with my
older sister. "Sit still, be quiet, don't act funny or
embarrass me," her voice would ring in my ears.
Now I'm by myself. I had trouble convincing them
to let me go, but nagging is a well-developed skill
in a 12-year-old.

The train is relatively empty for an evening
run between Toronto and the Ellington suburb, and
the people in the train seem to be fairly quiet. It

was never quiet like this when my sister was with me. There was always a baby crying or a group of office buddies talking amongst themselves. Everyone is sitting silently though—very silently. Just relaxing alone.

The silence seems to be growing—ominous. The train bucks, and I look outside, counting the lights as they go past—one, two, three, four, five ... I tear my blurred eyes away from the window and survey the train. All is still. Too still.

Then from the far corner of the train, a body stirs, covered in a long black overcoat. The man gets up and stands, smiling at me. His features are indistinct, except his eyes, which twitch when he smiles. I shift in my seat and swallow.

"Hi, sonny," he drawls, "how have you been? You mind if I sit beside you?" He walks towards me, smiling and twitching.

I grasp my leather seat with one hand while I reach up to tap the man in front of me on the shoulder: "Excuse me, sir." No response; the man continues reading the paper.

Meanwhile, the smiling face has drawn closer, and the man it belongs to eases himself into the cushioned chair beside mine. He clears his throat and rasps out, "That won't help, sonny. I just want to talk. No harm done." Again—that smile—and a frown. "How's your mother?" He spits on the floor.

My eyes race around the room, across the faces of hypnotically frozen passengers. The train hums smoothly, "Fine."

The man snarls from his throat, "She wasn't always so good you know. She was sometimes a very bad girl, very bad."

I look down, and then up again—the man has tears in his eyes. He sniffles loudly, "Your mother killed me. She killed me with her own two hands."

The words disgust me, "Who are you? You're crazy. I don't know who you are and you don't know who I am. Get out of my life!" Something must be wrong with me.

He smiles consolingly, "Oh, I guess I don't blame her. I just thought … " He ruffles my hair. "Well, you being such a good kid and all, I just thought you should know the truth."

I struggle to breathe against my tightening chest and fast heartbeat. I don't know what to do. The man isn't saying anything. Just waiting—testing me. I spring. In one leap, I'm over him and shaking people's shoulders.

The man laughs again. It slowly subsides as I back into a corner breathless. He smiles at me and his eyes twitch. He stands up, and offers his hand to me, "Come on, sonny, there's no need to be afraid. Sit over here, and I'll tell you a story. You deserve to know … the truth."

This time, as he talks, a great fear washes over me. Not just fear, but terror. Real and honest-to-goodness terror. Terror enough to make people do things that would seem crazy at any other moment. No thoughts of control or heroics encompass me. I just turn and start bashing my head against the double-paned, reinforced glass of the train window. Once, twice, three, four, five ... I tear my blurred eyes from the window and survey the train.

Everyone is acting very normal. A man is snoring in the corner and a mother is trying to quiet her crying child. Self-hypnosis. Somehow, I put myself under self-hypnosis and dreamed up that whole encounter. But why? I'm crazy. I just gotta calm down. I've been spooking myself the whole trip. Just calm down. Forget it.

The train starts slowing, grinding to a halt. I try to turn my thoughts from the train trip, but I can't. It all seemed too real.

Revenge?

I get off the train, carried by the milling crowd. I find Terminal 3, and sit down in a padded seat. Calm down. Grandma will be here right away. I look at myself in a mirror on the wall. I look terrible. My face is white and my hair plastered to my forehead with cold sweat. Where is she?

I try to clean myself up. For some reason, I think I'll feel embarrassed or maybe even guilty if she sees me this way. As I try to comb my hair in place, Grandma walks through the door. She seems a new woman. Smiling. She looks younger—eyes alive and smile bright, like a little girl. She walks quicker as she sees me and opens her arms wide.

I hug her warmly. "Hi, Grandma. How are you?"

"Fine. How was the trip?"

"All right, I guess."

She smiles and clasps my hand in hers. "C'mon, Billy, let's go. I want to show you something."

"All right, Grandma, let's go."

I follow her outside to her car. She turns and faces me, her eyes bright with excitement. "Get in, Billy." She opens the door. "I'd like you to meet your Grandpa." She smiles real wide.

"But Grandma, Grandpa is dead. Grandma, Grandpa's been dead since Mom was just a little girl." Oh God. "Grandma … " I scream, but she cuts me off and pushes me into the cushioned seat of her car, slamming the door behind me.

"Hi, sonny," a familiar voice says.

Without knowing why, I turn and face quietly twitching eyes.

▲▼▶▼▶▲▼▶▼▶▲▼▶▼▶▲▼▶▼▶

A HELL OF A STORY

by H. R. F. Keating

Old Pete thought it'd be a snap looking after a
young boy being held for ransom. But the
boy had ideas of his own.

They snatched the Oil Sheik's kid, exactly as
planned, at 11:06 precisely. There were no difficulties. The girl they'd got for the job distracted the
boy's bodyguard for just long enough. The boy
himself reacted to the little flying helicopter on a
string just as they'd calculated he would. But then a
kid of eight, and an Arab from the sticks first time
in London, that part couldn't have gone wrong.
Worth every penny of all it had cost, that toy.

Everything else had gone like clockwork, too.
No traffic holdups when they were moving away
from the park. No trouble in the changeover of
cars. No one about in the mews to see it, and not a
bit of fuss out of the lad. Quiet, big eyed, doing
what he was told, scared to death most likely.

So inside half an hour he was safely in the
room they'd prepared for him in the old house

waiting for demolition up over Kilburn way. No one had spotted them taking him in. He hadn't had time to see enough of the outside of the place to remember it again when they'd got the cash and let him go. And Old Pete was there minding him. Dead right for the job.

Forty years in and out of the nick[1] had soured Old Pete to such a point that anybody who met him accidentally began at once to think how they could get away. No one would come poking their nose into the Kilburn place when there was sixteen stone[2] of Old Pete there, fat but hard, never much of a one for shaving, always a bit of a smell to him. The kid was in as safe hands as could be while they conducted the negotiations.

They put in the first call to the rented Mayfair house at six o'clock that evening when they calculated the Sheik would have had just about enough time to have unpleasant thoughts and be ready quietly to agree to dodge the police and pay up. "The kid's safe," they said. "He'll be having his supper now. He's being well looked after."

It was true. Old Pete was just going into the room with the boy's supper, baked beans and a cup of tea, prepared on the picnic stove they'd put into the place. The boy looked at the extraordinary food—extraordinary to him—without seeming to be much put out by it. Old Pete even grunted a question at him, which he hadn't meant to. Only the kid's calm was a bit unexpected. It threw Old Pete a little. "All right, are you?" he grunted.

The boy looked at him, his large dark eyes clear and unwavering.

"Will you mind being in Hell?" he asked.

Old Pete, lumbering toward the door with its dangling padlock, stopped dead in his tracks and turned round.

"English," he said dazedly. "English. You speak English."

"Of course I do," the boy replied. "I always speak English with the Adviser. Talking with me is all he has to do, now that my father has the oil and doesn't need advice anymore."

Old Pete, crafty enough in his way but not one for confronting new situations easily, stood blinking, trying to fit this into the framework of his knowledge. And there was something else. Something at the back of his mind that had to be dealt with, too. And it was that, surprisingly, that pushed itself foward first.

" 'Ere," he said suddenly, "what d'you mean 'Hell'?"

"Will you mind being in Hell forever?" the boy asked.

"What d'you mean, me being in Hell?"

"Well, you will have to go there. Kidnapping is a sin. If you commit sins you go to Hell."

The simple, fundamental philosophy of the desert fell like drops of untarnished water from his lips.

Old Pete, tire tummied, dirt engrimed, looked at the kid for a long while without speaking a word. Then at last the machinery of his mind ground out his answer.

"Look, lad," he said, "that's all gone out. They finished with all that. Word may've not got round to where you come from, but they found out all that's wrong. Just tales. You know, what ain't so."

He stood, bending forward a little, examining the slight form of the boy in his neat, expensive Western shirt and shorts.

"Yes," he said, ramming it home, "you take my word for it, lad. That's all pastimes stuff now. Gone and forgotten."

He made his way out, an evil-smelling forty-ton tank, and carefully refitted the padlock to the little secure room.

But the next morning, when the Sheik was still holding out and the rest of them were considering what would be the easiest way of putting the pressure on a bit, the boy proved not to have absorbed the latest developments in Western thought at all. When Old Pete brought him his breakfast, the kid accepted the big bowl of corn-flakes eagerly enough, but in his conversation he was making no concessions to modernity.

"You will go to Hell, you know," he said, picking up from where they had left off. "You have to—you've done wrong."

"But I told yer," said Old Pete. "They changed all that."

"You can't," the boy said, with all the calm certainty of someone pointing out an accidental breach in the rules of a game. "If you do something wrong, you have to be punished for it. Isn't that so?"

"Well, I don't know about that," said Pete. "I mean, the cops don't always catch you. Not if you're sharp. They're not going to catch us for this lot, that's for sure. Those boys have it worked out a right treat."

"Yes," said the Sheik's son, "but that's just the reason."

"Just the reason?"

"Yes, if you do not get caught and punished here, you must be punished when you are dead. When you cross the Bridge of Al Sirat, which is only as wide as the breadth of a hair, the weight of your sin makes you fall. Into Hell."

His large brown eyes looked steadily into Pete's battered face.

"It's forever, of course," the boy added.

Old Pete left the room in too much of a hurry to collect last night's dirty baked beans plate.

He did not come back at lunchtime as he had meant to do. But at about six that evening—when the Sheik, after talk of making life hard for the boy, had just caved in and promised to deliver the cash—Old Pete once more removed the heavy padlock on the door and entered with another plate of steaming baked beans. The boy said nothing but seized eagerly on the beans. Old Pete turned to the door. But then he stopped, and began to gather up the two previous lots of dirty crockery. The boy ate steadily. Pete picked up the plates and put them down again. At last he broke out.

"Forever?" he said.

"Of course," the boy answered, knowing at once what they were talking about. "If you go to Paradise forever if you've been good, then you must go to Hell forever if you've been bad."

"Yeah," said Pete. And after a little he added, "Stands to reason, I suppose."

He put the now emptied second baked beans plate on top of the others.

"I'm not meant to tell yer," he said, "but you'll be going back 'ome soon. Yer old man's coming up with the dibbins."

"It won't make any difference," the boy said, again answering an unspoken question.

Pete blundered out the room, snapping the big padlock closed with a ferocious click. And entirely forgetting the dirty crockery.

But he was back within 20 minutes.

"Look," he said. "If I'd forgotten to lock the door when I brought you your nosh[3] just now, you could've sneaked out and nobody the wiser."

"No," said the boy. "You must *take* me home, all the way. Otherwise it wouldn't count."

Sweat broke out under the dirt of Pete's broad, fat, bulged face. "I can't do that. They'd catch me. Catch me for sure."

At the steps leading up to the door of the big corner house in Mayfair the boy turned to his companion.

"All right," he said. "I will ring myself. You can go now."

Pete swung away and lumbered off round the corner, fast as if he was a tanker lorry[4] out of control on an ice-slippery hill. But his legs were too jelly-like to support him for long, and once safely round the corner out of sight, he just had to stop and lean against the tall iron railing and let the waves of trembling flow over him.

For two whole minutes he did nothing but lean there, shaking. Then he began to relieve his feelings in dredging up from a well-stored memory every foul word he had ever heard. He only came to a halt, after some ten minutes, in order to draw breath.

When he did so the cool, clear, horribly familiar voice of the boy spoke from the open window over his head.

"I'm afraid with all that you will have to go to Hell after all," the boy said.

1. **the nick:** prison
2. **stone:** a British unit of mass, equal to 6.34 kg
3. **nosh:** food and drink
4. **lorry:** truck

3

In the Line
of Fire

▲▼▶▼▲▼▶▼▲▼▶▼▲▼▶▼▲▼▶▶▶

He had grown up in a country run by
politicians who sent the pilots to man the
bombers to kill the babies to make the
world safer for children to grow up in.

Ursula K. Le Guin,
from The Lathe of Heaven

▲▼▶▼▲▼▶▼▲▼▶▼▲▼▶▼▲▼▶▶▶

▲ ▶ ▼ ▲ ▶ ▼ ▲ ▶ ▼ ▲ ▶ ▼ ▲ ▶ ▼ ▲ ▶ ▼ ▲ ▶ ▶

HIJACKED!

by John Melady

What would you do if you found yourself holding two wires connected to a bomb? And then had to keep them from touching for over four hours? This is what happened to flight attendant Mary Dohey.

The big Air Canada jet lumbered out to the runway, received clearance for takeoff, and roared into the sky at precisely 4:15 p.m. Below and behind, Calgary looked like a toy town on the edge of the prairie. Tiny trucks raced along tiny roads, and the dots that had been cars disappeared. For a time the mountains were visible, but soon even they were gone.

Within minutes, Flight 812, bound for Toronto and Montreal, reached its cruising altitude. Far below, the checkerboard prairie was another world, familiar yet remote, for on this plane, as on every aircraft that has ever flown, reality is largely confined to the activities within the plane itself. And that night, on board that airliner, reality would become a horror beyond words.

It all came about because of one man.

Paul Joseph Cini was the 27-year-old son of a Maltese ship engineer. He grew up in Glasgow, Scotland, but when he was 17, he emigrated to Canada. He settled in Calgary and held a number of jobs there, one of which was rodman for the city survey department. After a while, however, he became disenchanted with surveying and decided to move to the United States. That was in 1964.

For the next seven years, his life was a litany of failures, both personal and professional. He became, among other things, a soldier, a car thief, a truck driver, and a father. When he boarded Air Canada's Flight 812 on November 12, 1971, he was employed as a record salesman. He had lost his only child when the infant's mother put him up for adoption soon after he was born. He saw the baby once.

During the summer and early autumn of 1971, the inadequacies of his life had been bothering Cini. His opinion of himself had never been high, but now it was even lower than usual. He felt he had to do something, anything, in order to prove to himself and to the whole world that he was important. That was why he decided to hijack a plane.

In order to prepare for his mad escapade, Paul Cini started acquiring the paraphernalia he would need. In due course, he purchased a black balaclava, a wig, some dynamite, a shotgun, and a parachute. With these, he reasoned, he could take over a plane, collect a ransom, and then parachute from the aircraft and disappear without a trace. As he went about securing the items he wanted, he drank, often to excess.

Finally he was ready. But he had not counted on meeting someone like Mary Dohey.

Dohey was a flight attendant on the plane Cini picked to hijack. And, while his life had been in turmoil as an adult, hers had been chaotic as a child. But Mary Dohey had overcome her upbringing and made a success of herself, while Paul Cini had traded his past for a present that was anything but praiseworthy.

Mary Dohey was the youngest in a family of 14. She was orphaned when she was only three, and in the years thereafter was passed around to several foster homes. She was abused in some, lonely in most, but unbelievably resilient in them all. She put herself through school, and for a time became a teacher in Newfoundland. When she realized that a career in teaching was not what she wanted, she went back to her studies and obtained her Registered Nurse's certificate, specializing in psychiatry.

At one time, a woman wishing to be a flight attendant had to be a nurse. It became almost natural, then, that Mary Dohey began looking for a career in the air. She longed to travel, and the idea of getting paid to do so was appealing. Air Canada, or Trans-Canada Airlines, as the company was formerly known, was looking for flight attendants. Dohey was accepted.

"I have enjoyed this life," she says today, "but of all the flying I've done, the night of the hijacking was something I will never forget. If I live to be a million, I will never get over that nightmare."

A Living Nightmare

For Dohey and the others on Air Canada Flight 812, the nightmare began less than an hour out of Calgary. A short, curly-haired, swarthy man sitting in seat 2B in the first-class section bolted down a vodka and orange and then left his seat to go to a washroom at the front of the plane. He wore a long, oversized beige trench coat and carried a shopping bag.

Five minutes later, John Arpin, the 48-year-old purser on the flight, heard a noise behind him. He turned and looked straight into the muzzle of a sawed-off, double-barrelled shotgun. A grotesque-looking figure in a trench coat, black balaclava, and black wig was sitting at a small table in the otherwise empty first-class lounge. The person holding the gun threatened to blow Arpin's head off unless he did what he was told.

"Sit over here," roared a male voice from under the black hood.

Arpin sat down.

"Take this and show it to the captain, and tell him to follow these instructions to a T," ordered the man.

He handed Arpin a sheet of yellow paper. The purser started to read.

"That's for the captain, not you," shrieked the man, and he jammed the gun into Arpin's face.

At that point, Mary Dohey walked into the lounge. She was about to speak to Arpin when she saw the gun.

"Sit down," demanded the figure in the black hood.

"Sit down, Mary," said Arpin. "It's for real."

As Mary took a seat beside the purser, the man in the mask swung the shotgun over to her and placed both barrels up against her forehead.

"Now, take that note to the captain," he said to Arpin, "and be quick about it. If you are not back right away, I'm killing your stewardess. Now you," he said, referring to Mary, "get over there by that window. Stand with your back against it and stare straight ahead. If you move, I'll blow your head off."

Mary went over to the window and Arpin disappeared into the cockpit. There he handed Captain Vern Ehman, a 43-year-old pilot from Montreal, the sheet of yellow paper. On it was a 506-word message that began with "Welcome aboard the original doomsday flight" and ended with "There'll be no heroes tonight, for tonight we all will die." The note demanded a ransom of $1.5 million and instructed the captain to fly to Great Falls, Montana. The money was to be collected there, and according to the note, had to be delivered to the plane by a woman.

While Arpin was on the flight deck delivering the note, the hijacker produced a 60-stick dynamite bomb. He handed Mary two wires protruding from it and told her to hold them apart. "If you don't," he snarled, "these wires will complete a circuit and this bomb will explode. If you want to die right now, you can let them touch." With that, he ordered her to sit beside him, with her back against the side of the plane. "Stare straight ahead," he repeated.

"I did exactly as he told me," Mary Dohey recalls. "I had one wire beside my little finger and another by my thumb, and I held them that way for over four hours. But my God, I was terrified, so terrified. I had to keep staring ahead, so I looked across to a window at the other side. I knew the awful situation we were in, and I thought I would likely be dead before Johnny Arpin got back from the cockpit. All this time I was praying, praying harder than I'd ever prayed before."

As the seconds ticked away and Arpin had still not returned, the man with the shotgun became more and more agitated.

"I could see his eyes through the slits in the black hood," Dohey says with a shiver, "and I could tell he was pretty jumpy. Then I noticed that his trigger finger was trembling.

"When I saw that, I was sure I was dead, so I made my peace with God. I was prepared to die. Then suddenly the gun started waving around and it went off."

Talking to the Hijacker

Today Mary grimaces as she recalls the incident.

"The barrel was right beside my ear when the shot was fired," she says. "My head was ringing from the sound as the shot went into the wall."

The blast thudded into the cockpit bulkhead and tore a fist-sized hole through it. Spent pellets, dust, and debris showered down on the second officer, and John Arpin was sure Mary was dead. He hurried back to the lounge.

As he did, he heard the hijacker say to Mary, "I'm sorry, I didn't mean to do that." She took up the cue.

"I know you didn't, dear. You don't want to hurt us, do you?" Her soft voice and sympathetic manner confused Paul Cini, the man in the disguise. She began to talk to him, hoping to gain his confidence. "My name is Mary," she said.

"Is that really your name?" Cini asked.

"Yes, it is," she answered. "Do you like it?"

"Yes, it's a nice name."

"Well, then, you may call me Mary. What is your name?"

"It's Dennis," lied Cini.

"Okay, Dennis," said the flight attendant, "may I hold your hand?" With that, she took the hijacker's hand in hers, all the while talking to him in a gentle, caring tone.

"I talked to him as I have never talked to anyone before or since," she recalls. "I asked him about himself and I told him about me. We covered almost every topic I could think of, from the weather to sports, to jobs, to children. When I told him I was one of 14 children, he laughed and told me that was a lot of kids. I knew then that he liked children, and I told myself that fact might be something I could use later on. I was trying to find anything I could to calm the guy. The talking was so hard, though. The saliva in my mouth kept drying up, I was so scared."

When Arpin returned from the flight deck, Cini demanded to know if the captain understood the message.

"Yes," answered Arpin. "We're to go to Montana, pick up the money, then go to Regina, release the passengers, load the aircraft full of guns and ammunition, and head for Ireland."

"That's right," Cini agreed.

"But where does the money come from?" Arpin asked.

"Air Canada supplies the money," Cini yelled. "Go and tell the captain that."

Arpin returned to the cockpit with the message. He also told Ehman that the hijacker's name was Dennis and that the flight attendant was sitting beside him holding his hand, trying to calm him down.

"Good," replied the pilot. "Keep me posted." With that he radioed Winnipeg ground control and passed on the new instructions. A few minutes earlier, at 5:15, it had been Winnipeg that gave Ehman the heading for Great Falls. Already the plane had been in the air for more than an hour.

During the flight into the United States, Cini would flare up at a moment's notice. Just when Mary began to feel that things might get better, they got worse. The hijacker complained of the heat in the plane, so the temperature was lowered. Arpin asked if he could put his coat on, but when he did, Cini saw the gold braid around the cuffs of the jacket and accused Arpin of being with the Federal Bureau of Investigation. When Arpin was asked about his nationality and said he was French, Cini shrieked, "It's good that you're not English, because I'm going to kill every Englishman on this plane."

Because the shotgun blast was loud enough to be heard by the passengers, Arpin asked Cini how the noise should be explained to them.

"Tell them a light bulb blew," the hijacker snapped. "Tell them whatever you want."

Arpin walked back to the first-class section and informed the passengers of the hijacking. "And if our guest comes back here," he warned, "don't let on that any of you are English. He told us he would kill anyone who was English."

Most of the passengers remained calm, although two got up and ran down the aisle towards the back of the plane. A few asked for drinks.

Shortly after Arpin returned to the lounge, assistant purser Phillip Bonné entered. Up to that point, he did not know of the hijacking, nor did most of the passengers in the rear economy section of the plane. Cini ordered Bonné to sit down beside Arpin.

"What nationality are you?" Cini asked him.

"I'm French Canadian."

"Well then, I'll blow your head off. The FLQ[1] would be proud of me and De Gaulle would turn over in his grave."

No one knew what this meant.

A few seconds later, Cini reached into the pocket of his trench coat and pulled out two bundles of dynamite. There were five sticks in each bundle.

"Now, I'm going to light these fuses and blow up the plane," he said.

Mary Dohey turned to him. "But Dennis, why would you do that, dear? You're going to hurt a lot of people. Do you know those people?"

Cini changed his mind. Instead, he took one stick of dynamite and pushed it into John Arpin's mouth. He then aimed the shotgun at Arpin's head.

Again Mary intereceded. "Dennis, dear," she whispered, "why don't you put the safety catch on the gun?"

Cini became confused.

"Sit over there," he roared at Bonné. The assistant purser moved to the seat across the table from Mary. "Now take her hands," Cini demanded.

Bonné did so.

"Hold her hands so tight I can see the whites of your knuckles," Cini snapped.

While this was happening, John Arpin slowly withdrew the dynamite from his mouth. Cini saw him and jammed the explosives back in again. Then he apparently changed his mind, grabbed the dynamite and ordered Mary Dohey to smell it.

"My darling, I don't know anything about dynamite," she protested.

Cini set the stick on the table.

Picking Up the Ransom Money

By this time, the plane had reached Great Falls, but Cini ordered it to circle the airport until the money he had demanded was ready. As soon as Captain Ehman received a radio message that the money was at the airport, he landed the DC-8. A police secretary walked out to the plane and tied the suitcase she carried onto a leather strap Bonné lowered from the aircraft. Bonné hauled the case containing the money into the plane and Ehman took off again. Fifteen minutes had passed.

As soon as the jet was at its cruising altitude, Cini ordered Arpin to count the money. As he did so, he realized, to his horror, that the suitcase contained only $50 000, not the $1.5 million Cini wanted. Fortunately the hijacker did not notice the discrepancy.

"By this time, I realized just how mad the

whole escapade was," recalls Mary. "It was a terrible, terrible nightmare, and I really expected we were all going to die. I made a pact with God at that time," she continues. "I told Him I would gladly die, but He had to show me a way to save the passengers. Then I recalled that the hijacker had seemed pleased when I told him I came from a family of 14, that he seemed to like kids."

Mary turned to Cini. "Dennis, I hear the children crying," she said.

"Do you mean there are kids on here?" Cini asked, apparently dumbfounded that that could be so.

"Oh yes," she said, "and I can hear them crying. The dear little things are so tired and hungry. They don't know what's happening."

Cini reacted in fury.

"Go up and tell that captain," he said to Arpin, "to go back to Great Falls and let the people off. I am going to need the space for the ammunition."

Ehman swung the plane around and returned to Great Falls. The 118 passengers began leaving.

"Now," Cini barked at Arpin, "I have a blue suitcase on this plane. I want you to get it—*now!* I'll give you ten minutes, and if you are not back with it then, I am going to kill this stewardess." He handed Arpin a baggage tag and checked his watch. Arpin scrambled down the ramp.

As soon as the purser had gone, Cini ordered Mary to turn around. Then he placed the muzzle of the shotgun against the back of her neck. She knew he was watching the time.

"Those minutes were some of the worst of my entire life," she says. "I could feel the cold steel on my neck and I really thought I would be killed—particularly when Johnny was delayed."

"Well, your time is up," Cini told her. Then he cocked the hammer of the gun. Mary asked if she could turn around. Cini consented.

"When I turned, he put the gun up against my forehead. But that was better than behind me, because I didn't think he could face me and kill me. I started pleading for him to give Johnny a bit more time. I told him how hard it would be to find one suitcase among all the others."

Just as Arpin returned, and after the last passenger was off, Cini leaned close to Mary and whispered, "Do you want to leave? If you want to leave, you can go."

Tough Decisions

Dohey was momentarily stunned by the sudden turn of events, but then she realized that if she left, the hijacker would blow up the plane. "I was worried about the pilot and the rest of the crew," she says. "I knew I had to fight to save them. By this time, I had developed some rapport with the hijacker and I knew that if I could not control him, we would all die."

"Do you want me to leave, dear?" Dohey asked.

"No, I want you to stay," muttered Cini.

"Then if you want me to stay, I'll stay."

"You're a fool for not going," Arpin told her as the plane left Great Falls for the second time that evening. "You should have left when you had the chance."

When the aircraft was well underway, this time towards Phoenix, Arizona, and not Regina as he had demanded earlier, Cini again changed his mind. He told Arpin to let the captain know they should fly to Calgary. Ehman agreed.

Then the already volatile hijacker became even more worked up. At one point, he accused the crew of piping lethal gas into the plane to kill him. On another occasion, he flew into a rage because he lit a cigarette and found that it was not his own brand. To ensure that this did not happen again, he ordered Dohey, Arpin and Bonné to sit down with him at the little table in the lounge.

When all four were seated, he took one cigarette from each of four packs, all different brands. He ordered Mary to light each and set them in an ashtray in the centre of the table. Then he turned the ashtray around and around, all the while telling his hostages that if the cigarette he selected from the ashtray was not his own, Mary would die.

He picked the right one and Mary Dohey almost collapsed with relief. "By this time, I was so tired, I almost gave up," she recalls.

As the big jet flew north, Cini embarked on

yet another mad endeavour. He suddenly sprang to his feet and rushed into the cockpit.

"The next thing I knew," Dohey says, "he came marching out of the cockpit, behind the captain, with the shotgun aimed at the back of Vern's head. The captain was carrying all the radio headsets."

The two went down the centre aisle of the plane, back towards the now empty economy section. When they reached the tail section, Cini told Ehman to open a door there, because he wanted to parachute out. Ehman refused, saying that opening the door would be impossible because of the slip stream. "Then I'll blow the back off the plane and jump out," Cini retorted.

Ehman dissuaded him, pointing out that if he really wanted to jump out, he could leave through one of the emergency windows over the wing. Cini agreed, but found that he could not open the window with one hand. When he set the shotgun down in order to free both his hands, Ehman saw his chance.

The pilot grabbed the shotgun and heaved it down the aisle. Then he lunged for Cini's throat, and at the same time yelled for help.

John Arpin raced to assist. Then Bonné and Dohey arrived. The four of them pinned Cini to the floor and he stopped struggling. Ehman said, "We've got to tie him up. Get some tape."

Suddenly Cini went berserk. He threw them off and began to thrash around like a wild animal.

Ehman grabbed the man's throat and the others fought to control him. They threw him down, but again he clambered to his feet.

"The axe, Phillip," Ehman yelled. "Hit him with the axe."

Phillip Bonné grabbed an emergency fire axe and belted Cini on the head with the blunt end. Cini shook off the blow and lunged at the captain. Bonné clouted him with the blade. Blood flew, but Cini was as ferocious as ever.

"Use the handle," yelled Ehman.

Bonné flipped the axe around, took the blade in both hands, and brought the handle down.

There was a crunching sound, and the hijacker's body went limp. Arpin pulled off the hood Cini wore and they tied him down. Captain Ehman returned to the cockpit. Half an hour later, he brought Flight 812 down on the tarmac at Calgary—just 20 minutes before a heavy fog closed the airport for two days. It was now midnight, but the terrible ordeal was over.

Later, after he had recovered from his head wounds, Paul Joseph Cini was sent to prison. John Arpin, Vern Ehman, Phillip Bonné, and Mary Dohey were all decorated for bravery, but Dohey alone received the Cross of Valour. She was the first person to win the award and live.

1. **FLQ:** a Quebec terrorist group in the '60s and early '70s. Their most notorious act was the 1970 kidnapping and murder of politician Pierre Laporte.

THE SHOOTING OF DAN McGREW

by Robert Service

Canadian poet Robert Service loved the frontier atmosphere of the Yukon. It was a place, he said, where "only the fit survive."

A bunch of the boys were whooping it up in the
    Malamute saloon;
The kid that handles the music-box was hitting a
    jag-time tune;
Back of the bar, in a solo game, sat Dangerous
    Dan McGrew,
And watching his luck was his light-o'-love, the
    lady that's known as Lou.

When out of the night, which was 50 below, and
    into the din and the glare,
There stumbled a miner fresh from the creeks,
    dog-dirty, and loaded for bear.
He looked like a man with a foot in the grave and
    scarcely the strength of a louse,

Yet he tilted a poke of dust on the bar, and he
    called for drinks for the house.
There was none could place the stranger's face,
    though we searched ourselves for a clue;
But we drank his health, and the last to drink was
    Dangerous Dan McGrew.

There's men that somehow just grip your eyes, and
    hold them hard like a spell;
And such was he, and he looked to me like a man
    who had lived in hell;
With a face most hair, and the dreary stare of a dog
    whose day is done,
As he watered the green stuff in his glass, and the
    drops fell one by one.
Then I got to figgering who he was, and wondering
    what he'd do,
And I turned my head—and there watching him
    was the lady that's known as Lou.

His eyes went rubbering round the room, and he
    seemed in a kind of daze,
Till at last that old piano fell in the way of his
    wandering gaze.
The rag-time kid was having a drink; there was no
    one else on the stool,
So the stranger stumbles across the room, and flops
    down there like a fool.

In a buckskin shirt that was glazed with dirt he sat,
    and I saw him sway;
Then he clutched the keys with his talon hands—
    my God! but that man could play.

Were you ever out in the Great Alone, when the
    moon was awful clear,
And the icy mountains hemmed you in with a
    silence you most could *hear*;
With only the howl of a timber wolf, and you
    camped there in the cold,
A half-dead thing in a stark, dead world, clean mad
    for the muck called gold;
While high overhead, green, yellow and red, the
    North Lights swept in bars?—
Then you've a hunch what the music meant …
    hunger and night and the stars.

And hunger not of the belly kind, that's banished
    with bacon and beans,
But gnawing hunger of lonely men for a home and
    all that it means;
For a fireside far from the cares that are, four walls
    and a roof above;
But oh! so cramful of cosy joy, and crowned with a
    woman's love—
A woman dearer than all the world, and true as
    Heaven is true—

(God! how ghastly she looks through her rouge,—
    the lady that's known as Lou.)

Then on a sudden the music changed, so soft that
    you scarce could hear;
But you felt that your life had been looted clean of
    all that it once held dear;
That someone had stolen the woman you loved;
    that her love was a devil's lie;
That your guts were gone, and the best for you was
    to crawl away and die.
'Twas the crowning cry of a heart's despair, and it
    thrilled you through and through—
"I guess I'll make it a spread misere," said
    Dangerous Dan McGrew.

The music almost died away … then it burst like a
    pent-up flood;
And it seemed to say, "Repay, repay," and my eyes
    were blind with blood.
The thought came back of an ancient wrong, and it
    stung like a frozen lash,
And the lust awoke to kill, to kill … then the music
    stopped with a crash,
And the stranger turned, and his eyes they burned
    in a most peculiar way;
In a buckskin shirt that was glazed with dirt he sat,
    and I saw him sway;

Then his lips went in in a kind of grin, and he
　　spoke, and his voice was calm,
And "Boys," says he, "you don't know me, and
　　none of you care a damn;
But I want to state, and my words are straight, and
　　I'll bet my poke they're true,
That one of you is a hound of hell ... and that one is
　　Dan McGrew."

Then I ducked my head, and the lights went out,
　　and two guns blazed in the dark,
And a woman screamed, and the lights went up,
　　and two men lay stiff and stark.
Pitched on his head, and pumped full of lead, was
　　Dangerous Dan McGrew,
While the man from the creeks lay clutched to the
　　breast of the lady that's known as Lou.

These are the simple facts of the case, and I guess I
　　ought to know.
They say that the stranger was crazed with
　　"hooch," and I'm not denying it's so.
I'm not so wise as the lawyer guys, but strictly
　　between us two—
The woman that kissed him and—pinched his
　　poke—was the lady that's known as Lou.

JUST LATHER, THAT'S ALL

by Hernando Téllez

Translated from the Spanish by Donald A. Yates

The barber's hated enemy is sitting in his chair. So close to the razor's edge. One slip of the hand, and many deaths would be avenged. Will the barber do it? Or will Captain Torres walk away?

He said nothing when he entered. I was passing the best of my razors back and forth on a strop. When I recognized him I started to tremble. But he didn't notice. Hoping to conceal my emotion, I continued sharpening the razor. I tested it on the meat of my thumb, and then held it up to the light. At that moment he took off the bullet-studded belt that his gun holster dangled from. He hung it up on a wall hook and placed his military cap over it. Then he turned to me, loosening the knot of his tie, and said, "It's hot as hell. Give me a shave." He sat in the chair.

I estimated he had a four-day beard. The four days taken up by the latest expedition in search of our troops. His face seemed reddened, burned by the sun. Carefully, I began to prepare the soap. I cut off a few slices, dropped them into the cup, mixed in a bit of warm water, and began to stir with the brush. Immediately the foam began to rise. "The other boys in the group should have this much beard, too." I continued stirring the lather.

"But we did all right, you know. We got the main ones. We brought back some dead, and we've got some others still alive. But pretty soon they'll all be dead."

"How many did you catch?" I asked.

"Fourteen. We had to go pretty deep into the woods to find them. But we'll get even. Not one of them comes out of this alive, not one."

He leaned back on the chair when he saw me with the lather-covered brush in my hand. I still had to put the sheet on him. No doubt about it, I was upset. I took a sheet out of a drawer and knotted it around my customer's neck. He wouldn't stop talking. He probably thought I was in sympathy with his party.

"The town must have learned a lesson from what we did the other day," he said.

"Yes," I replied, securing the knot at the base of his dark, sweaty neck.

"That was a fine show, eh?"

"Very good," I answered, turning back for the brush. The man closed his eyes with a gesture of fatigue and sat waiting for the cool caress of the soap. I had never had him so close to me. The day he ordered the whole town to file into the patio of the school to see the four rebels hanging there, I came face to face with him for an instant. But the sight of the mutilated bodies kept me from noticing the face of the man who had directed it all, the face I was now about to take into my hands. It was not an unpleasant face, certainly. And the beard, which made him seem a bit older than he was, didn't suit him badly at all. His name was Torres. Captain Torres. A man of imagination, because who else would have thought of hanging the naked rebels and then holding target practice on certain parts of their bodies? I began to apply the first layer of soap. With his eyes closed, he continued. "Without any effort I could go straight to sleep," he said, "but there's plenty to do this afternoon." I stopped the lathering and asked with a feigned lack of interest: "A firing squad?" "Something like that, but a little slower." I got on with the job of lathering his beard. My hands started trembling again. The man could not possibly realize it, and this was in my favor. But I would have preferred that he hadn't come. It was likely that many of our faction had seen him enter. And an enemy under one's roof imposes certain conditions. I would be obliged to shave that beard like any other one, carefully, gently, like that of any customer, taking pains to see that no single pore emitted a drop of blood. Being careful to see that the little tufts of hair did not lead the blade astray. Seeing that his skin ended up clean, soft, and healthy, so that passing the back of my hand over it I couldn't feel a hair. Yes, I was secretly a rebel, but I was also a conscientious barber, and proud of the preciseness of my profession. And this four-days' growth of beard was a fitting challenge.

I took the razor, opened up the two protective arms, exposed the blade and began the job, from one of the sideburns downward. The razor responded beautifully. His beard was inflexible and hard, not too long, but thick. Bit by bit the skin emerged. The razor rasped along, making its customary sound as fluffs of lather mixed with bits of hair gathered along the blade. I paused a moment to clean it, then took up the strop again to sharpen the razor, because I'm a barber who does things properly. The man, who had kept his eyes closed, opened them now, removed one of his hands from under the sheet, felt the spot on his face where the soap had been cleared off, and said, "Come to the school today at six o'clock." "The same thing as the other day?" I asked horrified. "It could be better," he replied. "What do you plan to do?" "I don't know yet. But we'll amuse ourselves." Once more he leaned back and closed his eyes. I approached him with the razor poised. "Do you plan to punish them all?" I ventured timidly. "All." The soap was drying on his face. I had to hurry. In the mirror I looked toward the street. It was the same as ever: the grocery store with two or three customers in it. Then I glanced at the clock: two-twenty in the afternoon. The razor continued on its downward stroke. Now from the other sideburn down. A thick, blue beard. He should have let it grow like some poets or priests do. It would suit him well. A lot of people wouldn't recognize him. Much to his benefit, I thought, as I attempted to cover the neck area smoothly. There, for sure, the razor had to be handled masterfully, since the hair, although softer, grew into little swirls. A curly beard. One of the tiny pores could be opened up and issue forth its pearl of blood. A good barber such as I prides himself on never allowing this to happen to a client. And this was a first-class client. How many of us had he ordered shot? How many of us had he ordered mutilated? It was better not to think about it. Torres did not know that I was his enemy. He did not know it nor did the rest. It was a secret shared by very few, precisely so that I could inform the revolutionaries of what Torres was doing in the town and of what he was planning each time he undertook a rebel-hunting excursion. So it was going to be very difficult to explain that I had him right in my hands and let him go peacefully—alive and shaved.

The beard was now almost completely gone. He seemed younger, less burdened by years than when he had arrived. I suppose this always happens with men who visit barber shops. Under the stroke of my razor Torres was being rejuvenated—rejuvenated because I am a good barber, the best in the town, if I may say so. A little more lather here, under his chin, on his Adam's apple, on this big vein. How hot it is getting! Torres must be sweating as much as I. But he is not afraid. He is a calm man, who is not even thinking about what he is going to do with the prisoners this afternoon. On the other hand I, with this razor in my hands, stroking and re-stroking this skin, trying to keep blood from oozing from these pores, can't even think clearly. Damn him for coming, because I'm a revolutionary and not a murderer. And how easy it would be to kill him. And he deserves it. Does he? No! What the devil! No one deserves to have someone else make the sacrifice of becoming a murderer. What do you gain by it? Nothing. Others come along and still others, and the first ones kill the second ones and they the next ones and it goes on like this until everything is a sea of blood. I could cut this throat just so, zip! zip! I wouldn't give him time to complain and since he has his eyes closed he wouldn't see the glistening knife blade or my glistening eyes. But I'm trembling like a real murderer. Out of his neck a gush of blood would spout onto the sheet, on the chair, on my hands, on the floor. I would have to close the door. And the blood would keep inching along the floor, warm, ineradicable, uncontainable, until it reached the street, like a little scarlet stream. I'm sure that one solid stroke, one deep incision, would prevent any pain. He wouldn't suffer. But what would I do with the body? Where would I hide it? I would have to flee, leaving all I have behind, and take refuge far away, far, far away. But they would follow until they found me. "Captain Torres' murderer. He slit

his throat while he was shaving him—a coward."
And then on the other side. "The avenger of us all.
A name to remember. (And here they would mention my name.) He was the town barber. No one
knew he was defending our cause."

And what of all this? Murderer or hero? My
destiny depends on the edge of this blade. I can
turn my hand a bit more, press a little harder on the
razor, and sink it in. The skin would give way like
silk, like rubber, like the strop. There is nothing
more tender than human skin and the blood is
always there, ready to pour forth. A blade like this
doesn't fail. It is my best. But I don't want to be a
murderer, no sir. You came to me for a shave. And
I perform my work honorably.... I don't want
blood on my hands. Just lather, that's all. You are
an executioner and I am only a barber. Each person
has his own place in the scheme of things. That's
right. His own place.

Now his chin had been stroked clean and
smooth. The man sat up and looked into the mirror. He rubbed his hands over his skin and felt it
fresh, like new.

"Thanks," he said. He went to the hanger for
his belt, pistol and cap. I must have been very pale;
my shirt felt soaked. Torres finished adjusting the
buckle, straightened his pistol in the holster and
after automatically smoothing down his hair, he
put on the cap. From his pants pocket he took out
several coins to pay me for my services. And he
began to head toward the door. In the doorway he

paused for a moment, and turning to me he said:

"They told me that you'd kill me. I came to find out. But killing isn't easy. You can take my word for it." And he headed on down the street.

4

Watch Your Back!

▲▼▶▼▲▼▶▼▲▼▶▼▲▼▶▼▲▼

Avoid running at all times. Don't look back.
Something might be gaining on you.

*Satchel Paige,
from* How to Stay Young

▲▼▶▼▲▼▶▼▲▼▶▼▲▼▶▼▲▼

▲▼►▼►▲▼►▼▲▼►▼►▲▼►▼▲▼►►

DIALOGUE BEHIND A CURTAIN

by Victor Canning

Smuggling is a very old crime, often carried out at sea. Is Tasso a smuggler, or just an honest fisherman, as he claims? His life depends on his ability to convince the authorities.

The Great Man stood at the window of the Winter Palace. Across the paved courtyard, beyond the long sweep of ornamental railings and the still line of grey-uniformed guards, lay the wide bowl of the only harbour the island possessed. He raised a hand and scratched the back of his neck and the movement made the early morning November sun glint on the gilt oak leaves of his epaulettes.

A respectful three paces behind him the Chief of Police stirred uncomfortably and said, "That's his boat coming in now. For a year this has been going on, and until now we have never known which of the many fishermen it might be. This time our information is reliable."

"Denunciation?" The word was harsh and bitter.

"Yes."

"Anonymous?"

"Yes."

"You have suspected him?"

"He and every other fisherman on the island, but until now I would have said that he was the last man—"

The figure at the window turned and a pair of cold, brown eyes regarded the Chief of Police shrewdly. They were eyes which missed nothing.

"You sound almost regretful. You like him?"

"Everyone on the island likes Tasso."

The Great Man walked past the Chief of Police towards his desk and from the shadow of the curtains at the window rose the brown and black length of his great Alsatian. As his master sat down the dog dropped heavily to the floor at the side of the desk.

"Your men are waiting for him?"

"Everything is ready."

"Go down yourself and arrest him and bring him here. Do not question him. Say nothing to him. Bring him here."

The face of the Chief of Police showed surprise. A large hand with a thick gold ring waved at him, and the ghost of a smile passed across the face of the Great Man. "Bring him here. For once I have time on my hands. I am curious to talk to a man who has found a soft corner in the heart of a Chief of Police. Such men are rare."

The Chief of Police would have spoken again

but the cold, brown eyes had grown colder, and the ghost of a smile had gone from the other's face. The Chief of Police saluted and left the room.

The Great Man lit a cigarette, eased his short powerful bulk back into the wide chair, and his left hand dropped to the neck of the Alsatian, the squat fingers teasing at the dog's thick fur. After a while there was the clatter of heavy boots on the wide marble stairway outside the room and then the door was opened. Tasso stood on the threshold, behind him two armed guards and behind them the Chief of Police. The Great Man eyed them in silence for a while and, in the long pause, the cries of the stallholders from the market along the quay front seeped faintly into the gilt and velvet stretches of the room.

"Let him come in alone," he said suddenly.

The doors closed behind Tasso and the fisherman came slowly down the room. The dog by the chairside stirred, beginning to rise, but the firm fingers tapped its head gently and the animal relaxed.

Tasso stood before the polished desk. He was a short, powerful man, much like the other in build. His eyes were brown, but with a warmth in them, his face tanned and creased with years of the sea, and about the wide lips clung a subdued smile. He showed no fear, nor embarrassment, though he knew well the identity of the man before him, had seen him resplendent at ceremonial parades and known those cold, brown eyes from a thousand photographs in a thousand public places. He stood there with his shabby blue jacket swung open to show a dirty red shirt, his trousers flaked with fish scales. In the lapel of his jacket he wore a half-opened yellow rose.

"Your name?"

"Tasso Susvid."

"Age?"

"Fifty-three."

"Occupation?"

"Fisherman."

"And smuggler."

"No man willingly puts his initials on a bullet." The frank brown eyes watched the plume of smoke rising from the other's cigarette.

"You have been denounced."

"The innocent as well as the guilty are often denounced."

The Great Man stirred comfortably and the ghost of a smile came back.

"Let us assume that you are a smuggler for the moment."

"Why not? I have time on my hands. My fish are caught and my wife will sell them."

"Why do you smuggle? It is against the interests of our country."

"If I do it—and we merely pass time with this game—it is to make myself more money. The better off the citizens of a country are, the better off the country."

"There are times when you smuggle out enemies of our country. A man who does that merits death."

"Why not a reward? Surely, a country is healthier without its enemies?"

The lips of the Great Man tightened and for a moment his eyes narrowed. Then he laughed gently.

"What do you bring in so valuable that it outweighs the risk of death?"

"Cigarettes."

"We make our own."

"But the one you smoke now is American."

"What else?"

"Whiskey."

"I prefer our own rakia[2]."

"I agree, but there are people in the capital who think differently. There are also nylons and perfumes."

"For the women in the capital?"

Tasso smiled and shook his head. "For any woman. Every goat girl on this island covets a pair of nylons, and if you tend goats you have need of perfumes."

The Great Man smiled, almost openly now, and stubbing out his cigarette, said, "And all these things you bring from over there?" He nodded towards the window and the blue patch of visible sea.

"If I were a smuggler I should bring them from there, yes."

"How long would it take—in your boat?"

"Ten hours across, four hours there, and ten

hours back. Twenty-four hours."

"When did you go out on this fishing trip?"

"At nine o'clock yesterday morning."

The Great Man glanced at the clock over the wide doors of the saloon. "It is now half-past nine. It's odd—your trip lasted exactly 24 hours."

"I ran into bad weather last night and we had to heave-to."

"We?"

"My son works the boat with me."

"Your boat is being searched now."

"They will find nothing."

"You have a radio? Maybe someone warned you—"

"There is no radio. No one warned me. Remember, we are only pretending that I am a smuggler."

"It is a game not without its dangers. During the war, you were a partisan?"

"Yes, I fought. Later, because I know the coast, I was a pilot for the Allied naval forces."

"You like the English?"

"They understand the sea, and they keep their heads in an emergency. Both qualities I admire."

"Who doesn't? But even so, everything is passing from their grasp. In politics, in art, in commerce, and in sport they are being swallowed up."

Tasso shrugged his shoulders. "In all these things, perhaps. But I like them still because of all these the one thing they will really care about is sport. Only being able to draw with our national football team yesterday—they will find that hard to swallow."

"You are interested in football?"

"Every man on this island is. My son is captain of the town team."

"He will be proud when you are shot for smuggling."

"The bullet has yet to be marked. Remember, this is a private game between us."

"You have been denounced. The game is finished."

"Denounced by whom?"

"I don't know, but I should say your wife."

"Why?"

"She is a woman. Women notice small things...." A large hand rubbed gently across a broad jowl for a moment, and the thick gold ring caught the light from the wide windows. "Four hours over there is not long, but it is long enough for a man to forget his wife. You wear a fresh rose in your lapel. A man who lands from sea after 24 hours with a fresh rose in his coat gives himself away. After a ten-hour trip from over there it would be fresh. Maybe you have made this mistake before. Maybe your wife has noticed it and grown jealous of the one who pins a flower to your coat before you leave. Jealousy makes all women dangerous. Yes, I think it was your wife who denounced you."

Tasso smiled and raised his hand to the rose. "I am 53. At 33 my wife was often jealous, but those years have gone. We are still playing our game. Look—" Tasso tossed the rose on to the desk. The movement made the Alsatian rise quickly, but a broad hand went out to restrain it. The Great Man picked up the rose and saw that it was artificial, made of wax-coated silk.

Tasso said, "It was the gift of an American nurse during the war. Ask any man in this town and he will tell you that I always wear it. After six years it is still fresh."

The Great Man was silent for a moment, turning the rose over in his hand. Then he looked up from under his heavy brows and smiled.

"A man who holds my power can resent the mistakes he makes. Out of hurt vanity I might take revenge and none would question my right. A snap of my fingers and our friend here … " he nodded to the Alsatian, "would tear your throat out. Maybe I should let him, for you are too frank and your tongue too ready."

But the smile still played about Tasso's mouth and he slowly raised his hand to the back of his neck, saying, "If you should try—there would be two throats cut. The dog's and your own." From the back of his coat he pulled a knife and placed it on the desk. "The Chief of Police is a conscientious man, but your presence here flusters him. He was so anxious to get me up here that he made a bad job of searching me."

The Great Man picked up the knife and gently tried the edge of the blade on his thumb. Then he said, reflectively, "There are a thousand men who would have liked the chance you've just thrown away."

"I am a fisherman, not an assassin."

"And also a smuggler. Some instinct told you to jettison your goods before coming in."

"I am a fisherman."

"No. I may have been mistaken about your wife, but not over the smuggling. Yesterday evening you were over there."

Tasso shook his head. "I was at sea—hove-to."

The Great Man went on, turning the knife in his hands as he spoke, "You left this island yesterday morning with your son. According to you, you have been 24 hours at sea, seeing no one, and without a radio of any kind."

"That is what I said."

"And you landed here a little less than half an hour ago and were brought straight up to me without a chance to talk to anyone?"

"That is so."

"And yet you knew that our International Football team had drawn with the English team? The game was played in London yesterday afternoon, after you left here. You heard the result over there when you landed. Both you and your son would be interested in the result. If you had been at sea 24 hours without a radio you could not have known the result. It is forbidden to go over there, but you went as you have so often gone."

Tasso's face never altered. For a moment the two men stared at one another. Then Tasso nodded slowly. "The game, it seems, is finished."

But the Great Man smiled and shook his head. "No. I have enjoyed the game too much to have it finish this way." He stood up. "You are free to go. What I know I shall keep to myself, and you will have no trouble with the Chief of Police."

"Why do you do this?" Tasso's face showed his surprise.

The other put his hand for a moment on Tasso's shoulder. "You made a mistake, one mistake that could have meant death. That can happen to the bravest and cleverest of men. It might happen to me one day. If it does, I shall know I have a friend on this island with a boat. A man can never have too many friends."

1. **quay** (pronounced "key"): a solid landing place where ships can load and unload
2. **rakia**: a brandy made in Yugoslavia

IF CORNERED, SCREAM

by Patricia J. Thurmond

On the way home late one night, a nurse stops for gas. Isn't she taking a chance by stopping?

On the night it happened she hurried across the hospital parking lot, unlocked her car door, and got in. She started the car, waved to her co-workers, honked to the security guard, and drove the half block to the freeway entrance. The late hour meant light traffic, and though she was a good driver, she was always relieved whenever she had negotiated an entrance ramp. That done, she settled back, driving easily.

Then in the dim dashboard light she saw the gas gauge indicating empty and remembered with annoyance that she hadn't had time to stop for gas. Working a late shift at the hospital was not an ideal situation, but it meant more money and allowed her to attend graduate classes during the days.

As she drove, she found herself gripping the steering wheel and made a conscious effort to relax and think pleasant thoughts. Each night during the drive home, she relived the safety lectures given to the nurses—make sure someone on the ward knows where you are at all times; leave the grounds in groups; avoid isolated places in the hospital; if cornered, scream.

Again she deliberately relaxed her grip on the wheel and took a deep breath.

Funny, she thought, she didn't know why, but she was even more uptight than usual. She was tired and looked forward to a long soak in the tub and her new magazine which had lain unread the last three days.

The gas gauge again caught her attention. She could probably make it home on what was still left in the tank, but she would have to fill up before class in the morning. If she stopped tonight at the station that Gabriel ran on Imperial Highway, she'd have a few extra minutes in the morning and wouldn't have to rush.

She approached Imperial Highway, flicked on the right blinker, headed down the off-ramp, waited at the stoplight, and then made a left turn. She pulled into the station at a pump and rolled down the window as Gabriel walked to the car.

Since he always spoke pleasantly on the nights she stopped for gas, she had automatically discounted the few disturbing rumours that accompanied his sudden appearance in the area.

"Hi, Florence Nightingale. Fill 'er up?"

"Hi, Gabriel. Yes, fill it up, please."

As she handed him the gas-tank key, he asked, "Any more ping-pong playing under the hood?"

"No, no more noise. It stopped when you did whatever you did."

Gabriel filled the tank, cleaned the windows and mirrors, and gave her the change from a 20. When he finished he said offhandedly, "By the way, my birthday was Sunday. Why don't you step inside the office and see what my sister gave me? You won't believe your eyes!"

"Oh, Gabriel, I'm in a really big hurry. I just can't stop tonight. But I will next time. I promise."

"Aw, come on. It won't be new any more by then. Besides, this is something extra-special. Come on. Only take a second."

As she and Gabriel talked back and forth, she realized she was wasting more time than if she went in and saw the silly gift.

Looking more agreeable than she felt, she said, "Okay, you win, Gabriel. Remember, this better be good!"

"It is. You'll see. Oh, before you get out, angle the car over this way—just in case anyone wants to pull in." Watching his gestures, she parked the car and followed him to the station office.

Once inside, Gabriel locked the door and quickly took a gun out of the drawer. Through the roar of her heartbeat in her ears she heard him say that there was no birthday and no present. Her fingers tingled. Nausea pitched and rolled through her body like seasickness. Each time the nausea crested, her legs felt like loosened moorings.

Her nose and toes were cold and she knew clinically, almost like an observer, that she was experiencing the symptoms of shock. She was unable to make a self-protective move, or even to scream. She tried to prepare to die, but didn't know how. Crazily, in the midst of her silent hysteria, the absurdity of it struck her, and she had a demented desire to laugh. Gabriel's lips were moving but she still couldn't hear above the roar in her ears.

Finally she heard sounds coming from his mouth. The sounds became words as her head cleared, and the words began to make sense.

"… sorry I had to scare you by telling you that. But don't feel bad, I was scared myself when I saw that dude on the floor in the back of your car. I had you angle the car that way so that I can see both doors from here. And if he tries to get out, he belongs to me. I'll call the cops now. It's okay. Good thing you stopped for gas tonight."

In a few minutes she was aware of the sirens, the flashing lights of the squad cars, and the bellow of the bullhorn.

▲ ▶ ▼▲ ▼ ▶ ▼▲ ▼ ▶ ▼▲ ▼ ▶ ▼▲ ▶ ▼▶

THE MOST DANGEROUS GAME

by Richard Connell

In this classic story of the hunter and the
hunted, the hero finds himself stranded on a
remote island. His host is General Zaroff, an
expert big-game hunter who has grown
bored with all the usual animal prey. Will
Rainsford manage to outwit this diabolical
master of the hunt?

Off there to the right—somewhere—is a large
island," said Whitney. "It's rather a mystery—"

"What island is it?" Rainsford asked.

"The old charts call it 'Ship-Trap Island',"
Whitney replied. "A suggestive name, isn't it?
Sailors have a curious dread of the place. I don't
know why. Some superstition—"

"Can't see it," remarked Rainsford, trying to
peer through the dank tropical night that was palpable as it pressed its thick, warm blackness in
upon the yacht.

"You've good eyes," said Whitney, with a
laugh, "and I've seen you pick off a moose moving

in the brown fall bush at four hundred yards, but even you can't see four miles or so through a moonless Caribbean night."

"Not four yards," admitted Rainsford. "Ugh! It's like moist black velvet."

"It will be light enough where we're going," promised Whitney. "We should make it in a few days. I hope the jaguar guns have come. We'll have good hunting up the Amazon. Great sport, hunting."

"The best sport in the world," agreed Rainsford.

"For the hunter," amended Whitney. "Not for the jaguar."

"Don't talk rot, Whitney," said Rainsford. "You're a big game hunter, not a philosopher. Who cares how a jaguar feels?"

"Perhaps the jaguar does," observed Whitney.

"Bah! They've no understanding."

"Even so, I rather think they understand one thing—fear. The fear of pain and the fear of death."

"Nonsense," laughed Rainsford. "This hot weather is making you soft, Whitney. Be a realist. The world is made up of two classes—the hunters and the hunted. Luckily, you and I are hunters. Do you think we've passed that island yet?"

"I can't tell in the dark. I hope so."

"Why?" asked Rainsford.

"The place has a reputation—a bad one."

"Cannibals?" suggested Rainsford.

"Hardly. Even cannibals wouldn't live in such

a God-forsaken place. But it's got into sailor lore, somehow. Didn't you notice that the crew's nerves seemed a bit jumpy today?"

"They were a bit strange, now that you mention it. Even Captain Nielsen—"

"Yes, even that tough-minded old Swede, who'd go up to the devil himself and ask him for a light. Those fishy blue eyes held a look I never saw there before. All I could get out of him was: 'This place has an evil name among seafaring men, sir.' Then he said to me, very gravely: 'Don't you feel anything?'—as if the air about us was actually poisonous. Now, you mustn't laugh when I tell you this—I did feel something like a sudden chill.

"There was no breeze. The sea was as flat as a plate-glass window. We were drawing near the island then. What I felt was a mental chill; a sort of sudden dread."

"Pure imagination," said Rainsford. "One superstitious sailor can taint the whole ship's company with his fear."

"Maybe. But sometimes I think sailors have an extra sense that tells them when they are in danger. Sometimes I think evil is a tangible thing—with wave lengths, just as sound and light have. An evil place can, so to speak, broadcast vibrations of evil. Anyhow, I'm glad we're getting out of this zone. Well, I think I'll turn in now, Rainsford."

"I'm not sleepy," said Rainsford. "I'm going to smoke another pipe up on the afterdeck."

"Good night, then, Rainsford. See you at

breakfast."

"Right. Good night, Whitney."

There was no sound in the night as Rainsford sat there, but the muffled throb of the engine that drove the yacht swiftly through the darkness, and the swish and ripple of the wash of the propeller.

Rainsford, reclining in a steamer chair, indolently puffed on his favorite briar. The sensuous drowsiness of the night was on him.

"It's so dark," he thought, "that I could sleep without closing my eyes; the night would be my eyelids—"

An abrupt sound startled him. Off to the right he heard it, and his ears, expert in such matters, could not be mistaken. Again he heard the sound, and again. Somewhere, off in the blackness, someone had fired a gun three times.

Rainsford sprang up and moved quickly to the rail, mystified. He strained his eyes in the direction from which the reports had come, but it was like trying to see through a blanket. He leaped upon the rail and balanced himself there, to get greater elevation; his pipe, striking a rope, was knocked from his mouth. He lunged for it; a short, hoarse cry came from his lips as he realized he had reached too far and had lost his balance. The cry was pinched off short as the blood-warm waters of the Caribbean Sea closed over his head.

He struggled up to the surface and tried to cry out, but the wash from the speeding yacht slapped him in the face and the salt water in his open mouth made him gag and strangle. Desperately he struck out with strong strokes after the receding lights of the yacht, but he stopped before he had swum fifty feet. A certain cool-headedness had come to him; it was not the first time he had been in a tight place. There was a chance that his cries could be heard by someone aboard the yacht, but that chance was slender, and grew more slender as the yacht raced on. He wrestled himself out of his clothes, and shouted with all his power. The lights of the yacht became faint and ever-vanishing fireflies; then they were blotted out entirely by the night.

Rainsford remembered the shots. They had come from the right, and doggedly he swam in that direction, swimming with slow, deliberate strokes, conserving his strength. For a seemingly endless time he fought the sea. He began to count his strokes; he could do possibly a hundred more and then—

Rainsford heard a sound. It came out of the darkness, a high screaming sound, the sound of an animal in an extremity of anguish and terror.

He did not recognize the animal that made the sound—he did not try to; with fresh vitality he swam toward the sound. He heard it again; then it was cut short by another noise, crisp, staccato.

"Pistol shot," muttered Rainsford, swimming on.

Ten minutes of determined effort brought another sound to his ears—the most welcome he had ever heard—the muttering and growling of the sea breaking on a rocky shore. He was almost on the rocks before he saw them; on a night less calm he would have been shattered against them. With his remaining strength he dragged himself from the swirling waters. Jagged crags appeared to jut into the opaqueness; he forced himself upward, hand over hand. Gasping, his hands raw, he reached a flat place at the top. Dense jungle came down to the very edge of the cliffs. What perils that tangle of trees and underbrush might hold for him did not concern Rainsford just then. All he knew was that he was safe from his enemy, the sea, and that utter weariness was on him. He flung himself down at the jungle edge and tumbled headlong into the deepest sleep of his life.

When he opened his eyes he knew from the position of the sun that it was late in the afternoon. Sleep had given him new vigor; a sharp hunger was picking at him. He looked about him, almost cheerfully.

"Where there are pistol shots, there are men. Where there are men, there is food," he thought. But what kind of men, he wondered, in so forbidding a place? An unbroken front of snarled and jagged jungle fringed the shore.

He saw no sign of a trail through the closely knit web of weeds and trees; it was easier to go along the shore, and Rainsford floundered along by the water. Not far from where he had landed, he stopped.

Some wounded thing, by the evidence a large animal, had thrashed about in the underbrush. The jungle weeds were crushed down and the moss was lacerated; one patch of weeds was stained crimson. A small, glittering object not far away caught Rainsford's eye and he picked it up. It was an empty cartridge.

"A twenty-two," he remarked. "That's odd. It must have been a fairly large animal too. The hunter had his nerve with him to tackle it with such a light gun. It's clear that the brute put up a good fight. I suppose the first three shots I heard were when the hunter flushed his quarry and wounded it. The last shot was when he trailed it here and finished it."

He examined the ground closely and found what he had hoped to find—the print of hunting-boots. They pointed along the cliff in the direction he had been going. Eagerly he hurried along, now slipping on a rotten log or a loose stone, but making headway; night was beginning to settle down on the island.

Bleak darkness was blacking out the sea and jungle when Rainsford sighted the lights. He came upon them as he turned a crook in the coast line, and his first thought was that he had come upon a village, for there were many lights. But as he forged along he saw to his astonishment that all the lights were in one enormous building—a lofty structure with pointed towers plunging upward into the gloom. His eyes made out the shadowy outlines of a palatial château; it was set on a high bluff, and on three sides of it cliffs dived down to where the sea licked greedy lips in the shadows.

"Mirage," thought Rainsford. But it was no mirage, he found, when he opened the tall spiked iron gate. The stone steps were real enough. The massive door with a leering gargoyle for a knocker was real enough. Yet about it all hung an air of unreality.

He lifted the knocker, and it creaked up stiffly, as if it had never before been used. He let it fall, and it startled him with its booming loudness. He thought he heard steps within; the door remained closed. Again Rainsford lifted the heavy knocker, and let it fall. The door opened then, opened as suddenly as if it were on a spring, and Rainsford stood blinking in the river of glaring gold light that poured out. The first thing Rainsford's eyes discerned was the largest man he had ever seen—a gigantic creature, solidly made and black-bearded to the waist. In his hand the man held a long-barreled revolver, and he was pointing it straight at Rainsford's heart.

Out of the snarl of beard two small eyes regarded Rainsford.

"Don't be alarmed," said Rainsford, with a smile which he hoped was disarming. "I'm no robber. I fell off a yacht. My name is Sanger Rainsford of New York City."

The menacing look in the eyes did not change. The revolver pointed as rigidly as if the giant were a statue. He gave no sign that he understood Rainsford's words, or that he had even heard them. He was dressed in uniform, a black uniform trimmed with gray astrakhan[1].

"I'm Sanger Rainsford of New York," Rainsford began again. "I fell off a yacht. I am hungry."

The man's only answer was to raise with his thumb the hammer of his revolver. Then Rainsford saw the man's free hand go to his forehead in a military salute, and he saw him click his heels together and stand at attention. Another man was coming down the broad marble steps, an erect, slender man in evening clothes. He advanced and held out his hand.

In a cultivated voice marked by a slight accent that gave it added precision and deliberateness, he said: "It is a very great pleasure and honor to welcome Mr. Sanger Rainsford, the celebrated hunter, to my home." Automatically Rainsford shook the man's hand.

"I've read your book about hunting snow leopards in Tibet, you see," explained the man. "I am General Zaroff."

Rainsford's first impression was that the man was singularly handsome; his second was that there was an original, almost bizarre quality about the general's face. He was a tall man past middle age, for his hair was a vivid white; but his thick eyebrows and pointed military mustache were as black as the night from which Rainsford had come. His eyes, too, were black and very bright. He had high cheekbones, a sharp-cut nose, a spare, dark face, the face of a man used to giving orders, the face of an aristocrat. Turning to the giant in uniform, the general made a sign. The giant put away his pistol, saluted, withdrew.

"Ivan is an incredibly strong fellow," remarked the general, "but he has the misfortune to be deaf and dumb. A simple fellow, but, I'm afraid, like all his race, a bit of a savage."

"Is he Russian?"

"He is a Cossack," said the general, and his smile showed red lips and pointed teeth. "So am I.

"Come," he said, "we shouldn't be chatting here. We can talk later. Now you want clothes, food, rest. You shall have them. This is a most restful spot."

Ivan had reappeared, and the general spoke to him with lips that moved but gave forth no sound.

"Follow Ivan, if you please, Mr. Rainsford," said the general. "I was about to have my dinner when you came. I'll wait for you. You'll find that my clothes will fit you, I think."

It was to a huge, beam-ceilinged bedroom with a canopied bed big enough for six men that Rainsford followed the silent giant. Ivan laid out an evening suit, and Rainsford, as he put it on, noticed that it came from a London tailor who ordinarily cut and sewed for none below the rank of duke.

The dining room to which Ivan conducted him was in many ways remarkable. There was a medieval magnificence about it; it suggested a baronial hall of feudal times with its oaken panels, its high ceiling, its vast refectory table where twoscore[2] men could sit down to eat. About the hall were the mounted heads of many animals—lions, tigers, elephants, moose, bears; larger or more perfect specimens Rainsford had never seen. At the great table the general was sitting alone.

"You'll have a cocktail, Mr. Rainsford," he suggested. The cocktail was surpassingly good; and, Rainsford noted, the table appointments were of the finest—the linen, the crystal, the silver, the china.

They were eating *borsch,* the rich, red soup with whipped cream so dear to Russian palates. Half apologetically General Zaroff said: "We do our best to preserve the amenities of civilization here. Please forgive any lapses. We are well off the beaten track, you know. Do you think the champagne has suffered from its long ocean trip?"

"Not in the least," declared Rainsford. He was finding the general a most thoughtful and affable host, a true cosmopolite. But there was one trait of the general's that made Rainsford uncomfortable. Whenever he looked up he found the general studying him, appraising him narrowly.

"Perhaps," said General Zaroff, "you were surprised that I recognized your name. You see, I read all books on hunting published in English, French, and Russian. I have but one passion in my life, Mr. Rainsford, and it is the hunt."

"You have some wonderful heads here," said Rainsford as he ate a particularly well-cooked filet mignon. "That Cape buffalo is the largest I ever saw."

"Oh, that fellow. Yes, he was a monster."

"Did he charge you?"

"Hurled me against a tree," said the general. "Fractured my skull. But I got the brute."

"I've always thought," said Rainsford, "that the Cape buffalo is the most dangerous of all big game."

For a moment the general did not reply; he was smiling his curious red-lipped smile. Then he said slowly: "No. You are wrong, sir. The Cape buffalo is not the most dangerous big game." He sipped his wine. "Here in my preserve on this island," he said in the same slow tone, "I hunt more dangerous game."

Rainsford expressed his surprise. "Is there big game on this island?"

The general nodded. "The biggest."

"Really?"

"Oh, it isn't here naturally, of course, I have to stock the island."

"What have you imported, General?" Rainsford asked. "Tigers?"

The general smiled. "No," he said. "Hunting tigers ceased to interest me some years ago. I exhausted their possibilities, you see. No thrill left in tigers, no real danger. I live for danger, Mr. Rainsford."

The general took from his pocket a gold cigarette case and offered his guest a long black cigarette with a silver tip; it was perfumed and gave off a smell like incense.

"We will have some capital hunting, you and I," said the general. "I shall be most glad to have your society."

"But what game—" began Rainsford.

"I'll tell you," said the general. "You will be amused, I know. I think I may say, in all modesty, that I have done a rare thing. I have invented a new sensation. May I pour you another glass of port, Mr. Rainsford?"

"Thank you, General."

The general filled both glasses, and said: "God makes some men poets. Some He makes kings, some beggars. Me He made a hunter. My hand was made for the trigger, my father said. He was a very rich man with a quarter of a million acres in the Crimea, and he was an ardent sportsman. When I was only five years old he gave me a little gun, specially made in Moscow for me, to shoot sparrows with. When I shot some of his prize turkeys with it, he did not punish me; he complimented me on my marksmanship. I killed my first bear in the Caucasus when I was ten. My whole life had been one prolonged hunt. I went into the army—it was expected of noblemen's sons—and for a time commanded a division of Cossack cavalry, but my real interest was always the hunt. I have hunted every kind of game in every land. It would be impossible for me to tell you how many animals I have killed."

The general puffed at his cigarette.

"After the debacle[3] in Russia I left the country, for it was imprudent for an officer of the Czar to stay there. Many noble Russians lost everything. I, luckily, had invested heavily in American securities, so I shall never have to open a tearoom in Monte Carlo or drive a taxi in Paris. Naturally, I continued to hunt—grizzlies in your Rockies, crocodiles in the Ganges, rhinoceroses in East Africa. It was in Africa that the Cape buffalo hit me and laid me up for six months. As soon as I recovered I started for the Amazon to hunt jaguars, for I had heard that they were unusually cunning. They weren't." The Cossack sighed. "They were no match at all for a hunter with his wits about him, and a high-powered rifle. I was bitterly disappointed. I was lying in my tent with a splitting headache one night when a terrible thought pushed its way into my mind. Hunting was beginning to bore me! And hunting, remember, had been my life. I have heard that in America businessmen often go to pieces when they give up the business that has been their life."

"Yes, that's so," said Rainsford.

The general smiled. "I had no wish to go to pieces," he said. "I must do something. Now, mine is an analytical mind, Mr. Rainsford. Doubtless that is why I enjoy the problems of the chase."

"No doubt, General Zaroff."

"So," continued the general, "I asked myself why the hunt no longer fascinated me. You are much younger than I am, Mr. Rainsford, and have not hunted as much, but you perhaps can guess the answer."

"What was it?"

"Simply this: hunting had ceased to be what you call 'a sporting proposition'. It had become too easy. I always got my quarry. Always. There is no greater bore than perfection."

The general lit a fresh cigarette.

"No animal had a chance with me any more. That is no boast; it is a mathematical certainty. The animal had nothing but his legs and his instinct. Instinct is no match for reason. When I thought of this it was a tragic moment for me, I can tell you."

Rainsford leaned across the table, absorbed in what his host was saying.

"It came to me as an inspiration what I must do," the general went on.

"And that was?"

The general smiled the quiet smile of one who has faced an obstacle and surmounted it with success. "I had to invent a new animal to hunt," he said.

"A new animal? You're joking."

"Not at all," said the general. "I never joke about hunting. I needed a new animal. I found one.

So I bought this island, built this house, and here I do my hunting. The island is perfect for my purposes—there are jungles with a maze of trails in them, hills, swamps—"

"But the animal, General Zaroff?"

"Oh," said the general, "it supplies me with the most exciting hunting in the world. No other hunting compares with it for an instant. Every day I hunt, and I never grow bored now, for I have a quarry with which I can match my wits."

Rainsford's bewilderment showed in his face.

"I wanted the ideal animal to hunt," explained the general. "So I said: 'What are the attributes of an ideal quarry?' And the answer was, of course: 'It must have courage, cunning, and, above all, it must be able to reason.'"

"But no animal can reason," objected Rainsford.

"My dear fellow," said the general, "there is one that can."

"But you can't mean—," gasped Rainsford.

"And why not?"

"I can't believe you are serious, General Zaroff. This is a grisly joke."

"Why should I not be serious? I am speaking of hunting."

"Hunting? Good God, General Zaroff, what you speak of is murder."

The general laughed with entire good nature. He regarded Rainsford quizzically. "I refuse to believe that so modern and civilized a young man as you harbors romantic ideas about the value of human life. Surely your experiences in the war—"

"Did not make me condone cold-blooded murder," finished Rainsford, stiffly.

Laughter shook the general. "How extraordinarily droll you are!" he said. "One does not expect nowadays to find a young man of the educated class, even in America, with such a naive, and, if I may say so, mid-Victorian point of view. It's like finding a snuffbox in a limousine. Ah, well, doubtless you had Puritan ancestors. So many Americans appear to have had. I'll wager you'll forget your notions when you go hunting with me. You've a genuine thrill in store for you, Mr. Rainsford."

"Thank you, I'm a hunter, not a murderer."

"Dear me," said the general, quite unruffled, "again that unpleasant word. But I think I can show you that your scruples are quite unfounded."

"Yes?"

"Life is for the strong, to be lived by the strong, and if needs be, taken by the strong. The weak of the world were put here to give the strong pleasure. I am strong. Why should I not use my gift? If I wish to hunt, why should I not? I hunt the scum of the earth. A thoroughbred horse or hound is worth more than a score of them."

"But they are men," said Rainsford hotly.

"Precisely," said the general. "That is why I use them. It gives me pleasure. They can reason, after a fashion. So they are dangerous."

"But where do you get them?"

The general's eyelid fluttered down in a wink. "This island is called 'Ship-Trap'," he answered. "Sometimes an angry god of the high seas sends them to me. Sometimes, when Providence is not so kind, I help Providence a bit. Come to the window with me."

Rainsford went to the window and looked out toward the sea.

"Watch! Out there!" exclaimed the general, pointing into the night. Rainsford's eyes saw only blackness, and then, as the general pressed a button, far out to sea Rainsford saw the flash of lights.

The general chuckled. "They indicate a channel," he said, "where there's none: giant rocks with razor edges crouch like a sea monster with wide open jaws. They can crush a ship as easily as I crush this nut." He dropped a walnut on the hardwood floor and brought his heel grinding down on it. "Oh, yes," he said, casually, as if in answer to a question, "I have electricity. We try to be civilized here."

"Civilized? And you shoot down men."

A trace of anger was in the general's black eyes, but it was there for but a second, and he said, in his most pleasant manner: "Dear me, what a righteous young man you are! I assure you I do not do the thing you suggest. That would be barbarous. I treat these visitors with every consideration. They get plenty of good food and exercise. They get into splendid physical condition. You shall see for yourself tomorrow."

"What do you mean?"

"We'll visit my training school," smiled the general. "It's in the cellar. I have about a dozen pupils down there now. They're from the Spanish bark, *San Lucar*, that had the bad luck to go on the rocks out there. A very inferior lot, I regret to say. Poor specimens and more accustomed to the deck than to the jungle."

He raised his hand, and Ivan, who served as waiter, brought thick Turkish coffee. Rainsford, with an effort, held his tongue in check.

"It's a game, you see," pursued the general, blandly. "I suggest to one of them that we go hunting. I give him a supply of food and an excellent hunting knife. I give him three hours' start. I am to follow, armed only with a pistol of the smallest caliber and range. If my quarry eludes me for three whole days, he wins the game. If I find him," the general smiled, "he loses."

"Suppose he refuses to be hunted?"

"Oh," said the general, "I give him his option, of course. He need not play that game if he doesn't wish to. If he does not wish to hunt I turn him over to Ivan. Ivan once had the honor of serving as official knouter[4] to the Great White Czar, and he has his own ideas of sport. Invariably, Mr. Rainsford, invariably they choose the hunt."

"And if they win?"

The smile on the general's face widened. "To date I have not lost," he said.

Then he added hastily: "I don't wish you to

think me a braggart, Mr. Rainsford. Many of them afford only the most elementary sort of problem. Occasionally I strike a tartar. One almost did win. I eventually had to use the dogs."

"The dogs?"

"This way, please. I'll show you."

The general steered Rainsford to a window. The lights from the window sent a flickering illumination that made grotesque patterns on the courtyard below, and Rainsford could see moving about there a dozen or so huge black shapes; as they turned toward him, their eyes glittered greenly.

"A rather good lot, I think," observed the general. "They are let out at seven every night. If anyone should try to get into my house—or out of it—something extremely regrettable would occur to him." He hummed a snatch of song from the Folies Bergère.

"And now," said the general, "I want to show you my new collection of heads. Will you come with me to the library?"

"I hope," said Rainsford, "that you will excuse me tonight, General Zaroff. I'm really not feeling at all well."

"Ah, indeed?" the general inquired solicitously. "Well, I suppose that's only natural, after your long swim. You need a good, restful night's sleep. Tomorrow you'll feel like a new man, I'll wager. Then we'll hunt, eh? I've one rather promising prospect—"

Rainsford was hurrying from the room.

"Sorry you can't go with me tonight," called the general. "I expect rather fair sport—a big, strong man. He looks resourceful. Well, good night, Mr. Rainsford. I hope you have a good night's rest."

The bed was good and the pajamas of the softest silk, and he was tired in every fiber of his being, but nevertheless Rainsford could not quiet his brain with the opiate of sleep. He lay, eyes wide open. Once he thought he heard stealthy steps in the corridor outside his room. He sought to throw open the door; it would not open. He went to the window and looked out. His room was high up in one of the towers. The lights of the château were out now, and it was dark and silent, but there was a fragment of sallow moon, and by its wan light he could see, dimly, the courtyard. There, weaving in and out in the pattern of shadow, were black, noiseless forms; the hounds heard him at the window and looked up, expectantly, with their green eyes. Rainsford went back to the bed and lay down. By many methods he tried to put himself to sleep. He had achieved a doze when, just as morning began to come, he heard, far off in the jungle, the faint report of a pistol.

General Zaroff did not appear until luncheon. He was dressed faultlessly in the tweeds of a country squire. He was solicitous about the state of Rainsford's health.

"As for me," sighed the general, "I do not feel

so well. I am worried, Mr. Rainsford. Last night I detected traces of my old complaint."

To Rainsford's questioning glance the general said: "Ennui. Boredom."

Then, taking a second helping of crêpe suzette, the general explained: "The hunting was not good last night. The fellow lost his head. He made a straight trail that offered no problems at all. That's the trouble with these sailors; they have dull brains to begin with, and they do not know how to get about in the woods. They do excessively stupid and obvious things. It's most annoying. Will you have another glass of Chablis, Mr. Rainsford?"

"General," said Rainsford, firmly, "I wish to leave this island at once."

The general raised his thickets of eyebrows; he seemed hurt. "But, my dear fellow," the general protested, "you've only just come. You've had no hunting—"

"I wish to go today," said Rainsford. He saw the dead black eyes of the general on him, studying him. General Zaroff's face suddenly brightened.

He filled Rainsford's glass with venerable Chablis from a dusty bottle.

"Tonight," said the general, "we will hunt—you and I."

Rainsford shook his head. "No, General," he said. "I will not hunt."

The general shrugged his shoulders and nibbled delicately at a hothouse grape. "As you wish, my friend," he said. "The choice rests entirely with you. But may I not venture to suggest that you will find my idea of sport more diverting than Ivan's?"

He nodded toward the corner where the giant stood, scowling, his thick arms crossed on his hogshead of chest.

"You don't mean—" cried Rainsford.

"My dear fellow," said the general, "have I not told you I always mean what I say about hunting? This is really an inspiration. I drink to a foeman worthy of my steel—at last."

The general raised his glass, but Rainsford sat staring at him.

"You'll find this game worth playing," the general said enthusiastically. "Your brain against mine. Your woodcraft against mine. Your strength and stamina against mine. Outdoor chess. And the stake is not without value, eh?"

"And if I win—" began Rainsford huskily.

"I'll cheerfully admit myself defeated if I do not find you by midnight of the third day," said General Zaroff. "My sloop will place you on the mainland near a town."

The general read what Rainsford was thinking.

"Oh, you can trust me," said the Cossack. "I will give you my word as a gentleman and a sportsman. Of course, you, in turn, must agree to say nothing of your visit here."

"I'll agree to nothing of the kind," said Rainsford.

"Oh," said the general, "in that case—but

why discuss that now? Three days hence we can discuss it over a bottle of Veuve Cliquot, unless—"

The general sipped his wine.

Then a businesslike air animated him. "Ivan," he said to Rainsford, "will supply you with hunting clothes, food, a knife. I suggest you wear moccasins; they leave a poorer trail. I should suggest too that you avoid the big swamp in the southeast corner of the island. We call it Death Swamp. There's quicksand there. One foolish fellow tried it. The deplorable part of it was that Lazarus followed him. You can imagine my feelings, Mr. Rainsford. I loved Lazarus; he was the finest hound in my pack. Well, I must beg you to excuse me now. I always take a siesta after lunch. You'll hardly have time for a nap, I fear. You'll want to start, no doubt. I shall not follow till dusk. Hunting at night is so much more exciting than by day, don't you think? Au revoir, Mr. Rainsford, au revoir."

General Zaroff, with a deep, courtly bow, strolled from the room.

From another door came Ivan. Under one arm he carried khaki hunting clothes, a haversack of food, a leather sheath containing a long-bladed hunting knife; his right hand rested on a cocked revolver thrust in the crimson sash about his waist....

Rainsford had fought his way through the bush for two hours.

"I must keep my nerve. I must keep my

nerve," he said through tight teeth.

He had not been entirely clear-headed when the château gates snapped shut behind him. His whole idea at first was to put distance between himself and General Zaroff, and, to this end, he had plunged along, spurred on by the sharp rowels of something very like panic. Now he had got a grip on himself, had stopped, and was taking stock of himself and the situation.

He saw that straight flight was futile; inevitably it would bring him face to face with the sea. He was in a picture with a frame of water, and his operations, clearly, must take place within that frame.

"I'll give him a trail to follow," muttered Rainsford, and he struck off from the rude path he had been following into the trackless wilderness. He executed a series of intricate loops; he doubled on his trail again and again, recalling all the lore of the fox hunt, and all the dodges of the fox. Night found him leg-weary, with hands and face lashed by the branches, on a thickly wooded ridge. He knew it would be insane to blunder on through the dark, even if he had the strength. His need for rest was imperative and he thought: "I have played the fox, now I must play the cat of the fable." A big tree with a thick trunk and outspread branches was near by, and, taking care to leave not the slightest mark, he climbed up into the crotch, and stretching out on one of the broad limbs, after a fashion, rested. Rest brought him new confidence and almost a feeling of security. Even so zealous a hunter as General Zaroff could not trace him there, he told himself; only the devil himself could follow that complicated trail through the jungle after dark. But, perhaps, the general was a devil....

An apprehensive night crawled slowly by like a wounded snake, and sleep did not visit Rainsford, although the silence of a dead world was on the jungle. Toward morning when a dingy gray was varnishing the sky, the cry of some startled bird focused Rainsford's attention in that direction. Something was coming through the bush, coming slowly, carefully, coming by the same winding way Rainsford had come. He flattened himself down on the limb, and through a screen of leaves almost as thick as tapestry, he watched. The thing that was approaching was a man.

It was General Zaroff. He made his way along with his eyes fixed in utmost concentration on the ground before him. He paused almost beneath the tree, dropped to his knees, and studied the ground before him. Rainsford's impulse was to hurl himself down like a panther, but he saw that the general's right hand held something small and metallic—an automatic pistol.

The hunter shook his head several times as if he were puzzled. Then he straightened up and took from his case one of his black cigarettes; its pungent incenselike smoke floated up to Rainsford's nostrils.

Rainsford held his breath. The general's eyes

had left the ground and were traveling inch by inch up the tree. Rainsford froze there, every muscle tensed for a spring. But the sharp eyes of the hunter stopped before they reached the limb where Rainsford lay; a smile spread over his brown face. Very deliberately he blew a smoke ring into the air; then he turned his back on the tree and walked carelessly away, back along the trail he had come. The swirls of the underbrush against his hunting boots grew fainter and fainter.

The pent-up air burst hotly from Rainsford's lungs. His first thought made him feel sick and numb. The general could follow a trail through the woods at night, he could follow an extremely difficult trail. He must have uncanny powers; only by the merest chance had the Cossack failed to see his quarry.

Rainsford's second thought was even more terrible. It sent a shudder of cold through his whole being. Why had the general smiled? Why had he turned back?

Rainsford did not want to believe what his reason told him was true, but the truth was as evident as the sun that had by now pushed through the morning mists. The general was playing with him. The general was saving him for another day's sport! The Cossack was the cat; he was the mouse. Then it was that Rainsford knew the full meaning of terror.

"I will not lose my nerve. I will not."

He slid down from the tree, and struck off

again into the woods. His face was set and he forced the machinery of his mind to function. Three hundred yards from his hiding place he stopped where a huge dead tree leaned precariously on a smaller living one. Throwing off his sack of food, Rainsford took his knife from its sheath and began to work with all his energy.

The job was finished at last, and he threw himself down behind a fallen log a hundred feet away. He did not have to wait long. The cat was coming again to play with the mouse.

Following the trail with the sureness of a bloodhound came General Zaroff. Nothing escaped those searching black eyes, no crushed blade of grass, no bent twig, no mark, no matter how faint, in the moss. So intent was the Cossack on his stalking that he was upon the thing Rainsford had made before he saw it. His foot touched the protruding bough that was the trigger. Even as he touched it, the general sensed his danger and leaped back with the agility of an ape. But he was not quite quick enough; the dead tree, delicately adjusted to rest on the cut living one, crashed down and struck the general a glancing blow on the shoulder as it fell. But for his alertness, he would have been smashed beneath it. He staggered, but he did not fall; nor did he drop his revolver. He stood there rubbing his injured shoulder, and Rainsford, with fear again gripping his heart, heard the general's mocking laugh ring through the jungle.

"Rainsford," called the general, "if you are

within sound of my voice, as I suppose you are, let me congratulate you. Not many men know how to make a Malay man-catcher. Luckily, for me, I too have hunted in Malacca. You are proving interesting, Mr. Rainsford. I am going now to have my wound dressed; it's only a slight one. But I shall be back. I shall be back."

When the general, nursing his bruised shoulder, had gone, Rainsford took up his flight again. It was flight now, a desperate, hopeless flight, that carried him on for some hours. Dusk came, then darkness, and still he pressed on. The ground grew softer under his moccasins; the vegetation grew ranker, denser; insects bit him savagely. Then as he stepped forward, his foot sank into the ooze. He tried to wrench it back, but the muck sucked viciously at his foot as if it were a giant leech. With a violent effort he tore his foot loose. He knew where he was now. Death Swamp and its quicksand.

His hands were tight closed as if his nerve were something tangible that someone in the darkness was trying to tear from his grip. The softness of the earth had given him an idea. He stepped back from the quicksand a dozen feet or so and, like some huge prehistoric beaver, he began to dig.

Rainsford had dug himself in France when a second's delay meant death. That had been a placid pastime compared to his digging now. The pit grew deeper; when it was above his shoulders, he climbed out and from some hard saplings cut stakes and sharpened them to a fine point. These stakes he planted in the bottom of the pit with the points sticking up. With flying fingers he wove a rough carpet of weeds and branches and with it he covered the mouth of the pit. Then, wet with sweat and aching with tiredness, he crouched behind the stump of a lightning-charred tree.

He knew his pursuer was coming; he heard the padding sound of feet on the soft earth, and the night breeze brought him the perfume of the general's cigarette. It seemed to Rainsford that the general was coming with unusual swiftness; he was not feeling his way along, foot by foot. Rainsford, crouching there, could not see the general, nor could he see the pit. He lived a year in a minute. Then he felt an impulse to cry aloud with joy, for he heard the sharp crackle of the breaking branches as the cover of the pit gave way; he heard the sharp scream of pain as the pointed stakes found their mark. He leaped up from his place of concealment. Then he cowered back. Three feet from the pit a man was standing, with an electric torch in his hand.

"You've done well, Rainsford," the voice of the general called. "Your Burmese tiger pit has claimed one of my best dogs. Again you score. I think, Mr. Rainsford, I'll see what you can do against my whole pack. I'm going home for a rest now. Thank you for a most amusing evening."

At daybreak Rainsford, lying near the swamp, was awakened by a sound that made him know that he had new things to learn about fear. It was a distant sound, faint and wavering, but he knew it.

It was the baying of a pack of hounds.

Rainsford knew he could do one of two things. He could stay where he was and wait. That was suicide. He could flee. That was postponing the inevitable. For a moment he stood there, thinking. An idea that held a wild chance came to him, and, tightening his belt, he headed away from the swamp. The baying of the hounds drew nearer, then still nearer, nearer, ever nearer. On a ridge Rainsford climbed a tree. Down a watercourse, not a quarter of a mile away, he could see the bush moving. Straining his eyes, he saw the lean figure whose wide shoulders surged through the tall jungle weeds; it was the giant Ivan, and he seemed pulled forward by some unseen force. Rainsford knew that Ivan must be holding the pack in leash.

They would be on him any minute now. His mind worked frantically. He thought of a native trick he had learned in Uganda. He slid down the tree. He caught hold of a springy young sapling and to it he fastened his hunting knife, with the blade pointing down the trail; with a bit of wild grapevine he tied back the sapling. Then he ran for his life. The hounds raised their voices as they hit the fresh scent. Rainsford knew now how an animal at bay feels.

He had to stop to get his breath. The baying of the hounds stopped abruptly, and Rainsford's heart stopped too. They must have reached the knife.

He shinned excitedly up a tree and looked back. His pursuers had stopped. But the hope that was in Rainsford's brain when he climbed died, for he saw in the shallow valley that General Zaroff was still on his feet. But Ivan was not. The knife, driven by the recoil of the springing tree, had not wholly failed.

Rainsford had hardly tumbled to the ground when the pack resumed the chase.

"Nerve, nerve, nerve!" he panted, as he dashed along. A blue gap showed between the trees dead ahead. Ever nearer drew the hounds. Rainsford forced himself on toward that gap. He reached it. It was the shore of the sea. Across a cove he could see the gloomy gray stone of the château. Twenty feet below him the sea rumbled and hissed. Rainsford hesitated. He heard the hounds. Then he leaped far out into the sea….

When the general and his pack reached the place by the sea, the Cossack stopped. For some minutes he stood regarding the blue-green expanse of water. He shrugged his shoulders. Then he sat down, and hummed a bit from *Madame Butterfly*.

General Zaroff had an exceedingly good dinner in his great paneled dining hall that evening. With it he had a bottle of Pol Roger and a half bottle of Chambertin. Two slight annoyances kept him from perfect enjoyment. One was the thought that it would be difficult to replace Ivan; the other was that his quarry had escaped him. Of course, the American hadn't played the game—so thought the general as he tasted his after-dinner liqueur. In his library he read, to soothe himself, from the works of Marcus Aurelius. At ten he went up to his bedroom. He was deliciously tired, he said to himself, as he locked himself in. There was a little moonlight, so before turning on his light, he went to the window and looked down at the courtyard. To the great hounds he called: "Better luck another time!" Then he switched on the light.

A man, who had been hiding in the curtains of the bed, was standing there.

"Rainsford!" screamed the general. "How in God's name did you get here?"

"Swam," said Rainsford. "I found it quicker than walking through the jungle."

The general sucked in his breath and smiled. "I congratulate you," he said. "You have won the game."

Rainsford did not smile. "I am still a beast at bay," he said, in a low, hoarse voice. "Get ready, General Zaroff."

The general made one of his deepest bows. "I see," he said. "Splendid! One of us is to furnish a repast for the hounds. The other will sleep in this very excellent bed. On guard, Rainsford." ...

He had never slept in a better bed, Rainsford decided.

1. **astrakhan:** the fur-like wool of young lambs from the Astrakhan area in Russia.
2. **twoscore:** 40
3. **debacle:** an overthrow; in this case, the Russian revolution of 1917.
4. **knouter:** a person who uses a whip called a knout to flog people.

ACKNOWLEDGEMENTS

Permission to reprint copyright material is gratefully acknowledged. Every reasonable effort to trace the copyright holders of materials appearing in this book has been made. Information that will enable the publisher to rectify any error or omission will be welcomed.

Flames on the Water (originally titled "Anna Lang") from *Cross of Valour* by John Melady. Copyright © 1985 by John Melady. All rights reserved. Used by permission of Scholastic Canada Ltd., 123 Newkirk Road, Richmond Hill, Ontario, L4C 3G5.

The Case of the Unused Seat Belt by Donald J. Sobol copyright © 1967 by Donald J. Sobol. Reprinted by permission of McIntosh and Otis, Inc.

Madeleine by Arthur Prager and Emily Prager © 1979 by Emily and Arthur Prager, from *World War II Resistance Stories*, reprinted with the permission of Wylie, Aitken & Stone, Inc.

Ordeal in the Arctic, originally titled "The Nick of Time" by Robert Mason Lee from *Death and Deliverance* by Robert Mason Lee, © copyright 1992, published by Macfarlane Walter & Ross, Toronto.

The Wish by Roald Dahl from *Someone Like You* by Roald Dahl. Copyright © 1953 by Roald Dahl. Reprinted by permission of Alfred A. Knopf, Inc.

Lot 87 by Joy Burnett from *Star Book of Horror, No. 1*, edited by Hugh Lamb, published in 1975 by W.H. Allen & Co. Ltd. Copyright © Joy Burnett.

Encounters of the Old Kind by Reid Van Melle originally published in *Windscript* Vol. 8 No. 1. Reprinted by permission of the author.

A Hell of a Story by H.R.F. Keating reprinted by permission of the Peters Fraser & Dunlop Group Ltd. Copyright © 1972 by H.R.F. Keating.

Unit 3 quotation "He had grown up...." Copyright © 1971 by Ursula K. Le Guin; from *The Lathe of Heaven*; reprinted by permission of the author and the author's agent, Virginia Kidd. Reprinted with the permission of Charles Scribner's Sons, an imprint of Macmillan Publishing Company from *The Lathe of Heaven* by Ursula Le Guin. Copyright © 1971 Ursula Le Guin.

Hijacked! (originally titled "Mary Dohey") from *Cross of Valour* by John Melady. Copyright © 1985 by John Melady. All rights reserved. Used by permission of Scholastic Canada Ltd., 123 Newkirk Road, Richmond Hill, Ontario, L4C 3G5.

The Shooting of Dan McGrew by Robert Service © 1910 Dodd, Mead & Co. Used by permission of the Estate of Robert Service.

Just Lather, That's All by Hernando Téllez, translated by Donald A. Yates, from *Great Spanish Short Stories*, selected and introduced by Angel Flores, copyright 1962, Dell Publishing Co., Inc. Used by permission of the Estate of Angel Flores.

Dialogue Behind a Curtain by Victor Canning from *Best Smuggling Stories*, edited by J. Welcome, published in 1967 by Faber and Faber Limited. Copyright © Victor Canning. Reproduced by permission of Curtis Brown Ltd. on behalf of The Estate of Victor Canning.

If Cornered, Scream by Patricia J. Thurmond first published in *Ellery Queen's Mystery Magazine*, January 1978. Copyright © 1977 by Patricia J. Thurmond. Reprinted by permission of the author.

The Most Dangerous Game by Richard Connell. Copyright 1924 by Richard Connell. Renewed © 1952 by Louise Fox Connell. Reprinted by permission of Brandt & Brandt Literary Agents.

THE EDITORS

James Barry is Chairman of the English Department at Brebeuf College School, North York, Ontario. He is the editor of the poetry anthologies *Themes on the Journey, Departures, Side by Side*, and *Poetry Express*, as well as an annual student writing anthology, *Triple Bronze*. Besides teaching, his special interests are sports (especially hockey), music, and student writing.

Christine McClymont was born in Scotland, but came to Canada at an early age. For many years, she has been compiling anthologies for Nelson Canada series such as *Networks, In Context*, and *Features*. Christine enjoys hiking and cross-country skiing, and is actively involved with the Toronto Chamber Society.

Glen Huser, a former teacher and librarian, is a learning resources consultant for the Edmonton Public School Board. He has won several newspaper literary competitions, and his novel, *Grace Lake*, was nominated for the W. H. Smith/Books in Canada First Novel Award in 1990. He also edits *Magpie*, a magazine of student writing and graphics.